THE ANCIENT HIGHWAY

THE ANCIENT HIGHWAY

JAMES OLIVER CURWOOD

A Novel of High Hearts and Open Woods

Originally published in 1924.
Published by Wildside Press, LLC.
Visit us online at wildsidepress.com.

To the Memory of
SIR WILLIAM PRICE

For the friendship, encouragement and active assistance of Sir William Price, of Kenagami, on the Saguenay, I feel myself deeply indebted. His tragic death seems an interwoven part of this book, for the very drama of the novel itself, as talked over and discussed with him, shaped itself with shocking suddenness in his own life. Sir William, with his great paper and pulp mills and his five thousand square miles of Quebec forests, was the heart and soul of the forest industry in the vast wooded Province which has grieved so deeply for him. His beautiful character, his love for the out-of-doors, his deep and sincere sympathy made him not only Canada's greatest conservationist but also her most loved citizen. Sir William was a man of the forests, and sent no man where he would not go himself. As this story was written, its typed pages went into his hands, and shortly after its last chapters were finished came the tragic day on the pitiless and mighty Saguenay, when Sir William, personally investigating a danger which was menacing some of his workmen, was caught in the avalanche which carried him to his death in the fury of the waters along which he had spent so much of his life. In that hour Canada suffered a loss of one who cannot be replaced. It is a satisfaction to me, mellowed by the grief of his loss, that Sir William played an important part in the writing of this novel.

—James Oliver Curwood.
Owosso, Michigan,
April 11, 1925.

CHAPTER I

Clifton Brant believed himself to be only one of innumerable flying grains of human dust in a world gone mad. And among these grains he knew himself to be a misfit. For which reason he was walking the wide highway from Brantford Town in Ontario to the ancient city of Quebec on the St. Lawrence, an unimportant matter of seven hundred miles or so, not counting the distance he would travel in crossing and recrossing the road on the way.

In the scale with which he was measuring life at the present moment time had no specific value for him, just as his objective was neither far nor near. People passed him, smothering him in the dust of their thirty and forty and fifty miles an hour, and wondered who he was. There was something picturesque about him, and worth remembering. He was, without shouting or advertising the fact, an adventurer. People sensed that quality about him after they had left him behind in a cloud of dirt. He caught their attention even as they bore down upon him—his lithe, khaki-clad form, the clean, free swing of his shoulders which bore a worn knapsack, his easy stride, as if he had walked from the beginning of the world—and then, as they passed him, the quick, flashing gray of his eyes, the debonair wave of his hand, a smile, a nod—and someone would ask, "Who do you think that man could be?"

"Out of a job and hoofing it to the next town," one would submit.

"An ex-soldier, by his walk," another would suggest.

"Or one of those walking idiots out on a week's vacation"—this from a man who curled up and snapped whenever his wife asked a question about another man.

And behind them, spitting out their dust, Clifton Brant wondered what life could hold for people who went through it always on four wheels questing out its beauties at a-mile-a-minute speed.

The golden sun was hanging low behind the spires and maple-clad hills of Brantford Town when he swung from the main highway into a road that angled southward. It was a modest and inconspicuous little road, slanting downward as it ran, carpeted with soft dust and winding between cool and shadowy thickets of bushes and trees in which the birds were beginning their evening song.

A thickening came into Clifton's throat and his heart beat a little faster as he looked ahead of him, for it was more than twenty years ago that his feet had last traveled this way. He was sixteen then, and barefooted. And time had been kind to the little road, he thought. The velvety dust was the same, and he caught himself looking for the imprints of his naked feet as he waded through it; and the trees were the same, seeming not to have grown in those twenty years, and the thickets of his boyhood sprang up one by one, with the big rocks between—only the rocks seemed smaller now than when he was a boy, and the hollows seemed a bit less steep, and the Big Woods, still uncut, held less of their old mystery and fearsomeness in the shadowing depths of sunset. A smile crept gently over his face, and in that smile were the pathos and joyous grief of reminiscence, of precious memories rising in his path and of faded years stirring with life again.

Verging on forty, he felt his boyhood was only yesterday. He was foolish, he told himself, to allow things to come back to him so vividly. And he had been unwise to return at all to this little road and its hallowed past. He had not thought it would hurt quite so much, or that such a vast and encompassing loneliness would descend upon him.

Almost as if a danger might lie in his path he paused hesitatingly at the top of a little hill which in childhood had been a big hill to him, and made his way through a fringe of thick brush and over a rail fence. The birds twittered about him. A yellow-breasted chat scolded him and a kingbird sent up a warning cry or two. Then he heard the twitter of swallows and caught the shiny flash of their wings over the clearing which lay just beyond the fence. A lump rose in his throat. It was as if the same swallows he had known and envied and loved as a boy were there still, dipping and shooting and sweeping the air as they cast about for their suppers among the insects that rose up from the earth at sunset. And there, just a little way ahead, was what he had once called *home*.

He was not ashamed of tears, in spite of the fact that he had passed through searing fires and had seen much that is hard for a man to look upon. He could not keep them back from his eyes and he did not try to wipe them away.

The old home was a ruin. Fire had gutted it and its walls of flat stones picked up from slate and sandstone ledges had fallen in. One end wall stood triumphant above the desolation, and this was the end which held the big fireplace chimney. He was born on a cold winter night when a fire had roared in that chimney. And before it he had dreamed his first dreams of conquest and adventure in the wonderful world which reached for such illimitable distances about him.

He went nearer and walked slowly about this ghost of a habitation which had once been home. He was surprised at its smallness. He had always carried with him the impression that this first and only home of his had been little less than a castle, at least three times as large as it now appeared to be. He chuckled, though he did not feel happy. Childhood memories were funny things. They were best left alone if one did not want to feel real grief. And what had been the inside of the house was pathetically small, now that he measured it with the eyes of a man.

The whole was overgrown with creeping vines and bushes. There were blackberry and dewberry vines with green fruit; bitter-sweet had tangled itself among the stones; wild cucumbers festooned one side of the chimney, and long grass had grown up quickly to cover the scars of dissolution. And other life was there. A pair of thrushes hopped about unafraid of him. A golden humming-bird flashed in and dipped at the honey-sweet hearts of red clover blooms. A yellow warbler dared to sing and the swallows were using the old chimney for a home.

Over near the fence he heard a red squirrel chatter, and the sound drew his eyes. There had always been a red squirrel in the old hollow oak near the fence, usually a family of them. The oak had changed amazingly, Clifton thought. He had remembered it as the biggest tree that had ever painted a picture of itself in his brain; now it was a most ordinary oak, not nearly as large as some he had seen up the road. His father had made him a swing in that tree, and his mother had played with him a thousand times in its shade.

His eyes turned from the tree, and suddenly his heart gave a queer jump.

For a moment his sensation was almost one of shock. Half a stone's throw away was a huge boulder from under which had always bubbled the icy water of a spring. Near this spring, looking at him, stood a boy—a boy and a dog. And this boy, as Clifton remembered himself, was the boy who had played about and drunk at that same spring a quarter of a century ago.

He was a pale, slim, rather pathetic-looking object who seemed to have grown mostly to legs. He had on the same old hat, too, a straw hat with a ragged brim and a broken crown; and his knee pants were too short, as Clifton's had always been, and were of the blue overall stuff which he could remember as clearly as he remembered Bim, his dog, who was buried down at the edge of the woods. And it seemed to Clifton the dog, as well as the boy, had come like an apparition out of the past. For it was a "hound-dog," a mongrel, just as loyal old Bim had been; a yellowish dog with loppy ears, big joints and over-grown feet and a clublike tail in which every joint was a knot.

Clifton saw all this as he drew nearer, smiling at them. The boy did not move, but remained staring, holding tightly to a stick, while the dog's big, lank body pressed closer to him, as if to protect him. Then, at close range, Clifton observed other things. The beast's ribs were as prominent as the knots in his tail, and in his eyes and attitude was a hungry look. The boy, too, was thinner than he should have been. His waist was ragged. The bottoms of his pants were in frayed tatters. He had blue eyes, wide-open, straight, strangely old but beautiful blue eyes, in a face which was too white and which was troubled with the same hungry look that was in the dog's.

"Hello, you and your dog," greeted Clifton, with a comradely grin. "Is the water still running?"

"Sure," replied the boy. "It always runs. We keep it dug out—me an' Bim."

"You and—*who*?"

"Bim. That's my dog, here."

Slowly Clifton took off his pack. "You and—*Bim*!" he repeated. "And your name doesn't happen to be Cliff, does it?—and your nickname Skinny?"

The boy eyed him wonderingly. "No. My name is Joe. What you carrying in that bag?"

"And where did you find that name—*Bim*—for your pup?" asked Clifton.

"Down there in a beech tree. It's cut deep in with a knife. An' there's figgers, but they've faded out. That's a funny-lookin' bag you got!"

Clifton turned away a moment. He could see the big beech tree under whose sheltering arms he had dug Bim's grave, and where he had worked the whole of one Sunday afternoon in carving his comrade's epitaph. His mother had helped him, and had comforted him when he cried. He was ten then, so it must have been twenty-eight years ago.

"Dear God, but life is even less than a dream," he whispered to himself.

The boy was inspecting his pack.

"What you got in this bag?" he demanded again. "It looks like a sojer's bag."

"It is," said Clifton.

The boy's blue eyes widened.

"You a sojer?"

"I was."

"An' you—you've killed people?"

"I'm afraid so, Joe."

For several seconds the boy held his breath. Bim was cautiously smelling the stranger, and Clifton laid a hand caressingly on his head. "Hello, Bim, old comrade. Are you glad *I've come back*?"

The mongrel licked his hand and wagged his knotty tail.

"What do you mean—come back?" asked the boy. "You been here before?"

10

"Sure," replied Clifton. "I used to live in that pile of stones when I was a boy, Joe. It was a house then. I was born there. And I had a dog named Bim. He died, and I buried him under the old beech tree down there, and carved his name in the trunk. This isn't your spring. It's *mine!*"

He tried to laugh as he knelt down to drink. But there was a choking in his heart that seemed to have taken away his thirst. When he got up the boy had tossed his old hat on the ground beside the pack. He was tow-headed, with freckles in his pale skin.

"What you got in this here bag?" he asked again.

An inspiration came to Clifton.

"I've got—supper," he said. "Do you suppose your folks will mind if you stay here and eat with me—you and Bim?"

A look of surprise, and then of pleasure, came into the boy's face.

"We'll stay," he said.

"But your folks? I don't want to get you and Bim into trouble. When I was a kid and wasn't home at supper time my father used to go to those big lilac bushes you see out there, and break off a switch—"

"I ain't got any folks," interrupted Joe hastily, as if to settle any possible objection the stranger might have. "We'll like as not get it anyway, if old Tooker is home, won't we, Bim?"—turning to his dog.

Bim wagged his tail affirmatively, but his hungry eyes did not leave the pack which the man was slowly opening.

"No folks?" queried Clifton softly. "Why not?"

"Dead, I guess. Old Tooker says I was wished on 'im. Mis' Tooker ain't so bad, but she's bad enough. They both hate Bim. He never goes home but just hangs around in the edge of the woods waiting for me. I get him what I can to eat an' we hunt the rest. That's a dandy kit, ain't it?"

Clifton was undoing his aluminum cooking outfit—a skillet, coffee pail, plates, cups, knives and forks—and paused for a moment with a brown parcel in his hand. Bim grew suddenly stiff-legged and thrust out his long neck to get a sniff of it.

"Meat!" exclaimed the boy. "Bim knows it. He can smell meat a mile away—meat an' chickens. Watch out or he'll lam it!"

"You mean—"

"Grab it. He's quick on meat an' chickens, Bim is!"

Clifton drew out two big onions, a link of bologna, half a loaf of bread made into buttered sandwiches, four oranges and a glass of marmalade. This stock, with a pound and a half of fresh beef ground into hamburger, he had planned as sufficient for both his supper and breakfast. The bologna was an emergency asset.

He smiled up at Joe, whose eyes had grown larger and rounder with each additional appearance of food. He had a hand gripped firmly in the folds of loose hide on Bim's neck.

"Look out for your bolony!" he gasped. "Bim's awful quick!"

Clifton held out a pack-strap. "Better tie Bim up until we're ready," he advised. "This bologna is especially for Bim, but we'll make him wait and eat with us like a gentleman. Heigh-ho! Now for some wood, Joe. We're going to have a great feast!"

He stood up, and for a moment watched Joe as he dragged the reluctant Bim to a near-by tree. And in this moment he became conscious of an amazing change in himself. The loneliness which had oppressed him all that day of his "home-coming" was gone. Tragedy and pain had crushed him a few minutes ago when he had looked upon the crumbled and over-grown ruin of what had once been his home, the shrine forever hallowed by the presence of mother, father, his dog—and boyhood. In those minutes he had felt and seen only the melancholy ghosts of dissolution and death, of broken dreams, of grief and the emptiness of life.

Now in the strange and swift reaction which swept through him he saw about him a sweet and wondrous beauty. There was no longer gloom or a suffocating heaviness weighing down his heart. The thrushes were singing their praise of the glorious sunset in the western sky. In the oak tree the red squirrel and his mate were scampering in play. Out of the woods came a low, familiar drone of life; a catbird offered up its incomparable melody from a thicket near the rail fence, and he sensed a new joyousness of greeting in the softer, lower twittering of the swallows skimming over his head. His heart beat a little faster. He raised his head and drank more deeply of the cool air of evening, and suddenly it came to him that the great and glorious nature which was his god had made itself a tenant here and lay like a benediction upon all that had ever been.

And then the truth pressed upon him as his eyes went back to the boy and the dog.

They had made this change for him!

He began to whistle as he gathered dry sticks of wood. The boy ran back and helped, his eyes shining and his voice a-tremble with the thrill of his wonderful adventure, while Bim settled back on his haunches after one mournful howl and waited like a stoic.

A thin white spiral of smoke rose in the sunset.

And in their new comradeship the boy became the inquisitor.

"What's your name?" he asked.

"Clifton Brant. You may call me Uncle Cliff."

"You got a dog?"

"Yes. You took my old Bim's name so I'm half owner in *your* Bim."

They peeled and cut up the onions. Water simmered in the coffee pail. The skillet grew hot and thick patties of hamburger sizzled as they were

12

dropped into it.

"You got any folks here?"

"I'm like you, Joe. I haven't any folks anywhere."

"Whadda you do?"

"Oh, I just sort of wander round. I'm what they call a—an adventurer."

"What's that?"

"Can you read, Joe?"

"I'm in the sixth grade. They make old Tooker send me to school."

"Ever read a pirate story?"

"You bet!"

"Well, a pirate is an adventurer."

The boy gave a sudden gasp.

"*Gee whiz*, are you a pirate?"

"A—sort of one," laughed Clifton.

"An' you kill people?"

"All adventurers don't kill people, Joe. Some of them just *pretty near* kill people, and then let them go."

The boy did not know the meaning of the steely flash which came for a moment into Clifton's eyes.

"You goin' to stay here?" he whispered worshipfully.

"No. I'm going on tomorrow."

A blue jay screamed in the oak. Bim howled again. For a space the boy no longer smelled the delicious aroma of frying hamburger and onions.

"Why don't you stay?" he asked. "What you goin' on for?"

Clifton laughed. He leaned over and took the boy's thin face between his two hands. Even with the laugh the steely glitter was not yet gone out of his eyes.

"I'm on my way to collect a debt of a million dollars, Joe," he said. "I've been on my way for a long time, and now I'm almost there. That's why I can't stay. Understand?"

The boy nodded. "I guess so," he said. "Can I bring Bim now?"

CHAPTER II

West of Brantford Town the sun sank behind maple hills as they ate.

Clifton was hungry, but he held his appetite in leash as he watched the boy and the dog, yet appeared not to notice them at all. For the boy's hunger was a thing that made him think of starvation, and Bim swallowed chunks of bologna with gulping sounds that emanated from the very depths of his being. Quite frankly Joe confided that he tried to smuggle to Bim a part of the food which was given him each day at old Tooker's.

"When we have milk an' boiled meal Bim goes pretty hungry because I can't sneak that in my pockets," he added.

"Who is Tooker, and what does he do?"

"He's just Tooker, an' I never see him do much of anything. Riley's boy told me once that his dad said Tooker peddled likker to the Indians on the reservation. When I asked Tooker if he did he whaled the life out of me an' told me if I didn't lick Riley's kid the next time I saw him he'd whale me ag'in. I tried it, but I couldn't lick Slippy Riley. He licked me. An' then old Tooker whaled me until Bim run in from the woods an' took a chunk out of his leg. Looky here—"

He bent over and pulled up his ragged waist. His {14} thin white back was streaked with the scars of a lash.

"He did that day before yesterday because Bim and me come on him way down in the swampiest part of Bumble's Holler cooking something in a queer-lookin' kettle over a fire."

"The devil!" said Clifton.

He changed the subject, and after a little the boy leaned back with a deep sigh, his hands on his stomach.

"I'm full," he said. "An' I guess Bim is, too. Want me to wash the dishes?"

They leaned together over the little pool and scrubbed the dishes with white sand, then dried them in the air. The last red glow of sunset was fading away when they climbed the rail fence and struck the soft white dust of the road.

The boy's face was filled with a grave anxiety as they walked down the road side by side.

"Where you goin' tonight?" he asked.

"As far as the little church and the cemetery."

"The old Indian church?"

"Yes."

"I'm goin' that far. Tooker's is the second house beyond."

He waited a moment, and his hand touched Clifton's arm timidly.

"You got anybody there—dead ones, I mean?"

"My mother, Joe."

"You ain't an Indian?"

"A part of me. My mother's grandmother was a Mohawk princess. She is buried there, too."

A silence fell upon them. The boy's bare feet made soft little pattering sounds in the thick dust, and behind them came Bim, so that looking back Clifton saw a trail which was very much like his own of many years ago. Twilight was falling and shadows were growing deeper in the thickets, and pale gloom descended like a veil upon the land about them. In the grass at the roadsides crickets chirped, and ahead and behind them tree-toads called their half-hearted promises of rain.

It was that part of evening which Clifton loved, yet in its stillness and peace was an unspeakable loneliness for him, and this loneliness seemed to fall upon the boy. A small hand gripped his sleeve and Clifton's fingers closed about it. For a little while longer they did not speak. A pair of night-hawks gave their musical calls over their heads, and from a long distance came the soft tolling of a bell. Then a rabbit scurried down the road like a torpedo shooting through the dust, and with a sudden wail Bim took after it.

The boy's fingers tightened. Ahead of them a darker glow grew in the twilight where the patch of maples and evergreens marked the churchyard.

"I'm sorry you're goin' on tomorrow," said Joe, and his voice seemed very faint and tired. "I wish we was goin' with you—Bim and me."

"I wish you were," said Clifton.

They came to the high bank where the church stood and the evergreens grew. And here, at the beginning of the worn foot-path which led up to the picket fence and the old-fashioned gate, Clifton stopped.

"You ain't goin' to stop here—*now*?" whispered Joe, with eyes that grew big in the dusk. "It's dark!"

"Adventurers aren't afraid of the dark," Clifton laughed softly, "or of graves. I'm going to sleep in the churchyard tonight. They're beautiful, Joe —churchyards, I mean. Everybody's your friend, there."

"*Ugh!*" shuddered the boy. "Bim—Bim—where you goin'?" The dog had moved away, but came back and snuggled close to his master's legs.

"You'd better run along now," urged Clifton. "I'll stand here until you are well down the road. Maybe—in the morning—I'll happen to see you again. Good night!"

"Good night!"

The boy drew away, and as he went it seemed to Clifton that something dragged itself out of him to accompany this ragged and barefoot youngster of the highway. Half a dozen times before he disappeared in the gloom Joe turned and looked back, and when at last the twilight swallowed him, with Bim trailing at his heels, Clifton went slowly up the little path and passed through the open gate.

He wondered, as he paused inside the gate, what the world would think of him if it could know what he was doing tonight. Would it call him a little mad? Or would it put him down as a sentimental fool in a day and age which had lost its sentiment? For surely it would not understand a man in his normal senses coming to sleep among the dead.

It still lacked a few minutes of darkness and he could make out the little cemetery quite clearly, with its crumbling gray headstones and the old board church. He knew there was no change, for this place never changed. It had not changed in nearly two hundred years. He went to the front of the church and looked up. There, indistinct in the dusk, was the time-worn tablet whose words he had learned by heart in boyhood, telling the occasional passer-by that this was the first church built in Ontario, and that it was erected by His Gracious Majesty King George the Third for his "children," the people of the Iroquois nation. It was Indian then. It was Indian now. In the plot of ground about him slept the dust of hundreds.

He took off his knapsack and hung it on the end of a box-like rack at the corner of the church. In the rack was a cracked bronze bell, and on the bell was the same ancient date as above. He had often played on it with sticks when a boy. Now he tapped it with his knuckles and found its melody still there.

He sat down and waited for the moon.

And now, it seemed to him, his mother came in the softness of the evening and sat beside him near the old bell.

The moon came up. It rose in the clear, where the trees thinned out. In their play his mother and he had had a lot of fun with the moon. It had been very much alive for them, and when dressed up in its various poses and humors they had given it different names. Sometimes it was a very gentlemanly old moon, with a stiff collar and a tilted chin; at others it was a Man out for Fun, with a cock-sure look in his eye. But best of all they had loved their Man in the Moon when he had the mumps. And it was the Mumpy Moon that came up tonight, with a head askew and one cheek swollen, as if he had been trampled under a cart and horse. But always, when the Man in the Moon had the mumps, he also had a jolly smile in his broad, fat face and a merry twinkle in his eyes.

"And when you are sick or things are going wrong you must always remember the Man in the Moon when he has the mumps," the mother had impressed upon Clifton. "It is then, when he is feeling very badly, that he laughs at us and winks. That is what the brave old moon does, and all brave men do the same."

Clifton remembered. He remembered so vividly that a strange thrill ran through him as he stood up to watch the transformation which the moon was making in the darkness and shadows about him. Objects began to take form and the trees grew out of night. Light played on the old bell and crept warmly over the church. It fell on the iron grating and stone tomb of Thayendanegea—of Joseph Brant, the Mohawk, greatest of the Iroquois. He saw the earth slowly taking new form on all sides of him, rising in little mounds that were marked with old and crumbling stones. And there were mounds and little hollows from which even the dust of stone had been eaten away by the centuries. Here were drama, romance, adventure and unspeakable tragedy—here where the last and the greatest of the chivalry of the Six Nations lay buried in a refuge given them by an English king when their blood-soaked empire was lost south of the friendly Canadas.

And they were his mother's people, and *his* people. He had always been proud of that. And the memory which came back to him so vividly now was of another night when his mother and he had watched the moon light up this acre of silence just as it was doing now. Their dead was what they had called these sleeping ones. His mother had known their tragic history and the stories and legends that reached back a hundred years beyond that; and she had told him they were so many here they slept one above another, and sometimes in twos and threes and with arms and shoulders touching— forgotten and nameless ones, buried even before King George built his church or ever a white man had come this way.

He passed out among them, and over him came a strange sense of restfulness and peace, as if he had reached home after a long and arduous struggle. He did not feel again the thickening in his throat or the tightening at his heart when he stood at last beside the spot where his mother lay. That had passed, and his emotion was one of gladness and a sort of exultation. It had taken him many years to achieve this moment, and he was amazed at the tranquillity which became almost instantly a part of it.

In a little while he spread out his blanket and sat down and then he lighted his pipe and began to smoke. The incongruity of it all did not strike him. He had sat and slept with the dead when they were above the ground and it did not embarrass him to be with them when they were a part of it.

The thought that remained with him was that he had been traveling in a circle for twenty-two years and had at last come back to the starting point.

He was rather disturbed by the fact that he soon {20} surrendered to the desire to stretch himself flat on his back with his pneumatic pillow under his head. It was his quixotic notion that the act was a selfish one. But he was tired, and the carpet of cedar needles under his blanket was soft to lie upon. Occasionally he closed his eyes as he looked up at the sky. The stars made him think of the tree-toads and the falseness of their prophecy. And he wondered if Joe had another whipping to his credit, and if old man Tooker was down in Bumble's Hollow cooking something in a queer-looking kettle over a fire.

Tomorrow he might look into it, for he knew that very spot where Tooker would undoubtedly hide.

Then, he planned sleepily, he would go on and collect his million dollars.

He smiled, and his eyes grew heavier. On that adventure the spirit of Molly Brant would go with him. For this she had waited, as he had waited, and they would collect the debt together.

And when it was over—

The wise-eyed old owl in the thick evergreen tops above him knew when he slept. The bird hooted softly and drifted out into the moonlight and away to its open hunting-fields. The night grew cooler and the aroma of the earth lay heavier as the hours passed. Overhead the moon climbed higher and began its descent into the west. The owl returned and croaked from the belfry tower. Darkness followed moonlight as the crickets and katydids hushed their cries, and out of the east crept dawn.

In that dawn Clifton dreamed. He stood with his mother in the cemetery, and he was a boy again. And Molly Brant was as he had so often seen her at his father's side, with her dark eyes afire with love and laughter and her long hair in a girlish braid down her back. They were alone, hand in hand, and suddenly all about them the earth began giving up its dead.

Chieftains rose to salute them and warriors sprang up so swiftly that very soon it was beyond his power to count them. They were in war-paint and feathers and ready for battle, and behind them, gathered in a great circle, were countless women and children. And in his dream Clifton saw that his mother and he were the center of this gathering host, and that his mother stood with her hand raised above her head, as if she were princess of them all.

The chieftains advanced toward them one by one, and he knew them as they came—first Red Jacket the eloquent young Seneca, with his eternal plea for peace with the white men on his lips; then Cornplanter, the terror of the Mohawk settlements, fierce and implacable, and Peter Martin the

18

Oneida, and after them—tall and calm and splendid in his power—Joseph Brant, the Mohawk, chief of all the Iroquois nation. And they bent their heads to his mother!

And then Thayendanegea began to speak.

"Tomorrow you seek vengeance," he said. "It is well. The Iroquois go with you!"

"You will find strife and death and unhappiness," interposed the peaceful Seneca. "The hatchet is rusty. Let it remain so."

"Only cowards like the backsliding Oneidas fear those three things," boomed the Mohawk in a voice that rolled like the deep beating of a drum.

"The Senecas are not cowards—yet I fear."

"I am an Oneida—and I do not fear," said Peter Martin.

In his dream Clifton saw a sudden break in the circle of warriors as an Indian girl ran through and knelt at the feet of his mother. It seemed she had run fast or far, for she could scarcely speak as she raised her bare arms. His mother bent down to her so that she could hear her whispered words, and in those few moments Clifton heard his own name spoken.

Then his mother stood erect, and faced the chiefs.

"Tomorrow we go," she said, and a murmur of approbation came from all except the Seneca, who stooped sadly to gather up a handful of earth and throw it westward over his shoulder.

A part of the earth struck Clifton in the face. It was soft and warm. And in that moment he saw a strange and amazing transformation in the girl kneeling at his mother's feet. She was no longer Indian, but a white girl, and she was looking straight at him with laughter on her lips and in her eyes. He felt himself grow uncomfortable and tried to wipe the wet dirt from his face, but no sooner did he remove it from one spot than it came back on another, and the greater effort he made the more amused she seemed to be.

In sudden rage he turned upon Red Jacket and found the Seneca gone. The Indian host was melting away and the going of the last of it was like the dissolution of shadow before swift dawn. He turned again, and his mother had disappeared. Only the girl and he were left, and it seemed to him this impertinent young person disfigured her pretty nose in making faces at him as she faded away, like the others, into nothingness.

A fresh bit of the warm, soft dirt struck Clifton on the cheek and roused him to a comprehension of other phenomena. He found himself suddenly lying flat on his back with his eyes wide open and he could see tree tops with the filtering gold of sunlight in them. A bird was singing.

Then appeared a grotesque head between him and the light above and Bim's warm and friendly tongue caressed him again.

He sat up.

19

"The deuce take me if it wasn't a perfectly ripping dream," he said; and then added, "Good morning, Bim!"

CHAPTER III

Clifton rose and stretched himself as Bim wagged his tail and contorted his loosely jointed body in greeting. It was at least an hour after his usual waking time. The sun was above the horizon, the birds were wide awake, and he heard the rattle of wagon wheels up the road and a distant voice calling cattle. He was pleased as he laid a friendly hand on Bim's homely head and looked about him. He could not remember a more restful night or a more interesting one and he was filled with a deep appreciation of the thoughtfulness which had inspired the dog's early visit. That was the way with dogs. They never forgot a courtesy. And that was one of the many reasons why he loved them more than all men and respected them more than most.

Dreams were remarkable things, he told himself, as the sun began finding its way in under the trees. For over there, as surely as he lived, was the very spot where the Indian maiden who had turned into a white girl had knelt at his mother's feet, and down that path which led toward the gate she had backed away from him at last, taunting him with her laughter. For a moment he almost fancied he could see Red Jacket's footprints in the bare patch of earth where he had stooped to fill his hand with dirt.

His vision went no farther. At the foot of the spruce tree his eyes fell upon a huddled, crumpled figure which he instantly recognized as Joe. The boy had fallen asleep with his back against the tree and had drooped forward until his head rested between his knees. His ragged hat had rolled away from him and his pale, thin hands were filled with the brown needles as if he had clutched at them in his last moment of wakefulness. There was something pathetically and tragically forlorn about him—in the droop of his slight shoulders, the raggedness of the wretched clothing that covered him, the brown thinness of his legs, the way his thick blond hair fell over his naked knees.

The smile that had been on Clifton's lips died away and the humor in his eyes lost itself in a gathering cloud. He drew nearer and looked down. On the back of the boy's bared neck was a black and blue mark, and one of the sleeves of his waist was torn to the shoulder. For half a minute Clifton made no effort to draw in a deep breath.

21

Then he saw something else. A little behind the boy, partly hidden by the tree, was a bundle. It was made up of burlaps tied with binder-twine, and through this twine was thrust a stick. Beside the bundle lay the oldest and queerest wreck of a gun that Clifton had ever seen—and he had been through the war. It was a muzzle-loading shotgun of ancient date. Its cracked stock was bound with wire; its one-time hammer had been replaced by a "zulu" slugger; its ramrod was a willow stick, and the sight-bead had been knocked from its end. Clifton picked it up, and the instrument of death wobbled loosely in his hands. Near the foot of the tree was a four-ounce bottle partly filled with shot and another containing powder.

The smile came back into Clifton's face.

Bim growled.

"I'm not going to steal it, you old fossil. Shut up!"

He replaced the gun on the ground as the boy slowly stirred himself to wakefulness. A little at a time, Joe sat up. He opened his eyes and blinked and rubbed them with the backs of two soiled hands. In this first moment out of sleep his face appeared strangely wan and frail. Life, it seemed, and not the joy of living struggled back into him.

Then he saw Clifton standing over him.

He climbed to his feet and his face flashed suddenly with last night's comradely smile.

"Good mornin'!"

"Good morning, Joe. When did you come?"

"I dunno. It wasn't light yet. Bim found where you was. We're goin' with you!"

"You're—what?"

"Goin' with you," repeated Joe confidently. "We told old Tooker last night and he gave us a heck of a whalin', didn't 'e, Bim?"

"Pinched your neck, too, didn't he?"

Joe nodded. "We'd better hurry," he urged. "If Tooker ever found us here—"

"Maybe that's him coming up the road," suggested Clifton. "Is it?"

A stifled breath came from the boy, as if his heart had suddenly skipped a beat or two. He looked from the road up at Clifton, and in his blue eyes was a terror which made Clifton's fingers slowly clench while the smile remained on his lips.

"That's him! It's Tooker! And he's after me!"

He made a grab for his gun, but Clifton's hand drew him back.

"Wait here, Joe," he commanded. "Stand right out in the open so that Tooker can't help seeing you."

"He sees us now!" gasped Joe. "He's coming toward the gate—"

"And that's where I'm going to meet him—right at the gate," reassured Clifton. "You stay here."

He measured his time and distance so that he had a moment in which to observe Tooker as he covered the last few steps between the road and the gate. He had seen ugly men but Tooker was one of the ugliest that had ever confronted his eyes. In the first place he was disgustingly dirty, even at a distance, and Clifton hated dirty people. His repellent face bristled with a reddish stubble of beard and one cheek was padded with an enormous quid of tobacco. His big body was clumsy and slouching; his eyes had the mean littleness of a pig's, and in one hand—as one might expect of a creature of this kind—he carried a heavy stick, shiny from use and quite suited to murderous assault in the dark.

Clifton was amazed. By what curious sociological argument had the people of the district allowed a beast of this kind to hold an abusive authority over a boy like Joe?

He had a way of smiling when he was ready to kill. He pulled a lone cigar out of his pocket and offered it to the man.

"Tooker, I believe?"

"Yes, I'm Tooker." The man accepted the cigar, looked at it, and flung it on the ground. "Who the devil are you, and what you doing with that brat?"

"Tut, tut, Mr. Tooker," soothed Clifton. "I'm merely a wandering officer of the law on a hunt for moonshiners. Incidentally, my name is Brant, and yesterday in Brantford Town I repurchased the old Brant homestead, which includes in its domain a nice bit of swamp known as Bumble's Hollow; and as I shall soon return to this place to live I want my property to have a clean reputation. And if it wasn't for Joe, my nephew—"

"Your—"

"My nephew, Tooker. If it wasn't for him and the disgrace it would be to the family I'd take you to jail this minute!"

Tobacco juice was leaking from Tooker's inanimate jaw.

"He's been squealin'—lying to you?"

"Nothing of the sort. We just happened to meet. I was coming to see you about him this morning. You see, I made myself his uncle last night, and today I'm taking him on to Montreal—and beyond."

He was no longer smiling, and as he advanced a step toward Tooker the other backed away. Clifton had put a hand into a pocket, and now—instead of something more dangerous—he drew out a wallet.

"I'm going to give you two things," he said. "First, the cleanest two hundred dollars you ever had in those unwashed hands of yours, Tooker. Here it is. Ten twenties so new you could hear them crackle if your ears were clean. That's for taking care of Joe so well."

The money was in Tooker's hands. An understanding gleam shot into his eyes as he pocketed it, and in the same moment he stooped and picked up the discarded cigar.

"That's right. It's a good one," approved Clifton.

He had measured his man correctly. Tooker was a pinch-fist skinflint, a coward, and quite easily subdued. He was, Clifton thought, the kind of human reptile whose eyesight is keenest in the dark.

"And the other thing I am going to give you is some advice, and it isn't bad like your moonshine, Tooker," he continued. "I'm going to leave my evidence with the authorities up at Brantford. I'll ask them to have a little mercy on you this time, for Joe's sake—and Bim's. My advice is to buy three or four cows with the money you have. And now we must leave you. I think we shall be back in about a year, and if you haven't acquired the habit of washing yourself and living like an honest man by that time—why, God help you, Tooker!"

And as Clifton returned to Joe and packed his blanket he sang blithely,

> *"At night I'd hear across the Bow the tom-tom and the wail begun,*
> *Which told Papoose had ceased to breathe, about the setting of the*
> *sun."*

The road claimed them again. This time the glory of the rising sun was in their faces.

For a space after they had started, Joe did not speak. He carried the burlap bundle over his shoulder and in his hand was the wreck of a gun. In his eyes was a light which day or night had never found there before.

When the curve in the road shut out the cemetery behind them, he asked, in a voice filled with worshipful awe, "How did you know all that?"

"All of what, Joe?"

"About old Tooker."

Clifton laughed. In his eyes, too, was a different look from that which sunset had left in them.

"I guessed it, just plumb guessed it from what you told me about Bumble's Hollow. Good Lord, I'm more likely to go to jail myself than to send Tooker there!"

"For taking me?"

"No, not for that. Remember, I'm your uncle, Joe. Tooker will stick to that story, for he wouldn't dare confess that he sold you—and he thinks too much of the money I've given him to tell the truth. You see, this uncle business saves you from being a runaway and me from being a kidnaper— which means a man who steals kids. I need a family, anyway. And now, by Jove, I've got one in you and Bim! I feel quite important. Let's see what you have in that bundle."

They stopped, and Joe untied his pack so that its contents lay exposed at the side of the road. There was a small matter of clothing, ragged and soiled, an old pair of shoes, half of an automobile tube, a monkey-wrench, hammer and nails, and a stuffed owl.

Clifton regarded Joe's possessions with serious eyes.

"What's the automobile tube for?"

"Sling-shots."

"And the monkey-wrench?"

"That—an' the hammer? Them's tools."

"And the owl?"

"That's for good luck. Carry an owl an' you can see in the dark."

"Oh!"

Clifton looked about.

"We're going on a big adventure, Joe, and these things won't help us. We must hide them somewhere. Behind that old log in the fence corner, for instance."

Joe picked up his gun and held it so tightly that his small hands grew bloodless.

"Not this!"

"No, you may take the gun."

They were soon traveling eastward again.

"You see, Joe, you are no longer a boy," Clifton explained. "You're a man. You're an adventurer yourself now, and we must outfit you like one. Does that gun work?"

"You mean does it shoot?"

"Yes."

"It does—sometimes. It's kinda slow-going, though. An' it blows powder in your face, but I don't mind that. She's good an' stout, with all this wire. Want to shoot it?"

"Not just now."

Straight to town Clifton led the way. In a restaurant reeking with the aromas of coffee and pork chops and fried potatoes they had breakfast, and Bim ate his fill of scraps in the kitchen. Then Joe was fitted out in a khaki suit, walking shoes, a Boy Scout hat and knapsack, handkerchiefs, shirts and a necktie. After that Clifton wrote a letter to Tooker, and when it was finished and mailed he hunted up a certain old minister in the town and sat with him in private conference for an hour. When he left he knew more about twelve-year-old Joseph Hood than Joe knew about himself.

Once more on their way they passed the little road which led down to the Indian church and settlement. Joe eyed it a bit wistfully.

"Was that a fib, too—about you buying Bumble's Holler?" he asked.

"No, that was the truth," said Clifton. "It's ours, Joe, every last leg of its eighty acres—the spring, the old house, the woods, everything. Some day we're coming back and will build another house near the old one."

"An' we'll leave the old chimney for the swallows."

"Every stone of it."

During this first day Joe proved himself a veteran at walking. And it seemed to him a thousand automobiles whizzed past them every hour. More frequently than before Clifton was offered the courtesy of rides, for the tall man, the slight boy and the gaunt dog traveling side by side were an unusual combination on the highway.

It was late in the afternoon, with the city of Hamilton half a dozen miles away, when a swiftly moving and luxurious sedan came up behind them. As it passed a man in the rear seat gave a sudden exclamation and turned to look behind. A cloud of dust shut out his vision, and with a word of apology he turned to the other occupants of the car.

"If it wasn't for the absurdity of the thing I would say I know that man," he said. "His resemblance to a remarkable person I once knew is almost shocking!"

"He had a pleasant face, and smiled at us as we passed. Why should the resemblance be shocking?" asked a girl who sat beside him.

"Because—under other circumstances I would swear that I saw him for the last time two years ago on the Yangtze Kiang, where he was in charge of the Chinese government's reforestation project. He had twenty-five million trees to plant. Six months later he was killed by natives north of Haipoong, in Indo-China. I feel as if I had looked upon a dead man, and one for whom I held a strange affection."

"Please stop the car!" commanded the girl.

The gentleman's bronzed face flushed slightly.

"Don't!" he entreated. "It is highly absurd. The man I am thinking of was a Princess Pat, and we came out of Belgium together. We were both laughing maniacs, and after the war he took to wandering. I heard from him occasionally. He said something or other was shot out of him—he couldn't just understand what—and that it was impossible for him to settle down to his old profession of forestry. He called himself an intermigrant—wanted to be constantly on the move. I called him the Walking Man. But he is dead now, shot up everlastingly north of Haipoong, the records have it. He gave a queer reason for not coming home."

The car had stopped. Behind it a cloud of dust drifted away with the wind.

"What was his reason?" the girl asked.

"He was afraid he would kill a certain man if he returned."

"They have left the road and are crossing a field."

"Of course," nodded the prematurely old man at her side. "Undoubtedly a farmer and his boy. Let us go on. And please pardon me for bringing about an interruption of this kind."

And the car continued on its way.

"Do farmers have such nice eyes?" asked the girl. And then: "What was the other man's name, Colonel Denis?"

"Brant—Clifton Brant," replied the Colonel. "He was somewhere in the woods of upper Quebec when the war broke out. He had made quite an unusual reputation as a forester, and was slated for an important post with the government at that time. I think his father had concessions there."

The girl was silent for a moment. Then in a low voice she said for the Colonel alone: "That terrible war seems to have happened only yesterday, yet it was ten years ago. I was a little girl then, and I kissed the men as they marched away."

"Yes, only yesterday," he nodded, "and with some of us it will always remain that near."

Clifton was following a creek into the green seclusion of a rolling wood-lot. Out of sight of the road he found a pool from which the water ran in a series of ripples that made a cooling, musical sound.

"Supper—and a bath," he announced. "The bath first, Joe. Strip—while I get out soap and towels. And scrub Bim while you're in. He's almost as dirty as old Tooker."

He stood guard while Joe spent twenty minutes in the water, then Joe took his turn, and fresh and cool from their purgation of dust and grime they began the preparation of supper. Tonight it was beefsteak, milk-fed and two years old the butcher had said, and when it was over Clifton leaned in contentment with his back against a tree. He noticed, too, that this one day had seemed to take much of the thinness and whiteness from the boy's face, and the restless and hunted look from his eyes.

"A fine place to sleep," he observed. "There is nothing like the open air to produce health, wealth and wisdom, Joe. Always remember that, and live up to it. If you do, and cultivate a sense of humor at the same time, you are sure to die happy. But you must see the funny things. If you don't you're a goner. God had to have His jokes when He was making the world. He intended there should be a lot of laughter, so you want to laugh. Why, *you're* funny, Joe—so is Bim, and so am I, and so is everybody else."

Joe sat cross-legged, with Bim squatted at his side, and both regarded Clifton with eager eyes. They were splendid listeners, and Clifton chuckled his appreciation as he lighted his pipe and held out at arm's length a newspaper which he had purchased in the last town.

"Here it is—the humor of life right on the front page," he went on, enjoying his monologue. "Picture of a girl with a million-dollar pair of legs!

27

They're the funniest of all, Joe—women, I mean. They're shockingly funny—all except our mothers. You must remember that mothers are never funny—our own, I mean, though the other fellow's mother may be deucedly funny. If *ours* bobs her hair it is all right; she is beautiful still. If *our* mother wants to carry about some kind of metal in the lobes of her ears it is perfectly proper for her to do it, for you mustn't see anything that isn't nice and beautiful about *her*. Now over on the next page—here we have it again!—something to laugh at if it doesn't bring on nausea first—a bobbed-haired Venus who is the millionth 'most beautiful girl in America.'"

"What's a Venus," interrupted Joe.

"A Venus is a woman."

"With short hair?"

"Not necessarily. She may have either short or long hair. But if she's a Venus with bobbed hair run for your life, particularly when you get a little older. Why, Joe, if there was only one woman on earth and she had bobbed hair I wouldn't marry her! I wouldn't marry her anyway, but the bobbed hair would make a certainty of it in case I got sick and weakened."

"It must be awful," suggested Joe.

"It is. Bobbed hair and million-dollar legs—they go together. Now—going back to the front page—"

As Joe waited he saw a strange change in the man. The lines in Clifton's face suddenly tightened and a staring directness took the place of the humor in his eyes. His body stiffened. He forgot Joe and Bim and slowly crumpled the paper until it was a mass in his hands. He rose to his feet and Joe got up with him, a little frightened.

Then Clifton took notice of the boy again, but this time the smile which came to his lips was a hard and terrible one which Joe had not seen before.

"And sometimes there are things which are not so funny," he said, as much to himself as to Joe. "For instance, I have just read that the man from whom I am to collect a million dollars sails from Montreal for Europe next Thursday. This is Tuesday. So we can't sleep here tonight, Joe. We have no time to lose."

Joe was bewildered by the strangeness and swiftness with which events happened after that. For the first time Clifton deliberately halted a car and asked for a ride. At Hamilton he hired another car and they were off for Toronto. A little later the rush and roar and electrical glare of the big city engulfed them. Joe clutched his gun and held so tightly to the string attached to Bim that it cut a crease in his hand. He was fascinated and appalled, held speechless and almost powerless to move, and Clifton placed an arm about his thin shoulders to give him confidence. Brantford had been the hub of activity and excitement in Joe's little world; Toronto with its hundreds of thousands was a monster of life and sound that at times made his heart stop beating.

They came to a building of colossal size about which hundreds of automobiles were moving like restless bees, and here their own car stopped and Clifton hurried him out and dragged him along so fast that he was compelled to trot at his side to keep up. They stopped at a window, then raced through a gate, and almost as it began to move they were boarding a train. Bim was hiccoughing and his eyes were bulging. A five-dollar bill placed him in charge of the porter.

That night with its dizzy swaying and incessant roar of wheels was a nightmare in Joe's life. The next day they arrived in Montreal.

Clifton found writing material at the station, and for half an hour he was busy while Joe sat watchfully quiet, holding to Bim. Then he used a telephone to find if a certain Benedict Aldous was in town. Aldous's housekeeper assured him that he was, whereupon Clifton pinned the letter he had written in the pocket of Joe's khaki coat.

"I'm sending you to a friend of mine," he explained, "and you must give him this letter at once. He will take good care of you and Bim. I will come to you sometime tonight, or tomorrow. Probably tonight. I'm going to send my dunnage with you. You aren't afraid, are you, Joe?"

"Not very, I guess. Why don't you come now?"

"I have some business to attend to."

"Is it the million dollars?"

"You've hit it, Joe. It's the million dollars."

He loaded them into a taxicab and gave the driver written instructions.

"Good-by!"

As far as his eyes could follow them he saw Joe's pale face looking back through the window.

For the first time in hours he drew a deep breath of relief. No matter what happened now Joe would be properly cared for. Benedict Aldous would see to that. He felt himself at least temporarily freed from a peculiarly embarrassing responsibility, and he found his good humor returning as he began to picture the Englishman's profound amazement when Joe presented himself with his letter.

He wondered if Aldous was as odd and thin and altogether lovable as in the old days when they had tramped India and Turkestan together. Of course he would be. It would be rather difficult to change him. But his blasé anatomy would receive a thrill when he learned that his old tramping companion and the savior of his soul and freedom in the Simla Hills was alive and in town.

Curiously, as he went up the street, Clifton thought of the vampish little blonde widow who had almost "got" Benedict during his convalescence from a fever. Maybe she was still hating him for smuggling Aldous away by force; maybe she had married again; maybe she was dead. Anyway, Aldous would always love him for the part he had played in his salvation. The world was a funny place to live in, filled with funny things and people! And especially the people, monumental egoists on two legs. They were never tired of playing out their trivial little comedies and tragedies, with absurd convictions of their importance.

Personally he was in the same boat himself. He was going to play a part of his own tonight. If possible he would make of it a comedy-drama instead of a drab and tiresome tragedy. There should be something to smile at even in the death of a man like Ivan Hurd, president and majority owner of the vast interests of the Hurd-Foy Paper and Pulp Company. At least he hoped there would be the saving grace of a touch of humor about it.

It was four o'clock by his watch when he came to the corner where the Hurd-Foy offices had been before the war. A new building had taken the place of the old one. Its size and massiveness were emblematic of power and wealth, and carved in stone over the arched entrance were the words *Hurd-Foy Building*. Clifton smiled at them cryptically. Here again was humor if one were of the disposition to look at it in that way.

He went in, and ascended by means of an elevator to the floor occupied by the Hurd-Foy offices. It was a quarter after four o'clock then.

His ears were greeted by the metallic clicking of typewriters, and he noted that a small army of employees were assembled on this floor. He took his time. The sumptuousness of the place interested him. He passed a mirror, and looking into it he wondered if Ivan Hurd would recognize him. The war had made quite a change in him. Ten years had increased it.

It was half-past four when he inquired if Ivan Hurd was in.

"He is busy. Will you wait?"

"No," said Clifton. He scribbled a few lines on a pad of paper. "Please take this to him. It is urgent."

The girl returned shortly. There was a clock on the wall, and Clifton made note of the fact that it was twenty-five minutes of five when she led the way for him to Ivan Hurd's office. She left him with a friendly smile. Something in Clifton's eyes invited her attention.

He passed in, and as the door closed behind him he turned and locked it. Even in this act he did not hurry or make an attempt to conceal his intention. He knew the man seated at the big walnut desk at the end of the room was watching him, and he had conceived a mental picture of his astonishment before he faced him. Casually he surveyed the room. It was very large, entirely done in walnut or mahogany, with a heavy rose-taupe rug on the floor. At its farther end was a smaller door sufficiently ajar to give

Clifton a glimpse of a lounge, and he tabulated it instantly as Ivan Hurd's rest room—and empty.

Hurd had turned so that he sat facing his visitor. He was a big man. The hands that gripped the arms of his chair were pudgy and large. His face and head were round, heavy, immense, throwing back to his German ancestors. His shoulders, trained down properly, would have expressed enormous strength. His eyes were light blue and steely with anger as Clifton tossed his hat carelessly upon a table, in the center of which stood a tall vase filled with flowers. In Hurd's mouth was a cigar. It was a mouth supported by a chin that might have been hewn out of granite. The man's age did not exceed Clifton's by more than a year or two.

"What did you do to that door?" he demanded.

"I locked it," said Clifton.

He sat down, with the long directors' table between him and Hurd. In the same movement he produced an automatic pistol and leveled it at the other's breast.

"Don't get up and don't make a sound that can be heard beyond that door," he warned. "Your one chance of remaining alive another half-hour depends upon the utter isolation of us two. I have traveled twenty thousand miles to keep myself from killing you, and now that nature is having her way I'm not going to make a mess of the job by doing it in business hours."

A deadly light was in Clifton's eyes. His voice was low but trembled with a dangerous thrill.

"Who are you, and what in God's name do you want?"

Ivan Hurd was not a coward. He leaned forward, demanding an answer. The flush was leaving his face. It was turning white.

"You don't know me?"

"No."

"Never saw me before?"

"No."

For the longest quarter-minute in Ivan Hurd's life Clifton's eyes remained steadily on his face.

"I think you believe you are telling the truth," he said then. "I am quite sure you are—or you would sweat instead of turning a little pale." He waited a moment, and then added: "I am the dead man of Haipoong come to life. I am Clifton Brant."

CHAPTER IV

Clifton was conscious of the ticking of a tiny ivory clock on the timber king's desk. He had not noticed it before, but now the sound seemed to break in excitedly upon the dead stillness which filled the room. From beyond the door came the dully subdued hum and movement of life which had not made itself noticeable until now. He heard faintly the passing of footsteps, a girl's laughter, the indistinct clang of an elevator door. And he fancied he heard a sound which came from Ivan Hurd's rest room. In that he was sure he must be mistaken.

In these moments even Hurd's massive chest did not seem to move as he breathed. He stared at Clifton, and as he stared the flesh of his body relaxed. The hands that had gripped the arms of his chair grew limp; his face and jaw began to show saggy lines; the light blue flame of anger that had leaped into his eyes at the other's cool impertinence was replaced by a filmy horror. At last he had recognized the dead man of Haipoong.

He forced himself to speak, and his voice was scarcely above a hoarse whisper as he looked into the black tube of the automatic and beyond that into the strangely smiling, terrible face of the man who held it. He thought of madness, for only a madman could smile as Clifton was smiling in this moment, without rage or venom, but with something more appalling in his eyes.

"What do you want?"

"You," said Clifton.

With his free hand he drew out his watch and laid it open on the table. It was two minutes slower than the little ivory clock.

"In eighteen minutes your offices will close," he went on. "Will anyone remain after that?"

"My secretary."

"And the janitor?"

"He comes at seven."

Clifton nodded toward the house telephone.

"Connect with your secretary and tell that person to leave promptly at five and see that no one remains after that hour. And if you make a mistake,

Hurd, if your voice is not natural, if you attempt to arouse the slightest suspicion at the other end of the wire—I shall kill you!"

Ivan hesitated with his hand on the telephone. Clifton could see him swallow. Then he took down the receiver and briefly gave the instructions to his secretary in a calm and even voice.

Clifton nodded his approbation when it was done.

"I am agreeably surprised with you," he said. "I was afraid one of your stripe and breed would turn entirely yellow in an hour of this kind. I don't like killing a coward. It seems too much like stepping on a worm just through spite."

Hurd made a fighting effort to regain his nerve by lighting the cigar that had gone out. He wet his lips.

"We can talk business now," he said. "We won't be interrupted."

"What business?"

For a moment Ivan Hurd caught himself as he was about to speak, and in that moment his eyes shifted to the partly open door of his rest room. Then he shrugged, as if he saw checkmate there.

"Money, of course. That's what you want, Brant. Money. How much?"

A flash of laughter leaped into Clifton's eyes and his face grew almost friendly as he regarded Hurd.

"I knew something funny would crop up, even here," he exclaimed. "It always does; it's just another proof that comedy lives next door to tragedy, and they're always playing in each other's back yard—granting you're built up to certain specifications that don't make you blind. Why, Hurd, I once saw two donkeys, a cart and a man wiped out of existence by a shell in Flanders and I almost fainted with horror, but when the smoke and dust cleared away I began to laugh, for while the donkeys and cart were gone forever there sat the man, black as a tar baby, without a scratch on him, and only a little deaf. *That* was funny. But this is funnier.

"I don't want your money. This building and all that is in it couldn't wipe out your debt to me. I want *you*. And in about nine minutes I'm going to have you. Imagine yourself, Hurd—how funny you will look when your friends find you, all lopsided and terrible, as I'm going to leave you. You are overfat, and will present a comical appearance in shrouds. How much do you weigh?"

"Good God, you are mad!"

"Possibly. You can't cut people up in a country like Haipoong, have them come to life again, and expect them to be entirely sane, can you? Just what do you think that you owe me?"

He waited. The sweat of agony was on Ivan Hurd's forehead now, and Clifton knew the torture that was in his soul.

"For instance," encouraged Clifton, "how much do you consider your life worth—to you? Not to the world, because the world would be better off without it, but to *you*? Be agreeable, Hurd, and answer me! It's worth more than all the money you've got, isn't it?"

The timber king nodded a throaty assent. He could see death in the steadiness with which the black pit of the gun found the center of his eyes.

"Of course," agreed Clifton. "One's life is quite frequently one's most precious asset. My father valued his life very highly, and it was worth a great deal to me. You killed my father, and I am his inheritor. You killed him while I was away helping to fight the battles which made it possible for you to pile up a profiteer's fortune of more than twenty millions. You grew fat on money while I lost everything I had in the world.

"Now I have come to collect. You were afraid I would come some day. I told you I would, when the story of my father's ruin and death reached me. You received the cards I sent?—one every six months for years! Of course you did—cards which bore those two unforgettable words of that country of yours which went to rot—'*der Tag.*' You knew you were a murderer and a thief, even though no technical law could touch you, and you grew afraid.

"For that reason, when your agents doing business with the Chinese Government found I was on the Yangtze Kiang job, and then at Haipoong, you took steps to have me put out of the way, and thought you were successful. It was a nice, out-of-the-ordinary place for the extermination of what little was left of the Brant family, and of course you didn't hear from me after that. Everybody collected their money. I understand the Haipoong assassins received eight hundred dollars in American exchange. Your agent, Gottlieb, must have secured a tidy bit. And now *I'm* on hand, Hurd. It lacks one minute of five o'clock. How much do you think you owe *me*?"

Clifton had leaned farther over the table. His finger, it seemed to Hurd, was pressing the trigger of the automatic. The man tried to speak. His ashen face was damp with sweat. His lips were white. Saggy lines hung under his eyes and in his cheeks. His hands and body twitched.

A silvery chime in the little ivory clock struck the hour of five. A distant door closed. In the stillness no sound of life came from the outer offices.

Clifton began to count.

"*One—two—*"

"Great God, don't shoot!"

"What price! What do you owe me?"

"Anything—anything you name!"

"Down on your knees, Hurd! *Down!*"

The great hulk of a man slid from his chair.

"I am giving you five minutes of life. Answer my questions. I want to hear the truth from your own lips. If you lie I will kill you instantly. By unfair and criminal methods, yet within the law, you robbed my father of the Brant timber concessions while I was away at war. Is it not true?"

The heavy lips moved. "Yes."

"You caused my father's death?"

"I—I—indirectly—yes—"

"Deliberately you plotted and hired assassins to kill me at Haipoong?"

The heavy head fell upon the kneeling man's chest, as if he had lost the strength to support it. A throaty cry came from his lips and his thick hands covered his face. It was confession.

In that moment if Clifton had looked beyond the man huddled on the floor he would have seen the restroom door slowly moving.

But his eyes did not leave Ivan Hurd. Here, at last, was vengeance. Here was justice measuring itself out in its own full measure. Every line in the timber king's sagging body proclaimed his hopelessness and his torture. With the stoicism of the breed from which he had come through two American generations he was waiting for the end. He was caught, and like his kind—knowing no mercy—he expected none. A great sack of quivering flesh, with his head bowed like a dull-witted ostrich, this man of millions, this power in finance, this war-evading political influence was stricken to the soul by the *little black tube of the automatic*!

And now, as he promised himself in this hour, Clifton laughed. It was a clean, joyous laugh, and in it was the ring of exultation and triumph. Ivan Hurd raised his head. His bloodless face met Clifton's. He saw the other's fingers working at the cartridge clip in the butt of the automatic. The clip came out. It sailed through the air toward him and fell with a tinny clatter at his knees. With pudgy, nervous fingers he picked it up. It was light. It was empty.

The automatic had not been loaded.

He pulled himself up, swaying, and sagged into his chair. The gasping breath that came into his body was like a sob.

Clifton's laughter had subdued itself to a chuckling smile. He laid his impotent gun upon the table.

"Did I frighten you, Ivan?"

"By God—"

The man wiped his face with his naked palms. Mottled spots appeared in his flesh where its ghastliness gave way to a rush of blood. The sagginess began to leave his body.

Clifton was taking off his coat.

"The trouble with you people of Hunnish blood is that you lack the artistic sense," he said, "and that is because you never have the true composition of humor. You make pretty baubles and paint fairly well, but when it comes to the art of dying, and of killing, you are absurdly crude. Now I have come to collect a million dollars, and I am going to show you how it can be done in a pretty way. I don't want it in cash because I hate money, generally speaking. But I am going to collect a million dollars' worth of satisfaction from you, and I am going to take it out of your hide. Killing with the naked hands has its virtue. Are you ready?"

He came around the end of the table. Hurd stared up, gripping the arms of his chair again. With the flat of his hand Clifton struck him in the face.

With an oath Hurd was on his feet. The Hun possessed him again. He no longer faced death, or even the threat of death. He had been terrified, humiliated, and now he was slapped! And all this by a man who had imposed upon him with an unloaded gun, a man who was lighter than he, smaller, slimmer, lithely boyish in comparison with his bulk.

Hun-like he sensed the atrociousness of it all, the unfairness of any enemy playing his own game, or tricking him, or touching him in that way with his hand. He was like a drowning devil, who, praying one moment, found his feet touching solid bottom in the next. His colossal egoism returned and his bullying nature leaped out from the concealment where fear had driven it. To Clifton the transformation was disgustingly amusing. He saw an ox shedding its skin and assuming the form of a lion.

Hurd was throwing off his coat. His cuff links rattled. His watch-chain flopped up and down his vest. He was surprisingly active for a man of his superfluous weight and there was something demoniacally murderous in his rush upon Clifton. He had seized the vase with its flowers, and it preceded him, touching Clifton's shoulder in its passage, and crashed into a thousand pieces against the wall. Then he let out a moaning grunt, for Clifton met him fairly in the face and slammed a fist deep into his fatty paunch.

They clinched. That was as Clifton wanted it. Pugilistic science would have been an insult to his intentions. He wanted Hurd to feel the tiger in him at close quarters, to come in touch flesh to flesh with the pent-up fury that had been gathering and waiting for this moment through many years. A possible blow might have settled it, but Hurd, inanimate or dead, was beyond the reach of his punishment; alive, choking, cursing; feeling himself losing inch by inch, at last facing blackness and the end—in that way he would be paying his debt. They crashed against the table, and in this first contact Clifton was amazed at the other's hardness. Hurd's arms and shoulders were more like solid wood than living tissue, and they possessed a strength he had not guessed at. A month in the woods and he would have been a giant.

His own strength, dominating every fiber of a body trained by walking and the out-of-doors, was like a voltaic force swiftly adjustable to given situations, and realizing instantly his error in judgment he struck up at

36

Hurd. He heard the man's jaw snap. They went down and under the table. Even then Clifton sensed a certain ludicrousness about it—two grown men rolling on a rug under a table! He could have wished the scene to have been attended with a little more dignity. The table upset. It came down sideways on them, then rolled over, so that they were flattened under it like two struggling insects under a chip.

But they were fighting. His fingers were at Hurd's throat. They came out, and he began pounding at the round, huge head, and then—being the first on his feet—he saw his opportunity to grip both hands under Hurd's chin and rip his collar, shirt and vest from his body. The rending of cloth was the last touch to the table-comedy. It left an exposure of Hurd's body up the middle from his belt-band to his chin. When he stood up his collar and tie hung down over one shoulder. His watch was out and dangled at the end of its chain. His fob and diamond pin were on the floor. And Clifton, a little disheveled and with a livid bruise on his forehead, was coolly laughing at him.

The sound Hurd made in his throat might have been that of a great frog. His eyes, it seemed to Clifton, were greenish-red in their rage. His mouth was a little open, and he was sucking in air in quick gasps as he made another rush. His powerful arms were out, his fingers extended like talons for Clifton's neck, when in a swift movement Clifton performed the boy's trick of making himself a stumbling-block in front of his adversary, and Hurd pitched over him and fell to the floor with a crash that sent a tremor through the room.

Clifton recovered himself in time to see the other's watch, rolling in a wobbly fashion across the rug, and Hurd's great legs half in the air, with a broken red and white garter trailing from the back of one shoe. In an instant he was at him, tearing at his garments and beating the bullish head each time it bobbed up.

Hurd had given him the inspiration!—it was a humiliation that would hurt more than physical defeat. The Imperial Instinct was in this Americanized Hun even more than he had thought it would be. To strip Hurd, to leave him naked, to make him a creature of helplessness and self-abasement in his own eyes, drinking to the dregs of humiliation and shame, would be worse than death, leaving in his soul a sore that would burn and fester as long as he lived. With brain and body Clifton leaped to the idea, and for a space he forgot every rule of the game and every instinct of conventional decency as he grappled with the man he hated and whom he had promised himself some day to kill.

And now, if Clifton had noticed, the rest-room door was wide open.

But blindness possessed him, blindness and a fury which until now he had held in leash behind a smile. Their bodies fought from side to side of

37

the room. Chairs fell about them, and one broke into wreckage under their weight. Twice they rolled close to the rest-room door. Hurd's breath came sobbingly and his mouth was open whenever Clifton saw it—open and bleeding; his garments were in rags, his arms naked, his hairy chest and puffy abdomen exposed. Then the reaction seized upon Clifton, and he sprang to his feet. Hurd followed, and Clifton knocked him down. He had never known a head which could stand half the beating which he gave Hurd's after that. The skull was either of iron—or enormously thick, he thought.

At last it was over. Hurd was still conscious, but utterly done for, and his puffy, half-open eyes looked up from the floor at Clifton with an expression of filmy inanity. Clifton, standing over him, recalled the incident of a huge fatted hog which he had helped to rescue from the mire of a shell hole in Belgium. Hurd was like that, wheezing and gulping and choking for breath in the same way, as if his lungs were filled with mud. Clifton straightened the desk armchair and dragged Hurd to it. All of his strength was required to get the heavy body into it, but the result was worth the effort.

As he stood back to observe his handiwork he laughed again.

Hurd, with his backbone gone, was two hundred pounds of formless flesh. He was not tragic, as Clifton viewed him. He was not even horrible, though he was puffed up and bloody and scarcely resembled a man. But he was grotesquely funny. There was something quizzical and bizarre in the glassy way his eyes held their focus on the man who had so successfully collected his debt. He was like a clown who had suffered mishap in the midst of his buffoonery. To Clifton the sublimity of the situation was in the fact that he knew Hurd was perfectly conscious of his own presence, of what had happened, and of his own monstrous appearance—yet was physically incapable of moving even one of his cumbrous hands.

The thrill in Clifton was one of immeasurable joy and satisfaction. How stupid it had been of him ever to have dreamed of killing Hurd! This was better. Memory of this hour would live through Hurd's life with the vividness of a scar branded across his face. It was like the breaking of the Kaiser, he thought. Better to let him live and suffer than to have him die and end it all.

He felt a growing dizziness. Hurd had struck him over the head with a rung from the broken chair and he had not sensed its effect until now. He drew nearer and bent over Hurd. The glassy eyes followed him without the visible movement of a muscle in Hurd's face and an apish desire to do mischief seized upon Clifton. He stuck a pen behind Hurd's ear. He placed an open book on his lap. From a humidor on the desk he took a big black cigar and thrust it into Hurd's mouth. The cigar hung there, a bit droopy, but fixed.

Then Clifton picked up his automatic and the clip and pulled himself together before a mirror. He looked at Hurd again, but the dizziness kept him from laughing as he wanted to laugh, and also it kept him from saying what he had intended to say before he left his victim—granting he was in a condition to understand. But even with his dizziness he saw a last possibility. He took Hurd's hat from a pedestal at the end of the desk and placed it at a rakish angle on the back of Hurd's head.

Then he turned to unlock the door. It was odd, he thought, how his fingers blundered. He opened the door and went out, closing it after him. In the railed enclosure just outside were several chairs and he sat down in one of these. His dizziness would leave in a minute or two, he told himself. But it was deucedly inconvenient just at the present moment.

He heard a big clock ticking on the wall and tried to make out the time, but the hands were muddled.

He noticed the sun coming in at a distant window, and between him and that sun the desks and chairs were confused and indistinct.

He covered his eyes with his hands and waited.

The big clock ticked on. The moments sped. And then an alarming thing startled him.

It was a peal of laughter. It was not loud. It was a girl's laughter, or a woman's, and there was a distinctly sweet and musical quality about it. Clifton started to his feet. The amazing thing was that the laughter had come from Ivan Hurd's room!

It was not repeated. For a space Clifton held his breath, and then the voice of merriment came again from beyond the timber king's door, and this time he heard it say:

"Oh, Mr. Hurd, you look so funny!"

CHAPTER V

A woman's scream coming from Hurd's room would have startled Clifton, but it would have sunk no deeper than what he whimsically called his secondary emotion. A scream was not an unusual thing. More often than not a woman screamed without reason or judgment—at a mouse, a bug, a splash of mud or water on her dress, and surely he would have expected one to scream if she had come suddenly upon a man sitting as Hurd was now sitting in his office chair.

But to *lagh* ...

He took a step toward the door, wondering how much his dizziness had to do with what he had heard. His first impulse was to open it and look in; his second held him back as the significance of a feminine presence in Hurd's room pressed itself upon him. Whoever she was he could hear her moving about, or possibly it was Hurd making an effort to get on his feet. Then the laugh came again. It was not loud or hysterical, but was very soft, and with a genuineness of humor in it that was like the spontaneity of water rippling over little stones. It was almost a giggle.

He drew a deep breath into his empty lungs. This, to say the least, was an unexpected and rather astounding situation. He had observed that Hurd's private office occupied the extreme corner of the building. Except through the main door there could be no other means of exit or ingress unless one climbed through a window seven floors above the street.

There remained only one conclusion and as its weight settled upon Clifton he drew cautiously away from the door. The rest room had concealed someone while he and Ivan Hurd were fighting. That person was young, if he could guess anything by her voice. She was with Hurd when the office girl had taken in his note saying he had five minutes in which personally to give the timber king an important message from certain large interests in Toronto. Hurd had asked her to step into the smaller room for a few moments, and from there she had witnessed the entire affair from its melodramatic beginning to its farcical ending. Now she had come out after the storm, was surveying its victim, and instead of being horrified or frightened she found him an object which had roused in her a most exceptional sense of humor—for her sex!

40

He made this mental reservation as he continued his retreat toward the main corridor. He would have expected a man to laugh, unless a certain part of his brain had gone completely dead. Hurd was funny as he had left him in his chair, pulpy and almost lifeless, his piggy eyes half open, the pen behind his ear, the cigar in his mouth, the hat at a rakish angle on his head!—unforgettably funny from a masculine point of view. But from a woman's, or a girl's—

Well, the world was changing, and changing swiftly. He had seen a lot of it during the last ten years. He had especially noticed it because he had spent recent years in places where there was never change. Women were different. They no longer ran true to type. They were smoking, and quarreling in public places, and fighting in politics, and everlastingly bobbing their heads. Their velvety sympathy was giving way to something else. They could box a man's ears as well as melt into tears. They cried less and fought more, and tears were a politic asset which frequently denoted wisdom instead of weakness. Quite logically they were also developing a new sense of humor as they became more intimate with men and their ways.

That was why the girl had laughed at Hurd, and Clifton found a strong undercurrent of approval running through him as he punched an elevator button.

His head grew muddled as the elevator went down with him. He saw several faces where there should have been one, and he was conscious of holding himself up stiffly, like an intoxicated person struggling to appear normal. It was impossible for him to get out of his vision the bobbed head of the girl who was running the car. It was like all other bobbed heads, irritatingly common and offensive to everything that was esthetic in man. Why didn't such women wear rings in their noses, he wondered, and blacken their teeth, and pull out what few hairs they had left in their eyebrows? Back of his dizziness he had the curious feeling that he had almost come in contact with at least one person who had not performed that idiotic amputation of her hair. She was the girl in Hurd's room. No "bobbed" girl would have a voice or a laugh like hers.

Clifton met the first draught of cool air from outside with an audible gasp. It was like a tonic, and helped to settle his stomach back in its place. For several minutes he stood leaning against the stone entrance, drinking it in. Then he took off his hat and ran a hand through his hair. There was a lump where the chair-rung had hit him. A little more and Hurd would have laid him out. He moved away from the Hurd-Foy Building and walked up the street. It was six o'clock when he dropped into an inconspicuous cafe and called for a pot of strong black tea.

After that he sauntered up Sherbrooke in the direction of Mount Royal. He was all right again and his old cheer began to return. With it came also a new sense of exhilaration, almost of freedom. He had dreaded this meeting with Ivan Hurd, not because he was afraid for himself but because of what might happen to the other. Now it was over, and luck had been entirely with him. His imagination could not have conceived a more satisfactory and at the same time a more harmless punishment for Hurd. He had scarred a soul without taking a life, and Hurd would die with the gall of it in his heart.

As he walked under the thick canopy of the trees that made a cool green corridor of the old highway he meditated on Joe's arrival at Benedict's, and what had happened there. Of course it would be a big surprise, dropping in on him like this—right out of the grave, you might call it. He could see Benedict pumping Joe down to the last drop of information that was in the boy, doubting to the very last that the dead man of Haipoong had actually turned up alive.

Good old Benedict! He began to moralize a little about him, that lovable, ungainly, preposterously careless and altogether fearless one man in the world who cared as little for entanglements with women as he did himself. His adventure with the little Simla widow was his one fall from grace so far as Clifton knew. Clifton wondered why it was that at infrequent intervals some pertinacious little devil would prod his memory with that particular incident. At those times he could see the widow as clearly as he had ever seen her in the flesh six years ago, with her romp of short gold curls, her vivid blue eyes, her mouth that was always pursing itself up into little round O's of delighted enthusiasm or attention—and the height of her—which was just enough to reach Benedict's arm when it was held straight out from his body. He had seen her standing in that silly way one day, measuring herself.

Of course she was pretty. Benedict's judgment wasn't wrong there. She was twenty-six, and seemed to tell the truth about it. The Afghans had shot up her subaltern husband six months after they were married, when she was twenty-one. Quite naturally she wanted another, and had made a strong play for Benedict. She would have got him, too, if it hadn't been for his own strategic generalship in the matter. Possibly he had been a little unfair, but as his opponent was a widow, and short-haired, his conscience had never pricked him.

Then it occurred to Clifton that he had heard in the widow's voice something of that same infectious sweetness which had come from Hurd's room. Funny. It was her laugh which had attracted Benedict first—made him crane his neck over the top of a hedge to see who it came from. Voices like that were dangerous and could cover up an enormous amount of deviltry. On the spur of the moment he had almost opened the door of Hurd's room, just because of such a voice. He was curious enough to reflect upon what he might have seen. Probably someone whom Hurd was going to take out to dinner. Yet there was a flaw in that supposition, for an invited guest would scarcely have found entertainment in what had happened.

He made no great mental effort to solve the mystery.

Nor did he make haste to reach the gloomy old stone house in the midst of its big garden, where Aldous lived. This place was ancestral down to its last stone, for an adventurous Aldous who was associated with the Hudson's Bay Company had come over from London and built it a hundred and sixty years before, and it never had been out of the hands of some scion of the English line since that day. Clifton remembered how the Simla widow had raved about its possibilities, its ghosts and its weirdly improbable stories, and how prosaic Benedict had fluffed up and colored like a pleased little child at her talk. The widow would have liked that place!

He came to it at last, away back in the deep gloom of the three-hundred-year-old trees where the Indians used to hold their councils with the white adventurers who were blazing trails into the hinterlands. It was aglow with light, just as Clifton had seen it on another night more than ten years ago— dully aglow, as if its illumination were still made by candles instead of electricity. The small windows gave that effect. Clifton's heart was beating a little faster when he reached the entrance. It was thrilling, this coming back from the dead. And he loved Benedict.

Scarcely had the dull clang of the knocker sounded from within when he heard approaching footsteps. He would have known them among a thousand, those steady, long-gaited steps of Benedict's, never excited or in undue haste, no matter what lay in front or what was coming from behind. The door opened, and Benedict's six feet three inches of oddly thin and slightly stooping figure filled his vision. Of course there was no change. He had expected none. Benedict's scarce blond hair was no thinner, the wisp of a mustache was still under his nose, his cravat had the same careless twist, there were ashes on his smoking-jacket, and his arms were—as they had always been—too long for his sleeves.

They looked at each other.

"By Jove, if it isn't the old boy himself, true as life!" exclaimed Benedict.

Clifton knew it would be something like that, a greeting with no emotional fireworks. They gripped hands, all four together, and the thrill went through them. It glowed in their eyes. It quivered on their voiceless lips. It twisted at their hearts and stirred their blood with a steady heat. They were two men who would die one for the other. For a few moments they did not speak or close the door. There was a moist glisten in Benedict's pale blue eyes. Clifton knew the same was in his own. Then he laughed. It was a bit nervous.

"How's Bones?" he asked. Bones was the nickname he had given Benedict the first time he had seen him stripped to the skin, with all of his joints revealed.

Benedict closed the door, put a long arm about Clifton's shoulders and walked with him down a low-ceilinged hall into a great room where half the odds and ends of the earth were hanging on the walls.

He picked up a cigaret case in which was a dent made by a partly spent bullet, and extended it to Clifton.

"Have one?" he asked.

By this time two tears had gathered triumphantly in the corners of his eyes, and Clifton, lighting a cigaret, brushed a hand across his own.

"Sure!" he said. "I haven't smoked a cigaret since our tiger hunt at Djharling."

That was the week they had separated, Benedict returning to an important matter in England, Clifton making his plans for China.

Neither sensed the passing of the first hour, or the beginning of the second. There was a lot to be talked about, when the talking began, without anything to interrupt them. Joe was in bed, Bim was in the garage, and the old house was very still. In that first hour of their renewed comradeship little that was ancient history repeated itself. Clifton told of the affair at Haipoong, and Benedict's eyes took on their old peculiar glitter when he heard of the thrills he had missed, and why Clifton had kept his escape to himself. The glitter became a deep and appreciative fire with laughter behind it when he learned of the final vengeance meted out to Ivan Hurd. He chuckled. Benedict's chuckle was infinitely more eloquent than laughter; it was something no one could forget, a mellow vibration of every vocal expression that was in him.

"I feel better now," finished Clifton. "I was a bit of a coward for a long time, afraid I would kill Hurd if I came back. Now it's settled, and in a better way. I feel good about it. I can settle down at last."

They talked about Joe, and of what had happened to them in the years since their parting at Djharling. Clifton, of course, had continued his wandering and had seen a large part of Asia. Benedict had slumped, he admitted. Actually began taking on flesh for a time. Lazed in England for a year, went over to Egypt, then came to the place he liked best of all quiet places —this house on the big hill overlooking Montreal. He loved Montreal. It was the one city in the world—that and Quebec—to dream one's dreams of the past in. Of course, if he had known Clifton was alive and in China, or Timbuctoo, or any place in the Antipodes—

He shrugged his baggy shoulders.

"I'd have looked you up, old chap," he said.

They fell back upon old days instead of making plans for new ones. Clifton had never been quite so happy, not for many years. He told Benedict so frankly. He never wanted another thrill or another shock. He was glad to be home, and didn't think he would ever go very far away again—unless Benedict insisted.

He picked up the silver cigaret case. Reminiscence twinkled in his eyes.

"Remember the Simla widow?" he asked.

Benedict was visibly flustered. He tried to laugh, and failed miserably. Clifton was delighted.

"Remember the day she tried to baby you out of this cigaret case?" he went on. "I was behind the hedge, and heard her!"

"You bally scoundrel—"

"Never saw her look cuter than she did that day, Bones, with her curls all freshly done up and the sun in them—that is, if you like short curls. She said that as this case had saved your life by stopping a Hun bullet she'd like to treasure it all her own, if you would be so kind as to let her have it. And you would have—if I hadn't appeared on the scene. Close shave for you, that was!"

"It was," agreed Benedict.

"Wonder what became of the widow," mused Clifton. "She's rather a setting to our Simla Hills adventures and I sometimes wonder what happened to her. She was a man-getter and I'll wager she laid one out at last."

Benedict hid himself behind a screen of cigaret smoke.

"No doubt, old chap. She wasn't the kind to give up."

"Never been sorry I got you away, have you?"

"I've been happier every day."

"I knew you would. You're not the sort to get married."

"I wouldn't marry the best woman in the world," said Benedict, reappearing through the smoke.

"Neither would I."

Benedict mixed himself a mild whisky and soda.

"You must admit she was rather nice," he argued.

"Who? The widow?"

"Yes."

"A nice little devil," agreed Clifton. "Yellow bobbed hair, blue eyes, a baby mouth—Lord, what a dance she would have led you into if I hadn't pulled you away from her bait! I'd rather be back in my grave at Haipoong than meet such a fate as that, Bones."

Benedict's chuckle filled the room.

"What are you going to do, now that you've settled with Hurd?" he asked in his slow, drawling voice. "Buy a farm?"

Clifton grew serious. He got up and walked slowly back and forth across the room.

"I've come back to begin where I left off," he said, stopping before the other and looking down at him. "Benedict, when I left Quebec woods ten years ago I had hope and ambition, and somehow—you know how as well as I—the war took everything out of me. Ruin and death came to the last of my family while I was over there trying to do something for the ones who brought it about. I wanted to kill a certain man. The disease worked in me. And the war itself made me learn to hate—not so much the men I was fighting against—but my own people, the stay-at-homes, the cowards, the money-grabbers; I saw delusion, fraud, hypocrisy, rotting principles, and I acknowledge I was a fool. I began to wander about, like a lot of others who went through that fuss, and the world soon let me know how funny I was. Three years with you helped me a lot, and I've picked up ever since. Now I'm back, and I'm never going away again!"

"Bravo!" applauded Benedict.

Clifton's face was radiant.

"I want quiet and peace forevermore," he went on. "I'm going back to the only love I have, the forests. First I'm going to take a walk up through French Quebec, where people live as quietly as they did two hundred years ago. From now on until I die I don't want to be startled or thrilled or excited. Those moments with Ivan Hurd were the last.

"I want nothing more than the stillness of the Peribonka, the swashbuckling roar of the glorious Mistassini, the sun-filled valleys of peace and quiet about Lake St. John, where the women still bake their bread outdoors and the men drive horses instead of automobiles. I want to go into the woods with the men from Metabetchewan again, and I'm homesick to walk down that one long street in Chicoutimi, with its smell of logs and pulpwood and its tolling of cathedral bells. I tell you, Benedict, I'm for all time tired of changes, emotions, surprises, shock. I want peace, quiet—"

Benedict's ungainly form was rising. He had a look in his face that stopped Clifton.

"Clifton—old chap—beg pardon!"

Clifton, with his mouth still open, turned about.

Benedict's hand sought his arm, as if to give him support, and from what seemed a vast distance away he heard Benedict's chuckle.

"My wife, old top!"

In the doorway, smiling at him, stood a little vision of white and gold. It was the Simla widow!

CHAPTER VI

There she stood, not a day older than she was six years ago—the same yellow hair, the same eyes, the same baby roundness to her smiling red mouth, the same white dress, the same flowery slimness, the same ineradicable *something* about her that proclaimed her a man-killing rogue right now!

For she was smiling at him, her eyes were shining, her mouth was a round O of delight as she looked at him—seductive—deceitful—impertinent—undeniably pretty!

Benedict's wife!

He continued to stare. His mouth closed slowly. The strength seemed to go out of his legs and body. There was no deception—he was looking at the only person on earth he had ever been afraid of, the woman who had tried to steal Benedict, and who at last had succeeded! Ivan Hurd's blow with the chair rung had had a less stunning effect than this. He gulped, struggling for a word. And he found three.

"Well, I'll be—"

She was laughing! He had always sworn that her round mouth and little white teeth were what had softened Benedict's brain for a time. They were still working, that mouth and the teeth—and the laugh, too. She had the same perfume, very faint but effective—something that stole upon one's senses unfairly, like a thief.

And then, before he could get out of its way, or guess at it, or raise so much as a finger to defend himself—something happened. The Simla widow—it was impossible for him to get that name for her out of his head! —was at his side. In that moment he could not have moved if death had been an inch away. It all happened in an instant. Her arms were around his neck—she was on tiptoe straining her slim body to reach him—she kissed him on the mouth!

That kiss was like an explosion inside him upsetting everything that it had taken him years to build up. It was not a quick, apologetic, Platonic kiss—it was warm, friendly, loving. The touch of the soft mouth was the newest, most astounding thing on earth to Clifton. It came and went like an electrical thrill. He gazed about him in a dazed fashion. He saw a chair, and sank into it.

"Lord, deliver us!" he gasped, looking up at them.

They stood before him like two children, hand in hand, one so ridiculously small and pretty and the other so absurdly tall and angular. And Benedict's face was foolish with happiness!

"Oh, I'm so glad you're not dead!" the widow was purring, and she freed her hand to clasp it with the other in an ecstatic movement at her breast. "When we heard the nasty Chinamen had killed you I cried for a week. Didn't I, lover?" she asked, looking up with adoration at Benedict.

Benedict's chortling chuckle accompanied his nod.

"We've been married for two years, three months and seventeen days counting from ten o'clock this morning," she went on. "Benedict and I were so sorry you didn't know about our happiness before you died!"

Her blue eyes were like a baby's, earnest and truthful and with the last glimmer of coquettishness and laughter gone out of them. It was that look which Clifton had feared most in the days when he had fought to save Benedict.

Then he noticed that her hair was no longer short or in curls. It was a glowing yellow mass about her small head. Its simplicity was stunning. She was quick to see his look.

"I began to let my hair grow three years ago—on account of you," she said. "Benedict said that was why you wouldn't let us get married. Didn't you, lover?"

Again Benedict nodded—like a big, overgrown baby, it seemed to Clifton.

Slowly Clifton rose from his chair. It was odd, he thought, that he felt neither foolish nor embarrassed. His sensation was more like that of an old man, as if years had somehow undermined his feet suddenly. He was sure of one thing—he would be white-headed before he ceased to be an idiot!

The Simla widow had beaten him—and he held out both hands.

"Now that it's all over, *I'm glad*," he said. "I guess, after all, poor old Bones needs a child like you to care for him. I'm not your enemy any more. I—by George, now that I see you together as you are, both stupidly in love after two years, three months and seventeen days—I love you almost as much as I do Bones!" In that moment the telephone rang.

"I'll answer it," said the widow, and left him alone with Benedict.

"Now, what the devil!" he demanded in a fierce whisper. "How did it happen? Why didn't you tell me?"

"She wouldn't let me," replied Benedict also *sotto voce*, answering the last question first. "Really, she wouldn't, old chap. When Joe brought the message that you were alive, and would be up tonight, she insisted on giving you a surprise—a pleasant one, she called it—and so she sent the children to bed early—"

"The—what?" gasped Clifton.

"The children," repeated Benedict. "We have two of our own—little Clairette, after her mother, and Benedict Junior, the rascal, after me—and with Joe that made three to get rid of."

"My God!" breathed Clifton.

"We want two more," said Benedict, "and then we're going to quit. Bally good job, I call it!"

The Simla widow reappeared.

"Benedict, there is a lady on the telephone asking for you—and at this hour! Who is she?"

"I can't guess," said Benedict. "I'll find out."

"Two of them—two of them already," mumbled Clifton, gazing after him. "Two—two—*two*—"

"I beg your pardon, Clifton?"

It was the first time she had called him by that name, and she was so absurdly friendly about it, as if she had been a sister to him all his life, that it was impossible for him not to smile back into her eyes.

"You're a—little brick!" he exclaimed. "Benedict just told me about the children. Is he spoofing me?"

"No, indeed."

"A boy and a girl?"

She nodded. They could hear Benedict's voice droning at the telephone. "Little Benedict is four months old day after tomorrow at a quarter after nine o'clock in the morning, and he looks just like his father," she explained.

"Oh!" Clifton grinned, and a frown puckered the Simla widow's white forehead.

"How did it happen?" he asked then. "Benedict was about to tell me when you called him to the telephone. I thought I had cured you both up in the Simla Hills!"

Benedict's wife dropped her eyes like a child under inquisition, and her fingers played together for a moment in front of her, as if she were puzzled to find an answer. No wonder poor Benedict had been unable to resist her!

"Well, you see, I followed him to England," she said.

"You did—that?"

"Yes. But when I got there he was gone again, so I followed him to Egypt."

She didn't look up, but she could hear Clifton swallow.

"I missed him there," she went on, a penitence so soft that it was almost tearful in her voice, "and I had to go back—and as I knew I couldn't be

49

happy without him—I followed him to Canada. We were married right away."

Clifton dropped back into Benedict's big armchair with a groan.

"And I returned to Canada to get away from changes, emotions, surprise, shock!" he mumbled to himself. "I came for a nice quiet time—and I find—"

Benedict interrupted him. He stood in the doorway. His face had a look in it that reminded Clifton of the days when they had listened to the smash of German shells.

"By Jove, the police are on their way!"

"The police?"

"That's what she says—the girl on the telephone. She won't give her name but seems to know a lot about what happened up at Hurd's. You didn't tell me about her."

"No, I didn't," said Clifton, rising. "Did she have a nice voice?"

"Deucedly to the point, old chap. She insists that Hurd knows you are here and that he has already left with the officers. She gives you five minutes in which to get away, and she wanted me to thank you for what you did to the infernal scoundrel. Said you'd better beat it. Those were the words she used—*beat it!*"

"I guess she is right," agreed Clifton. "I didn't think Hurd would go to the police."

Benedict's wife clutched his arm. He had never seen in her eyes anything like the fire that flashed in them now.

"The—the beast!" she exclaimed. "Why didn't you kill him instead of propping him up in that chair like a big pig? I'd have choked him with the cigar instead of leaving it in his mouth! I'd have—"

"What do you know about Hurd?" he asked in amazement. "You weren't—"

"Yes, I *was*," she interrupted him. "I couldn't help stealing down to see how you would take it when Benedict told you I was his wife. But he forgot, or was afraid, and so I listened to what you said about Hurd. I hate him! And if he dares to come *here*—"

Benedict had gone to the window.

"I can see the lights of a car through the trees," he announced in a mild voice. "It's stopping in front. If you want to be sure of that walk through French Quebec, old chap, I'd advise you to make a leg of it until the thing blows over a little. Ivan Hurd has a mean influence with the city police."

Clifton's face darkened and his hands slowly clenched.

"I thought we had ended it," he said. "I was sure Ivan Hurd would consider the beating I gave him a cheap way of canceling his debt to me. But if he is determined to go on—"

"I must tell you about Hurd," said Benedict, speaking hurriedly. "He is a member of the Provincial Parliament and heads the most powerful reactionary bloc that has ever existed in Quebec politics. He has grafted millions, and his wealth and influence are enormous. Up at Parliament House they call him *Le Taureau*—the Bull. He is merciless to those who dare to become his enemies, and therefore few oppose him. At the present moment —and especially for you—he is the most dangerous man in Canada!"

"And yet, only a few hours ago, I discovered him to be a yellow coward," said Clifton.

"Men of his type are always cowards—when the final moment comes. That is why Hurd will kill you if he ever gets the chance to do it or have it done in a way harmless to himself—because you are the only man living who has broken through his veneer to reveal him as he really is. If you two had been alone he might have kept the thing to himself and stalked you on the quiet. But you weren't, old chap. A woman or a girl was there, and when you strip a man to his yellow soul before someone he'd give half his life to keep that secret from, why—" Benedict paused with a suggestive shrug of his shoulders.

"Listen!" cried the Simla widow softly.

"They're coming up the gravel," said Benedict.

His voice had fallen back into its drawling coolness. He lighted a cigaret.

"Have you good evidence of the Haipoong affair?" he asked.

"Lost," replied Clifton tersely. "I think the evidence was killed. Anyway he disappeared a month before I left Indo-China."

Benedict nodded.

"Remember the day we ran away from the mud huts up on the Irawadi?" he asked. "We weren't afraid, old top. Just policy."

Clifton grinned.

"Good-by, Bones. I'll go. You'll hear from me soon. Do you suppose the Little Captain here will let you join me later up Mistassiniway, just for a peaceful hike?"

"If you hurry—yes," cried Benedict's wife, a sharp little tremble in her voice. "Quick—they're coming up the steps! Don't let them in, Benedict! We'll go out through the door in the cellar!"

She was gripping Clifton's thumb in her hand, and somehow he found himself hurrying at her side, across the hall, through a door and down a narrow stairway into cool darkness that in another moment was illuminated by an electric bulb. With a finger at the switch Benedict's wife pointed to Clifton's dunnage-pack, and as he took it in his hands they were in darkness again. In the gloom she unbolted a narrow door and a silvery glow of stars and moon lighted up her white dress and golden hair.

Her eyes were strangely bright as they stood for a moment in the light. Voices came to them faintly as Benedict played for time above.

And in this moment Clifton felt creeping over him a sense of humiliation and shame.

"Forgive me," he whispered. "That is all I can ask—and more than I can expect in return for the evil which I tried to do you. But I didn't understand. It was because I loved Benedict. And I thought you—you—"

"I know," she interrupted him, and her hand pressed his softly. "I understand. You thought I would bring him unhappiness. When I do that—-I want to die."

"You will care for Joe—for a little while?"

"This is Joe's home, and yours whenever you care to return to it."

He fitted the pack to his shoulders.

She seemed taller when he said good-bye. Her eyes were very bright and steady, and he thought that even in these moments of uncertainty and thrill a smile trembled on her lips.

Her voice had in it an odd ring of triumph as she partly closed the door behind him.

"I forgive you, and I pity you," she whispered after him. "You need a wife, just as poor, dear Benedict needed one. Women are different today, you know, and they don't sit around any more weeping and praying for what they want. They get up and go after it—and especially the bobbed-haired ones. And some day I hope another Simla widow will see you, Clifton, and want you, and go after you, and get you, and I pray—oh, yes, I pray dear God that she will have bobbed hair!"

And the door closed behind him, and he heard a little laugh from behind it, and then he walked up and straight out through the moonlight into the cool deep shadows of the trees between him and the freedom of the wide highway.

CHAPTER VII

Where that freedom lay Clifton paused. It did not lure him out of the shadows. The last tinkling laugh of the Simla widow—of Clairette Aldous —remained softly in his ears, and he felt like a coward running away from a humiliation as great as that which he had inflicted upon Ivan Hurd. He knew it had come from her heart, and its very triumph so gentle that it bore no note of malice or exultation pressed upon him now what seemed to be his own littleness and degradation. He had come triumphant; he was going away whipped—unmercifully impaled upon his own folly. And he knew he deserved it.

He concealed himself in a break in the thick hedge and faced the château. The door was open and he could hear voices. A little distance away he could see the motorcar. A figure was pacing up and down beside it and the moonlight revealed two others in it. He guessed that one of them was Hurd.

Benedict's drawling voice came to him. Another moment a little shiver ran through him as he heard Clairette's. It was like a sharp little barb striking him in a tender spot, for he knew what she was saying. She was covering his flight. She was directing the twin batteries of her prettiness and ingenuous naïveté upon the officers that he might get safely away.

He saw them come out through the door, the Simla widow talking so fast that Benedict was subdued; their feet crunched in the white gravel; he could see the moonlight glinting in her hair, and he heard her say good night, and saw Benedict strike a match to light a cigaret, and watched the officers as they stalked down the path on their return to the car. Then the château door closed with a defiant and aggressive slam.

It was over. She had fought for him instead of giving him up to the punishment he deserved. His face had been hot, now it cooled. He smiled in the darkness of his hiding-place and a little grimly at first his old humor returned. He thanked God she was like that.

Lovable old Bones deserved a woman like her—the best in the world. But what an ass he had made of himself those weeks in the Simla Hills!

A voice growled angrily from the car. It was Hurd's. There followed a consultation which lasted several minutes. Then the motor began to purr, but not before two figures had detached themselves from it, one entering the grounds and the other disappearing in the deep gloom of the avenue trees. Hurd had suspicions, if not convictions. The place was under surveillance.

Even at that Clifton was sure he could regain entrance into the château unobserved. But the desire to go back, though it was warm in his heart, did not move him in that direction. He considered himself a good riddance. So he kept to the shadows and stole to the east with much the same caution with which he and Benedict had left the mud huts on the Irawadi in the younger days of their adventuring.

For a long time after that he gave little attention to his progress except that he traveled a street which ran parallel with Sherbrooke and kept as much as possible in shadow. He had no motive or destination in mind. He was simply getting away from something in an entirely unplanned and desultory kind of way, and only the habit of his last few days of journeying kept him facing the east. Never in the memories of his adventuring had such a complexity of happenings fallen upon him as tonight, and he was still dazed by their unexpectedness and even more upset by the unaccountable emotions which they had stirred within him. Since five o'clock his world had been shaken in a bag.

He was surprised when he reached the borderland of the city. Time had passed swiftly, he had walked fast, and a sea of electric glow lay behind him. Life was obliterating itself in a pall of darkness mellowed by starglow. The moon was hidden beyond the forested crest of Mount Royal and the stillness of Canadian midnight gathered about darkened homes which had thinned from packed-in city dweller to suburbanite, and now to the less tenanted country of the still more fortunate.

Clifton threw back his shoulders and drank in the air deeply as he looked up at a million stars. Such as these were his hours of happiness, with the free earth under his feet and all the world to swing his arms in. He was traveling a dirt road that was soft and springy. The paved trail was farther south.

His anxieties melted away and questionings ceased. In their place came a pleasanter contemplation of what to him had been a series of interesting phenomena. He granted the possibility of unusual psychical happenings, and he seldom traveled alone even when to all appearance he was physically in utter isolation. It was then that life and comradeship drew nearer him and he felt himself gathered into a fraternalism so vast that it filled other universes besides his own.

He believed that to the human soul anything was conceivable once it understood the significance of space, and that somewhere among a billion other worlds and suns and solar systems the greater things in soul-progression were being enacted. And so, partly from a drop of blood that was inherited from the forests and partly from an understanding that was clearer than most men's he did not laugh at miracles and dreams any more than he accepted them as messages to be translated and obeyed. It was their mystery that interested him. For which reason, as he went on through the starlight, his thoughts returned to the old Indian cemetery at Brantford Town and the visions that had come to him there.

It occurred to him that the ghost of the peace-loving young Seneca chieftain might have been right and that he should have left the hatchet buried instead of stirring up all this mess with Hurd. But there had been his mother and Brant and all the warriors to urge him on in the decision which he had already made. He tried to beat around the bush by revisioning only those parts of the dream in which the young girl did not appear. But she broke in at last, and Clifton laughed as he confessed his own weakness and admitted that his mind had gone back to the cemetery especially on account of her.

There was about her much that reminded him of the girl in Hurd's room. She had laughed, she had run away from him, she had been completely elusive and mysterious. So was the girl who had warned him. Both were without a solution that he could think of, and a superstitious person might have fancied things and worked himself up into a curious mental state of hypothesis and conjecture, especially as one girl had knelt at his mother's feet and the other had saved him from his enemies; but as for himself, possessing both sanity and an unexcitable temperament—

"Neither of which I've got," he broke in on himself. "I'm an ass, and always have been!"

Relieved by this burden of confession he stood straighter, walked faster, and began to whistle.

In the cool of night, with a soft road under his feet, he was tireless. The hours and miles fell behind him and the glow of Montreal faded until it was a pale nimbus almost lost in the light of the stars. And now, in that hour of miracle and stillness that just precedes dawn, and with the city fifteen miles behind him, he knew that he had come into the heart of the country of L'Assomption—and the French habitant.

Here he was entering the edge of life as it had been lived nearly three centuries ago, and he looked ahead through the miles and days that would lead him deeper into this land that he loved, with its freedom and its illimitable space, its romance and its tragedy, and above all else its priceless heritage of a people untouched through twelve generations by the mad progress of the swift-moving civilization that shut it in—New France three hundred years ago, still New France today; assimilating instead of surrendering itself to the inroads of invasion, as true to itself as in the days when

Cartier and Champlain and Frontenac first came that way, and to Clifton the one hidden-away paradise in the world.

He knew that he had passed through but the first door of Old Quebec, yet even here, with one of the world's great cities less than a score of miles behind him, all its welcome swept upon him. He passed the sleeping habitant farms, with their barns built close to the road and their homes sometimes unseen. Here a cross and there a sheltered shrine rose in the starlight ahead of him, and always the figure of the Christ with His crown of thorns looked down at him as he passed them. The wayside churches with their doors that were never locked cheered him with the gossamer glow of burning candles and invited him to rest if he was tired.

Slumbering villages grew up like shadows in his path, and about him, it seemed, were remnants of the forests of the earliest pioneers, with oaks so great that they must have looked down on the first cavaliers and seigneurs who followed the trails of the Jesuit fathers, and maples that spread their arms over the road to form long aisles and pools of deepest gloom.

He paused at the top of a hill and from there he looked down both ways on the ancient highway. And behind him he could still faintly see Montreal. It was many years since he had last stood on this hill, and then the little old gray priest of St. Lin had stood at his side and had drawn pictures for him of the days when these wooded hills and green meadowlands had witnessed the making of the first and most terrible of all the blood-written pages of history in a new world.

He had never forgotten little Father Arnaud of St. Lin, who would rather have died a martyr like Chaumonot and De Brébeuf than to have lived in these days of peace. And the visions and pictures came to him again as he stood looking back at the dying glow of a great city, and he tried to fancy that he heard—as Father Arnaud with his strange, restless mind had heard until the day of his death—the footsteps and voices of those who had come centuries before to conquer or die.

In this dust under his feet and in this greensward at his side had traveled the feet of Cartier and Champlain and Joliet and Frontenac. Pierre Radisson, the greatest adventurer of them all, had looked down from this hill, and it may be that the great oak at its crest had shaded Tonty and La Salle; and it was here, the priest of St. Lin had told him, that the Iroquois had tortured Fathers De Brébeuf and Lallemant, plucking their fingers and their nails and tearing out their tongues and at the end of two days of torture pouring boiling water on their heads in imitation of baptism.

And as these priests had died so had others died in this amphitheater whose heart was now the glow of a city. Here the Jesuits had come to offer up their bodies on the sacrificial altar of martyrdom, just as little old Father Arnaud would have done in the same day—Father Daniel who had smiled his forgiveness as the Iroquois arrows killed him; Father Joseph Bressani, who lived through a month of tortures; Fathers Garnier and Chabanel and Jogues, who died at the stake—and scores of others who, the little old priest of St. Lin had declared, gave up their lives in horrible torture that the modern city of Montreal might have its God.

To Clifton, in his aloneness, there rose up much of the majesty and awesomeness of those years that were gone, and for a moment he fancied the dying glow of the distant city was made by the flaming homes of old Lachine, and that if he listened hard enough he might hear the triumphant yells of the Mohawks, the Oneidas and the Senecas as they turned the valley red with fire and blood. And suddenly it was the barking of a dog that roused him from his dreaming, and he went down the hill and noticed that the east was beginning to break with dawn.

This, at last, was the beginning of his homecoming, for there was less of grief here than in the boyhood memories of Brantford Town, and more of hope, and with it the thrilling nearness of that God's country which had claimed him when his body and soul were in the making. A little ahead of him lay the city of old Quebec, and beyond that the vastness of the Laurentian forests, and the great rivers that roared like lions out of the unmapped mysteries of the Upper Lands, and countless lakes shut in by their walls of primeval grandeur—and a people who regarded the English-speaking race as foreigners.

It was there he would find the trails blazed by his father and himself—half a century ago, it seemed to him. He felt himself touched suddenly by the spirit of a joyous adventuring, as it must have touched those others in days when the dust under his feet was a winding path in the wilderness. And then he laughed softly for calling himself an adventurer in a land that was gray with age, yet knowing that it was this very remoteness of its birth and the ancient ghosts that peopled it which gave him the thrill that would never die as long as he lived to vision its pictures under the fading stars.

He came to a stream which was the Achigan, and struck out from the road into the edge of a woodland where a monarchy of century-old elms and oaks reared their heads in a canopy that shut out what was left of the starlight, and here he spread his blanket and prepared to sleep. Fragrance of flowers filled the woods and the breath of earth and green foliage was like a delicate musk in the air, and as drowsiness stole over him he thought of Hurd, and of the police watching the château grounds, and he wondered if Benedict and the Simla widow were sleeping as soundly as he was going to sleep for hours to come, and if the mystery girl who had warned him was at home and in bed—as it was highly proper she should be.

A queer mess he had fallen into, he meditated, but he was out of it now; he chuckled drowsily as he thought a last time of the foolish disturbance he had made. Tomorrow he would write a letter to Benedict and his wife and another to Joe. He wished that Joe were with him, for he missed the little beggar—and Bim. Maybe he would have them come to Quebec later on. These two were last in his mind when he fell asleep.

The world began to rouse itself soon after that. Roosters stretched their necks and crowed while it was still dark. In the little homes with their vivid colorings of red and green and yellow paint the wicks of low-burning lamps were turned higher, multiplying their reflections on snow-white, naked floors and the polished nickel-work and spotless mirrors of the splendid cook-stove which was the grand piano and ultimate ambition of every habitant home. The clink of milk pails came from cool cellarettes built in the earth, and one dog answered another half a mile away, and birds fluffed themselves into wakefulness in the thickets, and with the first streaks of dawn the crows began cawing over the hay fields.

Even here, so near to the great city that its whistles sent faint echoes over the land on still days, there was no wakening bedlam of automobile or trailing blanket of dust stirred up by early travelers. A cool, sweet moisture dwelt in the purity of the air, waiting for the sun; it covered the earth with a shimmering mist and hung in tiny shining pendants from petaled flowers and the ends of thick, rich grass. Strokes of a distant ax drifted like mellow notes in a melody of home and peace and voices called out their morning cheer in the soft language of New France. A song rose, where a man was building a fire in a great outside oven whose bricks had been molded by the hands of his grandfather a hundred years before. And the early sun broke over it all, a rose-flush first, a crimson streak of fire, and next the glory of day itself.

In the wood where Clifton slept a pair of squirrels scolded at the monster who lay under the oak in which they had built their summer nest, and a jay screamed down to help them. But above their excitement rose the melody that was always like a benediction coming out of the forest to greet the summer sun, the voice of thrush and robin and catbird—drab brown nightingale of the Canada woods; of little brush-sparrows that were like silvery flutes, of the cardinal and the golden canary, and the lark with his winged song in the edge of the meadow—a glorious minstrelsy which Clifton slept through, yet sensed in the restfulness of his slumber, until the stillness of mid-forenoon lay heavily again through the greenwood.

He opened his eyes then and saw the gnarled and deep-foliaged limbs of the oak above him, and heard the droning hum of bees among the flowers intoned with the whispering breeze in the tree tops. The wings of the busy workers glistened in the filtered sunlight as he sat up, and his hand rested in a mass of wood-violets that his cheek had crushed. Sweet scent of silvery-petaled anemones and purple trillium filled the air he breathed, and crimson wild fox—sweeter than honey—nodded at him on long, thin stems that grew up out of little seas of broad-leaved mandrake, heavy with their yellow fruit.

It was here, amid dainty lilies-of-the-valley and star-flowers and lady's-slippers and golden love-apples that peace must everlastingly dwell. The thought came to him as he rose and stretched himself, and noted the position of the sun. Here there could be no Hurds, no police, no strife, no marring discord to break the symphony of life. In such a place as this he had often thought he would like to live forever.

And then he heard a sound that turned him with quickened ears, and eyes that sought to penetrate the deeper aisles of the wood. It was a strange and unusual sound. He walked toward it, leaving his pack on the ground and the sound grew more distinct as he advanced, as if a great flail were threshing about in some hidden thicket ahead of him.

He climbed a knoll, and then came to the edge of a tiny forest meadow, and there, looking down, he saw four men crash out from a clump of underbrush in what appeared to be the throes of a mortal combat.

CHAPTER VIII

The men were fighting. There was no doubt of that fact in Clifton's mind. He was so near he could hear their panting breaths, and suddenly one voice rose like the bellowing of a bull, and it was answered by a shrill and squeaking cry from almost at Clifton's feet.

He peered out from behind a concealing bush, and within reach of his hands was a squatted figure of a composition so startling that he swallowed his breath in amazement. The man was little and skinny and sat with his chin in the palms of his hands regarding the unequal battle—for Clifton had seen that one was fighting against three in the terrific combat a dozen yards away.

The onlooker's bent body was clothed in worn and shiny black, and his cadaverous face looked out from under a skull that was shaven like a monk's. In either hand he held a small stick, and these he waved as a band-master might have used his baton, keeping time to the swift-moving events in the little meadow below him. And as he waved his squeaking voice hurled down Latin words and phrases and his heels kicked furrows in the soil.

This much Clifton saw, and turned his eyes upon the fight.

His blood curdled, for if he had ever looked on murder it was happening here. The man who was fighting alone was a giant with a great moon-face and arms that swung like beams, but each of his three assailants was scarcely smaller, and bore down on him in a mighty rush. As they went to earth together in a mass of straining bodies and twisted legs and arms the yell that was like a bull's bellow came again out of their midst, and again it was answered by the squeaking death's-head sitting in the shade of the bush.

Clifton made a swift decision as he realized what was happening. Here among the habitants—even in a three-to-one fight—he knew there was no stand up and take, no warding of blows or pugilistic skill, but only biting and gouging and choking and rib-breaking, strength pitted against strength, teeth against teeth, thumbs against thumbs—and with three hulking brutes against one in that kind of shambles—

60

A sudden eruption in the mass of bodies stopped him as he was about to make sudden descent, and a shriek of approbation followed by a volley of Latin anathema came from the little man under the bush as the moon-faced giant disentangled himself, with an arm around the neck of one of his enemies. And then Clifton saw that it was this moon-faced man who bellowed like a bull, for his momentary yell of triumph made the woodland echo.

But it was choked in the middle by the other two, and down they went again in a scramble of horror, and this time only the lone fighter's heels remained above the melee. Heroically the monk-headed figure under the bush swung his sticks and screeched his encouragement, but the moon-faced man gave no answer, and the heels remained mutely where they were, and *ba'tams* and French oaths of greater quality rose from the triumphant three as they bit and gouged and tore at their victim, while a yellow-throated warbler split his throat in song near the scene of battle.

In another moment Clifton had leaped from his concealment and was close to the fighters. He saw that the ground was torn up as if pigs had been rooting it, and shredded bits of clothing were scattered about, and his toe kicked up a handful of brick-red hair. It was apparent that the bloody debate had been progressing for some time, and now, if he was any judge at all in such matter, it had almost reached a termination. The moon-faced man's legs continued to wave and kick in the air, and Clifton guessed it was his voice that came in muffled snorts and groans and bellows from underneath, but outside those manifestations of life he seemed to be done for. And his complete demise seemed imminent when one of the swearing Frenchmen dug himself out and with both arms pinioned the struggling legs, bent them back, and with a howl of triumph sunk his teeth in the moon-faced man's shank where a ripped trouser leg left it white and naked.

Clifton struck out and the Frenchman let go his hold. He swayed to his feet, mystified by the blow, and Clifton knocked him down so efficiently that he rolled over on his stomach and remained quiet. Then he seized a brick-red head and dragged a pair of huge shoulders after it and swatted their owner with both fists until the moon-faced man was left with only one assailant. For several minutes after that Clifton found himself with his hands full, until a lucky blow in the pit of the red-headed man's stomach laid him out beside his countryman. The moon-faced individual, staring at him through blood and dirt, sat astride the third man's body with his huge thumbs fastened at the nape of his neck ready to give him the *coup de grâce* if he dared to move. From that position he looked his amazement at Clifton.

Now that the peace of victory seemed to have descended upon the land the death's-head figure under the bush scrambled to his feet and hopped like a cricket to the edge of the arena.

"By the blessed St. Peter but that was a timely interruption!" he cackled joyously in French. "It was sweet manna for one¹who is frail in body yet strong in spirit, Monsieur, the lustihood of a seasonable David smiting an accursed Goliath, of a strong arm among the Philistines, of—"

"Shut up!" panted the moon-faced man as he swallowed a great lump in his throat. "Do you dare intimate I would not have wrecked these three with my own two hands, and without help of man or God, if this interloper had not spoiled my plans just as they were about to take form? What difference does it make to Gaspard St. Ives whether there be three or twenty! I've a notion to rattle your bones—"

"Tut, tut," interrupted the little man, dropping his sticks and rubbing his hands gleefully. "If I never have a full belly again you were done for this time, dear Gaspard! Only your heels were alive when the good St. Michael who delivers us from our enemies sent this friend of ours. Thank him, Gaspard. Rise like a gentleman and thank him!"

"*Ba'tam*, I say!"

"You would have had no ears in another two minutes, friend Gaspard."

"I would have thrown them off!"

"They were eating you alive. Even those great heels of yours were growing weak. Thank the gentleman, Gaspard, before he thinks you are bedeviled and an imbecile! Only the grace of God keeps me from doing it, for the words should come from your mouth."

With a huge grunt the moon-faced man rose from his enemy. He was stripped to the waist, and his immense body was stained with blood and dirt. One of his ears bore the marks of teeth, his neck was red from choking, and his left eye was closing.

"I am Gaspard, brother of Antoinette St. Ives, and if you did me a favor —which I doubt—I thank you," he said, in as good French as Clifton had ever heard in the province of Quebec. "And this little parcel of bones with the shaven head is Friar Alphonse, a back-sliding monk from the Trappist monastery of Mistassini at the head of Lake Saint John. If he says I cannot whip these three, or any other three men in Quebec, all at once and to-gether—"

"I am sorry that I interfered," said Clifton, smiling, and holding out a hand. "I can see now that they were almost spent. I am sure you would have finished them in the end."

The giant's round, smooth face with its mop of unruly blond hair grew clouded.

"You mean that?" he asked a bit dubiously. "Had I a chance, think you, Monsieur, with one of them at my throat, another with his teeth in my ear, and a third tearing like an angry dog at my shank? Were they weak when you put those two out—like that?"

"They were weak as children," said Clifton.

"He lies like a man without conscience," rasped the little monk.

And suddenly, without warning, St. Ives put his hands on his hips, threw back his head and roared with laughter. Then he seized Clifton's hand and near broke it in the heartiness of his clasp.

"No brother could love you more than I!" he cried. "You are a man of honor who will lie for a cause, and what better can there be than that? I was trained for the priesthood, Monsieur, but being of free mind and open disposition I loved fighting better, and know enough of it to guess that sweet Antoinette St. Ives would not have recognized her brother a week hence had you not interfered; and as for Angelique Fanchon, next prettiest to my sister of all women in the Province of Quebec, and who will not marry me because I do not love pigs and cows and a farm—why, the sight of me would have turned her gentle soul against me forever! *Ba'tam*, I thank you again, Monsieur!"

His French rolled out in a mellow cadence, and all at once Clifton felt a great liking for the man.

The other three men were pulling themselves together as St. Ives dusted himself and gathered up his clothes. Two of them sat up and one raised himself on an elbow, and smiling and nodding at them in a friendly fashion Clifton saw that Gaspard had given a magnificent account of himself. His enemies were in tatters and their faces were bruised and bleeding. One's nose was still running red, another's ear was streaming where Gaspard's teeth had got a good hold of it, and a third was blinking out of eyes almost shut. There was no more fight in them and they uttered no word as St. Ives led the way up over the knoll toward the river beside which Clifton had slept. Clifton explained the presence of his pack when they came to it, and how he had wakened to the sound of battle.

"You could hear it?" asked Gaspard with pride, as he stripped himself for a plunge. "It was that violent, you say?"

"It was your bull voice he heard howling with torment," chuckled Friar Alphonse. "Never did I hear a yell like yours when that red-headed disciple of the Devil had his teeth in your ear!"

Gaspard rumbled in his deep chest.

"What was the cause of the misunderstanding?" asked Clifton, loading his pipe.

"Pretty women and a liar, friend," grunted Gaspard. "The liar is this worthless rattle of bones Alphonse who tells tales that would hang him in perdition. To maintain my dignity while traveling in his company I am compelled to fight when people tell him what a dissembler and hypocrite he is. He perjures and bears false witness and therefore I have trouble."

"Yet my story was truth," averred the little monk, rubbing his hands as if to warm them. "I did set that hen on forty turtle eggs, and the turtles were hatched, and the hen did go crazy as I described; and in that other story the wolves did tree me, just as I set forth, and as they dug up one tree by the roots I jumped into another, and so kept them digging up trees all night, until I had a little clearing all ready for a cabin, with no work on my part but climbing from tree to tree as they fell. And as for the pet muskellunge, which followed me for days in the water, and into whose nose I strung a ring carrying the Holy Family—Jesus, Mary and Joseph—all brought from the sacred font at Sainte Anne de Beaupré, and in little forms of pewter neatly done in a box—"

"Shut up!" growled Gaspard.

His great body plunged into the stream.

"It was more the women than my stories, I assure you," confided Alphonse as his big friend disappeared under the water. "Wherever we meet in sociable discourse with village strangers he never misses the opportunity to tell them that the two most beautiful women in the world belong to him, his sister and the sweetheart who refuses to marry him until he settles down from his deviltry and becomes a farmer. I travel with him because I love him and hope some day to bring his soul to salvation.

"His sister and his sweetheart, and not the truthful tales which I occasionally relate, were the cause of our trouble at the neighborhood dance last night, for there were other swains present who, under the influence of strong beer, resented his boasts; and so it happened that he offered to fight the three strongest men in the Assomption country, come all at a time, and because he stood with his arm about the girls' waists between dances it was no difficult matter to arrange the meeting for this morning in the wood. It is true some of them did call me a liar because of my stories, but it was Gaspard's pretty sister and the sweetheart who won't have him that started the trouble. I swear it by sweet Sainte Pauline, who died of a most horrible toothache in a wood just like this!"

He was silent for a moment, and his hands grew quiet as he looked at St. Ives plunging about like a great porpoise in the river.

"And she is the prettiest and sweetest girl in all Quebec," he said musingly. "In that he is right. I mean his sister, Antoinette St. Ives. And how she worships this overgrown son of Satan who ambles about like a cock always in search of a new dunghill to conquer!"

Clifton bent over his pack to hide his amusement, but the next words of the talkative little monk put something besides laughter into his heart and took the smile from his lips.

"And when this trouble occurred we were just beginning our way homeward from that monstrous city behind us, where the Devil abides in all his glory—and where Antoinette St. Ives, who comes of the ancient blood of Martin and Herbert and Marrolet and all those others who have their names on the stone monument in Quebec City, has gone to see an unblessed limb of that same Devil named Ivan Hurd. Why, friend stranger, for you have not yet confided in us your name—"

"She—she has—a voice—" began Clifton, before he could stop himself.

"Of a certainty she has a voice, brother. Would you have it otherwise? And she sings like a golden warbler at the beginning of the love season. But look at that gross pig coming out of his wallow—I mean Gaspard St. Ives! How can any beast love him, much less a woman?"

"Yet you said that you had love for him."

"I have."

"Then why did you not help him in the fight?"

The little monk looked up with a grimace.

"Help him—*in a fight*? *Maudit*, you are the first man who ever did it and suffered no penalty afterward. Gaspard will have no help in a fight, even though he die in it. I helped him once, twice, three times—and that is why my bones are so loosely jointed now, because of the shakings he gave me. And so I sit and look on, and call upon all the sixty saints in my calendar, and pound our enemies with Latin, and count my beads and pray—and never in single combat, or even double, have we failed to win. Yet this three against one is sinful and against all the rules of common sense. But I would not have interfered a fourth time—not I!"

St. Ives had come out of the river, his smooth white skin adrip with water, and never had Clifton seen a better made body or muscles. It was the round, moon-like face of the man, wide between the eyes, fresh as a girl's in its color and topped by a riot of sunny hair that took away from the dramatic possibilities of him. Clifton would have judged him a peace-loving soul quicker to pray than to fight.

"I have a towel in my pack," he said. "May I lend it to you?"

"If you will, Monsieur. And you, Alphonse, go make our own things ready while I dress."

The monk drew away into the edge of the wood and Gaspard scrubbed himself with Clifton's towel.

"You must not give much account to Friar Alphonse's talk," he explained, pausing in his labor to give point to his words. "For years he was a Cistercian, in other words a Trappist monk. Then one day a tree fell on him and so cracked his head that it let in a little common sense—God forgive me my own weakness!—and from then on he has traveled the roads, talking all the time to make up for lost years.

"I keep him with me because I love him in spite of the accursed rattle of his bones and tongue, and because that twisted back of his—it is slight, but you may have noticed it—was caused by a beating among the rocks which he received one day years ago in the Mistassini when he saved my sister from drowning. So he may lie if it gives him pleasure—and there never was a greater liar born!—and I will continue to fight for him, come one come all, and break with my hands whoever dares to give voice to that truth that he is a liar. And so, because his words and his tales are the most unbelievable in the world, he is a constant brewer of trouble, and keeps me in good form as you have witnessed, Monsieur—

"Brant—Clifton Brant," nodded Clifton as the other waited for his name. "I am on my way to my old tramping grounds, the Saguenay, Chicoutimi, Metabetchewan, Lake Saint John and all the great rivers north."

Gaspard paused in his dressing and looked at Clifton. Then he stretched out two great hands in a new grip of fellowship.

"I knew it," he cried joyously. "I knew it by the little twists of your French and the way you spit. No other in the world can spit like a Metabetchewan man or a Lake Saint Johner! And I have seen you do it twice, Friend Clifton—twice—once when you hit a lily-of-the-valley squarely in the eye at a good six paces, and again when you shot over that log into the edge of the stream! We'll go on together, for I'm a Lake Saint John's man myself and it's on the streams of the north I live. *Sacré*, but this is luck!"

They left the river and found Alphonse with a big pack ready where he and Gaspard had slept in the wood not far from the place Clifton had chosen in the early dawn. Then the three crossed a green meadow to the highway.

Only half attention had Clifton paid to most of the talk since the derelict monk had dropped the extraordinary information that the sister of this moon-faced fighter whose ally he had become was associated in some way with Ivan Hurd.

It seemed, as he passed the circumstance over in his mind, that Fate was dogging his footsteps with a most unusual and complicated set of events. That it might have been Gaspard's sister who was concealed in Hurd's rest room during the struggle in his office had been his first thought. There was something about the name of Antoinette St. Ives that touched his imagination instantly, especially as he had witnessed the fighting qualities of her adventurous brother. If St. Ives had the nerve to tackle three men at a time it was surely reasonable to presume that his sister would not be afraid to laugh at Ivan Hurd.

But he kept back the question which several times had come to the end of his tongue. His curiosity, he believed, was getting the better of his sound judgment. Yet he said casually, as he walked between Gaspard and the monk: "It is strange that your sister knows this Ivan Hurd in Montreal, St. Ives. It is a long way from the country of Saint John, or even old Quebec for that matter."

Alphonse opened conversation with a curious click of his teeth, and scarce had this click sounded, giving notice of words about to follow, when St. Ives reached behind Clifton and caught the monk's arm in a grip that wrenched a grunt of pain from his bony comrade. In the same moment Clifton caught a swift change in the blond giant's face. It hardened in an instant and a warning flash of fire was in his eyes as he looked at Alphonse.

Then he laughed, and sunshine leaped back into his countenance again.

"It is hard, Monsieur, with a sister in Montreal and a sweetheart in that paradise valley at Saint Félicien, where I should be raising pigs and cattle and high-stepping horses if I were not a fool. It is sometimes hard to tell which pulls the strongest. If you could see my sister, and then Angelique, you would know what it means to be between the Devil and the sea."

"I already know," said Clifton with a careless laugh, as if he had not seen the change in his companion's face.

"A love affair, *ami*?"

The little monk interrupted with a contemptuous cackle that was half sneer and half laugh, and at the same time drew himself a safe distance from St. Ives.

"What fools women make of strong men!" he exclaimed. "Why don't you tell our friend the truth, Gaspard—that this black-eyed wench of an Angelique whom you call your sweetheart has wrecked your heart into a jelly, put water into your soul and turned you out on the highways half a lunatic—and not entirely because you won't turn farmer—but because her eyes are filled with a form even mightier than your own, none other than that of Ajax Trappier, who owns seven hundred arpents of grassy valley, a thousand head of stock, the fastest horses about Saint Félicien—and two legs, a body and a set of teeth of which I verily believe you are mortally afraid. Tell him all that, Gaspard, and you will tell the truth!"

The pink left Gaspard's face and gave place to white.

"It is true this Ajax Trappier is trying to buy her with his wealth," he said bitterly, "and when the humor comes to me I will crush him like an egg-shell for his villainy."

He paused in the road to lengthen a strap on his pack, and Alphonse had opportunity to whisper: "That is a weak spot I hit him in, and I must keep it up to get action. It is the only way to drive him back to Angelique, who truly loves him, and who uses this big fool Trappier only as a foil to work out her ends. If St. Ives will only go back and whip Ajax, and settle down, and become the respectable and God-fearing farmer that Angelique is praying for—by Sainte Marguerite what happiness and children there will be!"

He fell into a thoughtful silence which was not broken for many miles, and Clifton found that when the little monk was in this mood, and walked with bent head some distance behind them, St. Ives held his banter in leash and made no effort to rouse him either with serious talk or joking.

It was noon before they came to a village where they stopped for their morning and midday meals combined, and when this dinner was over St. Ives excused himself mysteriously and said he would return in half an hour.

Food and drink had put Alphonse in happy humor, and his thin face cracked with a smile as his eyes followed Gaspard's broad back until it disappeared.

"So long as there is a telephone and he has a penny in his pocket he will call up his sister," he said, and there was a gentleness in his voice which Clifton had not heard before. "They are all that is left to each other of what was once a great family in New France, and their devotion is like that of sweethearts rather than brother and sister. Abraham Martin, one of those forty first settlers of Quebec, whose name is on the big monument in the square, and after whom the Plains of Abraham were named, was their forefather; and the blood of the Marrolets and the Piverts is in their veins, so that—if it were two hundred years ago—Gaspard St. Ives would be wearing fine lace at his sleeves and carrying a rapier instead of a pack, and his sister would be the sweetest and most beautiful lady in the land.

"It's the spirit of the old days that moves them still, Monsieur. And like two children clinging to their dreams they hold to that ancient and ghost-filled house in Notre Dame Street, sheer under the rock walls of the citadel, which has come down without change of ownership through the Marrolets and St. Ives since Crepin Marrolet built it in sixteen hundred and seventy-two, when the Abitation de Quebec was in Lower Town and the prettiest maids in all the world strolled under the fortress walls instead of above them.

"If you could only see this Antoinette St. Ives, whom God once gave me grace to do slight favor, you would know that shoes of queen or saint were intended for her little feet. If Sainte Genevieve, whose husband went to war, had not toughened my heart until it is like whipcord in such matters I would long ago have died of love for her myself. Yet she will look on no man with favor but her brother."

He paused for breath, then fell silent again, and after a little rose from the table at which they were sitting and found himself a quiet corner in which to await the return of St. Ives.

Clifton, alone, found himself meditating with deep interest upon the strangeness and character of his new acquaintances. The association of a few brief hours had made him feel that he was an accepted part of this brotherhood of two, and an excitement of interest was growing in him which he now made no effort to keep down. For the first time since his adventure in Montreal he conceded without reservation that a real thrill of concern regarding a certain feminine human being had taken possession of him, and the sensation was far from being unpleasant. Whether the girl in Hurd's room and Gaspard's sister were the same or not, he wanted to see this descendant of ancient Quebec, Antoinette St. Ives. The name itself held him with a peculiar fascination, and coupled as it was with a pair of adventurous and unaccountable spirits like Gaspard and the monk its lure was one which he could not have shaken off had he so desired.

He went into the street while waiting for St. Ives and its primitive quaintness was like a forgotten song coming back to him. It was off the main thoroughfare and here the habitant spoke his French as he liked it, and little children shook their heads when Clifton experimented with them by speaking words of English. And then their white teeth flashed with sudden joyous understanding of his playfulness when he talked to them in the tongue of their mothers. He found himself wondering if Antoinette St. Ives was mistress of his language as well as her own. In a vague sort of way he hoped she knew as little of it as her brother. He loved French, and especially this tongue mellowed by three hundred years of great forests and streams such as no other country in the world could boast of. And he wondered—*did Antoinette St. Ives have bobbed hair?*

He bit a freshly lighted cigar half in two at that, and was laughing when St. Ives came up the street to meet him, oblivious to the admiring eyes of a pretty girl in a brightly colored little balcony under which he passed.

He greeted Clifton stiffly, and his face had a hardness in it that Clifton had caught a flash of before. He had little to say as they went out of the village, with the monk trailing behind them.

Half a mile down the road they came to a wayside shrine, and at the foot of the towering cross with its life-size figure of the bleeding Christ the big man paused and crossed himself.

Then he turned to Alphonse, and bared his head, and with the look of understanding that passed between the two the giant and the black-faced little man of God fell upon their knees in the shadow of the cross, and with a note that was both pride and bitterness in his voice Gaspard St. Ives said:

"Pray, Alphonse—and pray hard—to the glory of Antoinette St. Ives and the eternal damnation of Ivan Hurd!"

CHAPTER IX

The prayer that followed was a greater shock to Clifton than the command of St. Ives and his astounding revealment of Ivan Hurd's name in an undoubted moment of stress.

The monk began softly, his voice rising scarcely above a whisper, but with each moment it increased in volume until it was no longer cracked and rasping but filled with a weird melody of passion and intensity that would have filled cathedral walls.

In his amazement Clifton stood without movement and stared at the kneeling figures as the bitterness of excoriation fell like withering red-hot lead from the lips of the little man who looked up with clasped hands and bared head at the crucified Christ. All the plagues and devils of earth and hell he called down upon Ivan Hurd, and from one saint to another he skipped with amazing swiftness, calling upon each with eloquent entreaty to smite the object of his flaying right and left, to strike him deaf and dumb, to blast him with lightning, boil him in oil and deliver his eyes for hungry crows to torture.

And St. Ives nodded his great blond head and rolled his eyes heavenward and the monk's thin face and shiny pate grew damp with sweat as the sun beat down on them in the climax of his prayer. Then came the sharp click of his teeth, like an exclamation point at the end, and the two crossed themselves and rose.

To Clifton's further amazement the hardness was gone from St. Ives's face and Alphonse chuckled and rubbed his hands together as he looked at him.

"Was that sufficient, Friend Gaspard?"

"It was well done, Alphonse."

"Did I pickle him to your satisfaction?"

"None could have done it better."

"If you wish me to give him another broadside, kneeling in the shade of that tree to give me better wind—"

"No, it is enough."

Clifton addressed the monk.

"What is the reason for that prayer?" he asked bluntly. "I would like to know."

"So would I, Monsieur, now that it is finished. I know as little of the reason for it as you, except that my friend Gaspard asked me to send to perdition a certain individual whom he evidently has little love for. And— St. Peter!—I forgot to offer up a word to the glory of our Antoinette!"

"She will do well enough without," said St. Ives.

Then he fell in at Clifton's side and set a good pace along the highway.

"I feel like a new man," he explained. "Whenever the Devil gets hold of me I hand my job of praying over to Alphonse and he lifts me out of the blues in a hurry. Did you ever hear better than that? It would have taken a week of swearing for me to have accomplished what Alphonse did so neatly in less than five minutes."

But Clifton knew that deep down in this unusual man a fire was burning of which he made no disclosure, and glancing from St. Ives to the monk he saw there a pair of clenched hands and a face that was set and pale; and with these discoveries came a sudden and decisive realization that it was not their intention to let him become more than a passing companion of the highway or read what they were hiding in their hearts. Of their comrade-ship and good cheer they gave without end, but in the depths of these men —and he guessed it for the first time—was something more than mere love of adventurous vagabondage and the freedom of the roads.

In the monk he was beginning to detect an undercurrent of shrewdness and deep thought which at times betrayed itself in an undeniable way, and in the poise of Gaspard St. Ives's head and the straightness of his eyes was the revealment of an infinitely deeper character than he had first seen in the roistering fighter. As the pleasant hours of their progress continued his in-terest in them became greater, and he found that even Alphonse loved life and was filled with the humor of it, though his cadaverous face was at times the saturnine mask of a misanthrope.

As each hour drew them deeper into the habitant country of the old French an even more surprising change came over St. Ives. He spoke of the ancient seigneurs as if they had lived but yesterday, and told Clifton the names of their holdings as they passed, describing the charm of their old-world manners and the culture of their time as if he had lived in it himself. He might have known the chivalrous and gay-hearted families of Tascherau and De Lotbinière, Baby and Casgrain, Bouchère Le Moyne, De Salaberry and others whose names came to his lips so easily, for he described the daughters of one, and the sons of another, and how the Gentlemen of St. Sulpice became seigneurs of all the Island of Montreal as though he had been a boon companion with them.

That his heart and sympathy were still with this feudal aristocracy of the Old World transplanted to New France was evident, for there was regret in his voice when he spoke of the act of 1854, when the United Parliament of the Provinces of Upper and Lower Canada did away with the powers and vast dominions of the seigneuries of Old Quebec. His knowledge of history was amazing, and it seemed to Clifton that every treasured act and story of the great drama that had written itself in adventure and blood between the cities of Montreal and Quebec must have known the hand of St. Ives in its making.

Yet at no time did the man's talk have a suspicion of boastfulness, nor did it reveal a pride in his knowledge; and the genuineness of his courtesy and breeding could no longer be doubted when, with all the information he gave about himself and his country, he asked no questions of Clifton and expressed no hint or desire to learn whence he came or the more intimate object of his journey north.

That he was in the company of two of the strangest dual characters it had ever been his fortune to meet, Clifton readily believed, for he made up his mind that Gaspard St. Ives was a gentleman as well as a fighter and a wanderer of the roads, and in the warped and dried-up figure of the monk he saw at times the fierce and inextinguishable spirit of a tortured Jesuit who had returned to walk over his old trails again in a modern day.

His desire to learn more about the association of these men and the sister of St. Ives with Ivan Hurd was uncomfortably insistent as the afternoon lengthened. He even went so far as to remark upon the strangeness of the fact that he himself was acquainted with Ivan Hurd and that there were very good reasons why he regarded him as an enemy. Immediately there followed an embarrassing moment in which the lines about St. Ives's mouth hardened and the little monk looked straight ahead as if he had not heard. No questions followed, as Clifton had hoped, nor acknowledgment from either of the twain by word or look that his information had interested them.

It was after this that Clifton noticed the beginning of an aloofness on the part of St. Ives and his comrade. It was almost a hint of suspicion, and once or twice after that he caught the monk's eyes fixed upon him with burning intentness as if they were determined to eat into any secret he might have hidden away in his soul.

The tension was no less when they stopped at a village for their supper, or when they went to bed under the open sky as dusk was beginning to thicken into darkness about them. The politeness of St. Ives as he bade the others good night was cold and formal, and the monk rolled himself up in his single blanket with his knees under his chin and spoke no word after he had placed himself in this fashion upon the sweet-smelling grass. That the souring of their humor might possibly be ascribed to the exhaustion of the day, Clifton at first tried to make himself believe. But that, he told himself, was not possible in a man like St. Ives. The change had come with the mention of his acquaintanceship with Hurd, and behind that change, if he was not mistaken, lay a suspicion of his motive in joining their company. Deeply puzzled he fell asleep.

With the beginning of another day he was half determined to ask for an explanation, but both St. Ives and the monk seemed to have a hint of his intention and their manner toward him and toward each other was such that he was helplessly at a loss to find an opportunity such as the preceding afternoon had given him. Apparently they were as friendly as ever, but he could see they were watchful without appearing to be, and careful of their tongues.

St. Ives talked again of the country and of Quebec and of the ancient glories and romance of the centuries-old footway they were traveling, and once or twice he seemed to forget himself by breaking into brief snatches of habitant song. But Clifton was still conscious of the mysterious breach that had come between them—until they arrived at Grande Rivière du Loup.

Here they put up at an inn for the night and St. Ives and the monk excused themselves immediately after supper. Clifton nodded coolly when they left him, and made up his mind that tomorrow he would find a reason for continuing his journey alone, possibly by delaying his departure until the others were well on their way. He wrote a letter to Benedict and his wife and another to Joe. Then he went into the taproom and sat down with a mug of foaming beer.

He was at a little table, sitting apart from half a dozen others in the room, when the door crashed open suddenly and St. Ives came in with Friar Alphonse at his heels. In an instant Gaspard was at Clifton's side, his face flushed, and seized his hand.

"Forgive me, *ami*," he entreated in a low voice. "I should not have been gone so long without giving you a reason for my absence. It is poor courtesy to one who stood by me so nobly in that hour when three devils of L'Assomption had me with my heels in the air. But I have been talking with my sister in Montreal and I am happy again, for she has promised to be in Quebec when I get there and will have all the blood sausage in the great market between the Cathedral of Saint Marie and the College of the Jesuits bought up for me and ready for eating. If you ever had a passion for blood sausage, Monsieur, you may know what that means! There is nothing in this world like blood sausage for both the palate and the digestive organs of a man."

"Unless it be the wild blueberries from the hills or speckled trout from the streams of the Montmorency, to say nothing of eels half as thick as your leg," added Friar Alphonse.

"Or grapes that begin to come up at this season of the year from the Isle of Orleans," said Gaspard. "All these she will have for us, Friend Clifton, when you come—as you must—to the humble little place under the old guns of the citadel which we call our castle."

"Your humor has changed somewhat since last night," suggested Clifton.

"It has," acknowledged St. Ives. "I beg your pardon for bad dreams and bad thoughts."

"It was the fight," helped Friar Alphonse, his face cracking with the most genial smile Clifton had seen upon it. "It proves that Gaspard was near done for. His head was unsettled, his wits scattered and his good reasoning powers debauched by the pummeling he got."

Clifton smiled in their faces. They were a remarkable pair. "And I won't embarrass you by asking questions," he said, speaking his thought aloud.

"For which I am deeply grateful," replied St. Ives, without shifting his eyes a thousandth of an inch.

"I had planned to finish my journey alone."

"That is impossible. You must give us opportunity to do penance for our bad disposition of today."

"And yesterday," added the monk.

"Yes—and yesterday."

"I swear by St. Raphael the Good Angel of travelers that it was a biliousness caused by the poisonous teeth and wicked thumbs of those men of L'Assomption," averred Alphonse.

"Or possibly it was caused by a lack of blood sausage in your diet," hinted Clifton.

The monk nodded gravely: "That, too, Monsieur."

"Or by not having wild blueberries from the hills for breakfast, or fat eels for dinner—or an Ivan Hurd for the victim of your hands instead of your prayers."

A low laugh rumbled in St. Ives's chest.

"You are hard on a man when he is down, Monsieur. Shall we have the opportunity of doing penance? Will you continue to Quebec with us?"

"With pleasure."

It was Gaspard's fist pounding at his door that aroused him in the early dawn. For three hours they traveled before breakfast, and at such a pace that the little monk was trotting half the time to keep up with them. His toughness was astonishing and both his wind and his ability to keep his tongue wagging seemed inexhaustible.

"Why are you walking?" asked Clifton of St. Ives. "If you are in such haste to reach Quebec it seems to me you might employ to advantage some other device more progressive than your legs."

St. Ives laughed and drew in a lungful of the fresh morning air.

"Partly because I am one of those misfitted fools who still love dog-carts and rockaways more than I do motorcars and trains, but chiefly because my sister Antoinette would disclaim me as a brother if I did not love to walk."

Clifton felt a pleasing stirring in his blood.

"Mademoiselle Antoinette loves to walk?"

"She has walked every path and highway in Old and Upper Quebec," said Gaspard proudly. "Three times she has walked from Notre Dame Street in Quebec to the upper tributaries of Lake Saint John. It is a matter of history in our family that whenever we have the time to walk—we never ride."

"Thank God that a few are left alive like that," said Clifton devoutly. "For nine years I have been walking, and my reasons are the same."

"Hospitals and graves are filled with people who never walked, Monsieur."

"And hell is cluttered with their souls," piped the monk.

St. Ives gave Clifton a sudden fierce look.

"I take it you consider yourself some walker, then?"

"None better in this province or any other," said Clifton, seeing the other's challenge.

"Straight walking, without jog-trot, ranging or toddle?"

"We will leave it to Friar Alphonse, if he can follow us, and the first to break loses a wager."

"Our breakfasts and a round of beer at the next inn?"

"Done. Are you ready?"

St. Ives shot ahead with great strides; Clifton followed with shorter but swifter ones, and shoulder to shoulder they stirred up a little trail of dust in the highway. Four miles an hour increased to five, and five to six, at which their speed reached a maximum but continued without a break. In two or three minutes St. Ives glanced sidewise and looked his surprise. Never had he met a man who could walk like Clifton. Five minutes, and then ten— and with suspicion in his voice but without a halt in his speed he called back to the trotting monk.

"Are you watching his pace, Alphonse? Has he not broken yet?"

"He walks as true as ever the Devil rode on a stick!" panted the monk.

A quarter of an hour and Gaspard was sweating, though only the rose-flush of the sun had risen over the rim of the east. Dust mingled with his sweat, he took off his hat to let the coolness of the wind in his hair, and he saw Clifton loading his pipe!

"*Ba'tam*, has he not broken yet, Alphonse? Are you cheating, that you may taunt me with another beating?"

"As sweet Sainte Anne is my witness he walks straighter than at the beginning!" half sobbed the winded monk.

"And we have only begun," said Clifton softly. "Come, St. Ives, let us hit a real man's pace. This boy's play can bring us no honor or pride!"

"*Sacré vierge!*" gasped St. Ives, and he saw Clifton forge ahead of him an inch at a time until he was a foot in the lead, and then two, and three, and going steadily.

The monk dropped behind, choking for breath, and sat himself down in the shade of a tree. Now St. Ives could see for himself that Clifton was not breaking. Another five minutes and he stopped, calling out to the victor. When Clifton turned and came back Gaspard's wide-set eyes were half popping from his head.

"If Antoinette could have seen this!" he exclaimed. "Monsieur, she will not believe me when I tell her! And Alphonse—I shall have to kill him now or he will make my life a misery until I die!"

They waited until the monk came up with sagging steps, still breathing hard. He was too far gone to make his thrusts at St. Ives when he learned the outcome of the match. But at breakfast time, when they had finished their meal, one might have thought that Gaspard's defeat had wrecked his soul.

"It was not for him that I care," he explained to Clifton. "He was puffed up like a bladder with his own greatness and needed to be pricked. It is of his sister Antoinette I am thinking, and of Angelique Fanchon, whose ears have been filled with his boasts since they were babies—though I have my doubts that Angelique will care, for coming this autumn I feel it in my bones she will be the wife of Ajax Trappier."

"Then she will be a widow soon after," grunted St. Ives.

"His sister," continued Alphonse, as if he had not heard the other, "has set this bag of wind up on a pedestal so high that there will be nothing left but the jelly of him when he falls. And he has fallen. He is done for. Whipped by the ragtag and bobtail of a country dance, and now beaten by a chance comrade of the roads—it is enough to make me weep for Antoinette and Angelique when they hear of it!"

"Possibly the news may not come to their ears," suggested Clifton.

"It will—just as soon as our little friend can find the opportunity of bearing it to them," declared St. Ives. "And to rob him of that joy I shall tell them myself!"

"If he had half a backbone he dreams that he has he would leave for Saint Félicien before the month is out, Monsieur, whip this Ajax Trappier and marry Angelique Fanchon. If you could see her—with eyes like velvet and hair so shiny black that it hurts to look at it in the sun, and a mouth redder than a wild rose, and a plumpness that fills you with hunger—may Saint Peter and Saint Paul confound me with ghosts and thunder if any man with half a heart and an ounce of courage would not put up a fight for her!"

"But why fight?" asked Clifton.

"Because this Ajax is the mightiest man between Saint Félicien and the big rivers, and has spread the rumor about that he will make Gaspard St. Ives cross his thumbs and beg for mercy if ever the two of them meet. And Gaspard is a little nervous about coming upon him."

St. Ives leaned over the table, and in his eyes was a sullen blaze as he ignored the little monk's words and spoke directly to Clifton.

"You have fought?" he asked. "You have been through the war?"

Clifton nodded. "Yes."

"You have seen some good fights?"

"A few."

"And you are on your way north—you are going there soon?"

"Very soon."

"Then, without going out of your way, will you honor me with your presence at the greatest fight that will ever have been fought in all the Lake Saint John country? I mean when I go to meet this Ajax Trappier, sometime within the coming month?"

There was no humor back of his eyes. His great hands were clenched and his mouth was set tight.

"If it were a hundred years ago, Monsieur, I would have killed him for what he has said about me at Saint Félicien!"

Clifton thought of the years through which he had held back his vengeance from Ivan Hurd. And he guessed that St. Ives had been making the same kind of fight through a briefer period.

"If it is within the month," he said, "I will gladly join you in any trouble you may have, St. Ives."

And for the first time Clifton fancied that he saw real happiness shining in the little monk's face as they set out once more on their journey to Quebec.

Late in the afternoon of the third day after this, with Quebec only a few miles away, an excitement that was almost boyish began to possess St. Ives. His blond face was flushed and his wide eyes filled with dancing lights, and for the twentieth time he assured Clifton that since Crepin Marrolet brought his bride to the house in Notre Dame Street two hundred and fifty-two years ago never had that house been more welcome to a guest than it would be to him this night.

If his sister had not yet arrived from Montreal they would still make a good time of it, with old wine and plenty of the best beer in the province, and blood sausage in quantities to satisfy that belly-god Apicius himself. And Clifton, he was sure, would be interested in the old, true stories of his house that had come down with their family through so many generations, and in which they still lived in spite of the fact that Lower Town was now mostly inhabited by the canaille and was picturesque with begging children.

It was the glory that was gone which held them, St. Ives impressed on Clifton. The place was filled with ghosts. Its oak was shiny with age and the rail of its narrow stair worn smooth by the touch of the beauty and culture of two and a half centuries ago. Crepin, a fierce young blade of those times, had brought one of the three most beautiful girls in Quebec to this place as his bride in a day when his fortunes were low in the royal favor in France. And now Gaspard's sister Antoinette, by all odds the most beautiful girl in this decadent Quebec of today, slept in that very room where Adelaide Marrolet first lay in happiness at the side of her husband.

In that same room the sweet Adelaide had died in the third year of their married life, just one week after she had looked on the body of her husband, brought home dead from a duel. Antoinette swore that she often talked with the spirit of Adelaide, and that she was sure the young wife had poisoned herself. Others had died in the old house, too; so many of them that it was impossible for him to remember all their names and the stories they had to tell. But the place was filled with the whisper and queer perfume of ancient romance and tragedy, as if happiness and broken lives and bits of history had been done up in musk and buried between its walls. And there was a story, come down from sixteen hundred and something, that the place was built over the lost bones of Champlain. Antoinette St. Ives would tell him all about it. Gaspard repeated that he was sorry she would not be home that night, in all probability, but he was sure they would have an agreeable time together.

His talk stirred Clifton as he had never been stirred before. It seemed to him that a new discovery of life had come into his body, and it warmed him with an anticipation of events to come that was pleasanter than anything he had ever experienced. Here he had met a man of a kind he had sometimes built in his dreams—a misfit of the age, as he called himself, a dreamer, one whose thoughts brought into the present something of the idealism and glory and thrill of a wonderful past—a man who would live in the shambles of old stone because of the associations through which those

78

stones had lived. And there was a woman in the world who was like him—his sister!

They approached the city by way of Sainte Foy Road and crossed to Saint Louis Road, passing Wolfe's Field and the battle-ground of Sainte Foy and the Plains of Abraham on their way to the heights that looked down with towering walls and bristling rows of ancient guns into the lower town. They crossed the terrace and for the first time in many years Clifton found himself again on the great board walk, wider than a street, from the railing of which he could look down upon the firefly glow of a thousand lights along the river and between the age-old walls of the lower city.

Back of him rose the gigantic and brilliantly lighted Château Frontenac, like a Gargantuan castle built for ten thousand warriors to hold; below him lay a half of the history of the New World.

He recalled that day when as a youth just entering into the romance and thrill of manhood he had first stood at this dizzy edge of Dufferin Terrace with his father, who had pointed out to him below the spot where Champlain had landed, and where Montcalm had lived, and had told him of some of the happenings of two and three hundred years ago that had consecrated all that ground with its twisted little streets, quaint chimneys and odd roofs.

Vividly there stood out in his memory his father's thrilling story of the little old church of Notre Dame des Victoires, which had stood down there almost from the beginning of time, for Champlain himself had cleared a spot for it and had built a house there first. The tolling of its bell came up to him sweetly now out of the stillness of the summer evening, and he saw St. Ives make the sign of the cross as he looked down where in day he would have seen the steep roof and age-blackened spire of the edifice that had stood a bulwark of glorious inspiration in those hours of strife and blood and despair when the fortunes of New France were blackest.

"It is my sister's church," he said simply. "She loves to worship there."

Somehow the words, senseless as they were, came from Clifton, "Mademoiselle St. Ives is a Catholic?"

"She is—everything," replied St. Ives in a strangely low voice. "She is Catholic, yes—and she is everything else that looks toward God. If there were more like my sister there would not be this quarreling and ranting between sects and churches, and all people would see God with the same eyes. The Protestant would not be suspicious of the Catholic, nor the Pope of the Free Church, nor the believers in Christ of those who believe only in the Unity. All churches and all religions are holy to Antoinette St. Ives, Monsieur!"

There were pride and a little defiance in his voice, as if he half suspected that Clifton himself was accursed with the blighting narrowness of sectarianism.

They came to the elevator car that traveled like a huge beetle up and down the rock wall of the terrace, saving the winding walk by way of Mountain Hill and Break-Neck Stairs, and a few minutes later stood in Lower Town, and almost immediately after that reached Notre Dame Street.

Here Friar Alphonse stopped, and bade his companions good night.

"He has many friends among the priests and friars and monks, and is eager to see them," explained St. Ives after he was gone. "That is why I call him Friar. He is as much one as another, though cowled monk is the rascal's proper place if he had kept it."

And now, down this street so narrow that the span of two men's arms could have reached across it, a street of ancient brick and stone dimly lighted by the glow of narrow windows, Gaspard St. Ives led the way. And then, ahead of them, a lantern of hand-beaten iron glowed with its yellow light, suspended from ancient metal arms buried in the stone wall.

St. Ives paused under it with his hand on the latch of a deep-set door.

"This is it, Monsieur!"

The door was unlocked, and they passed into a little entrance hall not more than four feet square, with a second door of leaded glass behind which other light revealed a curtaining of filmy lace. This St. Ives also opened, and in another moment Clifton stood in a bit of the heart of Old Quebec and New France.

The room was large and low. Its woodwork was quaint and every darkly glowing beam and panel bore the irregular craftsmanship of hand and adz. With the tips of his fingers St. Ives could have touched the ceiling, yet Clifton felt no sense of being crowded. An indescribable atmosphere of peace and comfort surrounded him. It was as if he had stepped suddenly out of the world into a place where turmoil and strife could not reach him and from which the storms and vicissitudes of life were barred.

It had upon him the almost startling effect of a sanctuary, and he felt that here, no matter what might happen outside, one was safe. He did not see the furnishings of the room in detail; they were more like the parts of a picture impressing him as a whole. But he knew that everywhere was the presence of a great age, in the walls themselves and the narrow, winding stairway, in the shaded lamps, the pictures and the great dog-irons in the fireplace. In a glance he saw all this, and two doors deep-set between heavy beams of oak that opened into other rooms—and then he looked at his companion.

St. Ives was standing with bowed head before an ivory crucifix built in a deep niche in the wall. A moment there was silence, and as he raised his head and saw the look in Clifton's face he said:

"Pardon, Monsieur. I never forget this little duty, more for my sister's sake than my own. This ivory figure of the Christ has looked upon every happiness and tragedy and every laugh and tear in this house since Crepin Marrelot put it there two hundred and fifty years ago. It was on this floor under the Crucifix, with her hands reaching up to it even in death, that Adelaide Marrelot was found."

He had scarcely spoken when a slight sound drew them quickly about and both raised their eyes to the head of the stair. In that moment Clifton's heart seemed for one swift instant to stop its beating. In a mellow glory of light stood the slim figure of a girl, and by the radiance of welcome in her face he knew that she was Antoinette St. Ives.

He was grateful afterward that she seemed not to see him but was looking at her brother, for in that moment he also knew that a strange thing had happened within him and that it must have shown in his face, just as in another hour that same mystery and revealment had transformed the face of Benedict Aldous when he looked over the low hedge in the Simla Hills and saw for the first time the white and gold beauty and soft blue eyes of the Simla widow.

And then St. Ives was going up the stair three steps at a time, and from the top came a happy, thrilling little laugh and the girl's voice in greeting. Clifton pulled himself together and swallowed to keep a sudden thickening out of his throat. Nothing had ever disturbed him quite so much—not even the Simla widow—as the laugh and the voice as they came from Antoinette St. Ives.

For he had heard them before—in Hurd's room. It was Antoinette St. Ives who had watched the fight from her concealment in the rest room! It was she who had laughed at the wreck of Ivan Hurd as he had left him in his chair! And it was she—the sister of Gaspard St. Ives—who had sent the warning over the telephone, and who was now coming down the stair to welcome him to this little hidden corner of an ancient world in which she lived!

CHAPTER X

More than one emotion swept over Clifton in the few moments it took Antoinette St. Ives and her brother to reach the lower room. To him she was like a lovely presence that had suddenly taken flesh and form out of all the romance and beauty which the dark walls about him must have sheltered in their day. St. Ives had called her the loveliest girl in Quebec, and in this amazing hour when for the first time a woman took possession of his soul Clifton thought of her as the most beautiful in the world. Yet he could not have described her had darkness suddenly shut him in, except that the top of her head came to her brother's shoulder, and that soft brown curls touched her cheek and neck, and that her chin was very high as she seemed first to look at him coming down the stair.

And then he was looking into her eyes, steady and gray and sweeping him from his pinnacles of assurance with their calm loveliness, and—he thought—a bit disdainful as her lips smiled.

"My sister, Monsieur Clifton Brant!"

The head with its velvety ripple of curls inclined itself a little, and Clifton bowed. His ready tongue was gone. Words that had never faltered on his lips grew dumb. He might have stood before a princess or a queen and smiled back proudly his American heritage of freedom and superiority, but before Antoinette St. Ives he felt dumbness and littleness creeping upon him. He held her extended hand and its warmth and smallness thrilled him. The blood rose in his neck and cheeks and he hated himself for his weakness.

"I am happy that you have come, Monsieur Brant!" she said in the sweetest of French, as if the meeting had been an appointed one, "I have waited quite impatiently for your arrival since morning. You are welcome to what we are pleased to call our little Château St. Ives!"

"You were expecting me?" he asked, as she drew her hand away. "I thought—"

He was glad St. Ives broke in with one of his sonorous chuckles.

"I must depend upon Antoinette St. Ives to secure your forgiveness," he said, as Clifton hesitated, "though I am assured by Friar Alphonse that a fib in good cause is a Christian act. And what better cause could there be in this world than for the sweet sake of my sister, who told me all about you over the telephone that night at Grande Rivière du Loup, and asked me to bring you here dead or alive but to keep to myself the reason for it, and to breathe no word either asleep or awake that might lead you to suspect a trap was being laid for you. And so—"

"Gaspard!"

"It is true, Antoinette—and I must relieve my soul of its guileful mendacity before I take a bath!"

"I spoke of no trap!"

"Not in words, but I read your mind and there was that kind of witchcraft in it."

A flush came into the girl's cheek and a defiant tilt to her chin as she looked at Clifton. He could see the little golden flecks in her eyes, like the tiny freckles made by fairy kisses in petals of the wood-violet, and each little fleck was filled suddenly with the flash of diamonds.

"Did he not give you my message, Monsieur Brant—and my invitation?" she asked.

"The only message I received from you, Mademoiselle, came over the telephone to my friend Benedict Aldous. For that I am grateful."

"Did he not tell you other things—among them that it was of great importance to me that I see you here within a week?"

"Had I told him that, Antoinette, he would have insisted on greater haste by means of motor or train and thus have spoiled my walking trip," interrupted St. Ives.

Antoinette St. Ives turned on her brother with a toss of her head that sent her curls into an instant's riot of flashing lights and soft confusion.

"For this," she said fiercely, "I shall not give you a letter which has come for you from Angelique Fanchon!"

St. Ives raised his hands with a gesture of dismay.

"From Angelique, you say? I entreat you, Antoinette—"

"You shall not have it—at least not until you have had your bath and I have seen you suffer a little. Your playfulness, Gaspard, will one day reach a tragic point. Why did you not tell Monsieur Brant that I had asked for him to come to me?"

"Because I used my man's judgment, and wanted to measure him up as another man—without filling his head with thought of my beautiful sister to change his disposition. And a man's judgment, Antoinette—"

She interrupted him with a little shrug of her shoulders and turned to Clifton. He had been staring at her, and in his contemplation of her increasing loveliness had scarcely listened to the scolding she was giving St. Ives. At first, with a kind of shock, he had thought that her hair was cut short and curled as the Simla widow's had been in the old days; but then he saw that the curls were pinned up and that one which had broken loose from its silken company almost touched her shoulder. This curl Antoinette St. Ives tucked in its place as she turned her back upon her brother.

"I am sorry, Mr. Brant," she said, changing suddenly to English. "Gaspard should have told you. I saw Mrs. Aldous within a few hours after you had gone, and when my brother said over the telephone that he was traveling in the company of one named Clifton Brant I think my heart almost stopped, for you were the one man in the world I wanted to see very soon and I was afraid I might have lost you indefinitely. I told him to let you know that I was in Ivan Hurd's room when you—annoyed him that afternoon."

A humorous light lay in her eyes as she recalled this incident. It was a look that gave Clifton back his courage and mental balance. She was still laughing at Hurd as he had sat huddled in his chair. Then it came upon him that he had been unsettled by the presence of a very small person, one not a mote larger than the Simla widow who yet appeared to be taller by inches. He could have tossed her to a ceiling twice as high as that of the room in which they stood. She was exquisitely feminine, and yet he sensed in an instant the difference between her and Benedict's wife. The Simla widow, finding herself fighting, would win her way with softness and tears while Antoinette St. Ives would win or die with that same proud tilt to her head and with eyes that might fill with tears yet never lose the steady glow of gray fires that lay in their beautiful depths. He liked it that way better.

"I heard your voice," he said. "I am sure it would have drawn me back, but I was a little dizzy and sick from a blow on the head. Hearing your voice in that room was the greatest surprise of my life, just as meeting you now is the greatest pleasure that has ever come to me."

"That is strange, Monsieur Brant. I was afraid it would be an annoyance instead of a pleasure to you. You have such a terrible reputation as a woman-hater—"

"Clairette Aldous told you that?"

"—and detest women with short hair, though mine is not entirely that, and is curled by nature if you please—"

"She told you that?"

"Yes, and so many other things that I feel you are scarcely a stranger."

"Then she has helped me some, thank God!"

"But you are a fighter in spite of the hopelessness of your other shortcomings," she went on. "I have had a most unforgettable demonstration of that. Otherwise I am sure I should never have been interested in you."

St. Ives touched his sister gently on her shoulder.

"If you will give me Angelique Fanchon's letter—"

"Not until you have had your bath and dinner."

"But it may be important."

"I think it is, Gaspard."

"And you will not give it to me?"

"No."

"Then I may as well drag you away to water and soap, Friend Clifton, for this lovely sister of mine has a stubbornness like the Devil's own when her mind is once made up." He bent his big head and like a lover kissed her smooth hair where it was parted in the middle; and almost in the same moment Antoinette St. Ives's hand went to her bosom and drew forth a letter which she gave to her brother.

"That kiss does away with a hundred sins, Gaspard," she said softly. "I hope the letter brings you happiness!"

Clifton's heart throbbed warmly at the look of swift tenderness that had come into her face. As he followed St. Ives up the stair he thought of it as a flash of sunshine that had come suddenly out from behind the still tranquillity of a beautiful cloud. A look like that must fill a man's soul with the glory of loving!

St. Ives ushered him into a little bedroom with a low roof that sloped almost to the floor on one side, and returned for his pack. When Clifton had selected the best of his clothing, consisting of a clean outfit of walking togs, he was introduced to a smaller room half occupied by a porcelain tub. St. Ives, still clutching Angelique's letter in his big hand, made him an elaborate bow.

"Behold the chief luxury of Château St. Ives, Monsieur—our bathing urn, which Antoinette insists upon calling a vaporarium. There is hot water in the right spigot and cold in the left. The tub measures four feet in one direction by three in the other, so make your measurements carefully before diving into it. And if you will pardon me for leaving you while I read Angelique's letter—"

"Don't let me detain you another moment from that pleasure," urged Clifton. "I join your sister in hoping that it brings you joy."

He had partly finished with his bath when the door opened and St. Ives rushed in. His face was blazing and the letter was crumpled in his hand.

"Joy!" he exclaimed. "This thing brings me joy!—this two-paged parcel of impertinence, this woman's falseness and deceit flung like birdlime at a real man—this—this—"

"What does it say?" interrupted Clifton soothingly.

"Say? It says nothing about me! From beginning to end it is filled only with this Ajax Trappier, how fine his horses are, what a splendid man he is, how he supports the church like a saint and drives over to take her riding each Sunday! It is an insult, Monsieur, and I thirst for the blood of the man who is the cause of it! Why should she peddle me the gossip of this polisson who bought his way out of the war, this reptile who would sell himself to the Devil to get her, this—"

"I don't know," interrupted Clifton again, standing up in the tub. "Let me read it, Gaspard!"

St. Ives smoothed out the crumpled letter and placed it in his hands. As Clifton read he smiled, and Gaspard's face darkened with wrath.

"It is quite clear," said Clifton. "I think that in many things Friar Alphonse is right, and in this one particularly so. You are thick-headed, St. Ives. Angelique Fanchon wrote this letter because her heart is eating itself up with love for you, and she is taking a woman's way of bringing you to time. You have quarreled with her recently?"

"A little misunderstanding caused by a difference in viewpoint. She thinks I am a wanderer and a good-for-nothing because I love the woods and the big rivers more than I do a farm and horses and pigs."

"And you love her?"

"I would pull down the stars and give them to her if I could."

"Yet you would not become a habitant for her sake?"

"I will not be bullied by a woman and that priest at Saint Félicien who is urging her to marry Ajax Trappier and have twenty children."

"Then what are you going to do?"

St. Ives sucked in a hissing breath of vapor and air.

"I am going to break every bone in Ajax Trappier's overgrown body!"

"Good!" nodded Clifton, returning the letter. "And let us be about that business as soon as we can. It is my opinion that Angelique would cry her eyes out with fear if she knew you were going into this danger. But I also think it will do a lot of good, no matter who wins in the contest."

"You guess that she loves me?"

"I am sure of it."

Gaspard smoothed out the letter and read it again while Clifton dried himself.

"If that is true," he said in a softened voice, "I swear to Sainte Anne I will never sing in a tap-room again! And I wouldn't mind owning a farm if I could leave it fallow, and if it was near the big rivers, and if this skunk of an Ajax Trappier whose scent offends me lived in the next county."

"Have you asked her to marry you?"

"How could I unless I promised first to become a farmer? But she knows that I love her. I have told her that!"

"I wonder why she is so insistent?" mused Clifton, his words only half implying a question.

St. Ives was silent for a moment, then laughed softly.

"If it was not for this accursed Ajax Trappier I would not blame her. It is in her blood. Her great-great-grandfather settled in the Saint Félicien coun-

86

try a hundred and sixty years ago, and the Fanchons have lived on the same land all that time. Angelique is proud of all that and holds her head high. They are great land-owners and she is a princess in her country. And I—" St. Ives shrugged his shoulders hopelessly. "Tonight you will learn why I am almost a pauper, and a St. Ives is too proud to accept a Fanchon patrimony along with his wife. I have opened the shell and you have the meat of the thing now! If Angelique Fanchon marries St. Ives she must go with him to a place where he can build a home for her himself." He turned to the door. "Will you come down when you are ready, Monsieur Clifton?"

After he had gone Clifton shaved himself and dressed. For a quarter of an hour the same unanswerable questions repeated themselves in his mind, and by the time he finished he had worked himself into a fair state of mental excitement. Something told him he was on the edge of the greatest adventure of his life, and the probability that Antoinette St. Ives was included in this adventure and was possibly the heart and soul of it aroused every nerve in his body with eager anticipation.

She was waiting for him when he descended the stair, and St. Ives had disappeared. He caught her reading and as he looked down on her bowed head its color made him think of the rich tints of a chestnut burnished and ripened by heavy frosts. He was not a dissembler. His admiration shone in his eyes.

"The warrior!" she greeted him. "My brother has been telling me how you helped him out of the trouble at L'Assomption and then beat him in a walking match on the highway. You do not look so terrible, and unless I had seen with my own eyes I am quite sure I should doubt Gaspard a little."

Her reference to the battle in Hurd's office was accompanied by what Clifton accepted as a covert note of humor in her voice. She was laughing at him for some reason, and suddenly his choler began to rise as he thought of the many uncomplimentary truths which the Simla widow might have revealed about him.

"Won't you sit down?"

He seated himself stiffly.

"I am at your command," he said.

She bent her head a little so that the glow from above caught her curls with enrapturing lights. He could see her long lashes, a bit darker than her hair, the pink of her cheeks and the soft red of her mouth—and his heart rose up and choked him.

"Please do not be so uncomfortably formal," she entreated. "I can understand why you have such an outrageous opinion of me, and I am quite frank in expressing myself when I say that I do not like you—but such trivial matters must not come between us at the present time. Not, at least, until you understand the very important reason why I have had you come to Château St. Ives."

"Why should I have a bad opinion of you?" he demanded.

"Because I was concealed in Mr. Hurd's rest room, of course! Nice young ladies are not caught in such a compromising situation, are they?"

"And you don't like me? Why?"

"Because you have no heart, no soul, no romance—because—"

Clifton rose protestingly from his chair.

"It's Clairette Aldous! She told you a lot about me, didn't she? And you haven't hesitated to let me know about it, almost before I'm dry from the use of your vaporarium. In fact I dressed myself before I was dry. And why did I do it? Why was I in such haste? I'm going to be frank with you, too. I'm going to shock you. It was all because of you! I wanted to look at you again. I wanted the opportunity of telling you that from the moment I found you were acquainted with Ivan Hurd something told me you were the girl whose voice I fell in love with that day. But I did not dream that good fortune would compel me in self-defense to disclose the cataclysmic thing which happened when I first looked up and saw you at the head of the stair. You have forced me to make that disclosure by intimating that I have a bad opinion of you, have actually necessitated the confession that my heart turned somersaults, and that at no time in all the history of the world—in spite of the fact that I have no heart and no soul and no romance —has a man ever been readier to die for a woman than I am this very minute for you! So I repeat—I am at your command!"

He paused for breath.

"It's your turn, Mademoiselle!"

Antoinette St. Ives, looking up at him as he stood before her, had turned red and then white. And now he was laughing down into her face, even though his mouth was a little tense. There was something more than jest in his eyes. Clairette Aldous had told her he was a man of remarkable possibilities, and he was. She rose from her chair and stood so close to him that he might have touched her. Never had he seen anything so coldly, gloriously beautiful as her eyes looking straight into his.

"With one exception this is the most infamous piece of effrontery I have ever listened to!" she said in quiet disdain.

"And that exception?" asked Clifton undismayed.

"There is only one other capable of subjecting me to it—Ivan Hurd!"

"For which I shall cheerfully kill him when the opportunity arrives," he declared, bowing as if to a princess. "I am your slave, Mademoiselle. And to be most efficient a slave should love his mistress."

Not for a moment did her eyes waver. The changing light in them seemed to draw out his soul. He knew that he wanted to touch her. He wanted to put a hand on her shining head. She seemed to read the thought, and her chin tilted itself another fraction of an inch. It was a gesture which would have put an immense gulf between her and any man. Clifton liked it though it struck him like a barbed shaft.

The tenseness of the moment was interrupted by the opening of the street door, and Gaspard's voice came to them from the little vestibule. It was answered by another, and the look of pleasure that came suddenly into the girl's face pierced Clifton even more than the haughty tilt of her chin. For the first time in his life he knew jealousy. It was upon him with the swiftness of lightning—and in that abysmal moment when Antoinette St. Ives's face and eyes lighted up like that at the sound of a man's voice he knew how far he had fallen.

He turned slowly, getting a dogged hold of himself. He was a fool, and an old fool at that. He was almost forty, and Antoinette St. Ives could be scarcely more than twenty. There were hard lines about his mouth as he saw Gaspard's companion—a slender, pale-faced man with graying hair above his ears. He stared. He saw Gaspard standing a little behind, grinning. Antoinette St. Ives was regarding them both with shining eyes.

And then in the same instant both men advanced with a cry of greeting and outstretched hands.

"Denis—Colonel John Denis!"

"Captain Brant!"

CHAPTER XI

It was a surprise for Clifton—this sudden meeting with the old friend at whose side he had fought through the hells of Flanders. He had expected to look him up while in Quebec, for it was at Sanctuary Wood that Colonel Denis had dragged him half dead off a field that fifteen minutes later was pounded into a pulp by shell-fire—and after that day a friendship had developed which years and distance had failed to obliterate. If he had met him on the street the shock would have been less. But to find him here, another factor in the mystery and adventure which had drawn him in its web, and to see the eyes of Antoinette St. Ives light up so beautifully at his coming made his heart pump almost audibly as he wrung the other's hand.

With John Denis their meeting bore an aspect entirely apart from emotion aroused by its unexpectedness. Denis had known of his presence and had come purposely to see him within an hour after his arrival at Antoinette's home. That fact was quite evident in the manner of the Colonel's greeting. It lacked the agitation of sudden surprise. But his fingers clung like slender bands of steel to Clifton's and his voice trembled with the sincerity of his emotion. Here was more than friend meeting friend; it was comrade meeting comrade, brother meeting brother. St. Ives had drawn away and in Antoinette's eyes came a swift change, a soft glow with tears close behind it as she saw John Denis's lips atremble.

Then Clifton saw with another kind of sensation the marked change in this man whose gallantry and bravery had made him one of the conspicuous inspirations of the Princess Pats in their days of travail and death. He had aged many years. His shoulders were a little bent. A tragedy of some kind was hiding itself deep back in his eyes and he was clearly under an excitement which he was trying hard to conceal.

But it found voice in his words.

"Thank God, Clifton! All the world could not have sent me a man I want more than I want you!"

They were strange words coming from a man like Colonel Denis, and almost identical with those of Antoinette St. Ives. Clifton turned toward her and caught her regarding him in a way that added to the thumping agitation of his heart. But instantly, when she found herself discovered, there came the upward little tilt to her chin as if she was altogether beneath such an intimate observation on her part.

Then she was excusing herself, and left the room. With a word of apology, Gaspard headed up the stair for his bath.

Scarcely were they alone when Colonel Denis drew in a sharp breath.

"It is amazing how things have been happening during the last week, Clifton," he said. "I am not going to spoil Antoinette's dinner for you by going into unpleasant details. They always come better on a full stomach, don't you think? But there have been certain remarkable occurrences which I know will interest you while we are waiting. In the first place, do you remember the day when you were walking the highway this side of Brantford in the company of a boy and a dog? Well, an automobile passed you——"

Clifton nodded with a flash of his old humor.

"Many of them passed us, John!"

"But in this particular car were Antoinette St. Ives and myself. I saw you. And I was so upset by your resemblance to the man I thought was murdered at Haipoong that I gave voice to my emotion. Antoinette insisted on stopping the car, but when the dust had cleared away you and the boy and the dog were cutting across a field toward a wood. We went on and Antoinette urged me to tell her all about the man whose ghost I had just seen. I did. You know how friends smother us with flowers when we are dead, Clifton? Well, I did that for you. I pictured you for Mademoiselle St. Ives as the greatest, cleanest, squarest fighter in the world, and a woman-hater from the toes of your boots to——"

"The devil!"

"What?"

"Nothing. Go on!"

"And after that, knowing you so well from my description, you can imagine her surprise when you came to life in Ivan Hurd's office, declared yourself, told your story, made that scoundrel confess himself a criminal on his knees—and then punished him as you did. She was in the little room off Hurd's office and witnessed it all."

"I know it," nodded Clifton. "And I am mighty curious to discover why she gave no evidence of her presence when she thought I was going to kill Hurd, why she didn't run out and scream and throw a fit—as most women would have done. At least it would have shown good taste if she had fainted!"

"Of course. I think I expressed something like that when she told me about it and I had recovered from my amazement and joy in the knowledge that you were not dead but very much alive. And she told me an astonishing thing, swearing to it by that crucifix up there—and Antoinette would suffer death at the stake rather than commit such a sacrilege if she were not

91

telling the truth. She said that from the beginning—from the instant you declared yourself to Hurd—she knew you would not kill him. *And she wanted to learn the trth of that story of yon father's rin and death as it came from yon lips!* She saw Hurd on his knees and listened to his confession.

"Look about you! This typifies what she is. The most beautiful, sweetest, purest girl in this city of Quebec—yet a little tigress inspired by a pitiless determination when it comes to combating an evil or a wrong. She is of the New France of two hundred years ago, and the seigneurs' fighting blood and their culture and ideals of honor are a part of her. So she was not afraid when she saw you fighting Hurd, and was confident you would not kill him. For she knew you were right, and she confessed to me that in the little room she was praying for you, believing that God would bring you out safely. That was why she did not scream or faint."

John Denis finished with a gesture half of hope and half despair.

"And she is equally sure that confidence and prayer—and *you*—will save us from the ruin which confronts us now. She has a most monumental faith in Clifton Brant. Has she not told you so?"

"Rather the opposite," said Clifton. "She was abusing me when you came in."

For the first time the tense look in the other's face disappeared and humor flashed into it.

"I might have guessed it by the gladness of her greeting when I arrived. What had you been doing?"

"I used her vaporarium without protest."

"What besides?"

"I told her how my heart inverted itself when I first saw her at the top of the stair, and how lovely she was."

"Ye gods!"

"And then, when she began to abuse me, I told her that from the moment I heard her voice in Hurd's room I was in love with her, and had just found it out. I do not believe in dissembling. I spoke the truth."

"And Antoinette St. Ives stood for that!"

"No, John, she did not. I think she is my enemy for life, but I am going to follow the Lord's injunction and continue to love this particular person who hates me. That is—unless—you—"

Colonel Denis shook his head.

"It won't hurt me, Clifton. That part of my heart which should hold a woman's love must be dead."

"I thought that, too. It's a fool thought. And when a man wakes up to that discovery he is sure to make an ass of himself. But I haven't heard what I am waiting for, and what Antoinette St. Ives did not tell me. What is this ruin that faces you both? Why are you both involved? What is the big fight that seems to have been preparing itself for my arrival? I have already promised Gaspard to help him out in his love affair with Angelique Fanchon. I have also sworn to die for Antoinette St. Ives at any time she may call upon me for that trivial sacrifice. In addition to these little matters Ivan Hurd has set the police after me and I am in love with myself. And still the *big fight*—if I understand you and Mademoiselle Antoinette—has not yet been placed on my schedule. Please let me hear about it!"

"Not until after dinner. Antoinette made me promise that."

"And Colonel Denis always keeps a promise he has given," came a sweet voice from behind them. "Pardon me for overhearing your last few words. Dinner is ready, and Gaspard has come down raving with hunger. Captain Brant, will you humiliate yourself so much as to give me the courtesy of your arm? I promise to touch it lightly, merely with the tips of my fingers!"

"I wish it might carry you entirely," he whispered, bending over her as they preceded Colonel Denis through one of the doors.

The moment gave him a bewildering opportunity of looking at her when she was thrillingly near to him. He had never dreamed that anything could be quite so exquisite as her head and her hair as he looked down on them. He would have given half a year of his life if her short curls could suddenly have tumbled about her shoulders, for that was the way he was picturing them. They would just about reach to her shoulders if loosened from their bondage, he thought—a deadly disarray of velvety gloss and sheen that would have disrupted any man's soul! And she had told him, with a stinging note in her words, that they were not a result of that detestable maggot in the feminine brain—the passion for bobbing. He felt like bestowing upon her a verbal commendation, but the tilt of her chin had reached a dangerous angle as she intuitively guessed the advantage he was taking of her.

The room which they entered, like the first, seemed to Clifton to be a relic of a forgotten age. It was smaller, with huge beams in the ceiling and paneled walls of oak and a fireplace at one end in which the old cranes of hammered iron still remained. The table in the center of the room was small but massive and had been carved out by hand, as had the chairs about it. On the table, illumining it with a soft glow, was a candelabrum of such ancient and unusual design that Clifton's eyes involuntarily rested upon it as they seated themselves.

Antoinette St. Ives observed his interest as she tinkled a silvery little bell at her side.

"You are curious, Monsieur Brant," she said, with a formality that robbed his heart and his lips of any lightness of thought that might have been in one or on the other. "We are proud of our little place, and I am sure you would be interested in some of its tales and the relics we have in it."

And as he looked at her now, like a lovely princess presiding over royalty at her table, he could have bitten his tongue in two for its boldness and impertinence, of a previous moment. What must she think of him? A clown for his boldness, a venturesome boor because of his flippant tongue—and a fool above everything! Yet, in God's name, it had not been his intention to appear any one of these—and less so in her eyes than in the opinion of all the rest of the world!

His voice was subdued when he answered.

"All my life I have wished that I might have lived centuries ago in place of now," he said. "So you may understand a little how coming into a place like this kindles me with that old thought, Mademoiselle. I think that is why I have been a wanderer. It is because of restlessness, a desire which can never be attained, a taint of heritage in my blood that is a calamity in this age. You are fortunate. If this little place were mine I would not exchange it for the Château Frontenac which looks down on you from above!"

A glow of pleasure suffused the girl's face.

"I can guess a little of that, Monsieur, or you would not have slept in the old Indian cemetery of your forefathers near Brantford Town. Little Joe told me about it, and how you brought him to Montreal. In the Chapel of the Ursulines is a votive lamp given by Marie de Repentigny in seventeen hundred and seventeen, and in spite of the vicissitudes of centuries and long sieges in which shot and shell have many times torn the convent walls that lamp has been kept burning through all the years since then.

"You have undoubtedly seen the lamp, a reminder of the greatest romantic tragedy in New France, when Amélie de Repentigny, sweetest of all women then living, cut off her beautiful hair and became a nun because her brother in a moment of drunken insanity killed the father of her lover. In seventeen hundred and nineteen, the year Amélie died of heartbreak behind the convent walls, this candelabrum on our table was given to a Marrolet by the mother of Amélie, and here it has remained since then. Many ghosts walk in this little house. It was here Amélie met her lover. Can you question me for loving it?"

"I honor you," said Clifton, and in his heart he worshiped it.

He had believed that the hour at table would clear somewhat the mystery of the situation of which he had become a part. But if ruin and tragedy hovered over the three in whose company he sat, there was no revealment of it in either their bearing or their words.

Colonel Denis had thrown off the tenseness which had accompanied him into the home of Antoinette St. Ives and his face grew softer in the glow of the candles. Even Gaspard was a changed man and smiled and said pleasant things to his sister as if the bitterness of his love affair was not gnawing at his heart. Here, with their food, the troubles of the world were deliberately held away, and from the moment Antoinette St. Ives had bowed her lovely head to repeat in a sweet, low voice the words, "Be present at our table, Lord, be here and everywhere adored, these creatures bless and grant that we may feast in Paradise with Thee"—a spirit of peace and happiness seemed to fill the room. In those moments of serene stillness when the gentle lips of the girl sent up their prayer he thought of her as an angel, and when it was finished and he looked across at John Denis the thought lay in his eyes, "If prayers like hers are not answered there can be no God!"

And after that the little stories and bits of romance of the old home fell like epics in poetry from her lips, so deeply had she cherished them in her heart; and Gaspard told of the old swashbuckling days when half the excitement in New France was down below the citadel walls, and the dainty feet and clanking rapiers of beauty and chivalry came to worship at the Notre Dame des Victoires, or to see the pilloried rascals in front of it, or witness a hanging where the ancient scaffold stood in the square. And up and down these streets, old and decaying alleys now, were the homes of bright eyes and gallant hearts, and fluffs and lace and sweet perfume and love-making where dirty children now cried out for pennies from gaping men and women who came to look upon the decaying ruins of a glorious past. Clifton could have sworn he caught an instant's mist of tears in the eyes of Antoinette St. Ives as she said, "It is a sacrilege to let them disappear in ruin and beggary. Do we care so little for the honor of our forefathers, for the men and women whose courage and faith in God gave us a new world and a nation? And it began here, where these little streets now are, a part of it in this house—and at the very table where we are sitting!"

And then suddenly she smiled at John Denis and murmured an apology for speaking of an unpleasant subject at this time when there were so many beautiful things in the world to talk about.

It was after this that Clifton said, venturing upon the edge of a matter of which he was a little afraid, "I hope you like my friends Benedict Aldous—and his wife?"

"I do," she replied. "They insisted that I remain in their home as a guest when they found I did not live in Montreal. I was there three days. I fell in love with Joe and Bim, and think I shall adopt them."

"Adopt them?" gasped Clifton.

"Yes, adopt them," she repeated coolly. "They need a mothering influence, and Clairette Aldous has her hands full with two of their own, though she was planning to keep Joe and Bim until I told her how I felt about it and asked her to let me bring them to Quebec. Madame Aldous would not let Joe come until she could properly clothe him. She is one of the sweetest women I have ever met. I think there are very few like her in this world— and Monsieur Aldous is a lucky man to have her!"

With those last words her eyes met Clifton's. It was the nearest she had come to shooting another dagger at him.

"Of course it was understood that if you should have a serious objection to my taking Joe and Bim, or wished to retain a certain partnership interest in them—but we can discuss that tomorrow, Captain Brant, after Joe and Bim arrive. They are coming in the morning!"

"But Joe," insisted Clifton. "He—"

"Yes, he likes me, and is glad to come," she smiled, with a little flash back in her eyes. "At first I frightened him, due quite naturally to his training, Monsieur Brant. He seems to have a mysterious horror of short hair, and when he first saw me in the hallway near his room my hair was down, and as I held out my hands to him he backed away from me as if I were a plague. Afterward, when certain definitions were explained to him and he came to understand that short hair and million-dollar-something-or-others did not always go together, he became quite lovable. Won't you have another cup of coffee, Captain Brant?"

Clifton felt himself burning up, a fact of which Antoinette seemed sweetly oblivious. She poured his coffee and added sugar to it with her pretty fingers, and at the same time spoke to Colonel Denis about the new French opera, as if to drag his attention from any effect which her shot might have had upon Clifton.

"'Venus and the Graces' is a pretty name for it," she went on. "The Three Graces, Euphrosyne, Aglaia and Thalia are all quite modern. They wear crowns of purple grapes in the Greek style and have bobbed hair. Do you like bobbed hair, Captain Brant?" she asked, turning on him innocently.

"I—er—sometimes," he countered in cold desperation. "I love beautiful hair."

A soft regret filled the girl's voice.

"I have always wanted hair like Amélie de Repentigny's," she said. "The history book of the nuns tells us it was the most beautiful in all Quebec and that even Mère Mignon de la Nativité, the Superior of the convent, wept when her scissors snipped off the silken tresses. But such beautiful fortune has not come to me, and I have never had greater crowning glory than this." And with two slim fingers she straightened one of her lustrous curls for them to observe, and Clifton saw that his guess was right and that loosened they would have clustered about her shoulders.

The chuckle that was like a subdued laugh rose in Gaspard as he said:

"My sister knows her hair is the most beautiful in Quebec today, just as Amélie de Repentigny's was two hundred years ago, or she would not draw our attention so closely to it."

Antoinette St. Ives let the curl back suddenly and blushed to her eyes, and Clifton felt like shouting out his gratitude to the blundering Gaspard.

"I did not mean it to be taken in that way, Gaspard," she reproved.

"And it was not taken as he has intimated, at least not by me," emphasized Clifton, trying to smother a note of triumph in his voice. "And it is beautiful, Mademoiselle! Have you ever seen lovelier, Colonel Denis?"

"Never," said John Denis, and surreptitiously his eyes stole to an old wooden clock ticking off its seconds on an oaken mantel.

In spite of its secrecy and her own confusion, Antoinette caught the glance and understood its significance. A few minutes later they stood again in the room into which Clifton had first entered.

There was no longer an element of hesitation or repression in the manner of Colonel Denis. He was openly eager to get away and take Clifton with him, and Antoinette St. Ives let it be known quite frankly that the real hour in this night was about to strike and that it meant much to her. John Denis went a little ahead with Gaspard, and Clifton guessed that it was with the purpose of giving the girl a last word with him.

Never would he be able to wipe out of his memory the dignity and beauty of her or the quiet, proud appeal in her lovely eyes as she gave him her hand in parting.

"Colonel Denis will tell you everything, Captain Brant," she said. "And I pray God you are the man I have judged you to be—the only man I have ever known that I would commit myself so boldly to—and that you will help us in our hour of trial if you can. Why I should believe that through you we can be saved from a situation which seems hopeless is a mystery to me. But I do. That hour in Ivan Hurd's room gave me an infinite faith in you—as a fighting man!"

"But in another way, Mademoiselle—as a man without heart or soul or romance—"

"Forgive me, please! You have these things. It was a perverse whim that made me say otherwise."

"Then you do not despise me for—"

"For what?" she asked, forgetful for a moment.

"For that boldness which made me ready to lay down my life for you when I saw you at the head of the stair, and for afterward giving even bolder voice to that truth which my heart could not withhold—my love for you."

"*Monsieu!* "

He bent over her head, and did not look into her eyes.

"If my life can lighten the burden that is oppressing you it shall be lightened, Mademoiselle St. Ives," he said softly, and as he went out into the dark little street that clung to the great rock wall of the Terrace it was with the thrilling knowledge that for a single moment the fingers of the hand which he had held had tightened a little more closely about his own.

CHAPTER XII

Denis and St. Ives were waiting for him, but at the end of the short street Gaspard said good night and turned back.

Fifteen minutes later they entered Colonel Denis's private office in the small building occupied by the Laurentian Pulp and Paper Company. Clifton looked about him with a word of approbation and pleasure. This was like coming home. It was the same office, with the same great oaken desk from which John Denis had taken the last two cigars they had smoked together before they left for the war ten years ago. The same maps and blue-prints and pictures hung on the walls, it seemed to Clifton, and the same old-fashioned comfort and lack of stiffness were about him—the atmosphere of English gentlemen whose great business had been something more than a machine for making dollars and building fortunes. In their same positions against the walls were the oil paintings of Sir William Denis and the Honorable Cecil Stanford, founders of the Laurentian Pulp and Paper Company, both mighty names among the pioneers of Quebec's greatest industry, and dead these many years; and between them, with his rugged, fighting face and deep-set eyes, was the Colonel's grandfather, John Denis the first, who had given to the Provincial government its greatest knowledge of the vast timber resources beyond the emptying waters of the Mistassini, the Peribonka and the Ashuapmouchan. And from their frames looked down the faces of other men who had played their parts in building up the honor and varying fortunes of this oldest and proudest institution of its kind in Canada. Over the oaken desk was a plain birch frame carved by Sir William's jackknife forty years before, and in it the fading words, "*God before success. Honor before the dollar.*"

Clifton, seeing the words again after many years, read them aloud, and added:

"Sir William's Golden Rule has always remained an unforgettable thing in my heart. I wish I might have lived a little more closely to it. And you have not changed here! I can fairly breathe the inspiration of this room— that spirit which has made the Laurentian Pulp and Paper Company a classic among its fellows, a blazer of trails, a leader in thought and action and the savior of Quebec's forest lands if you want to put it that way."

99

"And tonight all this is—dead," said John Denis with a note of despair in his voice. "Sit down, Clifton. Make yourself at home—and light up a cigar."

"Dead!" exclaimed Clifton. "Dead!—with Sir William looking down at you with the benignity of a guardian angel, and Grandfather Denis watching with those fighting eyes of his, like a fierce old Recollet damning a horde of scalping savages to perdition? Why, man—"

"I'd give ten years of my life if Grandfather Denis could step down out of that frame and fill my shoes for six months, Clifton. It would be worth that much to me—and to Antoinette St. Ives. At least he would give an account of himself, if he died on the gallows for it. He was that sort of a man."

"No man ever lived, not even your Grandfather Denis, who would have fought harder for Antoinette St. Ives than I am willing to fight," said Clifton tensely. "I am ready. What is the trouble?"

"The same thing that happened to your father," said John Denis in a quiet voice. "That is why it has seemed to me a special act of Providence that you did not die at Haipoong but lived to make your appearance in that miraculous hour in Ivan Hurd's office. Antoinette is even more assured in her conviction that it was the hand of God. Otherwise why should you, of all men on earth, come like a ghost out of your grave at that very moment when Mademoiselle St. Ives was being asked to sell her soul to Ivan Hurd? There is something uncanny about it, Clifton!"

Clifton was on his feet. "Until now I have been patient, Colonel Denis. In God's name come to the point! What has Ivan Hurd to do with Antoinette St. Ives?"

"And with me, you might add," said Denis, with a shrug of his shoulders. "I wish I might snap a finger and let you see and understand the entire situation that quickly. But it is impossible. You have been away many years and must be given the fundamentals first. Otherwise you might be inclined to laugh at me. The details can only be prefaced by the fact that unless something incredibly unexpected happens very soon the Laurentian Pulp and Paper Company will go out of existence, a ragged bankrupt. And with it will go the hearts and souls of Antoinette and her brother. Of course you do not understand how they can be so intimately associated with my own ruin, but you will in a few minutes if you will have patience with me. It is not a matter of financial loss so far as it affects them personally. They care even less for that than I do. I face ruin as it is thought of in dollars and cents and loss of pride—but that is all. Antoinette St. Ives faces a more serious thing. Do you know Ivan Hurd? Not as he was years ago, but as he is today?"

"Only from my experience with him in his office. And Benedict Aldous told me he was a very wealthy man and a political power in the Province, and extremely dangerous to those who oppose him. *Le Taureau*, I think Benedict said they called him—the Bull. An all-round scoundrel, I should say, with plenty of friends to back him!"

"I cannot conceive how it would be possible for the situation to be any worse," said Colonel Denis bitterly. "You've got to know about Hurd before you can understand the rest. You know how he destroyed your father and what your father was building up. But Ivan Hurd was a pigmy then. He is a giant now. I don't want you to understand that our provincial legislators, taken as a whole, are rotten or dishonest. I am confident that even a majority of them would like to see Ivan Hurd go down and out. But those who are not with him are afraid of him. A dozen times in the last five years a David has risen to fight Hurd, and each time that David has gone down to ruin not only politically but in almost every instance in a personally financial way as well. Hurd is getting away with more than dishonesty and graft and the legislation he wants. He is simply too powerful to touch, and is getting away with crime as well. That is the man you humiliated and made your deadly enemy in Montreal!"

John Denis's voice had fallen into the short, sharp speech of his army days. His thin face had flushed. His eyes blazed, and he paced back and forth before Clifton as he talked, his hands clenched at his sides.

"I should have killed him," said Clifton. "But he is still alive, and my opportunity lives with him."

He was thinking of Antoinette St. Ives and his heart was throbbing with the suspense of waiting for the other's revealment of her relationship to Hurd. But he did not break in with the impetuous questioning which was at his tongue's end. He waited.

As he spread out a map on a table Colonel Denis said:

"I think you should. Your danger would have been scarcely greater than it is now. Hurd considers you a dangerous menace or he would not have attempted your assassination at Haipoong. Antoinette told me of that affair as it was given to her by Benedict Aldous. And Hurd knows that you are a greater menace than ever to him now. He acted in haste and passion when he called upon the police in Montreal, undoubtedly with the thought that he could easily send you to the penitentiary for twenty years for attempted murder. But it happened that Antoinette St. Ives was a witness and because of that his scheme went on the rocks. He could not send you to prison with a St. Ives giving testimony against him—at least there would be serious difficulties in the way. So he will attempt to get you some other way. And now, if you accept my invitation to join in what seems to be a hopeless fight against him, he will hate you more than any other man on the face of the earth, and will not sleep nights until you are utterly demolished. In the old days, possessing the power he has now, he would have had you burned at the stake!"

"Interesting," nodded Clifton, as the other paused. "Consider that I am a partner in this fight. I have already promised Mademoiselle Antoinette, and I now promise you. But the manner in which I am to fight is still a mystery to me, and until you become a little more specific I shall continue to sweat with suspense. If you would express yourself a little more clearly about Antoinette St. Ives—"

"Take a look at this map," said Denis shortly. "We are coming to that."

Clifton stood at his side and bent over the map on the table.

"Here is your old friend, the Mistassini River," Denis went on in a quieter voice. "The concessions of the Laurentian Pulp and Paper Company are outlined in red—two thousand square miles at an approximate cost to us of a thousand dollars a square mile. Our limits, as you can seen by looking at the scale, reach forty miles east and west and have a frontage of fifty miles on the river. Every feeding stream that brings timber out of our territory empties into the Mistassini. The Mistassini itself is the only road to Lake Saint John and our mills, which until three years ago were putting out more than a hundred thousand tons of paper a year. Shut off the waters of the Mistassini and you stop our life's blood—and we die!"

"I begin to understand!" said Clifton. "It's the same old system, only my father's petty limit was on a stream that wasn't more than a creek except at flood time—and Hurd didn't find it much of a job to take that life's blood away from us. But the Mistassini—the greatest stream that comes out of the north—"

"Has a carrying limit of five million logs, and not a thousand more," said Denis. "And our mills require a hundred and fifty thousand cords of pulpwood annually to run us eighty-five percent capacity—and you know that one hundred and fifty thousand cords of four-foot pulpwood figure up to just five million logs. At best, crowding every inch of water in the stream and using day and night of the driving months we can't run our mills more than eighty-five percent of their capacity. A little graft money, a little dishonesty, more of politics and less of that Honor and God which Sir William put up there and we might have had other concessions—or at least could have bought protection for our own. But we are on the Mistassini, and there only, with a four-million-dollar investment out of which Ivan Hurd has been slowly but surely choking blood and life. The final smash will come next spring, in the driving season—and unless a miracle comes to save us the Laurentian Pulp and Paper Company will not only turn over on its side and die but practically all that it ever possessed will fall into the waiting hands of Ivan Hurd and his grafting gang."

102

"You have forgotten Antoinette St. Ives," reminded Clifton.

Colonel Denis placed the tip of his forefinger on a small black patch almost in the center of the Laurentian concession, and touching the river.

"For more than a quarter of a century Gautier St. Ives, the father of Antoinette and Gaspard, was the backbone of all Sir William's activities in the forests. He was another Sir William, practical and yet a dreamer, a gentleman and yet a fighting man, a product of the old school whose ideals have been inherited by his children. His wife, Antoinette, died when the present Antoinette was six years old and Gaspard fourteen. I believe I have never seen anything more terrible than Gautier's grief. It was a quiet grief, and killed him by inches, in spite of his love for his children. He died two years after his wife left him, with the request that Gaspard be induced to enter the priesthood if he could be made to show a liking for it, and that little Antoinette, then eight years old, be educated in the Ursuline Convent.

"We tried to follow his wishes, but Gaspard was cut out for anything but a priest. A number of years before Gautier St. Ives died Sir William and his partner had deeded over to him—as a mark of their gratitude and esteem—this sub-concession of one hundred square miles which you see herein in black on the map. It was a gift of a fortune, of course, but the governors of the Laurentian Company were of the kind who took pleasure in showing their appreciation of unusual service. And before Sir William died he knew that Gaspard, like his father, belonged to the forests—so Gaspard took charge of this concession for himself and his sister, running camps which a year ago numbered more than a hundred men, and all of his product of pulpwood was bought in by the Laurentian Company.

"Under this arrangement the St. Ives limits have netted Gaspard and his sister between ten and fifteen thousand dollars annually, and the limits have been undercut if anything, for Gaspard loves trees more than he does people and will only cut timber that is fully ripe or crippled or seared by fire, which fact makes his operations somewhat expensive. But he has followed out in practice the one system of harvesting and conservation which will save our timber supply of the future, a policy which the Laurentian Company itself has always followed from the beginning along somewhat less strict lines. Now you understand one of the ways, and the least tragic one, in which Antoinette St. Ives is involved in this life-and-death struggle with Ivan Hurd. Before you can understand the blacker side of it, and the one which threatens her most, I must come up to the present situation in my own way. Have you patience?"

"I am following you closely," said Clifton. "Go on."

"You remember it was Hurd and his associates who first began pulling off the timberland colonization grafts before you went away," resumed Denis. "During your absence this scheme has become so highly organized that it is now one of the greatest menaces that confront our paper and pulp industry. According to all our agreements with the Provincial Government any part of our limits may be set aside at any time for so-called colonization purposes, and if enough political influence can be brought to bear in a certain direction the very heart of a concession representing an investment of millions of dollars can be preempted for 'colonist' purposes—and you know how big a chance a 'colonist' has of making a living in our wild timber country, when each settler can legally cut only five acres of his timber each year. But the government does allow him to cut *all* burned timber, whether on his land or government land, and so these non-bona-fide settlers brought in by men like Hurd start forest fires, and within forty-eight hours they have a vast burned territory in which they can legally work. They are the pirates of the forests, and not only give grafters like Hurd an opportunity to get cheap pulpwood but cause incalculable damage through their incendiarism.

"You know all about this, Clifton. And our first intimation that Hurd and his gangsters had their eyes on the Laurentian properties was when we were advised four years ago that two hundred square miles of our limits had been set aside for 'colonization' purposes. Of course the 'colonists' came, hired for the purpose, the forest fires followed, and the Hurd-Foy interests bought the pulpwood, though it is a matter of record that we offered fifty cents a cord more for it than they did—and as a result Hurd had two hundred thousand logs in the Mistassini that year, cutting down our drive by just that number.

"Almost simultaneously came our real shock. Options which we had on eight hundred square miles of timber *below* us on the Mistassini, and other options on the Rivière aux Rats were withheld at expiration by the government, and the properties were sold to Hurd. It was one of the boldest pieces of political dishonesty in the history of the Province. But there was no redress. We were hemmed in. And that spring, three years ago, Hurd and his interests ran a million and a half logs down the river, leaving only water enough to carry three and a half million of our own. That cut our pulp and paper production thirty percent in spite of all we could do. It was then Hurd offered us—*what*? Half a million dollars for Laurentian properties of six times that value!"

John Denis's voice trembled and his face was white with suppressed passion as he paused. He walked back and forth across the floor, not looking at Clifton.

"Of course we accepted war and ruin instead of alms and disgrace," he continued, after a moment. "The result was that two years ago we were cut down to fifty percent of our normal production, lost an enormous amount of money, and were compelled to cancel our oldest and most important contract with a New York publisher who uses seventy acres of forest in each Sunday edition of his paper. We tried to get help, but our best friends could see no hope against the handicap of political power that Hurd had brought against us. Our heavy mill investments were eating us up. So we did the only thing possible. We wiped a million and a quarter off our assets, closed our largest mill, and adjusted ourselves to a secondary rating and an output of two million logs a year. God knows I'm glad it happened after Sir William died! It would have broken his heart. And then—then—the *real rottenness* came out!"

In a moment's silence when Colonel Denis was fiercely lighting himself a cigar Clifton rose.

"Finish it, John," he said quietly. "I want to walk a little, if you don't mind—back and forth here across the room, while you are giving me the rest of it"—and his fingers unclenched, and then drew themselves up again, and his face was almost as white as that of Sir William's son.

Denis's voice broke into an unnatural laugh.

"Don't allow yourself to become disturbed—not now, Clifton! I'm only coming to that part of it which will make your blood boil, and which has weighed on me until I am no longer fit either physically or mentally. That is why I thank God you are here. I need you, if for nothing more than to be near me when the old ship gives up the ghost and sinks. Again I swear to you I'm not worrying so much about the money loss. It is the insult of it, the humiliation, the breaking down of my father's handiwork—and Antoinette. I'd willingly give a half of the remaining years of my life for a little of her faith. God bless her!"

"I encore that," approved Clifton. "But please don't get sentimental just now, John. You've let this man Hurd get the best of your nerves, but you're a long way from running up the white flag or going to the bottom. Cheer up, walk a little as you talk, whistle between times—and let's have the rest of it!"

Denis was about to answer when the telephone on his desk began to ring.

"At this hour! Only Antoinette and St. Ives know I am here!"

He took down the receiver. Clifton watched the expression in the face slowly change. He could hear an indistinct feminine voice at the other end of the wire, and during the next two or three minutes Colonel Denis interrupted it less than half a dozen times and then only with a word or two. A flush was in his pale cheeks and dampness of perspiration shone on his forehead when he finished and turned to Clifton. He smiled but there was a hardness in the twist of his lips.

"Antoinette St. Ives," he explained tersely. "Ivan Hurd is in town and has just got word to her. He is to be at her home in half an hour. Then will come the big explosion, Clifton. Hurd is coming with his final ultimatum and Antoinette is ready for it. After their meeting there will be—hell—and plenty of it."

The telephone communication seemed to have had an unusual effect on Colonel Denis. The tension in him had broken and with eyes that were coldly clear and almost smiling he faced Clifton.

"Rather unexpected," he said, "and—in a way—I'm glad. Hurd is bringing the thing to a head. After tonight there will be but one road to travel— and I like it that way. I never did fancy going over the top in the dark, did you? Always thought I'd rather go west with the sun shining than be struck by something hidden and unseen. And Antoinette will see to it that we have light from now on.

"Curious, too, that it should happen just as I was about to tell you about her. Maybe it's a lucky omen. That is what she said over the telephone, and she believed it! I could tell it by her voice. Her faith in prayer plus that fighting strain which is a part of her is—marvelously uplifting. At times it almost convinces me that we are going to pull out of this hole and that in this girl Hurd has more than met his match. Excuse me. I must go back to the point where the telephone interrupted us. Then you will know what is happening tonight down in the little house in Notre Dame Street."

He placed his finger again on the dark little patch on the map.

"When he wiped out almost a half of our assets and thus prepared ourselves to accept the inevitable, with a production of two million logs instead of five each year, Hurd was shot off his balance. He had not expected that, but had figured we would go down to ruin before making such a move. As it was, having accepted our loss in advance, we were in a position to carry on a sound but much smaller business—and Hurd could not salvage our concessions until we were literally against the wall. He set about finding other ways of putting us there, and hit upon the St. Ives sublimits. He knew that if he could get possession of these he would have us by the throats as he would then be located in the very heart of our property.

"So he offered Gaspard St. Ives as much for his two hundred square miles as he had offered us for our two thousand—a quarter of a million dollars! Think of it, Clifton!—twenty-five hundred dollars a square mile, more than Antoinette and her brother could expect to get out of it in a lifetime. Of course it was refused. It was then Ivan Hurd first met Antoinette. It isn't difficult for you to guess what happened. From that hour the beast was possessed by a passion that overrode all his other ambitions. He was clever enough to begin with apparent decency, if you can call a proposal of marriage at the end of the second week of a rather cool acquaintanceship decent—"

Clifton chuckled.

"Forgive me for interrupting you, John. I am tense, I am mad, I am ready to choke the life out of Ivan Hurd—but I must recall your attention to the fact that I didn't wait two weeks to tell Mademoiselle St. Ives what Hurd told her. I am quite sure I declared my love for her within the first hour—immediately after coming from her vaporarium. If Hurd wasn't decent what in Heaven's name was I?"

"Rather—indiscreet, I should say," replied Colonel Denis. "I am wondering you are not a rag. Antoinette must have a splendid opinion of you to let you get away with a thing like that. But of course she saw the difference. Hurd came to her from out of a reptilian age, and I guess she let him know it. She let him understand clearly how she despised him.

"But Hurd wasn't the kind of man to let go once he had set his heart on a thing. It was his nature to ride over obstacles as a steel tank goes through entanglements and over trenches. Antoinette's refusal and resentment merely served to increase his madness for her. He wasn't thinking of love, not on her part. That she hated him made no difference, unless it still more increased his desire and determination to possess her. He wanted her body and her beauty, and I believe that in this very hour down in Notre Dame Street he would turn over half his great fortune for those things.

"Along with his millions and his name he offered to give up his fight against the Laurentian Company and to turn over to it without cost all his grafted limits in our territory. He made this offer directly to me with the hope that I might help to influence Antoinette St. Ives. When he finally realized that nothing he possessed could possibly count with her he reverted to his type—the jungle beast. He had cornered us, and he began his schemes to corner her. If he could not buy her he would trap her—force her into giving her body to him no matter where her heart and soul might be. And to do this he began by bringing about one of the most contemptible pieces of civic legislation in the province.

"You know how Antoinette and her brother love the memories of what few stones and hallowed places are left of the ancient days when the pioneers of New France started a world over here? It is almost a religion with them. Their one ambition in making money is to save a few of the things that are going into ruin, and which in another quarter-century will have become only memories of the past. Hurd, discovering this, had painted visions of what his money could do, but even this lure failed to buy the soul of Antoinette St. Ives. She told me once that she would willingly give up her life to bring about the things she dreamed of but that her soul was not her own and she could not sacrifice it to an eternal damnation.

"Then Hurd, the jungle fiend, sprung his first trap on Antoinette, just as he had previously sprung one on the Laurentian Company. His agents worked with the slyness of foxes. He bought up a million dollars' worth of property in and about Quebec, including almost every historical point that could be purchased, and through his political influence had Notre Dame Street, Sous le Cap Street, Little Champlain and Cul-de-Sac *condemned*, and now owns practically every foot of them. In this scheme, of 'civic improvement' the St. Ives home must go with the others. And with it, and the disruption of those little streets, go the dreams, the heart and the happiness of Antoinette St. Ives. There is only one way in which she can save them— give herself to Hurd!"

He stopped, and his eyes met Clifton's. Each knew what lay behind the cold and quiet tenseness of the other's silence.

"And now," finished Denis after that interval of stillness, "you know why this is not entirely a fight for the salvation of the Laurentian Pulp and Paper Company. It is a fight that goes to the heart of two hundred years ago —to the life and happiness and honor of a beautiful girl—to the—"

"What else?"

John Denis slowly clenched and unclenched the fingers of his hands.

"If it happens—as Hurd has planned it—Antoinette St. Ives will be another Amélie de Repentigny. For Gaspard St. Ives will kill Ivan Hurd, and his sister will offer up her life for the salvation of his soul—by becoming a nun!"

"Good God!" exclaimed Clifton. "She would do that?"

"With her brother as a witness she has made that pledge before the crucifix of Adelaide Marrolet. It is the only thing that has thus far held back Gaspard St. Ives. If it was not for Antoinette's oath to the Virgin Mother Ivan Hurd would be as good as dead, and Gaspard would be forever gone into the big forests north—or at least until his love for his sister brought him back where the law could get him. It is this thought of what St. Ives may do that frightens me. He is like a man born two hundred years ago living over into this age. His ideals of honor are the warp and woof of his heart, and if Ivan Hurd wins and smashes us all and levels that little place in Notre Dame Street—I do not think that even his sister's pledge will hold Gaspard back.

"She is afraid of that, too. Of course the thought of going into the cloistered convent of the Ursulines holds no horror for her, although she loves life. It is merely a beautiful renunciation, like that made by Amélie de Repentigny. That is why Friar Alphonse never leaves Gaspard. Tonight you thought he had left you at the entrance to Notre Dame Street, but he was back again before you entered the St. Ives home. He is always within the call of Antoinette St. Ives and will see that Gaspard is kept out of Hurd's way."

Clinton was pacing back and forth across the room again, and his thoughts were running more wildly than his blood. "If St. Ives should kill

Hurd—you think Antoinette would keep her promise?"

"Only death would stop her."

"And St. Ives knows this?"

"Even better than I."

Something dropped from Clifton's lips which was unintelligible to Denis. "Then he would kill Hurd—*knowing that*?" he demanded savagely. "He would deliberately send her into convent walls—just to ease a passion?"

An almost gentle smile came into the face of John Denis.

"Not to ease a passion, Clifton. Not that. But to *right a wrong*—that would be St. Ives's way of looking at it. It is the old blood in him—something you cannot stop—the thing which impelled his forefathers to come out at dawn down there in Lower Town to adjust their grievances in an honorable way at the rapier point. For months Gaspard has been fighting against his desire. Days and weeks at a time he tramps the highways. On his knees he has entreated his sister to take back her pledge and allow him to right this trouble as he thinks a man should right it. It has brought distress into the heart of a sweet girl up at Saint Félicien, Angelique Fanchon —whom Gaspard loves, and who has also made a pledge—that if Gaspard so much as lays a hand on Ivan Hurd she will marry a man named Ajax Trappier—"

"So that's it!" interrupted Clifton. "John, how the light does begin to dawn upon me! And I see only one way out of this trouble—only one."

"And that?"

"I must kill Ivan Hurd myself!"

He laughed and there was a note of wild and almost joyous abandon in his voice.

Denis put a hand on his arm.

"That is the old voice, Clifton—with the ring of the days in it when I, too, was a whole man and not a half of one, and God knows I've wanted to hear such a voice a long time! You know—and I know—that you will not kill Ivan Hurd unless necessity and justice both demand it. Since I learned you were alive new hope has begun to burn in me. Canada has never had another man of the forests like you and my Grandfather Denis. With you up in the Laurentian woods, with your knowledge and skill as a forester, your fighting qualities and your ability to make men love and respect you —all pitted against Ivan Hurd and his forces—I still see the possibility of triumph in what until now has only been tragedy and defeat.

"Gaspard St. Ives is no longer dependable in this situation as a leader in the woods, and I have no other man capable of fending the final smash. I cannot do it myself. Physically I have been unfit for a year, and I have no great influence with men as you have. And that is what will triumph up

109

there, if anything triumphs. For Hurd's last assault, which will begin this coming winter and reach its climax in the spring, will be nothing short of robbery, murder and piracy. It was Antoinette who learned his plans, and we already begin to see the working of them.

"Labor trouble has come like disease into our mills through his endeavors. He has brought discord among men we have employed in the woods for years. From the States and other parts of this province he is importing a horde of men to work out his ends who are little better than outlaws. He has tried and is still trying to subsidize the Church—to buy the influence of certain priests and parishes through gifts and promises and a widespread propaganda of falsehood about ourselves. He has begun the building of certain dams to flood us out—and is deliberately setting our forests on fire.

"This winter and next spring the hell will break loose. He will have in the woods five hundred men of the worst type ever brought together under one organization, and we shall be compelled to use the same roads, the same bridges and the same portages with this hired banditry. There can be only one way to meet it, man to man, bullet for bullet if necessary. We have law and justice on our side—Ivan Hurd has political power and prestige. And—"

He paused, as if to give force to his next words. "This may shock you, Clifton. Antoinette St. Ives says this is no longer a man's job—*but a woman's*! It is her scheme, her plans, her ideas and spirit that we are going to follow in the final hours of our struggle with Hurd. That is why it was she, and not I, who was having that conference with Ivan Hurd when you came to his office in Montreal. Hurd had purposely given publicity to the lie that he was about to leave for Europe, thinking it would bring us to our knees more quickly, and Mademoiselle St. Ives was there in a last effort to bring about peace. Hurd asked her to step into the adjoining room while he had his word with you. Fate could not have arranged the situation better—and as a result Antoinette wants you to accompany her on a certain life-and-death expedition which leaves the city of Quebec for the north country day after tomorrow in the morning. How about it, Captain Brant? That is the story—all of it. Are you willing to fight at the side of this Jeanne d'Arc of ours?"

"Until I die," said Clifton in a low voice. "*Until I die.*"

He had taken his hat, and now placed it on his head. Then he looked at his watch, and held out a hand to Colonel Denis.

"If Ivan Hurd has kept his appointment promptly he has now been fifteen minutes with Mademoiselle St. Ives," he said in a coldly unemotional voice. "I think I should like to be down there, Colonel Denis. I should like to pass the little place once or twice during their conference, and I should like to meet him face to face as he comes out at the end of Notre Dame Street. Good night!"

"Good night!" said Colonel Denis.

CHAPTER XIII

Impelled by a great desire for action and by a fear of what might be happening in Notre Dame Street Clifton lost only a little time in descending to Lower Town. The miles he had walked that day seemed to have left no effect of exhaustion and every nerve and muscle in him was alert and sleepless.

The Frontenac orchestra was playing its final evening number on the Terrace and for a moment he paused to listen to it as he leaned over the dizzy height between him and the roofs of Lower Town. The thought came to him suddenly that he had stumbled out of earthly existence into something unreal and too beautiful to last long, a land of Prester John, a kingdom of Micomicon, a world made out of the dream of Alnaschar and filled with thick-coming visions and fancies. The music came to him softly, floating between the earth and sky, for a half of the world lay below him. Its lights burned with a velvety radiance so far away that in places they were like scattered stars.

He saw the little streets, so directly under him that he could have tossed a stone upon the roofs, and the faint glow of light that came out of narrow windows broke the darkness for him and made deeper patches of shadow in between. Flame-like points of light gleamed upon the great river; many of them were moving and some were still; a French warship lay where Cartier's tiny ship had moored itself for the first time in this new world three hundred and ninety-one years ago, and the lanterns of a British destroyer burned their signals where Champlain had first set his foot in the name of God and the King of France. Somebody was singing down in the mystic gloom and distance. It was a woman's voice rising very faintly toward the stars. There were millions of these stars above him and never had they seemed so bright or so large or so filled with the radiance of glory and promise.

He walked down Mountain Hill and the Break-Neck Stairs with the music growing fainter behind him, and with each step that he took the truth overwhelmed him still more and told him that it was in himself that the mighty change had come, and that because of it the world had leaped suddenly out of its drabness and sameness, and life was a new thing—thrilling him, crowding him with its closeness and stirring his heart and body and soul.

He laughed to himself from the sheer joy of what had come to him. As confession and acknowledgment swept upon him he thought of Benedict and Clairette Aldous and of the inanity and sheer inconsequence of man until touched by this miracle of love. For he loved Antoinette St. Ives. He kept repeating it like a wordless and voiceless song in his heart. It was more than love. It was a kind of worship. It was something which he had never dreamed could come to any man, though he had never denied love and its glory—in an ordinarily earthly way. But this was different. He told himself that, while his feet and his soul were treading enchanted ground. Then it occurred to him that Benedict must have felt like this, and Clairette Aldous, and Amélie de Repentigny—away back through the ages so far as true love went. The thought brought him back to earth—and his feet to Notre Dame Street.

He walked past Antoinette's home and saw the warm glow of light within as he had left it an hour ago. Hurd was probably there. He turned and paused for a moment in front of the windows. What would happen if he went in? His blood was filled with that desire—to stand face to face with Hurd again and to let him know as quickly as he could that it was to be a fight to the death now between himself and the murderer of his father. He walked on, going to the end of the street, and a dispassionate coolness began to possess him. He felt an immense confidence—and at the same time the necessity for caution and a deliberate command of himself.

They would beat Ivan Hurd! Not for an instant did a doubt of that fact oppress him. If it came to the worst he held the final key, the final solution. Hurd owed him a life in exchange for his father's, and it would not be so terribly hard to collect the debt—with the heart and happiness of Antoinette St. Ives dependent upon its fulfilment.

A third and a fourth time he walked past her door and windows, treading softly so that his feet made no sound, and he began turning over in his mind what the plans might be that were taking her into the north country. Colonel Denis would probably have explained if he had waited a little longer—but tomorrow would do. A *woman's* job! He thought again of Clairette Aldous and smiled in the gloom that lay between the narrow walls. The same pluck was in them both, and it was a more beautiful courage than man's. When he found himself saying that, half aloud, it was like an arrow driving into him where the light of wisdom had never found its way before.

Twice he had seen a shadowy figure at the end of the street and each time it had disappeared at his approach. Now he observed it a third time, and again it was swallowed up in gloom as he came toward it, as if one of

113

the old walls had opened and let it in. It was late and most people were asleep. Few lights were burning beyond the windows and stillness hung heavily in the little streets of Lower Town. And at this hour, Clifton thought, no one would be appearing and disappearing in that ghostly way unless he was a spy or some evil lay behind it. He recalled Colonel Denis's words regarding the little monk and wondered if it was Friar Alphonse who had also made this a night of vigil in Notre Dame Street.

The stillness was broken by the opening and closing of a door. The sound was like a pistol shot in the little street, sharp and with something of dramatic harshness about it.

It was the St. Ives door.

Clifton flattened himself against one of the walls. His position was good. Light shone in from the end of the street and Hurd would easily recognize him when he stepped forth.

He could hear Hurd's feet pounding heavily, like an animal's. That, and the slamming of the door, convinced him of the passion of the man. He sauntered out from the wall as Hurd came up. They met face to face with scarcely the reach of an arm between them.

Hurd's face had a strange look in it. His eyes were flaming. His full, heavy lips hung a little loosely and he was breathing shortly and quickly. Something that was more than passion—a touch almost of madness—seemed to have hold of the man. The instant he recognized Clifton a hand shot to his pocket. There it stopped, gripping something tightly.

Clifton smiled coldly into his eyes.

"We're not in the woods yet, Hurd," he admonished. "Better not shoot! Leave that kind of work to your hired assassins—only I'd advise you to get better ones than you had at Haipoong."

He gave Hurd no chance to reply.

"I've been waiting for you," he went on. "I want to tell you that I realize what a fool I was for not killing you in your office in Montreal. You owe me your life, and I'm going to have it. This time I am not playing with you. I am going to kill you—but not here. I am going to give you one chance— only one—and you'd better take it. If you do not, all your political power won't save you. I want you to understand that, Hurd—I'll kill you anywhere, in the woods, on the street, in your own home—if you go on with your plot against the Laurentian Company and Antoinette St. Ives!"

His voice was like ice, but in the face of it Hurd had recovered his nerve. His grinning teeth leered at Clifton. He laughed with low savagery. In a moment he was *Le Taureau*—the Bull—the human steam-roller preparing to ride over his enemies.

"You fool!" he snapped, thrusting his huge shoulders forward. "No, I won't shoot. I'll wait. I'll break you into little bits, an inch at a time. I'm

114

glad the police didn't get you, for that would have been too good for you—too good!" The bones of his fingers snapped in their clenching tenseness. "You miserable—bluffer!"

He made as if to pass but Clifton stood in his way.

"Are you not a trifle curious, Hurd?" he asked. "Are you so demoralized by your conference with Mademoiselle St. Ives that you do not want to know why I am going to kill you unless you put an end to the scheming deviltry through which you hope to force her into your possession?"

A momentary shock of amazement touched Hurd.

"What do you know—you—you—"

"What do I know?" interrupted Clifton. "Everything. And why shouldn't I, inasmuch as I am going to make Antoinette St. Ives my wife? Now you understand why it will be so easy for me to kill you!" And with these words he left Hurd.

His blood ran hot as he walked again up through the gloom of Notre Dame Street. No power could have kept the words back from his lips. He wanted Hurd to know, and he was glad he had spoken them. Yet his heart was frightened and his soul trembled as he came nearer to the door of Antoinette St. Ives.

For a moment Ivan Hurd stared after him and then crunched fiercely out through the mouth of the street.

As he disappeared Friar Alphonse came from his hiding-place within a dozen feet of where the two men had stood. Doubling himself over so that he became more than ever a part of the shadows he followed on the trail of Ivan Hurd.

For only a moment Clifton hesitated before the St. Ives door. Then he knocked, and entered the little vestibule. He tapped at the second door, and waited. He heard light footsteps and after that fell a silence in which he could hear his heart beating.

"It is Captain Brant who knocks, Mademoiselle," he called reassuringly.

The door was slowly opened.

After Ivan Hurd's visit he had expected to find Antoinette St. Ives with flaming cheeks and eyes filled with fire. She was that kind of little fighter, he believed—one who would die before showing the white flag of fear to her enemy. Her appearance now was something of a shock to him. She was deathly white—so white that the curling richness of her hair seemed to rest with almost metallic weight against her bloodless cheeks and forehead. Her eyes were luminous pools of a strange light which he had not seen in them before, and he could see a little throbbing place in her white throat as she faced him. In the mute tragedy of her whiteness and with that heart beating in her throat she was lovelier to Clifton than when he had first seen her at the top of the stair. Yet there was something frightening about this beauty

115

now. It was as if it had turned suddenly to snow, even to the hand that had risen to her breast as he entered. His impulse was not to let her know he saw the change in her, to pass over it if he could and to bring the rose flush of blood back into her face with the boundless optimism of his own confidence and strength.

So he said: "Pardon, Mademoiselle. It is late, but I could not sleep until I saw you again. I think Colonel Denis has told me most of the story. He is upset—tremendously so. A little off physically, I should say, and overworried, especially about you. That is why I came back—to make sure your mind was not unsettled for the night. I met our old friend Hurd in the alley —I mean in the street. Had a nice little chat with him. An unconscionable scoundrel and a hopeless ass, isn't he? Hurd is a type. I met them in the war. They are the same everywhere—in business as well as behind the gun. There is only one way of handling them, and I am glad I happened to come home with that method fresh in my mind. Please don't worry, Mademoiselle—Antoinette."

He dared the last word—her name. It was the only thing that came a little unsteadily from his lips. And he noticed that the pallor was beginning to go out of her cheeks.

"You are thoughtful, Captain Brant. And you are quite sure Colonel Denis left nothing untold?"

"I am quite sure—except that I did not wait for the details of the plan which is taking you into the north. I think he told me everything—even to your vow to consecrate yourself to the Church should your brother destroy Ivan Hurd. Such a thing will never be necessary, Mademoiselle. From this night on Ivan Hurd belongs to me. I told him that in our brief conversation out there, and the entirely satisfactory part of it all is that Hurd knows it!"

He was ready to go then. It was enough to have seen her and to have said this much. He inclined his head as if to say good night.

Her hand touched him. It rested on his arm and the feathery weight of it thrilled him. The heart-like little beat in her throat was gone. Her eyes shone for a moment with the softness of dawn breaking through a mist of morning dew, and almost unconsciously his hand rose and touched her own as it rested on his arm. She drew away.

"Forgive me," he said, "I had to do that—or touch your hair."

She ignored his words, as if he had not touched her or spoken. And he was looking at her hair, its shining beauty, its softness and its tempting nearness.

She made a little gesture with her hands.

"You, too, would kill Ivan Hurd?"

"If your life and happiness depends on his death—yes."

116

"But it isn't necessary!" she cried with a sudden passionate break in her voice. "It is not Ivan Hurd I am afraid of. He can destroy, he can drive us out of the forests, he can break up this home, he can do his worst and still there is life. It is my brother—Gaspard—who fills me with fear. There is a madness in him which frightens me. If Hurd goes on I know what will happen. It will end in—in—"

"I know," said Clifton. "John Denis told me. But it is not going to end that way. I am answering for your brother now. We are going north, and I am wagering twenty to one that we will beat Hurd on his own ground. As for your brother—I can give you the greatest guarantee in the world that he will never injure this man he hates."

Relief filled her face. His own assurance rose as he saw it flooding her eyes with a radiant glow. Lightsomeness swept his heart. It was impossible for him to see tragedy or even the shadow of tragedy. For him the world was a glory of hope, and he smiled his optimism and faith and happiness in her face that was suffused once more with a soft flush of color.

"The beast frightened you tonight?" he asked.

"It was unpleasant."

"And—it was final?"

"Yes, final."

"Then let us cheer up, *cara sposa*! That is a perfectly proper Hindu luck-name for one who has courage, pluck, determination and a great faith in prayer. It is extremely formal and I hope you don't mind my using it. *Cara sposa*! It is almost as pretty as Antoinette, and means so much, and the higher-caste Hindus believe it never fails to bring good luck when applied to one with all the sincerity of another's heart. You see I am a little superstitious. And now if you will go to bed and dream of nothing but sunshine and success—and possibly of me—"

The humor in his eyes was infectious. She smiled. Her shining head was near him when she said good night.

"I am glad you came back," she said; and he went away repeating those words—"I am glad you came back—*I am glad you came back*"—until his brain seemed to have heard no others since the beginning of the world.

From the end of the street someone watched as the night swallowed him, a bent and silent figure that was a part of the shadows. It was Friar Alphonse. A few minutes later he stood under the light in front of the St. Ives home. His mouth was twisted as if in pain. A look of grief was in his eyes. With an effort he seemed to shake himself, and straightened his shoulders, and forced a smile to his tense lips.

"God's will be done!" he muttered, and still like a shadow he disappeared through the door which a few moments before Antoinette St. Ives had closed upon Clifton.

CHAPTER XIV

It was after midnight when Clifton ceased walking and got himself a room. Even then it was not with the intention of immediately going to bed or trying to sleep. He bought a paper and cigars and explained quite plausibly to the hotel clerk why he had no luggage. The missing pack, of which Gaspard had taken possession, emphasized the general upsetting and bewildering readjustment of the entire universe during the last few hours.

The pack, now in the St. Ives home, was an unmistakable proof that at first Gaspard and his sister had planned to keep him there as a guest. But he remembered that nothing had been said about it when he left with Colonel Denis. Of course an unexpected thing had happened after that—the surprise visit of Ivan Hurd. Otherwise Denis would undoubtedly have escorted him back to Notre Dame Street. And Ivan Hurd had not produced the only shock in the St. Ives household that night! His visit must have been immeasurably less astonishing than this own attitude toward Antoinette St. Ives, and after what he had said to her it was of course inconceivable that she could think of him as a guest. She had even forgotten the pack which contained his belongings when she knew he was leaving for other lodging.

Clifton felt no regret. He was filled with a glowing exultation and happiness which persisted in keeping him wide awake and he was glad he had given voice to a daring truth instead of hiding it. That Antoinette St. Ives was thinking of him as impertinent and over-bold, even when regarding his action in a most charitable way, made no difference. He was glad for all that, glad the truth was out. And each hour and day she would know more and more that it was the truth he had spoken, and if God would only be with him a little he would prove to her in the end that they had never been strangers but that he had been waiting for her from the beginning of time—*yes, ever since that day long ago when she was the lovely Adelaide and he was Crepin Marrolet.*

That thought ran through him so sharply that it brought a little gasp to his lips. *Why not*? Had he not lived before—in all his dreams, his thoughts, his wide-awake visions of a day and age that had preceded this? Was it not thinkable that he was that Crepin Marrolet who was brought in dead from a

118

duel, and that it was Antoinette living in the body of Adelaide who had wept over him and died of grief three years later? Yes, it was thinkable—believable—it was so! If he could only tell her that—if he could let her know that it was Crepin who had come back to fight for her out of that life which they had both lived and loved so many years ago!

He pulled out a drawer, and there was paper. He began to write—not to Antoinette St. Ives but to Adelaide Marrolet. It was his soul that burned in the words, his love, his faith, his belief, his religion. He did not read them when he had finished. His face was hot with the fever of this thoughts, this miracle of revelation that had come to him, as he sealed and addressed the envelope. Now he knew what the open skies and the stars and the voiceless glory of nature had been trying to tell him all these years of his earthly wandering. He had been questing—seeking—and at last he had found that for which he had sought, that treasure which he had lost for a time at the end of a rapier point two hundred and forty-nine years ago. And Antoinette St. Ives must know!

He went down and got a messenger. And after that he paced back and forth in his room, looking at his watch, counting the steps that must be taken, until he knew that his message had reached her.

He did not feel that he had done an insane or foolish thing. Now that he had acted he tried to recall what he had written. It would amaze her, of course. At first she might think he was a little mad, and he could fancy her getting very angry, too. But she could not escape the truth that was in those pages. By this time she was up and was reading or had read what he had sent. He made his vision of her, all in lacy white, with her silken curls about her shoulders and the pages of his letter in her lap. What if she should think he was mad? A little stab of uneasiness went through him. Shell-shocked, gassed—afflicted with hypochondriasis, or dithyrambisis, maybe. He grinned. If he had thought of those words he would have used them. They would have been incontestable proof of his sanity.

It was three o'clock when he partly undressed and stretched himself out on the bed. It was not his intention to take more than a cat-nap if he slept at all. Joe and Bim were arriving at seven-thirty in the morning and probably Antoinette would be at the depot to meet them. He, also, would be there. It would be a splendid opportunity, and he could take them all to breakfast. He closed his eyes and firmly adjusted his mind upon a five o'clock awakening. He was confident as drowsiness stole over him. He was like an alarm clock, and when he set himself to awake at a certain hour it always happened.

But this morning there was an error somewhere in the mechanics of the system. It was ten o'clock when he looked at his watch. A high sun was pouring in at a window and a newsboy was calling out the noon edition of a paper.

He leaped from the bed in a panic. It was eleven o'clock before he had a shave and was in Notre Dame Street. Of course it was excusable for him to call there to see Joe and Bim. Antoinette would almost expect that.

As he knocked at the door he wished he had stopped somewhere to take a cup of coffee. He might need it, facing her this morning. He felt a little taggy. His nerves were not as steady as they should have been, and his heart was not pumping as strongly as last night. Afraid? His confidence a little gone? He shook himself and laughed the thought away. There was no answer to his knocking. He tried the outer door and found it locked, and then pommeled it more loudly. It was impossible for him to rouse an answer. He went down to the market, killed half an hour, and returned again. Still he could get no answer. Then he hunted up a telephone and persisted in that way. Funny he could not even get the maid!

It was almost noon when he went to Colonel Denis's office. Denis had evidently been awaiting him with some anxiety, for a look of unconcealed relief came into his face when Clifton entered.

"I was beginning to wonder if something had happened to you, too," he greeted. "Guess I'm in rotten shape. My nerves won't adjust themselves to the unexpected. Glad you've come, Clifton! There is your pack over there, and I have two letters for you—one from Antoinette and the other from Gaspard. The devil, but I thought maybe Hurd had got you!"

Clifton controlled his uneasiness.

"I overslept," he explained. "Then I went down to Notre Dame Street and could find no one there."

"They're gone!" shrugged Denis. "You never can tell exactly what Antoinette St. Ives is going to do—and she has done it again, if that makes me clear. She left by rail early this morning for Metabetchewan up on Lake Saint John, instead of taking the really beautiful water trip on a Saguenay boat. Don't know what started her so suddenly, but her brother and the monk are with her, and also the boy and dog. The *dog*, mind you! Can you beat it? And—can you tell me any more about it than she told me in the note which I found here this morning?"

"Probably less. You say you have letters for me?"

Denis gave him two envelopes that were on his desk. One was effeminately small and sealed with wax. Clifton opened it first. The handwriting was as exquisite as Antoinette St. Ives herself.

"If it were not that I need the assistance of a man of your experience and age I would be inclined to ask you not to follow us to Metabetchewan," she had written. "But your years soften the voluminous audacity of your letter, all of which I have not yet had time to read—and I doubt if I shall find the leisure to continue through so many words which seem to carry such a pitifully small expression of idea. I think we shall be at Metabetchewan for a day or two before leaving on the pilgrimage which Colonel Denis can tell you about. As one who wishes you well, however, I might suggest that you go to a psychopathic hospital first, at least for an examination if not for treatment." And then she added, "With good wishes for your health, Antoinette St. Ives."

Clifton was sallow when he turned to Colonel Denis.

"She says nothing," he mumbled.

He opened Gaspard's letter.

"My beloved sister has us running in circles with the unexpectedness of her departure," he wrote briefly. "This is only to call attention to your promise, Monsieur—that you are to be with God and me when I break the bones in Ajax Trappier's body. If you will come to Metabetchewan we will immediately make our plans."

Clifton felt better.

"I am to follow them on the next train. When does that leave?"

"Day after tomorrow," said Denis.

Clifton's heart fell like a chunk of lead.

"Not until then? No other way?"

"Not unless you walk through several hundred miles of wilderness." Suddenly Denis caught himself. "By George, Lucien Jeannot telephoned me not half an hour ago! Jeannot is one of the government hydroplane fliers who are mapping the northern timber country. His station is at Roberval on Lake Saint John, and he is flying back sometime early this afternoon. If you'd care to go that way—"

"*Care!*" Clifton fairly shouted the word. "For God's sake get hold of him and make it possible for me if you can, John! If I had it I would give a million dollars to be waiting at that little old Metabetchewan station when Antoinette St. Ives gets off the train! Where is Jeannot? Can you reach him? Will he take me—"

Denis was already at the telephone. Within ten minutes he had located Jeannot at the government offices. Yes, Jeannot would be glad to take Monsieur Brant. He would like his company. He was leaving at two o'clock.

Clifton emitted a groan of joy as he sank into a chair.

"Don't mind my emotion," he begged. "I am eager to be on the scene of battle. And I am confident, John—never was so sure of a thing in my life. We are going to beat Hurd. And you have until two o'clock to tell me many things I ought to know. First, what are the working plans that Mademoiselle St. Ives has proposed?"

121

Colonel Denis had prepared himself for that explanation. He had maps, papers and blue-prints laid out on the table and began where Clifton had interrupted him the preceding night. First he pointed out the positions of dams, bridges and roads and the locations of camps. It was like going over a battlefield. The blue-prints contained their enemy's possessions, and Clifton could easily see the drama of the situation. They were not only working on the same river with their foes, but shoulder to shoulder with them, in many instances using the same roads and bridges.

"We have seen a lot of fighting together, Clifton," said John Denis, "and with the battleground laid out before us like this we should at once recognize that one chance upon which our salvation depends. Here the conflicting forces will meet. Victory or ruin, as I see it now, will rest entirely upon superiority in manpower, but not so much in the strength of that manpower in numbers as in morale. Hurd has a great advantage of us now. His forces are organized, his machine oiled and working smoothly, not because of love or loyalty but by reason of unlimited money behind it. Our forces are broken, scattered and undermined by his agents and his propaganda and his promise of bonuses.

"He is an atheist and at heart hates Catholicism yet he has contributed money to a dozen parishes and has built a dozen shrines in the Lake Saint John country, where we are dependent for our men. If the Church could be convinced of his heart and his purpose I am sure it would repudiate his gifts and his influence, but by the time it has made that discovery Hurd will have achieved his ends. That is why Antoinette St. Ives has risen like a Jeanne d'Arc to take charge of the situation.

"She believes that women will see the truth where men have failed, and that what we must have in the woods this year are friends. So she is going north to make them—to meet the wives and children of the forest men as well as the men themselves, to live with them, and scatter the seeds of truth and loyalty where Hurd and his people have sown their poison. It is not selfishness that urges her, Clifton. She loves the people she is going among. She knows many of them. She worships the forests. It is a labor of love and justice and service to God she is on far more than that of her own welfare—those things and to save her brother from what she knows will happen if Ivan Hurd completes the devastation he has begun."

Clifton saw him hesitate.

"And that is all?" he asked.

"No," said Denis. "A few of the men will be leaving their homes for the woods late this month, and most of them will go during September and October. Antoinette is going to spend the winter with them in their camps and remain until the driving season closes after the flood waters of spring. It took me a long time to approve of that, but I had to, for she was determined

122

on the adventure whether I gave it official sanction or not. There is a danger about it, too, for Hurd now understands what her intentions are and he has the toughest crowd in the Province up there—a crowd that will grow worse as winter comes. And she is going in among that crowd. I cannot stop her. It is her intention to meet Hurd's ruffians in Hurd's own camps, become acquainted with them, sing for them, give them little talks on Sundays, and make them ashamed of their fight against a woman.

"A fascinatingly courageous program, don't you think?—no less an idea than driving Hurd out of his own household through the sheer force of decency and respect which she hopes to rouse in the better element of that horde which Hurd will have under the leadership of his professional bad men. Maybe it will work. Maybe it won't. If it doesn't, or if something should happen to her—then is when I want you to be ready to fight in another way.

"You are to have full authority over the men. Mademoiselle St. Ives has agreed to that, with the very emphatic reservation that you are to have no authority whatever over *her*." Denis laughed as he shrugged his thin shoulders. "Beyond that, Clifton, go your own lengths. I confess that I am beaten. I am now shifting the entire burden of the field management of the organization onto your shoulders, and not only the fate of the Laurentian Company but also that of Antoinette St. Ives and her brother rest almost entirely in your hands. It is a big job. But there is one glorious thing in it— and that is Antoinette. You won't lack for inspiration."

"No," said Clifton, "I won't."

Until half-past twelve they buried themselves in business details; then they had a quick luncheon. It was a quarter of two when they reached the launch that was to take them out to the hydroplane. Jeannot was waiting for them. He was a slim, keen-eyed Frenchman with a wisp of a mustache, and he greeted Clifton with a friendliness that at once made him a comrade.

At the last moment Clifton caught himself. "Is there a telegraph office near?" he asked.

"Up there, two blocks," directed Jeannot. "I just sent some wires to Roberval. Take your time."

Ten minutes later Clifton read over the message he was sending to Antoinette St. Ives, addressed to her aboard the train bound for Metabetchewan. It would reach her about half past three o'clock.

The message ran, "Have seen an alienist. He says I am mentally all right but need very tender attention and care. Love. Clifton."

A little later Colonel Denis stood alone and watched the government hydroplane as it rose like a bird from the water, righted itself, and disappeared swiftly in the direction of the northern wilderness.

CHAPTER XV

"This will be an unusual experience for me," Clifton had said to Jeannot as he adjusted his helmet and speaking-tube receivers before the Frenchman started his engine. "I have been up overseas but never have looked down on my own forests. We were not using flying-machines in the wilderness country back in nineteen-fourteen. Only lunatics and idiots were beginning to think of that."

"Some people call us idiots now," laughed Jeannot. "We smash machines, of course, and some of us count in on the wrecks, because if anything happens we have just one chance—and that is to hit for a lake or a river if it is big enough. And if one isn't near, or we mess up in our judgment in aiming at it—something happens. That is why we use hydroplanes. Water is our only hope. But for all that we are mapping and photographing new countries, putting out fires and bringing the farthest frontiers right up to our doors now."

Looking down on the city a few minutes later Clifton held his breath in wonderment, and in a flash his mind leaped to the slow-moving train that was bearing Antoinette St. Ives through the forests, and to the sacrifice he would willingly make if she could be gazing down upon this same earthly paradise with him. Jeannot was saying something through the transmitter but he paid little heed to the Frenchman's voice or words. Even the roar of the engine was lost in the thrill that swept his senses.

He had flown over Belgium and Alsace and a part of France; he had looked down into the streets of Paris and London, and had twice been over Hongkong and once with an English flier over Bombay—but nothing had ever pressed upon him so overwhelmingly the wonder-working forces of nature and God as this city of Quebec and the magnificent terrain about it. His mind sped with the swiftness of his vision, and it seemed to him that Cartier and Champlain and Roberval and the others must have possessed some power whereby they too had looked down on this wonderland before choosing it as the heart of the New World.

In other places Clifton had regarded with interest and curiosity the works of man, but here man's efforts were completely overridden and subdued by a colossal triumph of nature. He saw the Château Frontenac like a mighty castle at the edge of an abyss, the great churches in their squares, and the ancient fortifications and gleaming monuments and the gray walls of convent and monastery. The Plains of Abraham and the battlefield of Sainte Foy circled under him, and he saw the Tidal Basin and Victoria Park, and where Wolfe and his men crept up in the night, and the Samos Battery and Spencer Wood. But in a moment these details were obliterated and forgotten in a vast and awesome panorama that was spreading itself out under his eyes.

East and west lay the mighty Saint Lawrence, and reaching out like a protecting arm to hold Quebec in the cradle which it made was the Saint Charles. In all directions were the blue and silvery gleams of water. The Isle of Orleans stood out in its frame of almost royal purple and north of it the splendid River Montmorency lost itself in forests that were like great dark carpets spread upon the earth. He could see twenty rivers and lakes, and between them ancient towns and villages appeared from hidden valleys or screens of forest and disappeared again like living things. As Jeannot rose higher the earth widened beneath them until the rising Laurentians and the forests in the north shut out distance in a blue haze.

Not until these things had pressed upon him for a number of minutes did Clifton's mind and vision return to details. He saw the great castle of Frontenac again and it was like a child's toy. Quebec was dissolving swiftly into a gray and white tapestry of sunshine and shadow. Levis and Charlesbourg and Sainte Foy were gone. A cross gleamed at Indian-Lorette and disappeared in a golden flash, and the Saint Lawrence was growing narrower while the Montmorency and the Jacques Carder grew longer.

"A fine atmosphere," called back Jeannot. "You can see a half of the Seigneurie de la Cote and thirty miles or more into the Laurentides. We are heading for the country of Fief Hubert now and Lac Baliscan. With this wind and air we'll make Metabetchewan two hours ahead of the train you want to beat."

Clifton hunched himself close to the bell-shaped mouth of the transmitter.

"Will we see the train?" he asked.

"After Lac Baliscan I follow the line of rail," replied Jeanne. "We should pass your friends about four o'clock."

A thrill of exultation swept over Clifton.

"If you can make them see us," he exclaimed, "I'll buy you a new hat when I come to Roberval!"

Jeannot saw Clifton's face and eyes for a moment, and grinned. Denis had told him enough to rouse both his curiosity and his imagination and he was quick to seize upon the possibilities of the adventure.

"We'll have them all poking their heads out of the windows," he promised.

Clifton looked at his watch. It was half past two o'clock. At three they were over the splendid water-way country that began with the deep and unbroken wilderness of Fief Hubert. With Lac Croche and Lac Sainte Anne as the central point Clifton counted forty lakes within a radius of thirty miles, with Lac Baliscan reaching north and west like a huge emerald set between rugged walls and mountains of evergreen forest. Another half-hour and Jeannot hovered over a break in the wilderness that was like a long and attenuated thread. It was the railroad, and the Frenchman descended until the steel rails gleamed clearly in the sunlight.

In a little while they passed over a moving freight-train, that looked like a string of toy cars standing motionless; and after that, as Jeannot pointed out things of interest and told how Quebec's vast forests were going swiftly to destruction Clifton listened but kept his eyes on the line of rail ahead.

"It isn't what the timber people are *cutting*," Jeannot was saying bitterly, with a gesture that took in a thousand square miles of country. "That could go on forever with proper harvesting in place of slaughter and with real conservation instead of political control. Politicians don't know how to deal with bud-worms and bark beetles and fungi, and just as long as they are allowed to fill the positions in our forestry service with personal favorites we shall continue to see what we are seeing now. Look off there! That's what hydro-planes and sky-photography are bringing before the people! That dark patch is ten miles square—burned over last year. And we'll soon be over ten million dollars' worth of rotting spruce and jackpine —killed by the bud-worm and fungi.

"Those are the problems we are up against, and at the present time they are not being solved by technical science. You will see that destruction all over Old and New Quebec, and the government is just beginning to wake up. If it were not for the intelligence and technical ability behind some of the big timber-leasing companies I'd see no hope at all. But as it is I am one of those who believe that incompetency and graft and sheer political rottenness are about due for the undertaker."

"So am I," almost shouted Clifton. "That is why I am going north—to help out! Do you know Ivan Hurd?"

Jeannot answered with an eloquent shrug of his shoulders. "Yes—and his gang," he said. "If we could guillotine about a dozen of his kind we'd have an honest parliament left. Isn't it one of the amazing spectacles of the age how a few clever scoundrels can gag and hoodwink ten times their number of men who at heart really have the desire to be honest and constructive instead of otherwise? It is simply the old story of the leader and

126

the sheep. One clever leader is worth a hundred followers, and if that leader happens to be a grafter and a scoundrel—God help the people!"

"What would happen," asked Clifton, "if something should occur to destroy the power and political influence of Ivan Hurd? I have been away a long time and the situation here is quite new to me."

"It would mark the beginning of the break-up," said Jeannot, idling his engine for a moment. "And after that, within five years, we would be well on our way in the care of our forests, as a man cares for his orchards or a farmer for his fields. We would have real forestry men in our service, a technically fitted fire-control, the right kind of legislation and half-way decent funds for the biggest work that man has before him on earth today. We would get hold of the spruce bud-worm and the bark beetle and the borer and have specialists working out the problem of fungi destruction. Forest protection and propagation and harvesting would in time become a science as exact as that of chemistry and medicine.

"But before we can get at men like Hurd and his gang people must be made to realize that their lives are absolutely dependent upon wild life and forests. Without these things we would become extinct as a race. Without wood we would have no agriculture, no manufacture and no commerce, and civilization as we know it would come to an end. Those are the truths we must bring to the people, and when that time comes there will be a wholesale resignation of political incompetents and their replacement by men who are technically and professionally fitted to do what must be done if we escape ultimate ruin."

Jeannot had lost the line of rail in the heat of his enthusiasm. He swung back to it again and as the thin threads of steel gleamed under them he pointed suddenly ahead.

"Smoke!" he exclaimed. "Maybe you can't see it. Quite a trick to make out smoke from a hydroplane. But that's the train—ten miles ahead of us!"

Sight of smoke which Clifton could not yet see in the sky had changed the Frenchman. There was an eager attentiveness in the forward thrust of his head and mischievous lines had gathered at the corners of his mouth.

"I hope you won't get groggy if I duck about a little," he said. "It's the surest way of bringing their heads out, and if you want to get a look at St. Ives, or Mademoiselle Antoinette—"

"I do," said Clifton. He had no reason for keeping that fact from his companion. He rather liked the idea of being a little confidential with this newly discovered friend. "I'm trying my best to marry Mademoiselle St. Ives," he added.

"*Par Dieu*, I wish you luck!" exclaimed Jeannot. "Will she guess you are in the machine?"

"No."

To himself Clifton was laughing, and accompanying his humor was a thrill which was beginning to send little electrical flashes through his body. What would Antoinette St. Ives say and think if she knew he was in the machine which would soon be cutting capers about the train in which she was slowly plodding along? And what would be her reaction when he advanced in all the profound triumph of his achievement to greet her as she stepped off the train at the little Metabetchewan depot? He could fancy the amazement and shock of that unexpected moment. And now if Jeannot only knew enough of the jugglery of flying to write his initials or the letters of his name in the air his cup of happiness would be filled to overflowing. He had known of such things being done overseas. Dare-deviltry, of course, but he was willing to risk that, and intimated as much to the Frenchman.

Jeannot shrugged his shoulders and kept his opinion to himself. In a few minutes they saw the train. It seemed to be traveling at a ridiculously slow speed and Jeannot sailed over it a thousand feet high. On their right and ahead of them, running parallel with the line of rail for a number of miles was Kiskisink Lake, and after certain observations Jeannot made a wide circle and returned to the train scarcely more than half as high as before. The hydroplane was already observed. The engineer greeted it with shrill whistles and faces and heads began to appear at the open windows of the coaches. Clifton waved his hand, and then a white handkerchief. He shouted, forgetting for a moment that the roar of the engine would drown his voice. He felt like a small boy who wanted to jump up and down and wave his arms and yell. And then came a wild and delirious eternity of semi-oblivion.

With a shout of warning Jeannot swung high up over the open lake. What happened after that Clifton's mind was incapable of comprehending. Above all other things he was an earth-man, and from such a being he was suddenly shot into a nightmare existence of dives and twistings and somersaultings that stopped his heart and his breath and his power of vision, and which seemed to mix all his senses and the vital organs of his body into one anesthetized mess. His only intelligent thought was that Jeannot had gone mad and they were falling a million miles, turning over three or four times a second in that endless descent.

He could see trains, plenty of them. Now they were over him, and then under him, sometimes running away and at others coming head-on but never traveling in a reasonable kind of way. How long it was before there came a subdued shock, a rushing hiss of water and after than an easy and undulating motion Clifton would not have dared to guess. It might have been one minute—five—fifteen—or a week. Anyway, this fool of a Jeannot had not destroyed them and the hydroplane was sweeping along easily on the water.

And then came Jeannot's voice, "Take a look, Captain Brant! There isn't a head inside the windows, and if that is not Gaspard St. Ives in the third car—and his sister looking with him—I'll forfeit the hat you are going to get me at Roberval!"

Clifton's muddled wits were slow in assembling themselves and before he could make out the third car from the fifth or sixth a headland of forest drove the hydro-plane out into the lake, and two or three minutes later they were again in the air, with a thin trail of smoke swiftly disappearing behind them.

The Frenchman was debonair and smiling.

"Did you see them, Monsieur?"

Clifton indulged in a sickly grin.

"I must have. I saw everything from the beginning of the world up to the present time. Where did you learn that stuff?"

"Picked it up over there. Mostly along the Somme and at Verdun and the Ypres salient."

Clifton reached a hand over to Jeannot. Their grip was a long and understanding one. "I didn't know that," he said. "Colonel Denis said nothing about it. We were three times engaged at Ypres, and were at Courcelette and Vimy Ridge. Maybe I saw you there. The air fighting was superb."

"It was most interesting," agreed Jeannot.

At Saint André Junction he left the line of rail and swung a point or two eastward. Half an hour later the hydroplane lay on the smooth surface of Lake Saint John a hundred yards from the Metabetchewan shore and a skiff was rowing out to them.

"We have a government wire as far up as the junction of the Mistassini and Rivière aux Rats," said Jeannot when they parted. "If you ever want to get hold of me call Roberval. Accident, you know, or something like that. I can reach you in an hour. And, by the way, never mind the hat!"

His engine was roaring and he was off with a smile and a wave of his hand as Clifton shouted good-bye from the boat. When he stepped ashore Jeannot was a speck in the western sky.

Shouldering his pack Clifton walked up past the little old sawmill with its tall black smoke-stack, crossed the railroad and wandered up and down the two or three Metabetchewan streets which he remembered so well. Then he stopped at Price Brothers' outfitting depot and from the agent in charge learned that a few men were already beginning to leave for the big woods. Campbuilders, mostly, the man told him. His name was Tremblay, and Clifton wondered if the Tremblays were as thick as ever in the north country, and if the Gagnons had come up to them in their race for numerical supremacy.

He asked about the new baby, and found that Philip Tremblay was the father of twins born three months before, making a total of fourteen children to date, and all doing nicely. In time Philip hoped to have a family of which he could be proud, he said, and especially as he had promised the local priest to adopt two children from the family of the first man who was killed in the woods that year, which act would surely bring him good luck and reward. Clifton liked his optimism and sense of humor, and when Madame Tremblay dropped in for a few moments to see her husband he was delighted with her freshness and good looks and general appearance of happiness. Fourteen children had not taken the sparkle from her dark eyes or the quick blush from her cheeks.

The Tremblays invited him to a supper which he could finish before train time, and he accepted. The fourteen children were as clean as Madame Tremblay's scrubbed floors, and Philip's eyes danced with pride when he told of a reunion recently held by his father at which only Tremblays over sixty years of age could be crowded at the tables in the house, while all other Tremblays under that age had to be served in a field. It required four two-hundred-pound hogs to feed them, and all the people were quite closely related, second cousins being the most distant in kinship.

He was full of enthusiasm for his work, and expressed himself as not satisfied with the way things were going this year, although it was pretty early to judge conditions accurately. The jobbers were sticking to their old companies, and there seemed to be plenty of them, but there was restlessness and dissatisfaction among the men which he did not like. The head choppers, swampers and teamsters were not so easy to get, while the ordinary roustabouts or second choppers were hardest of all to enlist in sufficient numbers. He was afraid that jobbers who had contracted to cut from twenty to thirty thousand logs each for the company would find difficulty in getting out a half or two-thirds of that number.

One reason for the scarcity of men, he said, was that the big Hurd-Foy interests were opening up new districts north, and were promising men bonuses and better wages, and were generally upsetting conditions as they had previously existed. The Laurentian Company was especially hard hit, he had heard, because its men came mostly from the west and north shores of Lake Saint John between Saint Prime and Peribonka, while the Price Company had the advantage of drawing its working forces from the towns and villages south and east of Metabetchewan.

"We cut a hundred and fifteen million feet board measure last year," he declared with pride, "and Price Brothers are building another paper mill on the Little Discharge over at Alma in anticipation of beating that cut by a half. We've got to hustle—and we're going to!"

That was the spirit with which Clifton went to the depot. It was in the air and in his blood. Such a country as this, with all its glorious sunshine and freedom and cleanness would not permit a beast like Ivan Hurd to dominate it. He gazed out over Lake Saint John in the sunset. Twenty miles across the water the four mighty rivers of the north were emptying into it, the Little and the Big Peribonka, the Mistassini and the Ashuapmouchan. He fancied he could almost hear the roar of them as they came tumbling out of the wilderness, clean and strong and filled from shore to shore with the virility of the vast forests which man had just begun to enter.

He had known Louis Hémon, with his sensitive, finely strung soul and not overstrong body, and wondered if good old Samuel Bedard and his wife Maria, whom Hémon had put in his novel, still lived in the little village of Peribonka. Quite vividly he recalled a raw evening of autumn rain when Maria Chapdelaine had fried eggs and made coffee for him, and afterward how he had sat with Samuel in his little store and exchanged stories between pipes. He was sure the men of Maria Chapdelaine's country would be with them in their fight with Hurd.

He was thirty minutes ahead of time at the depot, and puffing at his pipe as he walked up and down the plank platform he began an analysis of certain thoughts and plans which his hydroplane experience had not permitted him to attempt until now. But as each minute passed his ability to reason grew less, until at last he concentrated himself entirely upon the movement of the hands of his watch. Never had he felt a sensation quite so pleasurably thrilling as that which these minutes brought to him. In a quarter of an hour he would see Antoinette St. Ives—if the train was not late. The agent told him it was on time, and that in itself set his blood running faster.

He was boyishly jubilant as he walked the last few minutes away. Antoinette would be glad to see him, he was quite sure, in spite of the acidity of her letter. He read the letter again as he listened for the engine whistle and endeavored to find something between the lines which would mellow its insinuation. He tried to picture Antoinette's lovely eyes filled with laughter and her lips smiling as she wrote it, and his hopefulness made him fairly successful.

Then he heard the whistle. A small crowd of people had gathered and he drew himself well back among these, and asked two or three foolish questions of a whiskered man who stood at the end of a buckboard which he had backed up against the platform. Just about where would the third coach stop, and from which end of it would the passengers alight? The whiskered man regarded him mildly and answered him as if he might have been a

131

child. "It stops most anywhere and they get off at both ends," he said, and then added gratuitously, "The engine comes in first, Monsieur!"

He was near the third coach when the train stopped. His heart thumped as passengers began to descend the steps nearest him—a fat woman first with three children clinging to her hands and skirts, an old man with a basket of eggs, a trio of woodsmen with packs and cowhide boots, and then a dog tugging at the end of a leash as it crowded its lank and bony head between the humans. It was Bim! Clifton almost cried out as the old hound made the platform, with Joe holding manfully to the other end of the strap. Following them came the beginning of an enormous bundle, and after the bundle Gaspard St. Ives himself, puffing and growling because of the size of it, and close behind him was Friar Alphonse, empty-handed but giving advice freely.

Clifton held his breath as he waited for Antoinette, who came immediately after her big brother and the little monk had cleared a way for her. For a moment she stood poised on the last step of the coach, a slim and boyish little goddess in gray knickers, with a Scotch tam on her head bearing a single feather at a saucy angle. Clifton felt the desire to cry out again. He wanted to run up to her and help her down before Friar Alphonse could perform that duty, but his legs failed to move.

He was stunned to inaction by her appearance now, so different from the lacy softness of her loveliness in the Château St. Ives, before which his optimism and man-egoism had failed to crumble. But here, in every exquisite inch of her, was something not only to worship but to be afraid of. From the tips of her trimly booted little feet to the curls that glowed under her tam she was vibrantly athrill with some new force which was manifesting itself to him for the first time. He had never dreamed that a pair of knickers and a jaunty tam-o'-shanter and a single feather that seemed to fling defiance into the teeth of the world could produce such a crushing effect.

He made a step forward, trying to recall the action and words which he had planned for this moment. Events began to shape themselves instantly. The monk had given his hand to Antoinette, and it was Gaspard who saw him first, staring with unbelieving eyes over the top of his bundle. In the same moment, Bim gave a muffled howl of recognition and leaped upon him with such force that his hat was sent to the ground and he reeled against the old man with the basket of eggs. Joe was only a step behind the dog, and by the time he had recovered from their greeting St. Ives had dropped his bundle and was shaking his hands, his huge bulk shutting out entirely the soldierly little figure in knickers and tam.

And to further wreck the joy of this hour upon which he had built so much Mademoiselle St. Ives herself took his hat from Joe, dusted it with her handkerchief, and gave it to him without a tremor of thrill or surprise in her voice as she said:

"A little gasoline will take this oil spot from your hat, Monsieur. It is too bad!"

And without further word of greeting she turned to the whiskered man whom Clifton had questioned and followed him to the waiting buckboard.

CHAPTER XVI

"This is marvelous!" St. Ives was crying. "So you were in that machine driven by Lucien Jeannot, who is crazier in the air than a lovesick loon at courting time! And my sister, the little rascal, said nothing when we were all guessing our heads off as to who it was with Jeannot in that fool's play that made our hearts come up between our teeth. But I might have guessed it from her whiteness and the way she trembled when it was over. For a little while it looked as though Jeannot was going to put an end to you, *mon frère*!"

"If she was white, and trembled, then it must have been for Jeannot—because she did not know I was in the machine," said Clifton.

The little monk chuckled.

"Our sweet Antoinette is not a dull-head like her brother," he said, and it seemed to Clifton his face was more than usually thin and pallid as he looked after the girl and Joe and the dog. "I think she made a very good guess, Monsieur—and as for the oil spot on your hat—gasoline *will* take it off!" And with that cryptic remark he left them, and joined Antoinette as the whiskered man turned back for Gaspard's dunnage.

Clifton walked along at the side of St. Ives. He had no plans now. His confidence was limp and unsettled. He had expected that his race to Metabetchewan, with all that it implied, would make a different impression on the girl who had inspired it. He had sensed the dramatic about it, almost the sensational, but more than all else he had intended it to prove his devotion and his sincerity, his determination to fight her fight with the same irrepressible energy with which he was making his own. That for some reason he had failed made him momentarily miserable. He began to see something of the opera bouffe in his action. Its anticlimax had been crushingly decisive. An oil spot on his hat! For a few moments he felt like choking Gaspard, and the monk, and especially Bim.

Antoinette had climbed into the one seat of the buckboard, and Joe was beside her. They were laughing over Bim, who had dragged his gaunt body up after them.

Then the whiskered man was at Gaspard's bundle. He seemed to be all whiskers, Clifton thought, now that he observed him more closely. For the owner of the buckboard was grinning at him openly—almost violently—as if he understood quite clearly why it was he had asked such silly questions before the train arrived. And Mademoiselle Antoinette was saying something to Friar Alphonse, smiling down at him. She turned and looked in his direction. Her pretty teeth flashed and the audacious feather bobbed. When Gaspard drew him up to the buckboard, with a friendly grip on his arm, she looked at him coldly.

Then as if a sudden thought had come to her she said to her brother: "Please take Joe and Bim with you, Gaspard. I will drive on alone with Captain Brant. I have something of importance to say to him."

Clifton's heart jumped. He lifted Joe down, asking him about the old gun. "Wish I had the old stuffed owl now—the one that never failed to bring good luck, Joe," he said, loud enough for Antoinette to hear. "I'm going to need it!"

As the girl's cool gray eyes looked down at him Clifton heard Gaspard making explanations.

"My sister loathes inns and closed rooms when we are in this country, Monsieur, so we camp and walk and live in the open air. Barnabe and our cook have camp made and our supper waiting for us at the lake shore. Get up—and *bon voyage*! You'll need to trot to beat us there for I am as empty as a drum!"

Clifton climbed into the seat occupied by the girl. She had drawn to her own side, leaving as much space as possible between them. Clifton looked at it, and then at her.

"Just enough room for the owl—if I had it," he said gloomily.

Barnabe the whiskered man was putting the last of the dunnage in the wagon. St. Ives surveyed it for a moment.

"Where is your pack?" he asked Clifton.

"At Price Brothers'."

"Then you can stop for it as you pass."

"Captain Brant will not need his pack, brother," said Mademoiselle St. Ives sweetly, yet with a little note of finality in her voice that was blasting. "I shall keep him only a few minutes."

She chirruped to the big black horse between the thills and they moved away. Clifton stole a glance at her, but the droop of her tam was on his side and hid her eyes from him.

"I'm sorry!" he thought aloud.

She was sitting very straight and rigid, her small hands gripping the lines more tightly than necessary.

"Sorry—for what?" she sniffed. "That you aren't more of a gentleman?"

"No. I am sorry I did not get on the other side of you, where your tam doesn't droop, so that I could look at your hair. From this side I can see

135

only your chin and the tip of your nose, and both look so ferocious that I am a little frightened. May I change?"

"If you wish."

The unexpectedness of her acquiescence as she stopped the horse and waited for him to alight made him feel foolish. In spite of a mighty effort to keep his blood back he knew his face was red when he climbed up on the opposite side of her. Her own coolness and the pitying smile on her lips made him more uncomfortable. She was bewitchingly lovely. Her hair was radiant in the fading sunlight. Her lips were rose-red. But in her eyes, soft as damask at times, were icy coldness and a smiling contempt.

She chirruped the horse into a trot. They passed Price Brothers', went up the hill and were in the glorious country of the habitant, with all of Lake Saint John shimmering softly in the last glow of the August sunset. Here, in this paradise which lay within a cup of the Laurentians, the hills and meadows were still verdantly green at the end of summer. It might have been springtime. The air was fresh and sweet. Flowers were blooming. Birds were singing. The sky was made of turquoise. And ahead of them ran the road, two hundred years old, dustless and winding—a road made first by Indians and then by cattle's feet, a thing of enchantment and of lure running into and through a country of peace, contentment and faith and ending only where the wilderness held it back in the north.

Clifton, stealing another glance sideways, saw the color in the girl's cheeks and an eager glow in her eyes.

"It is beautiful," he volunteered feebly. "And—this is a very ancient road."

"Thank you," she said. "I know it."

She managed to edge another half-inch away from him.

"If you please, Captain Brant, we will forget the scenery and take up another matter. Of course you think you are a very clever man. People who make exhibitions of themselves, as you love to do, are invariably possessed of that ego. You have made yourself ridiculous and—unbearable. You might amuse me if it were not for the fact that you have elected to practice your eccentricities on me. I believe I am charitable when I speak of your queerness as eccentricity. Others might call it a mania which would bear watching. But I know you went through the war, and it is possible something might have affected your mind during those horrible years. Shell-shock, for instance, or—"

She hesitated, seeking a word.

"Go on," pleaded Clifton. "The Germans never did anything like this to me. In a minute or two more it will kill. And all because I am mad enough to love the very dust you pick up on the soles of your feet!"

"*Love!*" She turned a look of withering scorn on him. "Could such a thing be accompanied by all the insult you have heaped on me?"

"Look out!" he admonished sharply. "You're driving into the ditch!"

She straightened herself with a sudden pull on one of the reins. "Could it?" she demanded.

"Could it what?" he asked stupidly. "You're making me nervous—the way you drive! If you wouldn't mind letting me take the lines—"

She passed them into his hand with a furious little gesture. She was beautifully angry. He could see that with half an eye. "I would cut off a hand—yes, I would kill myself before I would knowingly insult you," he said. "How have I done it?"

"How?" There was a note of amazement—of despair—in her voice. "Captain Brant, you are utterly hardened to all the conventions of decency, of ordinary courtesy, of—oh, I don't know the word that could tell it all!"

"It isn't born yet," he helped, regaining a little of his cheerfulness. "Here is a fork in the trail, Mademoiselle. Which do we take?"

"The right, of course. Isn't that the lake side?"

"I don't know—am so upset," he excused himself. "Nothing I do seems to be quite proper, even to choosing between roads. How have I insulted you? If you can prove it to me I will go out there and drown myself in your sight. I have promised to die for you anyway, if you ask it."

"You are insulting me even now!"

"God forgive me if I am. I don't intend to be."

She faced him as squarely as she could in the seat. Her cheeks were blazing. Her eyes were gloriously afire. "You began it—that first night—in my own home. I forgave you. I even allowed you to repeat the insult later, after your talk with Hurd, when you left me. I tried to think you were moved by an impulse of which you would be ashamed afterward, and that you would redeem yourself."

"I am not ashamed that I love you," said Clifton gently. "It is the first great glory that has come into my life."

"And that same night," she continued, her face flushing still more hotly, "you had the impertinence and audacity to tell Ivan Hurd that you were going to marry me!"

"If God is with me, I am," affirmed Clifton desperately. "That is not an insult, Antoinette. It is a statement of fact that has grown to be bigger than life in my heart. If I fail—if I don't marry you—I don't care to go on living!"

"Oh, if Gaspard was only here," almost sobbed the girl, facing the road again. "You call me Antoinette—and repeat the insult here—to my face! Oh, oh, oh! And then you called me *cara sposa*, which isn't Hindu at all, but Italian—and which doesn't mean what you said it did, but which—which means—"

"Lover, sweetheart, wife—everything that is dear and precious in the love of a human soul," finished Clifton, as words refused to come from her lips. "I ask your forgiveness there—and yet I meant it all!"

"And then the wire—the telegram that came to me on the train—and after that the hydroplane—and now—*this*! It is either madness or—I don't know what. You are old enough to know better. You are almost old enough to be my—my—father."

That was the deadly shot that hit. She had reached for the reins, and he surrendered them limply. His head drooped. And in that same moment the sweet soul of Antoinette St. Ives cried out against the crime she had committed. She looked up quickly into his hurt face. Her voice broke, and all the bitterness that had been in it was gone.

"Oh, I pray God you will forgive me for that," she cried. "It was wicked—untrue—ungrateful—and I didn't mean it. But maybe it was necessary for me to hurt you—to make you understand. You have said such shocking things to me—so—suddenly. And now you must go back. Please."

She stopped the horse.

Slowly, as if afflicted by that very hand of age with which she had taunted him, he climbed from the buckboard. Then he looked up at her. His face had grown older in those moments. His eyes seemed tired.

"I do love you, Antoinette," he said, and his voice was almost whispering in its worship. "And I am Crepin Marrolet come back to find you and fight for you after two hundred and fifty years. But"—and the old whimsical smile played for an instant over his face—"I *am* older than Crepin, I guess. Somewhere there has been a mistake in the passing of the centuries."

She struck the big black horse with the loose ends of the reins. "You are younger than Crepin ever was," she cried down to him, and there was a softness in her eyes which left his heart beating strangely as she disappeared down the road, a straight little figure that never once looked back as he watched her.

He walked back slowly. The sun had gone down and blue shadows were creeping softly over the lake. Yet a last glow had settled at the tip of a white cross on a distant hill, like a radiant bird resting for an instant in its flight. That cross seemed to rise like a comforting benediction as the world faded drowsily into the mellow shades of twilight. It was like a voice to Clifton, and its whisper seemed to be, "Men are seeking me, reaching out for me, crying for me—yet they do not find me. They are looking far, and I am very near—so far that they look over and beyond me when I am waiting at their feet. When at last they see me, and understand, then will they have discovered the greatest of all treasures—Faith and Contentment!"

It comforted him, and he felt joy creeping into his heart, and he fancied Antoinette at the foot of the cross with her sweet face bowed in prayer. Schisms and sects and religions might rend and rave in the outside world, tear at each other's throats and seek destruction—but here in this ancient land of horse and buggy and simple creed, of priest and cross and unbounded faith was the dream still true of peace on earth and good will toward men—except when the outside world sent in its poisons and its dissensions to break down and jeer at a childlike belief in God and the preachers of God which two centuries of simple living had built up.

He was not a Catholic, yet because of the cross and these thoughts his confidence pressed upon him stronger than ever, and he knew that a just people and an honest people—and the priests in their little churches—would be behind them in their struggle with Hurd if they could be made to understand.

As the tip of the cross dissolved into the soft gray of the sky he heard boisterous voices in song, and in a few moments came upon St. Ives and the whiskered man singing, while the monk and Joe and Bim trailed a little behind. For a moment depression fell upon him. He was no longer one of these. Antoinette had made him understand quite clearly that she did not desire his company. Then at sight of Joe and Bim the little god of hope and resolution bobbed up in him again. She could not steal them and leave him out!

St. Ives was carrying a pack.

"It's yours," he said, and stopped at the roadside until the others were well ahead. When they were out of hearing he questioned, "She sent you back, Monsieur?"

"What is left of me," nodded Clifton.

St. Ives laughed and bared his blond head to the coolness of the evening. "*Mon Dieu*, but she is a little tyrant when the spirit takes her," he gloated, "and I love her for it! I brought your pack because I knew that after she had said it all she would be sorry. What is the trouble, friend?"

Clifton looked St. Ives squarely in the eyes.

"I think I should tell you," he said. "You are her brother and—father. I love your sister. She knows it, and resents it. I love her more than any woman was ever loved from the beginning of time. I—"

A scowl gathered in Gaspard's face.

"That is false, Monsieur," he rumbled. "It is a monstrous lie. No other woman was ever loved as I love Angelique Fanchon! And if you repeat it again—"

"Then you know how I feel, Gaspard. Without her I don't want to live —"

"*Pouf!*" snorted St. Ives. "Is that all, Monsieur? Well, without Angelique I *won't* live! That is the difference between us. You simply don't want to live and I am determined not to live. Is that proof, or shall we settle it in another way here where the grass is soft and green, and your falls will be less violent?"

Clifton stared at the other in amazement.

"Are you mad, as Friar Alphonse has so often declared?" he gasped. "Did you not hear me? I love your sister! I have told her, and because I dared do that she is in a rage at me. Are you not surprised, shocked, angry at me yourself? Break my neck if you want to! I promise not to lift a hand in resistance—"

The incomprehensible St. Ives chuckled and rubbed his great hands as if he perceived a huge joke.

"You have told me nothing," he said. "Of course you love my sister. You would be blind and deaf and a fool if you did not. And it has been no secret with me—since early candlelight this morning. My sister left your letter on her bed, and in the excitement of getting away so unexpectedly I read a little of it to see what was being so carelessly left about—and having read a little of it I read more, and then the Devil himself could not have stopped me from finishing it. But she does not know it, Monsieur, and by Saints Peter and Paul I would give five years of my life to be able to write a letter like that to my Angelique!"

"And the fact that I wrote it does not outrage you?"

"*Maudit*, no! My respect for you has grown. To write such a letter is a virtue and not a crime. Besides, I have never known a man I like more than you. Only you must take back what you said about Angelique Fanchon and apologize to her through me!" And Gaspard shifted Clifton's pack with a ferocious hunch of his shoulders.

"I said nothing about her."

"But you implied a great deal—that she is not beautiful and good enough to be loved as you think you love my sister!"

"I apologize. And now if you will give me my pack—"

"I will carry it, brother."

"But I am going the other way."

"You are going *this* way," said Gaspard stoutly, and set off at a good pace after the monk and Joe and Barnabe the camp man.

"But she sent me back," insisted Clifton, dropping in at his side. "She is angry—"

"And she will be angrier if you take her at her word," declared St. Ives.

They walked a distance in silence.

It was still day, though the hour was close to eight o'clock in the evening. Shadows were deepening and distances were melting away but there were bird-chirpings and sleepy twitterings along the roadside, and out of nowhere had come a silence that was like a mothering hand caressing the world to rest. To Clifton it seemed a thing that could be felt and touched. He looked at St. Ives. In his face, too, the miracle of it was revealed. Lightness of thought and humor were gone as he looked off into the beauty and stillness of coming night.

"It is in this country that I want to live—and die," he said.

"And I," said Clifton, and drew so near that his elbow touched St. Ives. They were thinking of the same thing.

"If it can be brought to pass—

"It can!" Clifton's hand rested on the other's arm, and he heard John Denis's voice telling him again what it was that lay at the bottom of St. Ives's heart—the demon of vengeance ambushed and waiting there for its final hour with Hurd. "It can," he repeated in a low voice, "if you will leave Ivan Hurd to me."

"And if you fail—"

"I cannot fail."

St. Ives looked straight ahead.

"By which you mean that if all other things fail you will do what I have determined to do—ahead of you?"

"It may be our thought is the same. But I have no sister, and no Angelique Fanchon who loves me."

St. Ives drew a deep breath. "If it were not for them—for those two holding me back—it would have been ended now. God knows it would be just and honorable for me to kill Hurd!"

"Then it is not all this Ajax Trappier? Angelique Fanchon has made a vow, as well as your sister—and they will make sacrifice together if you destroy Hurd? That is the truth, Gaspard. Why not speak it?"

"It is," acknowledged St. Ives. "And Ajax Trappier, while he does not know this truth, is trying to take advantage of me in the absence which Angelique's vow has made necessary. That is why I am going to break his bones!"

"Of that I approve," replied Clifton. "But the other—what good would be done by killing Hurd?"

"I would rid the earth of a monster—a beast who wants my sister, who would buy her, ruin her, destroy her happiness—do anything to possess her —and who has heaped insult upon her that I should wipe out."

"Yet in doing this you would make another Amélie de Repentigny of your sister?"

"I would have achieved justice."

141

"As it was reckoned two hundred years ago—yes. And in achieving it you would also destroy another whom you love—Angelique Fanchon? St. Ives, you are a fool!"

"It may be, Monsieur."

"And you would become an outcast yourself—to be hanged by the neck until dead if caught. A pretty mess you would make of it. Again I say you are a fool!"

"It may be, Monsieur."

"And Angelique will marry Trappier."

"That is her vow, foolishly made. But there will be no Trappier when I am finished, with him. And—"

"What?"

"Hurd is coming up into the woods. He will spend the fall and winter among his men. I shall kill him when he is alone, and no one will know. That is my hope."

Clifton gave a sigh of despair.

"You would deliberately murder—and then lie to your sister and Angelique. I believe Friar Alphonse now. Your soul is lost."

"And you, Monsieur? If you take my place, and kill Hurd, will your soul not be lost, and will you not become an outcast—and hang by the neck as gracefully as I?"

"I have no sister, no Angelique—"

"But you have an Antoinette."

St. Ives's voice held something hidden and quietly thrilling, as if back of it lay a secret.

Yet in the face of it, even as his heart leaped to the thrill, Clifton tried to laugh.

"I had forgotten. We must be near the camp. If you will give me my pack—"

"It is not heavy, Monsieur."

"But I am going back."

"No, you are going on," said Gaspard with unruffled stubbornness. "You would be a coward if you turned back. Besides—my sister is expecting you."

"Expecting—the devil!" exclaimed Clifton. "A little more and I believe she would have horsewhipped me."

"Possibly—and then have cried her eyes out about it all night. You are a dunce among women. I know them!"

"Why do you think she—may—expect me?" stammered Clifton dubiously. "I am afraid—"

"*Pouf*! I know. She read that long letter of yours again on the train, trying to hide it behind a magazine. And when the telegram came and I asked

142

to see it she blushed until I thought she was going to cry. I swear she knew you were in the hydroplane, too—and when you were done with those fool stunts in which it looked as though you were bound to break your necks she was whiter than chalk. *Maudit*, it would take a wise man to tell who the fool is—you or me—or both!"

A moment more and they made a turn in the road. Lakeward, partly hidden by a fringe of trees, was a green little meadow through which a creek ran, and in it were two tents. Sweet-smelling pine smoke was rising lazily from a camp-fire, and about this fire a man was busy among various pans and pots and kettles.

St. Ives sniffed at the air.

"There is duck in the wind—roast duck with onions," he said. "In all the county of Lac Saint Jean there is no cook can roast a duck like Napoleon Plante, or cook a fish or sirloin of moose so well. And I am pinched with hunger, Monsieur!"

Clifton held back. He could see the big black horse grazing beyond the tents and the buckboard wagon near them. From the creek, whose cooling splash among pebbles and rocks he could clearly hear.

Barnabe came with a pail of water. The cook was whistling. But there was no sign or sound of Antoinette, or of Joe and Bim.

"Even now I think I shall turn back, if you will give me my pack," he said.

A dog's howl came up from the shadowy edge of the lake.

"She is down there," said St. Ives, and raised his voice in a sudden mighty shout that carried half a mile. In a moment it was answered by a girl's halloo, and Joe and Bim raced up through the dusky twilight of the slope.

St. Ives had seized Clifton's arm and there was no escaping the hold.

"You should be happy, *ami*. Come!"

As they advanced Clifton saw a slim figure approaching from the shore. Joe and Bim were on him in another moment, and he seized the hand of one and patted the bony head of the other, but his eyes were on the figure coming up the slope, and a quaking was in his heart.

She was bareheaded. She had loosened her curls and the cool breeze was playing with them as they clustered about her neck and shoulders. She made no effort to fasten them back as the distance between them grew thrillingly shorter. She was like a glorious, beautiful child, Clifton thought, and it amazed him that the glad smile did not leave her lips or the soft light fade from her eyes when she saw he was with her brother. He stood silent and a little grim, still holding Joe's hand. He was having difficulty in keeping his heart working steadily, and his effort gave to his face a look of

143

sternness and to his posture a rigid and almost soldier-like stiffness. She greeted Gaspard and then turned to him.

"You have come so slowly, and I am starving," she protested. "Joe and Bim and Barnabe arrived a quarter of an hour ago, and Alphonse came ahead of them. I can scarcely believe that you two are famous walkers, Monsieur Clifton!"

She turned quickly away.

Was it a mistake—or had she deliberately called him Clifton? And had there come a sudden instant of change in her face in that same moment—or was it his imagination of the illusive shadowings of the twilight?

She seated him opposite her at the narrow camp table over which Barnabe had suspended a gasoline lamp. Joe was beside her and Gaspard was at one end and Friar Alphonse at the other. And the lamp was so hung, or her chair so placed beneath it, that her hair was lighted up gloriously in its radiance.

He looked at her, and the little god of unchained thought came to his tongue again.

"It is lovely, Mademoiselle. How fortunate is the wind!"

"Thank you," she said, and bowed her head a little. "You are observing —and appreciative, Monsieur Clifton"—and this time he knew there was no error or slip of tongue in the quiet and deliberate way in which she spoke his name.

144

CHAPTER XVII

Near them Barnabe had built up the fire and later in the glow of this fire Antoinette St. Ives sat brushing out her hair, apparently oblivious of Clifton's presence and interested only in Joe and Bim. The hound lay at her feet while Joe sat cross-legged on the ground where he could look at her as one after another she brushed out her curls and talked to him.

The monk was gone. In the circle of light Gaspard discussed with Barnabe the fine points of the big black gelding, and a little beyond it the cook was cleaning up the supper things. Though touching elbows with his company Clifton felt the spell of aloneness upon him. It had been that way at supper. After the two thrilling moments in which she had called him Clifton the girl had seemed almost to forget him in her attentiveness to Joe. He was glad Gaspard insisted on pulling him into the discussion about horses finally, for it gave him a screen behind which he could hide while he stole occasional glances at Antoinette and the boy.

As she sat with Joe, laughing softly and telling him things of which Clifton could only now and then catch a word it seemed to him that one was only a little older than the other in the golden glow of the jack-pine and poplar. In a moment of anger and forgetfulness Antoinette St. Ives had spoken the truth, though she had asked his forgiveness for it afterward. He was older, and the truth weighed heavily upon him as he looked at the two on the other side of the fire. She was even nearer to Joe than to him. She drew Joe to her now, and brushed his hair where an untrained cowlick persisted in standing up straight, and when she had done this she kissed him on the tip of his freckled nose and turned her head a little so that she caught Clifton's eyes upon her. And never had he dreamed she could look so like a child as in that moment, with her boyish littleness and her soft red mouth and her hair falling so sweetly about her face and shoulders.

Then he heard her say, "You must go to bed. It is time, Joe. Kiss your Uncle Clifton good night—and when you are ready I will tuck you in."

So Joe came and held up his face to Clifton.

"She said I should kiss you good night," he apologized, and as Clifton bent down he added in a whisper, "She makes me get on my knees and say a prayer. I don't like that!"

"You will—in time," Clifton assured him. "Whatever she tells you to do is right, Joe—dead right."

He walked with the boy to the big tent in which the men-folk were to sleep, and when he returned Gaspard and Barnabe had left the fire and Mademoiselle St. Ives was humming a little tune to herself as she finished the last of her curls. She looked up at him when he paused at her side.

"I have been sitting over there watching you and thinking of you as a beautiful child," he said. "Do you mind my saying so—in a paternal kind of way?"

"I do mind it—very much," she replied, attending to her task again. "I don't trust paternalism in men of your kind and I am quite sure I do not need it."

"I have come to say good night."

"You might have said it before, Captain Brant."

"A few minutes ago you called me Clifton. Now it is Captain Brant. Why?"

"You were at my table then. Now you are about to leave on your return to Metabetchewan."

"I am not going to Metabetchewan," he said.

She was silent but her brush worked faster.

He persisted, bending a little over her. "As one who is infinitely your superior in age—yes, as one who has reached that ripe and even mellow maturity wherein you can safely show a daughterly interest and compassion I ask you to let me touch your hair with the tips of my fingers before I say good night."

Before he could straighten up she was on her feet.

"You are unkind to taunt me with that! I have asked your pardon for words spoken in anger and haste. If you possessed only a little of Crepin Marrolet's chivalry and gentleness, would you remind me of them?"

"No. Crepin was an active chap in his day. He would have touched your hair and asked permission afterward. But this situation is different. Crepin had youth in his veins, while I—with almost forty years behind me—"

"Are possessed of a most aggravating senility," helped Mademoiselle St. Ives, the tilt of her chin beginning to reach the danger point. "Good night, Captain Brant. I am going to my tent."

"Not until we have settled about Joe and Bim," objected Clifton coolly. "They are mine. I paid two hundred dollars for them and I am going to take them unless you make it right with me. First you must tell me why you want Joe."

"I need him!" cried Antoinette quickly. "I do, Captain Brant. I need someone to care for like that. I love Joe. I must have him. Having him gives me courage—keeps my mind from other things—helps me to—to—

"Then you must return to me what I have invested in him, or its equivalent, Mademoiselle. And I prefer the equivalent."

"You mean—you want me to pay?"

"Exactly."

"What? How much?"

"If I sell Joe, with Bim thrown in, it must be for one of those curls which you would not allow me to touch with the tips of my fingers. That is my one and only price."

She had drawn away from him. In the firelight her eyes were a liquid flame.

"Have you a knife?" she asked chokingly.

He drew one from his pocket and opened a blade.

"It is like a razor," he said. "Be careful!"

The steel glittered. Its sharp edge lay against the curl which she had gathered in her fingers. Then Clifton called out quickly, "Stop! I don't want it cut! It can be mine and still remain where it is. I can then think that a little of you belongs to me—and you can have Joe and Bim just the same. I'd rather have you cut off my finger than cut that!"

"Then—consider it your finger, Monsieur!"

It was done! He could hear the quick little cutting sound even as a sharper cry of protest came to his lips. It was hard for him to meet the contemptuous flash in her eyes as she dropped the curl and the knife at his feet.

"Your finger, Captain Brant," she repeated, and with that she was going away from him, and he watched her like one stunned by a blow until she disappeared in her tent.

The naked knife gleamed at his feet. The curl, catching the light of the fire, lay across the blade that had severed it. He picked them up and as Barnabe and St. Ives came back he returned the knife to his pocket and placed the curl in a fold of his wallet. He would sleep on the sand, he told St. Ives—and with this explanation shouldered his pack and left them. He went down to the shore and continued to walk along the smooth beach. It was cool, a sweet night filled with more than usual darkness, but not enough to make his way obscure or difficult. The white sands seemed to have held something of daylight though clouds had gathered in the sky. Between two huge rocks he found a place for his pack so that he could walk without its burden resting on his shoulders.

He had gone a quarter of a mile beyond these rocks when he discovered he was not alone. Padding softly in the sand behind him was Bim. He waited and rubbed the hound's head and talked to him a little before going on. He walked steadily and for a long time, and like a gaunt shadow Bim kept pace at his heels or his side. He put miles behind him before he

147

turned. The late moon came up through a bulwark of ragged clouds. When he came back to the rocks where he had left his pack it was midnight. He spread out a blanket and sat down with his back to one of the boulders.

It was Bim, at last, who made him suddenly conscious of something approaching along the edge of the lake. And then through a thinner curtain of cloud a pallid light from the moon shone down, revealing a figure with bent head and slow step walking along the shore. It was Alphonse the monk. With chin sunken forward on his chest and hands clasped behind him he passed and disappeared in the gloom. The ghost of something which was more than solitariness had seemed to walk with him, and the word of greeting which Clifton would have spoken stuck in his throat.

Then came light. The mass of cloud that had smothered the moon was driven on by storm winds high up above the earth and a mellow radiance illuminated the shore and the silvery unrest of the lake. He sat rigidly as he saw the monk returning.

The bent and solitary figure passed near him again, and a hundred paces from him it turned once more; and after that, with head never lifting itself to the sky and shoulders that seemed to droop more and more as the minutes sped the monk passed and repassed the two big rocks until in the moonlight Clifton could see the path made by his feet in the smooth sand near the water's edge. It was Bim who broke the tense stillness after that. A smothered howl rose in his throat. For a few moments Friar Alphonse gave no sign that he had heard it. Then he faced the rock and saw Clifton sitting with his back against it.

Clifton stood up, and as the two met in a light that was fighting its way once more through a thickening mask of cloud the monk's thin face made him think of a death's-head advancing out of a sea of gloom. Its eyes amazed him. He could see them burning, even in half darkness. But the monk's voice, when he spoke, was so soft and quiet that it bore almost the thrilling contrast of madness.

"Pardon, Monsieur, if I have disturbed you. It is a night of unrest with the shifting possibilities of quicksilver between the earth and the sky, and I cannot sleep."

"Nor I," said Clifton. "I think it is going to storm."

They were looking at each other, and the little monk smiled while his eyes held their strange light. He had found something in Clifton's face that made him place a hand on the other's arm.

"It is the kind of night and the hour in which a man may measure himself well," he said. "I have been doing that. And so have you. What conclusion have you arrived at, friend?"

"That I am a fool and very much smaller than I ever thought myself to be," said Clifton. "And you?"

"Let us walk," said the monk.

And so side by side they went up the shore in darkness that was thickening swiftly about them, with Bim a silent shadow behind.

And after a little Friar Alphonse answered the question which Clifton had asked.

"I have discovered myself to be a man," he said, and in his voice lay a ghostly whisper of tragedy. "And so, being that and nothing more, I must return to a monastery—after our task up here is done. That is what this night has revealed to me!"

For a space Clifton found nothing to say, and he looked up where the moon was blotted out and felt himself walking hand in hand with a spirit that was prisoned in strange torment in the twisted body of the man who walked with him.

At last he said, "I am leaving the St. Iveses in the morning to travel more quickly into the north. It may be I will not see you again for a long time."

"You are going to the depots and the woods?"

"I am taking charge up there."

"And are leaving sooner than you had planned?"

"A little, yes. But I shall meet Gaspard at Saint Félicien on the day he appoints for his battle with Ajax Trappier. I have promised that."

"Yes, yes—Saint Félicien and Ajax Trappier," muttered the monk. "You must meet again there. But something is hurrying you away, friend—the happening on the road this evening and that other beside the camp-fire tonight—" His voice choked suddenly in his throat.

"You know——"

"She told me of her words with you when I came, and found her crying. And that last in the firelight I saw—and heard. You are running away from Antoinette St. Ives."

"She will be happier for that."

"Blind!" muttered the monk, as if to himself. "Blind—while I can see so clearly! She might have struck you. But she did not do that. She gave you the thing for which you asked. If she had done that for me I would have thanked God all my life, even though she flung it at my feet as she did to you."

"It was my price for Joe and Bim," said Clifton, staring hard to make out the face of his companion in the dark.

"And with it she gave you her heart."

The monk's hand touched his and the chill of it was that of a bloodless thing.

"I have known Antoinette St. Ives from little girlhood," he added gently. "She loves you."

"Impossible," said Clifton after a moment. "I am so sure of it that I wish you would relieve me of—this"——and he fumbled in his wallet until he found the curl, and placed it in the ice-cold hand of Friar Alphonse.

A flash of lightning cut the sky far in the west and a sombrous roll of thunder accompanied it, while a silence so great fell for a space about them that even the murmuring unrest of the lake seemed hushed. In that silence Clifton knew that he had guessed the truth. He had felt the passionate closing of his companion's hand about the curl, and now the little monk's breath had stopped, and he stood like a dead man in the darkness. Blackness hid the tragedy. But Clifton's hand reached out and found the other's bent shoulder, and rested gently there.

"You, too, love her?" he whispered softly.

"More than life—more than God," said the monk, and his voice seemed strangely far away and very cold, as if coming out of a fathomless place from which all passion and life and warmth had died. "I loved her as a child, when my back was broken in the Mistassini. I love her now as a woman. May God forgive me and cleanse my soul of its sin!"

"It is not sin," said Clifton, but as he spoke Friar Alphonse drew away from under his hand, and after a little when Clifton called his name there came no answer. He reached out gropingly in the darkness, and called again.

"Alphonse—Friar Alphonse—"

He could hear Bim sniffing in the sand. But the monk, if he was near, made no sound. The lightning came again. It showed inky ramparts of cloud in the sky. The wailing of wind high up was like the droning of a distant waterfall and Clifton knew there was more than rain in the night.

"The storm will soon be upon us. Let us go to Gaspard's tent," he said.

Only Bim answered him, making a sound with his jaws as he followed. Clifton guessed his distance, and turning away from the beach stumbled across higher ground. Then a point of light appeared to guide him, a lantern in Gaspard's tent, and he waited once more, staring back into the gloom out of which he had come. A huge drop of rain fell on his hand, another on his face. He could hear the distant moaning of wind and rain as they advanced together, and half ran up the slope to beat them. Antoinette's tent, without a light, was lost in a chaos of darkness. Probably she was asleep. He wondered if Joe was with her and if she was afraid of storm.

He entered Gaspard's tent quietly. It was a big tent, with ample room for half a dozen sleepers. The lantern was burning low. Its light revealed St. Ives sprawled out on his eiderdown robe, sound asleep. Barnabe and the cook were snoring gently. Joe was curled up on a pile of blankets near them. Another bed, which must have been for Friar Alphonse, was empty.

The rain began beating like little hammers against the canvas—a thousand tiny fists demanding entrance, seeking shelter from the fury that was driving them on. Then came the deluge. Clifton sat down, making himself comfortable with his back against a box, and he wondered what kind of shelter the monk had found. Years ago he had spent a night like this in the sticky clay country east of Lake Saint John and had nearly died of mud and water. He could still taste clay and feel it at times like an adhesive plaster all about him. Even Flanders could not compare with that clay of the East Shore, and the rain that came to smother him in it.

But this was worse—that is, the rain was. It came in a solid sheet. The tent sagged under it, and he wondered how the others could sleep through it together with the thunder and lightning. The inundation passed on over the lake and wind followed it—a biting, snapping wind filled with fierce maelstroms and eddies and with a growing roar behind it that made Clifton get up on his feet again.

He roused St. Ives with the toe of his boot. The other sat up, stripped to his pajamas.

"The devil!" he said, his ears filled with the tumult.

"A hurricane, or the edge of one," said Clifton, getting a searchlight out of his pack. "If it hits us the tents won't hold. You'd better go to your sister."

St. Ives jumped up and flung off his sleeping garments. In a moment of stark nakedness he made a dive for his clothes, and in that same moment all the savagery of the night was upon them. Clifton had a swift glimpse of changing things. He saw Joe and Barnabe and the cook suddenly waking as if struck by whips, and of the three Joe was on his feet first, with eyes popping. The roar was deafening, a shrieking, monstrous thing that seemed to be tearing the earth as well as the air into bits.

Then the end of the tent burst in like an exploding balloon. It had all happened in those few seconds of St. Ives's nakedness, and the last of Clifton's vision was filled with Gaspard's hugeness struggling with a garment. It was then the lantern went out, smashed all in an instant, and the tent fell about them, wrapping them in its sodden folds like a living thing.

He was conscious of crying out loudly to Joe, telling him not to be frightened but to remain quietly under the canvas that had flattened them all to the earth. He had himself gone down as if struck by a club and was flat on his back, clutching the flashlight in one hand. Close to him he could hear St. Ives cursing above the roar of the hurricane at being caught in such a mess without even his nightdress on. By shouting at the top of his voice he got Gaspard's attention.

"I'll care for Antoinette," he yelled. "You stay here with Joe!"

He began fighting his way out, twisting over on his face, and for two or three minutes was hopelessly tangled in a pocket made by the side and the roof of the tent coming together. But he got himself out at last. There was less roaring about him and he could hear the sound charging steadily eastward, like a bull half as big as the earth itself. In the wake of the wind came rain again. It fell steadily and straight down. The lake was moaning. There was moaning in the air. The whole world seemed moaning. The strange part of it was that all the wind was now either far away or high up in the darkness overhead. There was scarcely a breeze against his cheek.

He shot his flashlight here and there as he gathered his wits and a sense of direction. Then he ran, and stumbled upon the canvas of Mademoiselle St. Ives's tent. It was flat, beaten down and utterly sodden. He heard a faint voice. "Gaspard!" it was calling. "Gaspard!"

"I'm here!" he sung out. "Don't be frightened!"

He had never known that canvas could be so devilish. He pulled and heaved and tore at it without apparently making headway, and all the time he could hear Antoinette's voice in terror as she called her brother's name. It did not enter his head to correct that error—not even when at last he found an entrance and felt a pair of arms clasping him convulsively about the neck. But at the same time he did find a blanket and had the presence of mind to wrap it about the girl's slender body as he drew her out and picked her up in his arms. In that moment he had a vision of a habitant's home a quarter of a mile down the road.

"I'll take you there," he shouted, telling her about it. "Everybody's all right in the other tent—Joe—everybody—"

She still thought he was Gaspard. The rain beat on them. The moaning tumult was about them. And her head was half buried in the blanket.

He held her closely, so closely that she seemed all pressed against his breast. Her arms tightened about his neck. He felt her face, warm, soft, wet. Her mouth was so near his own that he kissed it, and so sweet and wonderful was the experience that he kissed it again.

"Don't be frightened," he cried, but he did not speak too loudly.

Her face nestled against his cheek and neck as he started toward the road with her. He had dropped his flashlight, and if he had possessed two lives he would have given one of them for miles of darkness and storm. His lips touched her hair, and he kissed that. Then he kissed her eyes, one after the other.

"Dear Gaspard!" he heard her say.

His heart was suffocating him, his blood dancing with madness. He found the road. One of Antoinette's hands caressed his cheek. Out of the blanket she was asking him about Joe, Friar Alphonse, the other tent, and—last—*Clifton Brant*! Her hand pressed his cheek a little harder when she

152

came to that name. He bent down, with his ear almost at her lips, so he would not lose a word.

"I hope he never comes back," she cried. "If he does you must get rid of him for me, Gaspard. I hate him!"

He hugged her tighter, and made no other answer. But that pressure of her little form in his arms carried sympathy and understanding—an affirmative response without words.

The rain had lulled. Now it came again in a sudden spurt. In that downpour he could use his voice again—safely, deepening it as much as he could, like Gaspard's.

"You won't see him again after tonight," he said. "He is going away—for good."

He felt his precious burden grow suddenly a little tense against him. There was silence—silence of a full half-minute as he trod along through water and puddles of liquid sand, though he knew she had heard him clearly. "He is a scoundrel," he added, with the bitterness of a hateful truth. "It is unfortunate that he loves you!"

The blanket, the rain, the moaning of the wind, the slush of water under his feet all helped to keep his secret.

He walked faster, bowing his face in her wet hair, caressing it softly with his lips. She felt and sensed his solicitude, his tenderness and adoration. It was a glorious thing in a brother, and in another lull of rain her hand lay against his cheek again.

Only a little distance ahead was the habitant's home. A few minutes more and it would be over—and after that would follow years and years of life in which he would think of this night. How mistaken Friar Alphonse had been! Love him? She despised him, loathed him. But she would never be able to rob him of this quarter-mile of mud and water and darkness, with her in his arms. Tomorrow she would learn the truth, of course—or, possibly, tonight. In her opinion there would then be little to choose between himself and Ivan Hurd.

In the blackness ahead he saw a light where the habitant's all-night kerosene lamp was burning. Then came a sudden blur. Wind and rain broke out of the west in a fresh fury, and he twisted the blanket about Antoinette until only an air-space for her mouth was left open. He heard her cry out for him to let her down that she might walk, but he held her closer and made headway a yard at a time in the teeth of the storm. Then he turned in, found a picket fence, a gate, and came up panting and half drowned to the shelter of the cottage. The door was not locked and as he opened it he called loudly to awaken the owners of the place.

He entered boldly, a miracle of change sweeping over him. Now that it was over he would not try to hide himself. To wait for tomorrow to reveal his hypocrisy would be cowardly. He had stolen love, but he would not run away with his pilfering like a sneak-thief with somebody's pocketbook. That thought came to him suddenly.

The room was dimly lighted and he stopped in the middle of it with his burden. Mademoiselle St. Ives was entirely enveloped in her blanket. The water ran from them in streams and gathered quickly in pools on the white-scrubbed board floor under their feet. From an adjoining room a man and woman looked out, wide-eyed and startled, in nightgowns that fell to their toes.

Clifton did not speak. The situation would be clear in a moment, and he would leave the girl to explain. Against the wall was an old sofa, and he placed her on this.

First he saw her little bare feet. Then the water-soaked blanket fell aside so that her head and shoulders were revealed, and one white, bare arm that was shivering. She was wet, drippingly wet. Her curls clung heavily against her face and neck. Clifton wanted to fall on his knees. But he waited stiffly in the lamplight, water running from him everywhere. She was smiling—trying to laugh in the face of such ridiculous misfortune. Then she saw him, and her eyes were suddenly ablaze with horror and incredulity.

"*You!*" she gasped.

She did not notice the man and woman—did not even see them as they came through the door. She hid her bare arm. Her fingers clutched at the wet blanket, hugging it to her. If eyes could have killed, Clifton would have fallen dead. He was sure of that.

He backed to the door, bowing a little—a drenched, wind-blown, disreputable-looking scoundrel if the way she was looking at him was a reflection of the truth. He was lost now, so completely that his face was dead-white under its trickle of water. The lips and eyes he had kissed were damning him, though after that one word of amazement and shock Antoinette St. Ives did not speak again. As he opened the door he did not look at her.

"Good-by, Mademoiselle," he said.

Storm and blackness roared their welcome to him. He went out and the door slammed behind him. And as he found the road again he thought of Friar Alphonse the monk, and knew what it was at last to have a heart without hope and a soul that was dead.

Yet in the face of it he smiled, for no power on earth or in heaven could take away from him the warmth and softness of the lips and eyes he had kissed.

CHAPTER XVIII

Wind died away. A warm drizzle followed the deluge. Then came a clearing sky, the crowing of roosters at the habitant's farm—and the beginning of dawn.

In that first glow of light the big tent was set up, and Clifton settled a matter definitely with St. Ives.

"Mademoiselle and you will need at least two weeks to do your work between here and Saint Methode," he said. "In one way or another your sister must become acquainted with every habitant in the valley while I am working along the Mistassini. I shall go across from Roberval. Twenty days from today I will meet you at Saint Félicien and help you settle your affair with Ajax Trappier."

A decisive note was in his voice which settled matters without argument, and St. Ives felt and saw the change. "I feel I am back in uniform again," he explained when he saw that Gaspard was a little puzzled. "Until now ours has been a pleasant adventure, a kind of preparatory holiday. But the real business begins from this morning. If Jeannot and his hydroplane are in Roberval night will find me in Laurentian headquarters on the Mistassini."

It was still morning twilight when he walked into Metabetchewan.

He roused Tremblay and they hunted up a man who had an automobile for hire. A flush of rose was in the sky when they drove out the road going north and west.

They passed the drenched camp. Barnabe and the cook were working about a smoky fire of damp wood. Antoinette's tent was up and he saw Gaspard hanging wet things on a line. There was no sign of Joe or the monk. He waved a hand and heard Gaspard's shout. Then came the habitant's cottage, and he told the driver to slow down. It was a happy place—he could see that. The French farmer's passion for color and flowers revealed itself everywhere about it. The little house was banked with flowers. Double rows of them ran down to the gate and the picket fence was streaming with morning-glories. It was a cleanly whitewashed cottage with vivid green doors and blinds and red chimneys and the pickets in the fence were white with red caps. The barn was white with red doors slashed by green

155

bars. Smoke was coming out of the cottage chimney and also from a big outside oven which was large enough to hold a small wagonload of bread at one baking.

As they went on, and the sun rose, and people came to life, the primitiveness and simplicity of the world they were in together with its rain-washed cleanness and beauty filled Clifton with a comfort which he felt no physical or mental torture could ever quite wipe out entirely. Here there were no crowds. The habitants' homes seemed far apart, with great reaches of meadow and slope and valley between them, and the little villages, each with its single street along the highway, were like rare old paintings come into drowsy, peaceful life. At times it seemed to him the presence of their automobile with its noise and odor of gas was almost a desecration.

Thank God he was not a religious fool and could see that here the little churches with their welcoming doors and the priests with their sunny faces and undying cheer had achieved a work which he had not been able to find anywhere in the outside world of money-madness, social rot and mechanical insanity. For here in this little world that nestled like a paradise around Lake Saint John were peace and love and good will toward men and the soul-inspiring presence of faith and an abiding happiness. What more could God Himself give, though all the fanatical religious intolerants on earth lifted their rabid voices in a scream against thoughts and methods and preachings which did not follow their own narrow-gauge line of mentality?

About him were the living symbols of Christ's richly beautiful vocabulary—seed, light, leaven, life; and that these people had ox-carts instead of trucks, horses in place of automobiles, and clean air, sunshine and green trees instead of belching factory chimneys—and a Church that believed in children—were not in Clifton's eyes evidence of soul retrogression. Alexis, who sat beside him, might believe in ghosts and miracles and never have seen Quebec—but Alexis also believed in God.

They went on and came to the sleepy edge of Roberval.

He did not find Jeannot, but the Peribonka boat was leaving at noon, which gave him time to purchase the bush necessities he required. At four o'clock that afternoon Samuel Chapdelaine was driving him across the blueberry plains in a horse and buggy and he ate supper at the Company's depot on the Mistassini.

Eugene Bolduc, the manager at Mistassini, had maps, figures and information awaiting him. They added a hundred details to what Colonel Denis had told him in Quebec, and until after midnight the two sat up and worked over them.

Eugene continued to add to the apparent hopelessness of the situation, and at times the blood seemed almost ready to burst out of the veins in his forehead. From the Lake Saint John country both companies were compelled to use the same trails for sixty miles, and he and his brother Delphis had counted every head that had gone up under the Hurd contracts. Only a hundred and fourteen had gone in, yet there were two hundred and fifty in the woods. That meant Hurd was sending in men through the mountains and back ways, secretly and with sinister purpose. He was gathering an army and hiding its strength from the Laurentian people.

To do this he had a detail of twenty rangers patrolling the boundaries and no man without a written permit in his pocket could enter the concessions. So strict was this surveillance that Delphis had gathered most of his information at night. And up the north trail an enormous amount of material had gone in for the Hurd people. Tons of dynamite, for instance. Whole wagon-trains of food supplies. Thirty horses were at work in the camps and on the trails. Six of these teams had worked for the Laurentian company last year.

Eugene was sweating when he came to these details. It was enough to make a man sweat, he said, and he was only beginning to tell the worst of it. In the face of all this early activity in the camps of their enemy the Laurentian camps were positively dead. Only forty-two men were in the woods, including fire-rangers and a gang of six engineers, as against Hurd's two-hundred and fifty. As early as this, six of their last year's jobbers had signed Hurd contracts, bought over by bonuses which did not appear on their papers.

At least forty of the hundred and fourteen men who had gone in were last year's Laurentian men. Those who were entering by way of the mountains and back ways were strangers. Delphis knew none of them. But they were a tough lot, only partly French—many of them from Ontario. Delphis had heard that others were coming a little later from Maine. Eugene clearly showed his distress. He doubted if the Laurentian company would have a hundred men in the woods by snow time, while at the rate they were going the Hurd-Foy company would have five hundred. With those odds against them and hemmed in as they were on both sides and below, what chance could they have when the spring drive came?

In his opinion unless something was done—and done quickly—the Laurentian company might as well burn its camps and give up.

The icy coolness with which Clifton received all this disheartening information rather upset Eugene. When he had finished, Clifton wrote a brief letter to Colonel Denis, in which he said, "I am sure my talk with Eugene Bolduc has given me a good vision of the situation. It is interesting. I like it. We are going to beat Hurd."

He showed these lines to Eugene, and for a moment the Frenchman stared at him. Then with an exclamation of joy he gripped his hand. "*Par Dieu*, that is what we have been saying—Delphis and I!" he cried. "Maybe we have grown a bit disheartened, but with you to help us we will keep up that cry forever. By the Saints, Monsieur, I know now that we are going to beat this black curse of a Hurd!"

The next day saw Clifton and Eugene on their way north. At the first camp they were joined by Delphis, a man whose leathery visage and sinewy body seemed made out of whipcord. Each day after that added to the mass of facts which Clifton was gathering. From the beginning he made himself one of the men, eating and sleeping with them and accepting no privileges which all could not enjoy. They liked him. First impressions grew swiftly into real friendships, and by the end of the first week he began to see about him the beginning of an organization in which he could place his confidence.

He was frank with the men. Individually and collectively he told them what Hurd's motives were and that the Laurentian Company was fighting for its life. On the evening of the tenth day he held a mass meeting at the main depot and with maps and blue-prints explained in detail just how the Hurd-Foy gangs expected to drive them out of the woods. He made no effort to screen the desperateness of the situation. He appealed not only to their pride and honor but to the fighting instinct which lives in the breast of every man who is a part of the forests. Fiercely Delphis told what he knew about the foreigners Hurd was bringing in, and their contempt for the French woodsmen.

"The *canaille*!" he cried. "Shall we let them buy us? And if they cannot buy us, shall we let them drive us out?"

A roar of voices applauded him.

There were forty in the big store-room of the depot, which had been cleared for the purpose. Clifton was more than satisfied. These men who had already remained loyal against the advances of his enemy would stand with him to the last. He was sure of that. They were only a handful, forty against six times their number as the odds were figured against them tonight—but such a forty! He looked into their blazing faces, from youth to bearded age, and counted hearts beating as eagerly and as swiftly as his own. Around this forty he would build his fighting machine. His enthusiasm was like a fire as he told them how he would do it, and what he expected. Then he called upon them for individual expressions of opinion, and among those who rose to their feet was a ragged giant as huge as Gaspard St. Ives, who bellowed through a beard as red as fire that he hoped the Devil would take his soul if he lived to run from all the foreigners that could be crowded between the St. Maurice and the State of Maine.

This man's name was Romeo Lesage, and the following morning Clifton and the Bolducs added him to their private council, and made him their chief fighting man. It was Romeo's suggestion which made Clifton

158

write to Colonel Denis and ask among other things for the immediate shipment of one hundred baseball bats.

During the next week Clifton slept not more than half a dozen hours out of the twenty-four, and each day he saw improvement in the definiteness and morale of his organization. Men began dribbling in. Samuel Chapdelaine sent up two families including six men from Peribonka. From the Roberval office then came copies of the first contracts signed by Antoinette St. Ives. They were a pleasurable shock to Clifton. Men followed—men, women and children, and especially children. Each jobber had from two to six. One had seven. The Bolducs were amazed. Clifton was alarmed as well as astonished. This, of all years, was not a year for women and children in the woods. It was bound to be a winter of disturbance and fighting, possibly of extreme tragedy.

Early in September the climax came when two young women arrived at the Mistassini headquarters. They were extremely nice to look at. One gave Clifton a letter addressed to himself. It was very brief, very much to the point, and signed by Antoinette St. Ives.

Dear Sir [it began stiffly]:
We need women and children in the woods this winter. Their presence will be a curb on Satan and an inspiration to their men. Wherever a man's woman and child are, there also is his home. Each jobber will have a camp, and in his camp from six to a dozen men. The women and children in these camps will be our chief allies. Therefore I am arranging jobbers' contracts with men who have large families.

The two young women who will give you this letter are good Quebec friends of mine. They are school-teachers. You will note the new clause in the contracts which guarantees that four schools shall be built at central locations, and that in each school the children in its vicinity shall receive instruction three days out of each week. Please have these buildings put up at once, and make each large enough for concerts, recitals and religious services. Also give Miss Clamart and Miss Gervais every opportunity to become acquainted with the mothers and their children. I suggest placing at their disposal two riding-horses, and, until they are familiar with the trails, competent guides.

And the letter ended coldly,

"Yours truly, A. St. Ives."

Clifton read the letter twice before he dared look up at Mesdemoiselles Clamart and Gervais. He wondered if in all his life he had seen prettier teeth than those that were smiling at him. Antoinette had shown exquisite judgment in the selection of her friends!

"I am Anne Gervais," smiled one.

"And I am Catherine Clamart," said the other, in a voice that was liquid music.

"And we have heard so much about you, Monsieur Clifton, that I am a bit awed and frightened," said the one who called herself Anne, and whose dark eyes were pools of laughter as she looked at him.

"Indeed we are," agreed the other, with a pretty bowing of a head that caught soft golden lights.

"Through Colonel Denis, of course," added Anne.

"Yes—Colonel Denis—of course," parroted the golden Catherine, and it seemed to Clifton that her blue eyes were laughing the truth at him already.

"You mean," he nodded, "that Mademoiselle St. Ives has properly warned you against me?"

"Our honor pledges us to secrecy—except that we believe you to be a very desperate man," said Anne, and jet-black lashes covered her eyes for an instant. Clifton's heart gave a little jump. Next to Antoinette she was the loveliest girl he had ever seen!

He felt himself coloring.

"In spite of which I'll build the schools," he said.

Anne unveiled her eyes. She took off her boyish hat, carelessly revealing the glossy richness of her thick dark hair, and Clifton walked between the two as he escorted them to a cabin which was built and furnished especially for company guests. And Catherine took her hat in her hand, as Anne had done, so that looking down on one pretty head and then on the other he observed, as any man not utterly blind must have done, the lovely coils of hair which the hats had concealed, on one head velvety black and on the other soft gold. Scarcely had he made note of this pleasant fact when Anne looked up at him with disturbing quickness and caught his admiration trying to hide itself like a thief in his face.

He left them at the cabin and instructed the depot clerk to see that everything was done for their comfort. Then he sought the privacy of the manager's office and found Eugene ahead of him, his big body shrinking back in the desk chair while over him stood a mysterious and weather-worn figure enthusiastically threatening his life.

"And on top of that may the Devil take your soul and stand it on end if you so much as open your mouth in the matter," this individual was saying. "And also on top of that—"

He turned about suddenly as Clifton entered.

It was Alphonse the monk.

Instantly his thin face was crinkling in a smile and he held out his two hands as if about to give a benediction. He was even thinner than when Clifton had last seen him. His clothes were ragged and his hair had grown lank and uneven about his ears.

"Forgive me, dear Clifton, for disturbing your ears with this excoriation of a hopeless sinner," he cried. "He took me for a tramp and not a priest and I have put him properly in his place."

Clifton seized the little man's hands, and in his amazement his first words were, "You came with *them*?"

"With whom?" asked the monk.

"Mesdemoiselles Gervais and Clamart."

"The two pretty demoiselles I saw through your windows? The Saints forbid! It is my opinion the dark-haired wench is unsafe to travel with, unless one carries with him a potion against the witchcraft of black lashes and the bottomless pools they sometimes cover."

"You have noted her closely," grunted Clifton.

"Very," said Alphonse, unabashed. "I scarce noticed the other. If Mademoiselle St. Ives knew this dark-eyed one was here, with lashes black as jet and half as long as her finger—"

"She sent them," interrupted Clifton, and he gave Antoinette's letter to the monk.

Alphonse read the letter slowly and with undisguised amazement, and when he was done he stood for a full half-minute staring at nothing at all through the window.

"It may be she is right, Monsieur," he said then.

"Surely men alone cannot win for us in this fight. I know—because for ten days I have been in the camps of the Philistines, an humble missioner carrying the word of God among Ivan Hurd's lawless scoundrels, and my eyes have been open and my ears wide awake night and day." Suddenly his voice filled and his cavernous eyes burned with a swift flash of excitement and understanding. "*Cher Dieu*, I think I perceive what Antoinette St. Ives has foreseen a million miles ahead of us! There will be outlawry in the woods this year and mayhap desperate happenings and fighting and even deaths! The government will come—its investigation must come. On one side it will find Hurd and his political power and his foreigners from Ontario and Maine. And on ours it will find *women and children and schools and music and the word of God on Sundays*. My dear Sainte Anne, the knell has struck! Justice must be given where there are women and children and these other things—even against the might of Ivan Hurd!"

The little monk's thin hands were atremble and a flush had gathered in the hollows of his cheeks. Eugene Bolduc had risen to his feet and seemed to hold his breath as he listened. Clifton felt his heart throbbing harder

161

against his ribs as the amazing truth of the thing rushed upon them with a numbing effect. For a few moments it held them speechless.

The brief interval of silence was broken by laughter and light footsteps.

Through the open doorway came Anne Gervais. Her cheeks and eyes were aglow. Her red lips seemed painted.

"Pardon!" she cried. "But, Monsieur—"

And then, facing her, she saw Alphonse the monk. Instantly words died on her lips. She drew in a quick breath, and her eyes slowly widened as she stared at the half bowed, shaven head and unkempt figure of the little missioner.

Then the monk raised his head and looked at her calmly.

"It is me you should pardon," he said gently. "I can see that you are shocked, child, at beholding a member of the priesthood in such disreputable attire, but Monsieur Brant will tell you I have just come in from arduous travel in the forest. Are you Anne—or Catherine?" And a quizzical smile twisted his face as he advanced and took her hand, and bowed his broken shoulders a little over it.

"I am Anne," she said in a low voice that was filled with relief. "Forgive me, Father. Won't you come to our cabin? We have soap and towels, and it will be a pleasure for us to serve you."

"I will come," said the monk without hesitation. "Monsieur Clifton, you will surely excuse us, for such unexpected happiness and promise of comfort I cannot put away from me. Gladly would I place this lovely Anne on the calendar of saints if I had the power!"

And as he went with Mademoiselle Gervais, without waiting for Clifton to answer, he turned and added in a low voice over his shoulder:

"Remember, Monsieur. *This is the eighteenth day.*"

CHAPTER XIX

Clifton turned to Eugene and found him staring through the window.

"He fills me with chills, like a dead man's ghost," said Eugene, without looking behind him. "And he left me a curse strong enough to loosen the teeth in my head if my tongue forgets itself! What did he mean by that eighteenth day, Monsieur?"

"It was a reminder that I am contracted to meet Gaspard St. Ives in Saint Félicien on the twentieth day after my departure from Metabetchewan," explained Clifton.

"He is talking with great earnestness to Mademoiselle Gervais," grunted Eugene.

"I don't blame him," said Clifton.

"And they have swerved from the path that leads to the cabin and are wandering toward the big rocks at the river's edge."

"Which proves him man as well as monk, Eugene."

Eugene turned about with a shrug of his shoulders.

"He has aged ten years since I saw him last, six months ago," he said. He caught himself almost sharply. "That is why I mistook him for a vagabond, as you heard him say. He is like a dried-up dead man walking about. *Ugh*!" And he shivered.

"You make a poor liar, Eugene," laughed Clifton good-humoredly. "But I am not curious enough just now to ask questions. I am excited by all these happenings and what they mean to us. How long will it take to build the schools? Logs, of course, and say twenty by forty feet inside measurement."

Eugene set to figuring on a pad of paper.

"Seventy-two logs in each, nine-foot walls, without counting floor or roof," he said after a few moments. "Six men to a building, one day for the logs, three for the raising and three for roof and floor. Seven days, Monsieur, or the four in a month."

"Good!" approved Clifton. "Choose the six men, Eugene—the best with ax and saw we have. I'll give you plans and locations at supper time, and tonight I'll send out an order for four of the finest little-red-schoolhouse bells that can be bought in Quebec or Montreal."

He felt a curious sense of elation as he went to his own room, set off at the end of the building in which were the store and the office. This feeling was more than optimism. It was the conviction that something had happened which had completely changed his footing in the approaching struggle with Hurd. He had feared a certain crisis; now he found himself looking forward with almost eager anticipation to the event which had worried him—the government investigation which was bound to follow serious troubles in the woods, and which was equally bound to make somebody pay. Hurd's gangs might overwhelm the Laurentian men in fighting strength, but they could not drive out or harm women and children—or Antoinette St. Ives or Anne Gervais and Catherine Clamart. And school bells would be ringing when the government men came!

At first he accepted this unexpected change in the situation as the one cause of his rising spirits. But as he shaved himself another factor came creeping in despite a mental protest which crumbled away before he had finished one half of his face. This factor was Anne Gervais—and behind was Antoinette St. Ives. A part of Antoinette had seemed to come into the woods with Anne. It had looked at him out of her bewitching eyes. The poise of her pretty head made him think of it, the slim likeness of her body —and even more than all these things something else which he could not define, and which was not a part of Catherine, though a quieter and rarer beauty might be found in the latter. He dressed himself with unusual care.

After his toilet he spent an hour drawing the plans for a school and deciding on their locations. Then he went to the guest cabin.

Evidently the monk had received his grooming and was gone. Anne and Catherine had slipped into fresh things. It was Anne who filled Clifton's eyes, though he kept that fact to himself. Outwardly he may have looked a little oftener at Catherine—a bit longer at Anne.

Anne had put on a simple white waist with a simple black tie, and with this her black hair was parted in the middle and smoothed like shining silk, with the heavy coil of it on her neck, so that if Clifton had been an artist he would have thought of but one picture to paint—the Mother Madonna.

While they were checking up the schoolhouse plans and talking business seriously, Anne's face was filled with the gentleness and sincerity of an angel's.

But when, a quarter of an hour before supper, she walked alone with Clifton at the edge of the river little devils of mischief lurked in the corners of her eyes as she looked up at him from under her long lashes.

"Like all other men who know her, I suppose you have fallen in love with Antoinette St. Ives," she said, and she put a hand tightly on his arm to steady herself over the rocks.

"I admire her," said Clifton.

Anne laughed softly, and looking down Clifton saw nothing but the sheen of her hair and the pink in her cheeks.

"I hope she marries Colonel Denis," she breathed gently. "I have tried to bring about the match for years. But I think—"

"What?" asked Clifton in spite of himself, when she did not finish.

"That she loves another man," said Anne.

Clifton's heart stopped beating. Against his most powerful effort his body stiffened.

"And the tragedy of it is that this man is the one man in the world who does not love her," continued Anne, looking straight ahead of her. "Is he not a fool?" Before he could force words out of his thickening throat, Anne asked, "Do you know Monsieur Gaspard St. Ives?"

"Yes. Very well," said Clifton. "I am to join him day after tomorrow."

The hand on his arm rested a bit more heavily.

"Where?" she asked.

"Oh—I think—at Roberval," he lied, keeping his pledge to St. Ives. There was a moment of silence. He looked at his watch. "Supper is about ready."

They walked back.

"Gaspard St. Ives is an—an unusually splendid man," persisted Anne.

"A prince among them," agreed Clifton, quickly catching at the way the wind was drifting. "You love him, Mademoiselle?"

"*What?*"

She faced him, her dark eyes glowing with fire, her cheeks like wild red phlox. Clifton smiled at her. How amazingly long her lashes were! Slowly they fell.

"Well, what if I do?" she asked. "Am I to be ashamed of it? Or shall I pine away and die because he happens not to love me?" And suddenly her milky teeth were laughing at him and her hand rested on his arm again. "But there is always hope," she said as they came to the door of the company dining-room, where Eugene and Catherine and one of the young engineers were waiting for them, "Remember that, Monsieur Clifton, when you dream of Antoinette St. Ives—*there is always hope.*" And from then until bedtime she gave him no further opportunity for words alone with her.

But in the morning, when he was ready to leave with Alphonse for St. Félicien so that they might be at the trysting-place bright and early the second day, she gave him a letter, and with a fierce little tempest which was not more than a whisper in her voice she said:

"If it were not for that hateful Angelique Fanchon at St. Félicien I could marry Gaspard St. Ives! Will you help me a little, Monsieur?"

"Help you?" Clifton felt his heart opening wide to accept her. Was Gaspard an absolute fool? Would he put away from him a little angel like Anne

Gervais for this plump and strong-headed farmer girl Angelique Fanchon, no matter how much land or how many cows and horses her father might own? "I'll help you," he said warmly. "I'll do everything I can."

"Then give him this letter," said Anne, and she placed a small sealed envelope in his hand. With a toss of her head she added, "Angelique Fanchon has made a fool of herself so long that she doesn't deserve him, and what it is in this stupid Gaspard's head that keeps him faithful to her I cannot understand. She should be whipped!"

"I have heard enough to incline me to that same opinion," agreed Clifton.

Anne looked up sharply. "From whom?" she asked.

"From Gaspard St. Ives, of course, and from Friar Alphonse as well."

"Oh-h!" said Anne, making a red _O_ of her mouth. "One would think they had a bad opinion of this Angelique Fanchon, the wicked thing!"

"They have," helped Clifton. "A very decided opinion. And I hope this letter from you will take the blindness from that ass of a Gaspard's eyes, and bring him to you."

"I hope so," said Anne faintly. "Good-by, Monsieur."

"Good-by, Mademoiselle."

He looked back from the crest of a hill a quarter of a mile away, and she was standing where he had left her, before the cabin in the clearing. She waved a handkerchief to him, and Clifton waved back, and Alphonse the monk gave a chuckle that was almost a laugh.

"A pretty wench," he exclaimed, "and one with eyes that would rock the reason of the Devil! There should be a Church canon against lashes as long as hers, for they have no righteous place among men." And he chuckled again.

"I am beginning to think that Gaspard has lost his mind," said Clifton. "She is adorable."

"A beautiful triumvirate, Monsieur Clifton, counting Antoinette. The children will love them. Also the women. And I fancy the schools will be filled when there is dancing or other nonsense. Our men will fight now, trust _them_! And it is a God's blessing, for I have brought information from the Hurd camps which will make you sick to hear. Ivan Hurd is there."

"The deuce!" cried Clifton.

"He came three days before I left, and with him half a dozen men who are as ugly-looking dogs as their master. Three of them are members of parliament, just up to look through the woods so they can testify to Hurd's splendid activities later on, two are men I have not been able to mark, and the sixth is Hurd's lawyer from Montreal."

Clifton drew his trotting horse down to a walk.

"They are planning on six hundred men by the middle of January," continued the monk, "and at least four hundred of them will be Americans and English Canadians—foreigners from Ontario and Maine. No matter what we can do, our Church will have little influence among them. And in the face of declining wages Hurd has raised last year's scale by twenty percent and is pledging a bonus of one hundred dollars to every man who sticks until the spring drive is over. That means a sixty-thousand-dollar bonus plus a forty-five-thousand-dollar increase in wage. And against all that we will have—"

"Three girls and four schoolhouses," Clifton finished for him. "And with good luck two hundred men. *Avance donc!*"—and he touched the horse into a trot again.

A third time Alphonse chuckled.

"Your humor is right, Friend Clifton. Why borrow trouble about gloomy matters when pleasanter ones are pending?" he philosophized. "For instance—tomorrow's bout between Gaspard St. Ives and Ajax Trappier should be a most agreeable and interesting affair, out of which, as the ancient saying goes, much honor may be expected."

"The fight shall not happen if I can prevent it," said Clifton.

Alphonse almost hopped from his seat.

"You would stop it?"

"I would."

"Then may your teeth ache everlastingly afterward if you succeed!" the monk shot at him fiercely. "Son, this is to be a greater fight than when Samson went among the Philistines with the jaw-bone of an ass! It is to be the greatest fight—"

"That two asses can possibly bring about," agreed Clifton. "But I think I can stop it when I tell our friend about Anne Gervais and give him her letter."

"She has written him a letter?"

"I have it in my pocket."

The little monk sank back in his seat. "If this fight is spoiled I shall never again believe in the virtue of prayer," he said.

And later that day, when the afternoon grew exceedingly warm and Clifton took off his coat, Alphonse found occasion to purloin the letter and hide it within the secret folds of his own.

Thereafter his spirits continued to rise until they entered the little village of Saint Methode, still a three-hour ride from Saint Félicien. And scarcely had they passed the priest's house and the small wooden church and come to the blacksmith's shop, the store and the little old inn which had a customer once or twice a week when a roaring voice greeted them joyously, and Gaspard St. Ives came out with the wild rush of a great Newfoundland dog from the door of the tavern. Before Clifton was out of the rig he had him in his arms, and was shaking the monk's two hands till the little man's bones seemed threatened with dissolution.

"*Bon Dieu!*" he cried. "I have been waiting since morning, knowing you had to come by this road. I left my sister at Normandin yesterday and have not slept a wink since, fearing you had forgotten your promise. But tonight I shall sleep long and sweetly, like a baby, and dream pleasantly of Ajax Trappier's cracking bones. Is there room in this buggy for three, Monsieur Clifton—two great men like you and me plus this shriveled minnow of a monk?"

"Enough," said Clifton, "for as far as we are going. Get in."

The overweighted buggy made its way out of the village at a sleepy jog.

"What do you mean?" demanded Gaspard, making a place for the half-crushed monk between them.

"For twenty days I have been thinking," said Clifton.

"A most extraordinary task," wheezed the monk.

"I have been thinking," persisted Clifton, ignoring him, "and I have come to the conclusion that you will be the biggest fool in Quebec if you fight this fellow at St. Félicien."

"You think he may beat me?"

"No. Not that. But this Angelique Fanchon, if she is the angel you have painted her, will think less of you for the fight; and if she does honor you for it, then she is a most ordinary creature, and not worthy the dirtying of your hands. How you can allow yourself to think of her as you do while a real angel like Anne Gervais is in love with you—"

"Anne Gervais!" gasped St. Ives.

"Yes, the school-teacher your sister sent up to our camps along with Catherine Clamart."

"*What*! That skinny little Anne Gervais whose eyes give me a chill every time they look at me! Compare her with my lovely Angelique Fanchon, would you, Monsieur Brant? You are mad!"

"As daft as a moonstruck loon," added the monk.

"A girl with feet twice as large as my Angelique—"

"And teeth that can bite through a hickory nut like a squirrel's," echoed the monk.

"It is monstrous!"

"She is very beautiful," defended Clifton. "Even Alphonse declared as much, and he spoke of the witchcraft of her lashes—"

"Because they looked hell-born to me," interrupted the monk. "Pay no attention to what he says, Gaspard. You cannot compare Angelique Fanchon with this Mademoiselle Gervais any more than you can set up a golden moon beside a hollow pumpkin with a lighted candle in it! And as for the fight—if you turn back now, even though you may be a little nervous—"

"Nervous?" rumbled St. Ives. "I am only nervous to be at it! I won't feel like a man again until I have whipped this overgrown horse-breeder under the very eyes of Angelique herself. That is my plan, friends, to whip him with Angelique looking on! So let us hurry, Monsieur Clifton, for I am anxious to find how the land lies at the Fanchon home. Tomorrow is Sunday, the day of all days to wreak the vengeance of the Lord upon Ajax Trappier!"

"Sweet are the thoughts that savor of content," approved the monk softly. "All that remains of your arguments, Monseiur Clifton, is the letter Mademoiselle Gervais placed in your care for our friend. Give it to him. We will be fair in the stand we have taken, by all means."

Clifton began searching in the pockets of his coat.

"This Anne Gervais sent a letter to me?" demanded St. Ives suspiciously.

"Yes. A love letter."

"Then God deliver me from it!" said Gaspard.

"It is gone," said Clifton, puzzled. "I have gone through my pockets twice. If it is lost I shall never forgive myself."

"Probably it fell into the road when you so carelessly put your coat over the back of the seat," suggested Alphonse.

St. Ives heaved a sigh of relief. "Don't mind it," he said. "It is profit instead of loss, for the last thing in this world I want is a letter from Anne Gervais. Will you give me the reins, Friend Clifton? I shall die of old age unless we make this road a bit faster."

"Go to it," yielded Clifton. "I'm through and you can make a fool of yourself if you want to. But I still insist that I wouldn't trade one Anne Gervais for a hundred of these Angelique Fanchons of Saint Félicien!"

And to his amazement the little monk whispered in his ear, "Neither would I, Friend Clifton, but we must let the Devil have his way—*this time*!"

CHAPTER XX

An emotion more stirring than thought of the approaching duel, yet stoically hidden, was in Clifton's breast. He wanted to hear about Antoinette St. Ives, even though he knew this desire was a weakness in himself, and he had half hoped that Gaspard would have something to say which would help to fill the emptiness in his heart. This feeling had increased since his brief acquaintance with Anne. That her love for Gaspard was a futile and despised thing was an absurd miscarriage of what ought to be. He began thinking of her almost affectionately. Even Antoinette was scarcely sweeter or more adorable. If there had been no Antoinette…

He jerked himself out of his thoughts as if someone had touched him with the end of a whip, just as Gaspard spoke the name of his sister.

"She has changed strangely since that night of the storm," he said, a puzzled note in his voice. "Possibly it is the strain of this business with Hurd. When she is not working among the people she is too much alone with herself, or with Joe. She has an armful of books and is teaching the boy from them. But along with that she has become too quiet, and I don't like it."

"Quietness hath its virtue," consoled the monk.

Clifton felt a depressing clutch at his heart. She had changed, St. Ives had said, since the night of the storm. Probably Gaspard did not know what had happened that night or he would have hurled him from the buggy. Now, looking back on it all, he could see how terribly he must have hurt her. The shameful advantage he had taken of her must have gone deep down into her heart and soul, like a blight. With his lips set tight he hated himself, and listened to St. Ives as he told about their work.

Night and day and Sunday they had been busy, and Gaspard did not think there was a villager's house or habitant's farm between Point Bleu and Saint Félicien they had not visited. Antoinette and Joe had spent five days at Saint Félicien, at Angelique's home, of course. But he had kept away—had gone to Normandin. Not for his life would he show his face to Angelique until he had broken Ajax Trappier.

As his own humor became gloomier that of Gaspard and the monk rose with each step that shortened the distance between them and St. Félicien. It

170

was as if Gaspard was on his way to some festive event, and Alphonse grew visibly brighter. It seemed that in some mysterious way he had already arranged for their night's lodging at a farmhouse which was less than two miles from the Fanchon home, and about an equal distance from that of Ajax Trappier, where their presence and mission would be held in strict confidence. So they avoided the town and came to Adrien Clamart's on a back road.

Clifton received a pleasant shock. Adrien, who was tall and slim and blue-eyed, and a married man, was a brother to Catherine Clamart, who was with Anne Gervais up on the Mistassini. He was in love with his sister as well as his wife, and shook Clifton's hand warmly. But he had to agree with St. Ives when Alphonse told about the difference of opinion regarding Anne Gervais.

"She is disagreeable, and has made a nuisance of herself, Monsieur, and I cannot blame Gaspard for his stand in the matter," he said. "I pity my sister if they are very long together."

Alone in his room that night Clifton took mental stock of himself. Was it conceivable that in some way he was blinded to the truth of Anne's personal appearance and qualities? He was puzzled. He fell asleep on a thick feather bed with Anne's lovely eyes and her long lashes filling his vision and pleading with him to fight her battle.

He was awakened early by a knocking at his door. It was seven o'clock when breakfast was over and he climbed into a buggy with Gaspard and the monk. Adrien cut across certain fields, and Adrien's wife kept away from him the shadow of doubt that had grown in her eyes. Last night they had talked to her about spending this day together seeing certain people in the interests of the Laurentian company. But she sensed excitement, even as Clifton could feel it as he sat next to St. Ives. Not until they were well away did either the monk or Gaspard give voice to it.

"The good Lord hath blessed us," Alphonse was first to say. "Madame and Monsieur Fanchon will leave for church at a quarter to nine, but Angelique—having received my message saying that Antoinette is coming at ten—will remain at home. She is delighted, Friend Gaspard, to know your sister is making her this unexpected visit. *Mon Dieu*, what a lie! But it had to be. And personally I saw to it that Angelique's note, written by myself— a finer woman's hand than mine you never saw, Monsieur!—was delivered to Ajax Trappier last night. He will be on hand in all his splendor at half past nine to take Angelique for a drive, as the note specially requested. Could that old fox, Richelieu himself, have done better, Gaspard?"

"You are a treasure, Alphonse!"

"It may be you will have a different opinion of me at half past ten, when you are beaten up like a bag of hops," exulted the little monk. "Ajax Trappier is in fine fettle!"

"So am I," boasted Gaspard.

In spite of the disgust which Clifton tried to impose upon himself he could not keep a growing thrill out of his blood. This was bound to be a memorable affair, a tremendous combat between two giants, and if it had not been for a certain dishonesty of action which seemed to be accompanying it he would have given himself up more to the spirit of anticipation which animated the monk.

As it was he asked, "And how have you insured yourself that Mademoiselle Fanchon will witness this fight?"

"I will arrange that," answered the monk. "The battleground is to be a greensward behind the house, Monsieur, and overlooking it, not fifty paces away, is a big window filled with flowers. And among these flowers will be Mademoiselle's face, so that until Gaspard's eyes are closed shut by Ajax he may see her every time he looks in that direction. Oh, that is the easiest part of it—arranging for Mademoiselle to see her baby Gaspard mauled unmercifully by this ferocious breeder of horses!"

After a time they entered through a gate into a wood, and in the heart of this wood they fastened the horse and went on afoot. A few hundred yards brought them to vast green meadows broken here and there by trees and thickets. This was the Fanchon farm, and half a mile across the meadows they came to a smaller wood, and just beyond this were the great barns and snow-white dwelling. A distance from the house the three concealed themselves, and St. Ives and Clifton smoked the time away until, at exactly twenty minutes of nine, Madame and Monsieur Fanchon drove off in great style in a rubber-tired buggy behind a high-stepping black horse whose sleek coat shone like silk even at four hundred yards. Scarcely were they gone up the road when Alphonse hopped like a rabbit from his cover.

"Give me twenty minutes!" he cried. "I will then be with Angelique in the house. After that come up behind the smallest barn, and make yourself ready, Gaspard. Within another twenty minutes Ajax Trappier will be driving down the road. And when he *does*, Monsieur Clifton, you are to be at the hitching-post to meet him and will tell him that a gentleman is behind the house who is very anxious to have a word with him. In that way you will lead him to the greensward we have mentioned, and Gaspard will advance at the same time from the barn, so measuring his steps that the twain shall meet in full view of the big window with flowers in it. And I swear that if you do these things properly Angelique will be looking on when the action begins!"

He was gone before even St. Ives had answered him, and Clifton looked at his watch.

Twenty minutes later they sallied forth from the wood, and found entrance through a back door into the barn. Here without further loss of time Gaspard began to prepare himself for battle. First he emptied his pockets of all articles and placed them neatly in a pile on a barrel-head. Then he began divesting himself of his upper garments, beginning with his tie and cravat, until his huge body stood naked to the waist. After that he drew in great breaths and blew out like a porpoise, and swung his mighty arms until he had given himself a general loosening up.

Clifton was beginning to enjoy himself. And he was also beginning to wonder what he would do if Ajax should get the best of St. Ives. Could he stand quietly by and see the brother of the girl he loved beaten up under the very eyes of that brother's sweetheart? He saw himself facing a serious problem.

Then a cloud of dust came shooting swiftly down the road. Clifton hurried to meet it and arrived at the hitching-post just as Ajax was making the last leg of the journey at a stupendous speed. The buggy arrived. It stopped. And Clifton stared.

Never in all his life had he looked upon anything in man-shape quite equal to the magnificence of Ajax Trappier. The man fairly glowed and glittered, dimming the glory of his splendid horse and wire-wheeled *voiture*. He was big, even bigger than Gaspard. But he hopped from his vehicle lightly and with debonair éclat fastened his horse to the post. He sensed his importance like a major-domo on parade.

His splendor began not alone with his size, or his fierce black mustache, or the shine of his polished face, but also with his cravat, which was a brilliant yellow. From that point down he was a feast for the eyes. His suit was a tan with whitish stripes, his vest was black-and-white check, and his shoes were shining enamel. The sun played on him effulgently. It reflected itself from a huge jewel in his cravat, from two enormous rings on his fingers, and from a double-hitch of gold watch-chain that dangled with the weight of half a pound across his upper abdomen. His chest was thrown out like a pouter pigeon's as he faced the house.

For the first time he seemed to notice Clifton.

"*Bon jour*," he said airily, with a greeting smile that revealed to Clifton the widest, whitest, longest, most powerful set of teeth he had ever seen.

"*Bon jour*," responded Clifton; and then he added, "Pardon, Monsieur, but there is a gentleman back of the house who will be grateful if you will come around and speak with him for a moment."

"Ah-h!" said Ajax. "With pleasure!"—and he passed through the gate with a splendid flourish, looking out of the corner of his eye to see if Angelique by any chance was observing him from a window or a door.

So it happened as the monk had planned, and Ajax came face to face with Gaspard on the greensward.

And Clifton's heart leaped full into his mouth when he glanced at the flower-filled window and saw the face of Angelique Fanchon staring out. It was partly screened, and withdrawn a little from the glass, but he knew it was Angelique by the wild look of triumph in Gaspard's face as he first greeted Trappier, and then pointed to the window. Ajax looked, and swallowed a great gulp. Then he smiled brightly and gracefully waved a hand to the girl.

"Mademoiselle Fanchon," said he.

"Yes, Mademoiselle Fanchon," said St. Ives.

Clifton was amazed by the paucity of words between them. Evidently the understanding of what would happen when they met was mutual. There was no abuse, no working up of their passions. In spite of his fealty to Gaspard, Clifton began to admire his gorgeous rival. Ajax's smile was a wonder. It was a perpetual thing, disclosing the deadly weapons behind it—his great teeth. He looked about him and calmly plucked a few flowers. These he carefully placed at a safe distance on the grass.

"I shall put them in your hands when it is over," he said to St. Ives, and smiled pleasantly at him.

He went into the barn and stripped, while Gaspard strutted up and down, apparently oblivious of the white and frightened face of the girl discernible through the flower-room window.

When Ajax returned he was smiling widely and he walked with the same cheerful animation, though he had on nothing but his trousers and enamel shoes. It was quite evident that his *gaieté de coeur* was in no way disturbed by this unexpected incident in his life. He twisted his mustache as he advanced, and again waved lightly to the girl in the window. Gaspard was gritting his teeth to hold back his rage. Nothing could have infuriated him more than his rival's pleasant behavior and stage-like complacency, and so fascinated was Clifton that he was almost startled when he heard the delighted chuckle of the monk close at his side.

"Is not this Ajax Trappier the flower of all flocks?" he asked. "And look at our Gaspard! A pin-prick and he would go up with a great explosion, for he is filled to the neck with the desire to get at this fellow. *Bon Dieu*, take a look at Ajax's teeth! They win his battles, Monsieur—those teeth!—longer than a boar's and stouter than iron nails. It is said he can bite a man's leg half in two with them, and when he lays hold of a man's ear—*per saltum!*—it is gone."

The two combatants were now facing each other, and for a few moments they moved slowly about, like two roosters making observations. Then they hunched themselves over, with a good six or eight feet between them, and like gorillas, with their heads low and their arms hanging down, continued their cautious circling.

With these actions began the preliminaries of a habitant duel.

"So you have come to break my bones, have you, Monsieur St. Ives?" smiled Ajax without a ruffle in his voice.

"Now that I am here I am going to do more than that," retorted Gaspard. "With Angelique looking on I am first going to pull out that greasy mustache of yours."

This was a good hit, for Trappier's mustache was his pride, and for a flash the smile left his face as they continued to circle about each other.

"A mustache will grow," he said then, exposing his great teeth again. "But what are you going to do without a nose, or ears, or eyes? I am going to take them all, but will let you live so that people may laugh at you and say that I, Ajax Trappier, was the one who plucked you so nicely. When I am through I am going to sing *Alouette* over what is left of you!"

This was too much for Gaspard. He shortened the diameter of their circle a foot, and Ajax promptly shortened it another. The monk began muttering under his breath—praying again, Clifton knew. Then with one impulse the two fighters came together in a terrific head-on collision, and at the same time grunts and roars rose from both of them. So far as Clifton could see, no effort was made to strike a blow with the fists. But the feet of the fighters became active, and he understood why they had kept on their shoes. In the first twenty seconds one of Trappier's shiny enamels caught Gaspard in the pit of the stomach and drew out of him a roar that could have been heard at the back end of the farm. At the sound of that roar, Adrien Clamart, who was hidden in the second barn, thrust his head out through the opening he had made by loosening a board and did not pull it in again until the combat was over.

From then on the action became so swift that Clifton could not keep track of it. The two giants rolled to earth, arms and legs interwoven—doubling, twisting, grunting and choking, now one on top and then the other, and at times turning over and over like a pinwheel, as Clifton had liked to roll down-hill when a boy. He knew that things were happening, desperate things, but only by the vocal manifestations of the combatants could he keep any record of them during the first few minutes.

A blood-curdling howl from Gaspard told him when Ajax's teeth first got into play, and a howl in a slightly different key likewise assured him when Gaspard put in a good stroke of business. The plot of green in which the combatants were laboring very quickly took on the aspect of a place where pigs had been rooting. Clods of turf flew up. Dust rose. Grass floated away on the air. Thuds, groans, mutterings, great gasps and occasional bellows came with these other evidences of ferocity from Gaspard and Ajax. They began to remind Clifton of those rubber dolls that respond when pinched and shriek loudly when suddenly bitten by a dog, for neither of the two was born to suffer in silence, and every hurt, every momentary advantage, had its immediate announcement in a properly pitched key of triumph or dismay.

Gaspard made the most noise. There was no doubt of that from the beginning. And it was not all inspired by triumph. Certain gasps and grunts were coming out of the very depths of him. Clifton saw his face, and it had been shoved firmly and deeply into the earth where there had been no grass to soften the effect. In that moment Clifton observed that his mouth was open and his eyes were bulging and he was spitting out soil. Then the gladiators creaked and twisted and strained, and he was gone out of sight again.

But the haunting things in this epic struggle which was being fought without a blow between four hundred and fifty pounds of human flesh and bone were Ajax's teeth. They were constantly bared, and no movement was so swift that the sunlight did not catch them in a sudden ivory flashing. The creature, it seemed to Clifton, was constantly smiling under his fiercely bristling mustache!

Then three things followed in swift succession, each of which seemed to promise the finish of the struggle. In number one it appeared definitely settled that Gaspard was receiving his *coup de grâce*. Ajax had him face down, with his huge hands at the back of his neck, and Clifton's blood went cold. A single blow of Trappier's mighty fist and St. Ives would be done for. But no true habitant thinks of his fist in a fight. So, following the usual method of one in his triumphant position, Ajax began the process of obliterating Gaspard's countenance in the soil. He rubbed and thumped and scrubbed it ferociously, and as he did this the little monk began to hop about the two excitedly swinging his arms in the air and forgetting his prayers to shriek out terrified advice to his friend. Evidently Gaspard was done for, for even howls and groans could no longer come from him, so intimately had his face become a part of the earth.

In this moment of dismay and horror Clifton looked toward the window. Was it conceivable that Angelique would remain an inactive witness of this catastrophe to her lover? Disgust and loathing filled him when he saw her white and frightened face staring through the flowers!

That instant the unexpected happened. As if in a dying fit Gaspard performed an extraordinary contortion which brought his two legs about Ajax's neck, where they fastened themselves like the two arms of a deadly, choking vise, and seeing them thus Alphonse emitted a wild and piercing cry of joy. Ajax made an effort to dislodge the grip with one hand, still keeping the other in Gaspard's hair. Failing in this he brought up the other, which movement freed St. Ives so that he could turn his head and suck in a little fresh air. The legs tightened more, and out of Ajax's mouth came a yell which ended in a gurgle. But so far as outward appearance went Ajax was still smiling. It was the effect of the man's confounded teeth, Clifton thought! He would die smiling. And when he was dead he would lie smiling in his coffin.

A feeling of intense relief swept over him. This, at last, must be the end. Ajax was gazing skyward, as if looking at a single star. His mustache bristled skyward. His eyes began to bulge skyward. His extraordinary teeth seemed to grow longer, reaching skyward. Everything was skyward, and it seemed to Clifton that even his soul was mounting in a debonair kind of way. Never had he felt such a feeling of admiration for Ajax Trappier as in this moment when he was helplessly waiting for the last of his wind to give out. It would be impossible for him to exist more than a minute or two.

He was thinking this, and preparing himself to pry apart Gaspard's legs before he murdered Ajax, when a third unexpected happening followed the first and second.

Ajax had loosened his hands and was reaching out slowly and somewhat blindly as if groping for something. This, Clifton thought, was the last act of a man about to give up the ghost, and he had already taken a step forward to end the affair when Ajax's two hands fastened themselves about Gaspard's ankle, and he saw that ankle and the lower leg to which it was attached slowly but surely bending toward the big, white, grinning teeth. Clifton held his breath. Could Ajax make it! He did—and not only made it, but shoved up Gaspard's pant-leg and pulled down his sock. Then his magnificent teeth sank in.

In his time Clifton had heard the wild shouting of men—of men frenzied by hatred and passion and the desire to kill, but in all his days no yell had split his ears like that which came from Gaspard St. Ives. It was more than a yell. It was one long and continuous roar and had he been blindfolded Clifton would have doubted that a human throat could have made it. Gaspard's legs loosened and Ajax's popping eyes began going back into their proper places in his head. Grimly and steadily he settled down to his work, putting every ounce of the increasing strength of his jaw into the labor at hand.

With Gaspard in this grim and tragic situation Clifton could not remain unconscious to the suffering of Alphonse the monk. The little man was almost sobbing in his despair, for surely St. Ives was being hamstrung before his eyes! Ajax was now complete master of the situation and would probably remain so until the end unless his teeth gave out, for Gaspard's legs were so twisted that they had no power with which to escape from the other's grip, and he was so firmly fixed upon his face, with Ajax on top of him, that his own hands were helpless. An invisible force seemed to drag

Clifton about to the window, and there he saw Angelique Fanchon, but not a movement was she making as she listened to Gaspard's wild yells of pain.

These yells were manifest evidence that for the present Gaspard had entirely forgotten Angelique. Not so with Ajax. In these precious moments of his triumph his thoughts went to the window and the eyes behind it, and there filled him an overwhelming desire to see Angelique looking out on his victory. So he began to twist himself a little at a time so that his eyes might come within range of the coveted spot.

He succeeded, but in the achievement it was necessary for him to change the angle of Gaspard's off leg, and the error was fatal. With one mighty effort Gaspard twisted himself half over, freed his leg, doubled it up, and sent it back with desperate force. The chance blow caught Ajax somewhere in front and sent him through the air like a bag of wheat. He struck the earth with a lifeless thud, and there he lay, stretched out nicely on his back with his arms and legs out spider-like, his eyes shut, his teeth smiling up at the sky and his mustache bristling in the sunlight.

For a moment the monk bent over the unconscious Ajax. Then with mysterious swiftness he departed for the front gate, and half a minute later was flying down the road behind Trappier's black horse.

Was it possible that Ajax was dead? Clifton bent over him fearfully. He was breathing, sucking in air mournfully, and his teeth clicked with each count. Then Gaspard limped painfully to his victim and triumphantly faced the window. Clifton was attending once more to Ajax when a different kind of cry came from St. Ives. Looking over his shoulder he saw the man rushing like mad for the kitchen door.

Quickly he followed. Possibly the pain he had suffered had turned Gaspard's head. Only a step behind him Clifton entered the room with the flower-filled window, and in this room, securely trussed up with rope in a chair and placed so that she could not help seeing the inspiring duel on the green outside, was a young woman. She had turned herself so that her horrified eyes encountered their own as they entered. She was deadly white, and sniffling. Her hair was sleek and straight. Her plumpness overflowed the chair. If this was the beauteous Angelique...

Gaspard gave a great gasp that filled the room. Slowly he circled about the girl. He tried to speak, and choked. Through the layer of soil which Ajax had scoured into his face his eyes bulged in amazement and shock. Finally words came from him—faint, weak, gasping, like a dying man's.

"It—it—isn't—Angelique—"

The girl's tongue came to life. Moaning and weeping and swaying herself until she threatened to overturn the chair she entered into a mild delirium of pleading and passionate explanation, out of which stood the main fact that the stranger monk had threatened her soul with eternal perdition unless she played the part before the window which he had demanded of her; and to make doubly sure he had tied her there with a rope. She wasn't Angelique Fanchon, and didn't know anybody was going to take her for Mademoiselle Angelique. She was only the cook, and the stranger monk had told her there was going to be a cock-fight in the yard, and he wanted her as a witness if anything unfair should happen. And he had threatened her with a thousand devils if she failed him!

In her excitement Clifton saw a letter fall from her lap to the floor. He picked it up and handed it to St. Ives.

"There is the letter Anne Gervais sent you. Alphonse must have taken it from my pocket. Read it!"

He felt an odd kind of thrill creeping over him as he cut the girl's bonds. Gaspard's big fingers worked clumsily as he opened the envelope. Stupidly he began looking at the writing, with Clifton watching him again after the girl had run out of the room like a scared rabbit. They could hear her continued blubbering as the kitchen door slammed, at least Clifton could. But St. Ives had suffered some kind of shock. He continued to stare at the school-teacher's writing; and then, without warning, he dashed from the room, limping as he ran.

Clifton followed, and found the girl on the kitchen floor, rocking herself back and forth in a hysterical spasm. For a few moments he paused to comfort her. When he got outside he saw Ajax sitting up and Gaspard vigorously shaking one of his limp hands. Then St. Ives hurried limpingly toward the barn, and Ajax remained in his unstable sitting posture, his head wobbling, his white teeth smiling, every hair in his mustache bristling and his eyes slowly assuming a light of intelligence and understanding. Clifton shook the hand which Gaspard had dropped and it seemed to him that Ajax's vacant smile widened a little.

Not until he was making a dive for the back door of the barn with his garments under his arm did St. Ives appear to think of Clifton. He paused then and held back the letter. Through its coating of soil his face blazed with a great light.

"Read that!" he cried. "I'm going down to the creek and take a bath!"

Outside the barn door Clifton read the few lines which Anne Gervais had written:

My own Gaspard:

Antoinette almost made me promise not to let you know I am here, but I cannot help it. She thinks it will disturb your work with her if I tell you now that I am sorry, and that I love you so much more than I ever have, and that I have made up my mind to do as you

179

wish, and be with you, and work with you, and care for you from this moment until I die. Monsieur Brant will tell you what I am doing here. He is so nice, and I am sorry Antoinette has such a feeling against him. Truly, Gaspard, I think she is shamming, and that she loves him.

And then came a signature which made Clifton's heart jump.

This Anne Gervais up at Mistassini was not Anne Gervais! *She was Angelique Fanchon!*

CHAPTER XXI

Clifton did not hurry after he had read Anne's letter. Like Gaspard he read it a second and a third time and by the end of the third perusal the surprising effect of the discovery that Anne Gervais was Angelique Fanchon had given way to a warm and thrilling sensation produced by the last line and a half she had written.

He followed in the direction Gaspard had taken, with the letter in his hand. When he came to a point where he could see St. Ives at his bath he waited until the other had dried himself and was dressed. Gaspard's slowness rather surprised him. He seemed in no great haste, and when he had finished he stood looking down at the pool until Clifton came up. His face was very red and bruised in places, and it wore a look which was almost a betrayal of embarrassment, with a whimsically humorous light behind it. He did not speak at once but took the letter again, with fingers that were clumsily gentle, and for a time his eyes seemed to linger on each word.

"I am not worth that," he said then, without looking up. "I think I have been a little mad. But reason has returned to me. A little while ago I was filled with the desire to destroy Ajax before Angelique's eyes. Now I am praying God that neither she nor my sister will ever hear of this fool thing I have done. Will you help me keep it from them?"

"If it is possible, yes. But there are others to remember—Ajax, the girl in the window, Adrien and Alphonse—"

"I am going back," interrupted St. Ives. "I am bound to tell Ajax I am sorry. He is a big-hearted fellow after all, and when I speak truth about him, and along with that he won't want the story of the affair to get out. Between us we will fix it up with the girl and Adrien, and I have thought we might loose a few pigs from the field to explain the uprooting of the yard. If you can find Alphonse, and keep his tongue quiet—"

"He ran away with Trappier's horse—to escape your wrath for the trick he played on you, I think," said Clifton. "Who is that coming into the edge of the field over there?"

"It is Ajax!" exclaimed St. Ives. "I will go and meet him. Good-by, my dear friend. You know what is in my heart, so tell as much of it as you can to Angelique—and that I shall come to her the happiest man in the world

181

the instant my sister's work and mine is finished. I would go now, but I knew she would not like that. And if you can get hold of Alphonse, who probably fears death at my hands, and is already on his way to the woods —"

"You are sure that you and Ajax will not become engaged in another fight?" interrupted Clifton doubtfully.

"Yes, I am sure."

"Possibly I should go back with you."

Gaspard laughed, and shook his head. "It would humiliate me greatly to have you hear the apologies I am going to offer Ajax." For a moment they stood with hands clasped. "You have—some word for my sister, Clifton?

"The best of good wishes."

He watched St. Ives as he returned limpingly across the great field. Ajax came more slowly, and at last stopped—probably anticipating further hostilities, Clifton thought. He could see Gaspard waving his hand in a friendly fashion, and after that they came together. For several minutes they stood without movement, and at the end of that time turned about and walked side by side toward the Fanchon barns. Twice Gaspard waved to Clifton. A third time and Ajax waved a hand. Clifton smiled. The dove of peace had strangely spread its wings.

Alone he returned into the woods, found the buggy, and came out upon the winding highway, thankful that he was started upon his lonely journey back to the Mistassini forests—and Anne Gervais. He felt a new sense of restfulness—was glad to get away from St. Ives, glad the monk had disappeared. He wanted a little time alone with thoughts which seemed out of place in their company. Here, with a sleepy wood on each side of him, the soft dust of an almost untraveled road underfoot, and his horse falling into his humor by plodding along at a slow walk, he felt privileged again—privileged to dream, to hope, to build his castles high up once more, as he built them not so long ago.

It was Anne Gervais who helped him. The spirit of her seemed near him, whispering softly in words what she had written in her letter—that it all was possible, that in Antoinette's heart *might* be something for him that was not hatred, something that was—love. He allowed the thought and even the word itself to possess him, and in the same breath he repeated to himself the impossibility of it—yet that impossibility did not keep his heart from trembling. And with the thrill of this nearness of hope it occurred to him that on the beach the night of the big storm Alphonse the monk had told him this same thing even more clearly than had Anne.

After a little he tried not to think of it any more. It was folly—a folly which would leave an abiding bitterness behind. Antoinette despised him. He knew, while the others could only guess. Yet he could not get rid of

Anne and her faith. They rode with him in the buggy. They sang with the birds along the way. They were a part of the flowers he passed. They gave a softness to the sunshine, a greater beauty to the sky. He found himself humming a tune, and talking aloud to the horse. That was his old self. And a part of the emptiness and loneliness which he had felt for many days was gone.

He wondered why Anne had come into the woods as Anne Gervais and not as Angelique Fanchon. Of course there was some reason for her masquerading under another person's name. Antoinette was mixed up in it, too —and the monk undoubtedly. He seemed to be the inspiring angel, or devil, wherever things were happening. Why had he played all this apparent trickery on St. Ives? Why had he plotted and encouraged the fight when he knew Angelique Fanchon was on the Mistassini? One question added itself to another until Clifton gave up trying to answer them.

He had almost come to the turning of the back road onto the main highway when a figure darted out from a cover of underbrush ahead of him.

It was Alphonse!

He was dusty and covered with perspiration, and he nervously looked up and down the road as Clifton reined in his horse. Then he smiled. Clifton did not return his greeting. Suspicion of the monk and the unpleasant effect of his sudden appearance at the roadside were revealed clearly in his face and attitude. He made no attempt to hide them. But Alphonse passed them over with a mirthless cackle as he climbed into the buggy.

As he drove on Clifton became oppressed by a strange sensation. Something about the monk began to stir him deeply. The little man looked straight ahead and his hands twisted nervously on his knees. He seemed to be trembling, too, and looking down at him Clifton saw his lips moving silently; age had settled more than ever in his face, leaving it pinched and thin and sickly white. What Clifton saw was more like sickness than fear.

Until they came to the turning of the road into the main highway silence rode with them in the buggy. Clifton's tongue clove to the roof of his mouth as he thought of madness and fancied that he saw it in the other's face. Then Alphonse seemed to come out of himself with a struggle, and looked up at him, and laughed. But there was no lightness in the laugh.

"Where is your friend Gaspard?" he asked.

"Making apologies to Ajax Trappier," answered Clifton. "They had a love-feast after you ran away—and both are anxious that no rumor of this foolishness reaches the ears of Mesdemoiselles St. Ives and Fanchon. I accepted the obligation of guaranteeing the secrecy of your own tongue. Was I right?"

"Perfectly," nodded Alphonse. "I have no reason for telling Angelique, and I never expect to see Antoinette again."

Coldly and clearly spoken, the words were a shock to Clifton.

"I think my work is coming to an end," the monk went on in a strangely even voice. "And you are the one man in the world who should know a little something about it, Monsieur Clifton, because there is between us a bond which even my ugliness and what you think is half madness cannot break—our love for Antoinette. Mine will die with me. Yours will go on living. But I am not mad, as you think, and as Gaspard sometimes thinks. There are times when I can see too far, too clearly, too deeply into matters which others cannot see.

"That is why I brought this fight about, and made the girl take Angelique's place in the window. I knew that until the feud between Gaspard and Ajax had burned itself out there would be no peace in Gaspard's mind, and one thing alone would destroy their enmity and make friends of the two—a spectacle which, when over, would prove them ridiculous in their own eyes.

"So when Antoinette suggested schools in the woods I secretly plotted with her to make Angelique one of the teachers. Mademoiselle Fanchon did not guess my part in the scheme, and so she almost betrayed herself when we met on the Mistassini, for she had come up there under the name of Anne Gervais for—I don't know what reason. That is her secret and Mademoiselle Antoinette's. Anne Gervais is a pretty name, but Anne Gervais herself is a skinny old maid of Quebec who has pestered the life out of Gaspard with her adoration. No matter what Angelique's reason for taking another's name may have been, it has helped me. There is one more task ahead of me, and then—"

"What?" asked Clifford, as the other hesitated.

"My work will be done. Those I love more than my own life will then understand. And Antoinette—may God forever bless her!—will be happy. And you, Monsieur—I am telling you this so that some day you may also tell it to them, when otherwise they might despise me. Oh, I am not mad! I am terribly sane! Too sane! For madness of a kind is often better than sanity. And when it is over—when my work is finished—I want enough of the truth to be known so that you, and those two I love, may sometimes be kind enough to pray for the salvation of a soul that once inspired a man of God and which now struggles weakly in the body of a sinner. Monsieur— there is a spring of cold water in the corner of this wood. Are you thirsty?"

"No, but I will wait for you," said Clifton, stopping in a patch of shade.

For a moment he was laboring against an almost irresistible impulse. It was not common for him to feel affectionately inclined toward men, so that he desired to put his hand on them. Benedict was the big exception. But in this moment of strange emotion that passed over him it was only a little thing that restrained him from placing an arm about the monk's shoulders,

184

as he would have done in comforting Joe. And before that instant of self-repression was gone the little monk stood in the road. He looked up and tried to smile. Then Clifton watched the dusty and broken figure as it passed through the roadside thicket and over the fence into the wood, and his heart was filled suddenly with compassion and sympathy.

He waited. Where the monk had disappeared a brown-coated warbler sang, as if welcoming a creature as drab and aloof from the world as itself. A squirrel ran along the rail fence. From the edge of the wood came the soft droning of bees, the rasping music of a locust, and the calls and whisperings and almost unheard murmuring of life deeper in. As far under the roofs of the trees as he could see Clifton caught the mellow gleaming of golden pools and streams of sunshine on the cool earth.

In among these the monk had gone, and he did not come out again.

Clifton listened for his footsteps and the sound of disturbed brush. On an old stub a woodpecker hammered. Closer about him crept the *cheep, cheep, cheep* and *twit, twit, twit* of little brown brush-birds. The squirrel scolded impudently from the fence, and down the road a fat woodchuck waddled across on his daily adventures into a clover patch.

It was taking the monk a long time, Clifton thought.

He got out and fastened the horse to a poplar sapling. Then he climbed the fence and came upon a tiny trickle of water which he trailed back for a hundred steps or so until he found its birthplace—the spring.

The monk was not there, and he had not been there, for no trace of footsteps was left in the soft mold about it. Clifton called his name and his only answer was a mysterious hushing of the wood about him.

He stood silent as the truth grew upon him. The monk had not come for a drink. He was gone, and had no intention of returning.

Yet Clifton waited for half an hour at the spring, looking through the lonely hush of the trees to catch any flash of movement which the yellow pools and streams of sun-glow might reveal.

After that he returned to the buggy and drove eastward on the dirt highway that led to Saint Methode. From the cool stillness of the byway he found himself suddenly in a moving stream of life and light and laughter. The habitants were returning from church. The younger swains and country gallants passed him first, each vying with the others in showing off the virtues of his horsemanship and steed—when the gallants rode alone. But when beside one sat a clear-eyed, pink-cheeked daughter of the land the young Saint Johnite wooer held his seat with stiff and dignified solemnity, knowing that the eyes of the young lady's elders were on them from behind.

And Clifton walked, letting them all pass him—long-legged Arab and lightning-swift galloway, fillies as spirited as young girls, thoroughbreds as

185

sleek as silk and geldings born for the fields, all bearing their happy burdens of love and cheer and faith in God that helped to make the glory of the day. The swiftest gone, the others followed—carts and blackboards crowded with children, sometimes two and three vehicles to a family; sweethearts, little loath to let the miles drag slowly within the vision of watchful mothers and fathers behind, and last of all half a dozen dog-carts whose juvenile drivers taunted Clifton good-naturedly for his slowness as they passed him.

Yet with all this there seemed something missing for Clifton, and slowly he continued his way until the gray trail of dust had completely settled ahead of him. Even after that he did not hurry. He could not get the monk out of his mind, or the strangeness of his departure, and behind the gaiety and happiness of the country folk who had passed him there remained a cloud which gathered itself more about him as the day lengthened. It was after midnight when he reached the Mistassini.

When he went to breakfast in the morning he had slept only three or four hours, and he did not leave his room until he saw Angelique and Catherine come from the door of their cabin, booted and dressed in riding-breeches and khaki shirts, each with a diminutive packsack over her shoulder. As he hurried to meet them his heart warmed at their sportsmanship. They were prepared for roughing it. Even their boots were made for the stress of water and mud and rock.

Clifton noticed this, and the other things, but more than all else Angelique's face and eyes filled his vision. Her greeting, though she tried to make it as gay as Catherine Clamart's, was subdued by what he saw there. She wanted to know about St. Ives; how her message had been received, and what word he had sent to her in return.

When breakfast was finished Clifton asked her for a few minutes alone.

They walked toward the river, leaving Catherine with the young engineer who had horses waiting, and who was to guide them on their first journey among the camps and jobbers.

"We had planned to start an hour earlier," said Angelique to Clifton, "but Catherine could never quite finish fussing with that hair of hers. It's glorious, and I don't blame her. She is desperately in love, and so is young Vincent, and each is trying to hide it from the other until a decently proper time has passed. Yesterday he blundered on us when we were sunning our hair where we thought no one would see us down among the rocks, and it was funny to see the look of incredulity and abject adoration in his face. It was all for Catherine. She was a veritable golden goddess aflame with a smother of tresses almost to her knees. If I hadn't been there I think Vincent would have fallen on his knees. Isn't it silly for a man to feel like

186

that?" And she shot a quick look up at him, as if daring him to answer in the affirmative.

"Maybe it is," he said, appearing not to notice her challenge, "but, somehow, it happens just the same. Men will persist in making fools of themselves, if not in one way then in another. There is Gaspard St. Ives, for instance. The first day I met him he raved to me about the beauty of some little country girl—Angelique Fanchon, I think her name was—and when I smiled at his enthusiasm he wanted to fight me. But I never heard him breathe a word about a girl named Anne Gervais!"

"I have been foolish," murmured Angelique.

"Very," agreed Clifton.

"You—gave Gaspard the note?"

"When I told him I had a letter from Anne Gervais he refused to accept it."

"What!"

"But I forced it on him, and he read it."

Angelique gave a deep sigh of relief.

"And then—are you playing with me, Monsieur Brant? If you are—if you think it is so very amusing to keep me in suspense—" A little dark flash of lightning passed up to him from her eyes.

"Play with you?" Clifton laughed softly. "Only because I am happy in your happiness, little friend! I don't think I ever knew St. Ives until he read that letter. It was like a flame that showed me the true depths of him for the first time. I believe he had grown a little hopeless, and your letter lifted him shoulder-high with the gods. He said very little, but it was the way he said it that counted. He gave me this message: 'Tell her that I shall come to her the happiest man in the world the instant my sister's work and mine is finished. I would go now, but I know she would not like that.' And—he let me read the letter!"

He could feel the tremble of Angelique's hand on his arm.

"He let me read the letter," he repeated.

"Yes, I understand," replied Angelique, and her head was bowed so that he could not see her face, and her voice was almost a whisper.

"In it you spoke of me," he went on. "I am grateful for your good opinion of me. And if it is true that you think Mademoiselle Antoinette has not this feeling against me—well, if you tell me that, I think I shall be almost as happy as Gaspard St. Ives. But if you wrote the lines thoughtlessly—"

He looked down to meet Angelique's eyes, beautifully soft and glowing.

"They were true," she said, and it seemed to him that her words were three little electric dynamos that set to work in his heart and body and blood. "I am more certain of it now than when I wrote them. You have done something terrible, Clifton, and Antoinette is trying to punish you, as

187

I tried to punish Gaspard, and it is hurting her as much as it is hurting you. If that were not true, why should she—

"Please go on," entreated Clifton, as she hesitated.

"Why should her eyes be red at times from weeping?" asked Angelique. "My own were that way many times during the past half year because I loved Gaspard and still tried to make him believe I hated him."

"It may be she weeps because of the strain and torment the machinations of Ivan Hurd have placed her under," suggested Clifton, his voice beating in his own ears.

"No, there is a flash in her eyes when she thinks of Ivan Hurd, or speaks of his work. She cries—at night."

"You know?"

"Twice, when I slept with her."

"It must be for other cause than me."

"But I have overheard her talk to little Joe about you. She tells me she dislikes you, repeats it too often for truth, Clifton—and in secret she tells Joe you are the finest man in the world and that he must grow up to be very much as you are. Once I heard those very words, and I did eavesdrop, I confess, when I heard her speaking them."

"It is because she is too finely honorable to prejudice Joe against me."

"And I have happened to look into a little box, in which I was hunting for powder for my nose," continued Angelique, "and in this box was a letter and a telegram, and on one I saw your name—and got out of the box as quickly as I could! In just that way I kept Gaspard's letters, not because I hated him but because I loved him."

Clifton drew in a breath that almost choked him.

"If only half of what you set me hoping for could come true!" he said.

"Was it so very terrible, that wrong which you must have done her?" asked Angelique Fanchon softly.

"I told her I loved her."

"Not a very great sin."

"But I happened to say what was in my heart the first time I saw her— the first night, in her home."

"Ugh-h-h!" shivered Angelique.

"And I told her so each day thereafter; and the third night, during a storm on Lake Saint John of which she has probably had something to say to you, I carried her in my arms to a habitant's home and kissed her considerably on the way."

"And she let you do that?"

"She thought I was her brother."

Angelique feigned a little scream.

"That was terrible," she cried. "But if Gaspard had done that with me I don't think I should have tried to hate him so much. Unless—"

"What?"

"He blundered inexcusably afterward. For instance, are you certain Antoinette really believed you were Gaspard? Isn't it just possible she knew it was *you*, and that the experience gave her happiness instead of torment until you were silly enough to reveal your identity to her in the light of the habitant's home? Oh, yes, she told me about the storm, and your carrying her, but she didn't say anything about the kisses, of course. And when you stood there like a dunce, and left her not a shred of pride to hide herself under, was there anything she could do but make up her mind to hate you? Of course, there wasn't! I tried to hate Gaspard for six months for less than that!"

"I thought it was the honest thing to do."

"And it was the very silliest thing to do. If she was shamming a little, and you spoiled it for her, your crime was inexcusable—and I doubt if she will come into your arms again too easily. But she loves you. I am quite sure of that. There come Catherine and Vincent! Observe how he drops a step or two behind her as she picks her way among the rocks, just so that he may drink his eyes full of that wondrous braid of hair! Oh, we all have our pretty little trickeries, Clifton, and it is sinful to discover them!"

"I shall always think of you as the good angel in my life," said Clifton gratefully. "I think you have made me happy. And always, when you seem nearest and dearest to me, I must think of you as Anne—Anne Gervais."

"Only another little hypocrisy," breathed Angelique, as the other two came nearer. "We are full of it, Clifton, so full of it that it is a wonder we do not sometimes wreck the world. I ask your forgiveness. The real Anne Gervais was coming up, until the last moment, when the poor, dear thing met a widower who needed mothering and married him on short notice. That will please Gaspard. So when I filled her place, and asked Catherine to come with me, I also took her name. It was a whim. A little fun. And it may be that Angelique Fanchon thought it might be a bit embarrassing to meet Clifton Brant, under the circumstances. But we got over it quickly, didn't we?"

She was smiling at Catherine and Vincent as she spoke the last words, but the tips of her fingers pressed Clifton's arm.

"Antoinette will join us within ten days or two weeks," she finished. "Then, if your eyes are sharp and your judgment is good—you will see!"

Half an hour later he watched them ride away, Vincent between the two, and until they disappeared entirely in the thickening forest he could see the flash of sunshine in Catherine's golden hair.

CHAPTER XXII

Clifton resumed his work with an enthusiasm which had not possessed him for years. Angelique Fanchon had swept away the cloud that had oppressed him so grimly, and he was inspired now by a glorious desire to achieve and succeed where only duty and a somber determination had spurred him on before. Antoinette did not hate him. She did not even dislike him, but kept what he had written her, and talked nicely to Joe about him, and—if Angelique Fanchon was right at all—cared a little for him! His mind was filled with dreams and inspiring visions, and he felt equal to a dozen Ivan Hurds—to a hundred.

He plunged into his work with a kind of ferocity which reminded him of certain fighting days in Belgium. The third day after his return from Saint Félicien the boat from Roberval brought Colonel Denis. His confidence then was like a mass of rock which dynamite could not blow up. They went from camp to camp together, and not an hour passed that Clifton did not point out some fresh reason why they would beat Hurd. Denis threw off ten years from his shoulders during the five days in the forests. Two of these days Angelique Fanchon and Catherine Clamart were in their company, and the souls of the girls had risen to the fight like Clifton's.

One of the schools was well under construction and the others were plotted and logs were being cut. The girls were already building their programs and arranging classes, and to the amazement of Clifton and John Denis they had brought a thrill of anticipation and excitement into every camp and jobber's home by arranging classes for the teaching of English to the men and women. There was not an adult in the woods who did not realize the value of an understanding of this language, no matter how small it might be, in adding to his or her earning capacity with the big English companies that ran ninety percent of the mills and timber concessions of the province.

"We cannot lose when we have a spirit like this behind us," Clifton said for the twentieth time to Colonel Denis. "If we get the timber cut nothing that Hurd can do will keep it from going down to the mills. Your big work now is to encourage the right side of the Government to come up here on an investigating junket or two when we are ready. The work we are doing will please the Premier. He is a constructionist and despises Hurd.

"Get his crowd up here, let them hear our school bells and see what our people are doing and Hurd won't dare to loose his foreigners on the criminal stuff he has planned. Arrange for the newspapers to have men with them. We've got a tremendous break ahead of us, and if we fail there are no such principles as honor and honesty on the face of the earth!"

He was like a tremendously charged dynamo in his enthusiasm, and only Angelique Fanchon knew the inspiring flame that was at the bottom of it.

"I'm going to cut two million logs," he said to Denis, *and I'm going to get them down!*"

The day after John Denis returned to Quebec he saw Angelique Fanchon again.

"Since the Archbishop has prohibited dancing among Catholics in the Province of Quebec we have decided to give a weekly musical entertainment and play at each of the schools," she announced. "We will need four pianos."

Clifton sent out an order for them that same day.

From then until the middle of September Clifton had no word from Antoinette or Gaspard St. Ives either directly or through Angelique. But the people continued to come in. By the fifteenth a hundred and eighty men were in the woods, and with them forty women and sixty children. On the seventeenth the first school bell ever heard in this northern wilderness sent its silvery chimes through the forest.

On the eighteenth came a cold and brief announcement to Clifton from Antoinette St. Ives saying that she and her brother would arrive at Mistassini on the twentieth.

This was the day that Delphis Bolduc came in with fresh information regarding Hurd's activities. Hurd had already begun cutting all along the streams below the Laurentian Company's timber. His object in forcing the work so early and waiting for the drive was quite clear. Among other things he was determined to have ready and waiting for the drive every log the Mistassini could hold when the spring floods came, and as these logs would all be below the Laurentian cut there was a great danger of the latter being crowded out entirely. That, of course, was Hurd's plot. If he could use all of the Mistassini's available raftage water for his own timber and thus hold back the Laurentian logs until the high water had passed the ruin of the latter company would be complete.

But Delphis did not bring down gloom with him. He had been thinking in the woods, he said, and there was a way to beat Hurd at that game. Forty miles up the river from their last timber operations, and hidden completely back in a pocket of mountains, was a big lake which he knew well. Its out-leading into the Mistassini was a stream between mountain walls of rock. It could be easily dammed and the water in the lake raised forty feet, he thought.

Of course it would be necessary to do the work secretly or Hurd would checkmate it. But granting this could be accomplished the Laurentian people could get their logs into the Mistassini ahead of Hurd, then blow up the dam with dynamite, and before Hurd knew what was happening the sudden rush of water would carry their logs well down the river, below Hurd, where they would have all the advantage of the spring floods when they came.

The idea was staggering in its immensity. If Bolduc's scheme could be worked Hurd would not only be beaten but a half of his season's cut could be left high and dry after the floods had passed, if Denis was correct in his statement that the Mistassini would carry five million logs, and no more during the high-water driving season.

In the company of Vincent, the young chief of his engineering staff, and with Bolduc guiding them, Clifton left the upper Mistassini on the same day that Delphis arrived from the Hurd Concessions. He left a brief letter for Antoinette explaining the importance of his mission and apologizing for not remaining.

At the first depot up the river he had a few minutes with Mademoiselle Fanchon.

"Of course you will be there to welcome them," he said.

"Of course I shall not!" declared Angelique warmly. "Do you suppose I am going to run after Gaspard St. Ives? He must come to me, wherever I am!"

"But Antoinette?" protested Clifton. "Someone should be there—"

"And he is running away!" taunted Angelique, raising her long lashes so that she was looking straight in his eyes.

"It is necessary that I go north."

"Yet not so necessary that you could not wait another thirty days!"

Clifton flushed.

"You are afraid!"

"I confess it—a little, yes. I rather seized this opportunity of getting away. That will permit her to become acquainted with the work through others, and not myself. I don't want to force myself on her any more. Frankly, where I used to be so bold—I am now—a coward."

Angelique gave a delightful little laugh, and the flush in her cheeks and the glow in her eyes were inspiring to look at.

"You are using good judgment now, Monsieur Clifton," she approved. "Unless a woman believes herself to be vital enough to frighten the man she loves she does not want him. Of course she will not know you are running away, unless I tell her. But before that, if I reveal the truth at all, I shall build you up so magnificently in her eyes that she may feel a little afraid of herself. Possibly it is well for her to see what you have done and hear what Catherine and I think of you before she sees you. So please hurry away on your important business and don't come back for a few days!"

So Clifton continued north, happier than when he had started.

What he found increased the new thrill that life was holding for him. Delphis Bolduc was right. Vincent's voice had a trembling note of triumph in it when he explained how easily the lake could be turned into a mighty reservoir. The dam could be chiefly built of timber and rock, with just enough steel and cement to reinforce it in places and plug up the leakages. Three or four charges of dynamite would utterly demolish it when the proper hour came, and something like five million cubic feet of water would be turned into the Mistassini, if the surface of the lake was raised twenty feet.

The outlet between the rock walls was a little less than sixty feet. Vincent figured and drew plans in the sand. He would undertake to do the work in ten days with twenty men, but inasmuch as secrecy was absolutely vital to their success he recommended six men, carefully chosen, and a month for the work. Before the day was over he had eliminated steel and cement almost entirely from his plans.

"Work should begin immediately," he said, after they had paddled around the lake, investigating each trickle of water that ran into it. "There will be no more rains, and very little water finds its way into the lake during the wintry months. Under normal conditions the lake will fall another foot between now and January. Our storage will accumulate very slowly, and it is important not to lose time." Aside to Clifton, he said a bit whimsically, "Of course you understand it's going to be a lonesome job up here."

Clifton thought of Catherine, and placed a hand affectionately on Vincent's arm.

"Maybe—but with a golden inspiration behind it," he consoled.

They set out on their return the next day.

This was Thursday, and Antoinette had arrived at Depot Number One on Wednesday. Gaspard, of course, had hunted up Angelique immediately, and this day would undoubtedly be one of excitement and prodigious happiness on the lower river. His own heart tuned itself to the pleasant happenings he was imagining. He did not hurry, but made an excuse of studying the shores of the river as they passed. Frequently he landed with Vincent and Bolduc to make a closer inspection, and every moment he was thinking of Antoinette.

That night he lay awake for hours. His blood was restless. His mind refused to rest from its incessant building of possibilities, and these pictures that he conceived were not disturbing, but built up his optimism until hope became an actual happiness.

It was supper time of the second day when they arrived at the lower depot. Clifton was grateful for the hour. It would give him time to clean up and dress, and get over a bit of nervousness that had begun to possess him. With Vincent he climbed a narrow path from the river, coming to his own door in an inconspicuous way.

Vincent's eyes had gone swiftly to the cabin set apart for the girls, and he gave a sudden exclamation of pleasure.

"There's Catherine!" he cried.

Clifton saw her. On this day when she knew they would return she was waiting for Vincent—with her magnificent hair in the heavy braid.

Vincent was off, forgetful of dirt and unshaven face, and Clifton heard Catherine's glad voice in greeting as he entered his room. Each minute after that he expected Gaspard to arrive. But Gaspard did not come. No one came. He had bathed and shaved and almost finished his dressing when Eugene Bolduc knocked.

"Thought I'd give you time to clean up," he explained, as he came in.

"The St. Iveses are here?" Clifton asked, his heart pounding.

"They came day before yesterday. And forty men and half as many women and children have arrived during the last two days," added Eugene exultantly. "We expect half a hundred more this week."

"Splendid!" exclaimed Clifton. "And St. Ives? Where is he?"

"Started for Depot Number Three with Mademoiselle Fanchon this morning."

"Was Mademoiselle here when the St. Iveses arrived?"

"Mademoiselle Clamart, yes; but Mademoiselle Fanchon was at Number One, and St. Ives went up to bring her down." Eugene's eyes twinkled and he gave his shoulders a significant shrug. "A pretty joke she played on him, with that name of Anne Gervais!"

Confound the man, why didn't he mention Antoinette!

Clifton fastened his tie.

"His sister is comfortable? And—where is she?"

Eugene had looked out the window.

"There she is. Just finished supper. On her way to the cabin."

Clifton sauntered to the window and looked. He caught a glimpse of her, the same slim, straight, adorable little figure, the uptilted chin, the brown hair he worshiped glowing in the last of the sun.

Something unleashed itself in him then. His heart choked him, but it had also choked out fear. He sprang to the door, and before Antoinette had

194

reached her own he was calling to her. She did not pause or turn until she reached the cabin. Then, casually, she saw him. His eagerness shone in his face. It glowed in his eyes. It trembled in his voice when he spoke.

"Only God knows how glad I am that you are here," he cried. "I've been counting the days and the hours——"

Then he saw there was no change in the beautiful gray eyes that were looking at him, no flash of joy or sunshine in them, no softening glow of welcome or gladness. Her hand rested on the latch of the door. And she had only half turned toward him.

"Thank you, Monsieur Brant," she said in a quiet, calm voice. "I am sure my arrival can add nothing to the wonderful work you have been doing."

The latch clicked and the door opened a few inches, and something snapped in Clifton's heart. He did not try to speak again. For a moment Antoinette hesitated, and then she added:

"Possibly I may see you tomorrow, Monsieur. But this evening I am tired. And——by the way——I sent Joe up to the school with Mademoiselle Fanchon. Of course Bim and the gun are with him."

She did not offer him her hand. No warmth of friendship crept into the cold evenness of her voice. The door opened wider and she entered the cabin. Clifton did not wait for it to close. He turned and stalked back to his room.

His heart was dead, emotionless. His body and brain were numbed. Something that was deathlike in its icy chill possessed him. After a time he had the cook prepare him something to eat. He learned that Vincent had not come to supper and smiled a bit grimly. Golden Catherine was filling the emptiness in a hungry man's stomach. Love was a wonderful thing——when successful!

With a woodsman bound north Clifton set out in a canoe before it was light the next morning.

The second day after, at Depot Number Three, he found Angelique Fanchon.

He was glad that Gaspard was out with the depot manager on an inspection of the first cutting operations. Angelique was busy at her work in the school when he called her out. She was happy. He could see that. She had never looked so beautiful. But when she saw who it was outside the door a look of distress came into her face.

"There is something——terrible——about you," she said, staring into his hard eyes. "And I know, *I know*. Oh, it's my fault, and I've been such a fool."

Her warm little hands were clutching one of his, and their tenderness softened the hard look that had settled in his face.

"Why your fault, little friend?" he asked.

"Because I made such a mess of it, Clifton. I know she wanted to see you when she came. It was impossible for her to hide it from me, or keep the disappointment out of her eyes when she learned you were up north. And that night, the *first* night, mind you, I spoiled it all! I was so happy at what I thought I saw that I came out all at once and told her how you loved her and that every move in your life was inspired by her.

"That would have been splendid if I had stopped there. But I didn't. I went on, and told her that I knew—was *absolutely positive*—that she loved you, and that it was only her foolish pride that kept her from letting you know. Dear Mother, you should have seen her then! She was furious, and accused both you and me of plotting together and betraying confidences—and she said she knew you were back of it all and that this was only another of your hateful and impossible tricks to gain her favor.

"Oh, she did flagellate you, Clifton, and me, too—and told me clearly not to mix myself up in her affairs. And all the time I knew her heart was almost breaking between that pride of hers and love for you, and that she was punishing me mostly to keep herself from crying. She did cry afterward. She said it was because of the humiliation I had brought on her. But that wasn't the reason. She cried because her pride is almost broken, and she wants you so badly."

Clifton was smiling. Angelique had never seen that same kind of smile on his face before.

"Dear little mother-girl, you have been awfully good to me, and because of it I shall help Gaspard fight for your happiness to the end of your days," he said. "But in all this you have thought and said you are wrong. I have no doubt now. I only stopped on my way into the woods to see if all was well between you and Gaspard. And I see that it is. God be praised for that! Gaspard is a prince, and you are an angel. Just now I don't feel like seeing Joe, so don't tell him I have been here. The school work is going well?"

"Beautifully," whispered Angelique, and her long lashes were shining with tears.

"Good-by!"

"Good-by, Clifton!"

As he turned away her dark eyes were filled with the fire of stars, and she called after him very softly:

"But remember, Clifton, wherever you go—Antoinette St. Ives does truly love you!"

CHAPTER XXIII

He went farther north—to the upper cuttings. From then on, day after day, he made himself a part of the forest work, passing from camp to camp and from jobber to jobber, locating new arrivals, urging and inspiring earlier ones to greater endeavor, overseeing the building of sluices and creek clearways and dams, and by the tenth of November had three hundred and twenty-five men at work. During these six weeks he saw Gaspard twice and Angelique Fanchon only once, and was careful to avoid situations which would bring him into contact with Antoinette. Until the middle of November it was not difficult for him to arrange his movements so that this result was brought about without creating a very great suspicion that he was purposely avoiding her, for there was work ahead of him night and day. But the time came when, as Bolduc put it, the whole Laurentian outfit was working like a well-oiled machine. With greater surety than ever Clifton wrote Colonel Denis that two million logs would be along the driveways when high water came.

Vincent finished his dam, and a guard of three trusted men armed with rifles watched the premises day and night, eight hours at a stretch. Clifton was sure Hurd had no suspicion of what had been done.

The Bolducs kept him in intimate touch with Hurd's activities. The attitude of their enemy puzzled Eugene and Delphis. Hurd did not seem to be at all disturbed by the Laurentian Company's success in getting its timber down and cut. Delphis believed that he had completely changed his plans, and that instead of "roughing it," as he had first designed, he had something tremendously more effective up his sleeve, and was waiting with a confidence which puzzled and alarmed Bolduc. Hurd was constantly in the woods. He had toned down his men so there had been no trouble at all between his own and the Laurentian people. And he was piling up pulpwood in enormous quantities.

Between the fifteenth of November and the first of December Hurd sprung two amazing coups.

Unannounced he visited two of the four schools during class hours, accompanied by several professional-looking strangers, and talked freely with Mesdemoiselles Fanchon and Clamart, assuring them that if their

197

schools were a success, which he could readily believe they were, he would institute the same splendid idea in his own holdings the following year.

His second inexplicable move was expressed in a letter which went simultaneously to both Clifton and Antoinette St. Ives, and in which Hurd asked for permission to send a number of children belonging to his own people to the Laurentian schools. "It would give the splendid idea an impetus among my own workers," he said; and then added, "I will gladly pay a part of your school expenses for this privilege and accommodation."

It was this letter which necessitated a meeting between Colonel Denis, Antoinette St. Ives and Clifton on the first of December.

The meeting was in Bolduc's office at Mistassini, at nine o'clock in the morning.

Two months and a half had passed since Clifton had seen Antoinette. Others had noted the change in him during these weeks. Angelique Fanchon had been a little frightened at it, as if something in him had killed the intimacy of their friendship. The three times he had seen Joe he had found it difficult to live up to the old chumship which had existed between them. He had found little to laugh at, or about, and had pursued his work with a grimness whose effect showed itself in his face now. Hard lines had grown about his mouth. The same lines were about his eyes. There was hardness in his attitude, in his glance, in the squareness of his chin. He could not have met Hurd now with a careless smile, and he found it more and more difficult to remain a part of Gaspard's light-heartedness and bonhomie.

With this physical change had come another, a dulling of certain emotions. The thought of meeting Antoinette no longer filled him with a nervous dread. He expected the meeting would be unpleasant. He knew it would be, but he also expected that the necessity of the meeting would be sufficient excuse in Antoinette's eyes for bringing him into her presence again.

He arrived at Mistassini at eight o'clock and went directly from his canoe to Bolduc's office, and was there when Colonel Denis and Antoinette came from a late breakfast at a quarter of nine.

He rose to meet them, and stood like a bronzed Indian when they entered. He had never looked quite so much like an Indian as now, with lips unbroken by a smile as he bowed to Antoinette and shook hands with Denis. He was years older in the face.

As he stood with Colonel Denis a look almost of terror swept like a hot flame through Antoinette's eyes. It was gone in an instant. But her fingers were closed tightly, and she was white. This man she was looking at was not Clifton Brant! This was not the man who had fathered Joe and Bim, who had fought for her brother, who had loved the whole world—and who

198

had outraged her so unforgivably! He was a savage. Even his greeting to Colonel Denis was coldly unemotional. She noticed his clothing, weather-stained, torn in two or three places, his hands calloused and hard, and his hair a bit ragged, and she turned to the window a moment to hide a sudden twitching of her lips and keep from the hard eyes of the man who had once loved her a betrayal of her own emotion.

Clifton did not guess the correct significance of her action, and brought the business quickly to a head. He was in a desperate hurry, he said, and wanted to get back to Depot Number Two as soon as possible. Bluntly he told what he believed Hurd's motives were, and sharply disagreed with both Antoinette St. Ives and Colonel Denis in their opinion that Hurd had at last come to a point where he had accepted decency as the better part of valor.

"To me your changed opinion of Hurd is as amusing as anything can be up here," he said to Antoinette. "With spring a tragedy of some kind will come, and I shall go on preparing for it. No one can tell who will be sacrificed, but I trust it will not be you, Mademoiselle."

Even Denis saw the little beating in Antoinette's soft throat.

"And besides," added Clifton, "you must both understand that I have my own case against Hurd. He is threatening you in a way, Mademoiselle, and he is threatening you in another, Colonel Denis—but—he killed my father. You may accept peace if it is offered you, but I have come to the conclusion that I must go through with what I came from China to achieve. Hurd may flatter and blind you two. But he owes me a debt which, God willing, he is going to pay!

"But I shall not jeopardize either of you, or your interests. I shall wait until the spring drive is over, at which time my association with your company must necessarily end. It really was unnecessary for me to come down here, for whether you allow Hurd to send some of his people to our schools or not does not change the situation at all. Personally I am sure he was laughing in his sleeve when he made that request. He is simply piling up written evidence which at some future time can be made public as showing his friendship for us. I would advise you to let him send the children, if we have room. It can do no harm, and will do the children good."

At half past nine he was ready to leave.

"You are not returning before dinner?" asked Colonel Denis in astonishment.

"I am returning immediately," Clifton assured him.

He shook hands again, and bowed to Antoinette without advancing a step across the width of the room which separated them. He did not see the little movement she made, as if to meet him half-way. He was blind to the whiteness in her cheeks, except as it was a part of the strain and discomfort of an enforced meeting with one whom she disliked so sincerely. He went out and walked down toward his canoe without looking back.

In sheer amazement Colonel Denis turned to Antoinette.

"What in God's name has happened to Clifton Brant?" he demanded.

He had noted her unusual pallor before, and that pallor was accentuated now by eyes that were shining brimful of tears.

Denis's gaze slowly turned from her and followed after Clifton. "Antoinette, *it is you!*"

"Yes, I am afraid so, Colonel Denis."

There was a little break in her voice, a breath caught short and smothered before it was a sob.

Clifton was bending over his canoe, and Denis watched him.

"I didn't think that of Clifton," he said after a moment. "I didn't think a woman could ever do *that* to him. But I suppose it's reasonable, if one knows the facts. It has hit him hard because—well—I don't think Clifton ever looked at a woman until he saw you. I'm sorry!"

"So am I," whispered Antoinette's trembling lips, but Denis did not hear her. Outside the door he was shouting good-bye to Clifton.

For three weeks thereafter Clifton lived and slept and worked with his men, and the logs piled up in the working camps with amazing speed. He saw Gaspard twice, and Joe and Bim spent two weekends with him. But he did not see Antoinette, Angelique or Catherine, though he knew where they were at all times. Antoinette was now working with the other two, and through the Bolducs, one or the other of whom was with him most of the time, he helped in the activities for the big Christmas and New Year's festivities which the girls were planning.

That week was destined to remain long in the memories of the forest people. A dozen entertainments and plays were given in the four schools. A Christmas tree as tall as the ceiling, ablaze with candles and weighted with presents, was in each building. Clifton went with Vincent to the school in charge of Catherine Clamart, and the day after Christmas he left for a fortnight in Quebec. He sent a Christmas greeting to each of the three girls and half a canoeload of presents to Joe.

When he returned from Quebec the men were back at work again. And a letter from Antoinette St. Ives was awaiting him at Mistassini.

It was different from any of the few things she had ever written him. All spirit and pride seemed gone from her writing. Very simply she greeted him, thanked him for his thoughtfulness in sending her a holiday token, and then in several pages poured out her heart to him in a matter which was causing her great unrest. Where was Alphonse? Why had he disappeared? And why did he not return? Only answers to those questions could possibly quiet her misgiving and worry. Gaspard had been able to tell her very little,

200

except about the rumors that Alphonse was wandering through the wilderness, preaching in the camps. She thanked him again for the wonderful work he had done, and assured him that nothing she could ever do for him would sufficiently recompense him.

Clifton smiled when he read these last lines. It was a rare bit of humor, he thought.

Then he answered her, and at length. But his letter, also, was unlike anything he had ever written her. It was not strained or formal, but no breath of his soul crept into it. He told her that for some time he had felt it to be his duty to tell her certain things about the monk, but circumstances had seemed to put themselves between him and the opportunity.

Without betraying the secret of Gaspard's fight he told her of his last minutes with Alphonse, and his disappearance. Since then he had learned that Alphonse was spending a part of his time among Hurd's camps, where of course his acquaintanceship with the St. Iveses was unknown. At other times rumors had come to him of a little wandering missioner farther west, whom he believed to be the monk. Frankly he did not believe Alphonse would return until he had accomplished a certain work which he had in mind. And maybe not then. She could judge for herself by the monk's last words to him, which he had quoted correctly.

Then he thanked her, in turn, for her kind appreciation of what little he had helped to accomplish. He was grateful to her for her well-wishes, but he was sure that her own example and the inspiration of her ideas had almost wholly achieved their success. This inspiration he assured her would always be a guiding light in his own work, and especially would it help him in a rather difficult task which he would face in the spring when he left to take charge of the Chinese Government's reforestation work.

Antoinette was at Depot Number Two when he wrote this letter, and the next day, when he went north, he passed Depot Number Two without stopping and slept that night at Depot Number Three.

With the beginning of the hard snows the winter passed quickly for Clifton. He had nearly four hundred men at work now and the camps were humming with activity. A score of important details outside of cutting the timber occupied his mind and time. Thousands of cords of pulpwood had to be teamed over the snow to the edge of the waterways, and as the loosening of the dam at the upper lake would raise the water only in the Mistassini the problem confronted him of getting back-country timber to the edge of the big river. While he had planned so that sixty percent of his cut was along the shores of the Mistassini, it was necessary for him to set twenty teams at work on the back timber late in January.

It was a wonderful Canadian winter, cold and clear and with the snow firm and not too heavy underfoot. Occasionally he saw Angelique and

Catherine, and he was delighted with their enthusiasm and growing love for the forests. They never wanted to leave them, they declared. With a radiant face Vincent confided his secret to Clifton. The glorious Catherine and he were to be married in the spring. They had planned to spend their lives in the wilderness, doing the forest work which he loved—and which Catherine had grown to love. God had been mighty good to him, he said; for when one possessed a love like Catherine's one had to believe in God. They went together. A love like that was a part of God, and he was proud of his conviction in the matter.

Angelique went home for a visit late in January and did not return until early in March, which added considerably to the work of Antoinette and Catherine. Twice in February Clifton met Antoinette, but he made no effort and showed no desire to be alone with her. A third time, in March, he saw the three girls at Depot Number Three, where they gave an evening's entertainment of music and singing. He complimented the three together.

His eyes revealed nothing when he looked coolly at Antoinette, and told her how wonderful the evening had been, and what an inspiration it was to the forest people. She had flushed at his coming and his first words, but when a moment later he bowed in that cold, hard way that had become a part of him and left them to mingle with the men and women and children who crowded the school-room the color left her cheeks and she stood strangely white.

Angelique's dark eyes had seen the color come and go and the look that had followed Clifton, and a little later she tore herself away from Gaspard long enough to catch Clifton alone as he was prepared to leave.

For the first time in his experience her eyes flashed at him angrily and her little hands were clenched as she cornered him.

"Now it is you who are the fool!" she cried hotly, but in a voice so low that only he could hear it. "Antoinette sang her song tonight for you—for you! And you're running away again. Oh!" And she stamped her foot to give emphasis to her feeling.

"It was a beautiful song," he said, "and Antoinette was lovelier than an angel. But until I approached her to offer my felicitation she had not looked in my direction once this evening, Angelique. I thank you, but you don't know how wrong you are in your judgment of her emotions."

Angelique drew herself up until it seemed that every inch in her slim little body was straining to come to a level with Clifton's eyes.

"You are a bigger fool than I ever dreamed a man could be—when it comes to understanding a woman!" she declared.

"I know it," he conceded amiably. "I've made an unforgettable ass of myself."

She heaved a sigh of despair. "Then you believe that Antoinette St. Ives does not care for you?"

"I believe that if she were a man she would deliberately force a fight upon me."

"Dear Mother, have pity on him!" gasped Angelique, her eyes devouring him with their fire. "Why—why—are you so stupid that you did not see the color leap into her cheeks when you came to her, or know that they went as suddenly white when you left her?"

"Other emotions than love produce those same effects," answered Clifton. "Extreme dislike, for instance."

Angelique settled back to her normal height.

"Hopeless, hopeless," she breathed. "I can do nothing with her, and I can do nothing with you, yet I know that the hearts of both of you are sick for that very thing which neither of you will bring about. Sometimes I grow faint when I think that for a time I was that way with Gaspard. If you two could have the sense of Vincent and Catherine—if you—there comes Gaspard, shoving everybody out of his way in his search for me! And—Clifton—*Antoinette leaves for Quebec tomorrow morning!*"

A few minutes later Clifton was on his way to Depot Number Four, eight miles up the river. It was a moonlight night, splendid for driving over a snowy trail beaten hard by the teamsters.

Late the following afternoon he received a telephone message from Bolduc, at Mistassini. Incidentally he learned that Antoinette St. Ives had arrived and arrangements had been made to drive her over the ice of the lake to Roberval the following morning.

The next day was Thursday. Clifton rose to his work with a strange feeling of despair and a still stranger feeling of relief.

Antoinette St. Ives was gone out of his life, probably for all time. He could concentrate himself now on the last great step he must take before collecting his debt from Hurd.

And on this day of her going something else went out of the forests for Clifton. Light, sunshine, hope and a part of his soul. And a great loneliness crept in their place.

203

CHAPTER XXIV

Clifton now applied every energy and thought to making preparations for the spring drive, and a subdued thrill of excitement and suspense began to possess those who would be responsible for its success or its failure. Hurd had his pulpwood piled high along the Mistassini and the tributaries which he was working, and there could be no secrecy in the efforts Clifton had made to get his own timber down to the shore of the big river in order to compete more favorably with his enemy when the first high water came.

On the first of April the Bolducs reported that the boundary line between the Laurentian and Hurd-Foy properties was patrolled by Hurd's men night and day and that especial caution was being employed along the river. Through a friend in the other camps Delphis learned that Hurd had seemed to be highly amused when he first discovered that Clifton was bringing down his wood from the back-timber and piling it along the Mistassini instead of waiting for spring to flood the creeks and do the work of the teams.

"Hurd has something up his sleeve," Delphis declared up to the last moment. "I can't guess what it is. But it's something that makes him mighty confident."

Clifton personally went up and down the streams and into the back-country watching the progress of the days and marking the first softening of the snows.

One day Romeo Lesage came to him about the baseball bats.

"I'm going to have them in handy places along the drive," he said. "If we need them it will be sudden—and no time to lose."

With the tenth of April came softening weather, warm suns, a melting wind, and water began to run. Colonel Denis had reached Mistassini, and came up to Depot Number Four.

Suspense crept into every man's blood. It found an outlet in the cautious voices of women. There was a restlessness in the schools during their last days. The shadow of impending drama, and possibly of tragedy, hovered over the forests.

On the fifteenth Angelique Fanchon got Clifton on the telephone from Depot Number Three.

"Antoinette St. Ives is at Roberval," she told him. "She was just talking with me over the telephone. She will arrive at Mistassini tomorrow. She said she must be here during the drive—with you and the men. She said *with you*. And she asked about you—if you were well, where you were!"

For a moment Clifton found no words with which to answer.

"Do you hear me?" asked Angelique.

"Yes, I hear you."

"And are you glad?"

"Yes, I am glad."

A triumphant little laugh sounded at the other end.

"That's all I want, Clifton. I wanted you to say that so I could tell Antoinette you said you were glad. Maybe I can do something yet! Good-by!"

Then Delphis Bolduc brought him word that added to the thrills of Angelique's message. Alphonse the monk was in Hurd's camps. There was no doubt now. Delphis, spying like an Indian, had seen him. And his friend had told him that this strange little missioner was quite frequently with Hurd.

What could that mean?

Clifton slept not more than five or six hours out of each twenty-four now. He went up to the dam with Vincent. The lake was full. Twenty feet of water waited to be released.

A light telephone wire had been strung during the past month, apparently running to an engineers' camp which the company had built three miles from the lake. Here Vincent remained, waiting for the word to blow up the dam.

When Clifton returned Antoinette was at Depot Number Two, on the edge of Hurd's concession. It was here, and below, that he knew trouble would come. And Antoinette had placed herself where the big fight would begin, if there was to be fighting at all. Angelique and Catherine were with her.

The ice was breaking. That word, sent up first from Mistassini, and then coming down from Vincent on the upper waters, passed like an electric shock from heart to heart. Each springtime the women dreaded these terrible days that were coming, when their menfolk took their lives in their hands, but this year a more oppressive suspense and fear possessed them. But the word passing from lip to lip and from camp to camp inspired the men. They were like men preparing to go into battle. Their blood ran restlessly. The great thrill which comes with the facing of a mighty hazard was in them.

The warm, gray night of April twentieth came without a moon. There were stars and a dull light in the sky. Until dusk not a soul but Clifton, the

Bolducs, Lesage, Gaspard and Vincent up at the lake knew this was the night on which the great coup was to be sprung on Ivan Hurd.

Even Denis, at Depot Number Two, was unaware of the exact time.

It was a little after midnight when a pounding at the door of their cabin roused the three girls.

A voice called from outside, "Colonel Denis wants you to dress and come to the office!"

In a panic of excitement they obeyed. Antoinette's curls smothered her neck and shoulders. Catherine's golden braid was half undone and she did not wait to plait it. Angelique failed to wipe the beauty-cream entirely from her face.

Denis was walking back and forth over the bare wood floor of the office when they came in together. His tense face twisted itself in a smile when he saw how evidently they had hastened to obey his summons.

"I didn't mean to alarm you," he said. "But you have been three faithful goddesses to the cause, and I promised to let you know the minute I received word that the final hour had struck." He looked up at the clock on the wall. It was a quarter after twelve. "Since nine o'clock last night Clifton Brant and three hundred men have been throwing logs into the Mistassini!" he added, and there was a strange tremble in his voice.

"God bless Clifton Brant!" whispered Angelique Fanchon.

Their faces had grown whiter and more tense, with Colonel Denis's.

The eyes of Antoinette St. Ives were like blazing stars.

"Yes, God be with him and help him," she said, and in the pale lamp-glow her white hand made the sign of the cross on her breast.

Denis tried to appear calm.

"In fifteen minutes—exactly thirty minutes after twelve—Vincent will blow up the dam!"

A stifled sob came from Catherine Clamart. For a moment she covered her face with her hands.

"God bless him, too," Angelique said, trying to laugh a little. "And my Gaspard? I suppose he is pitching logs!"

"He is at the head of fifty men whose duty it will be to keep the logs moving and free from jams," said Denis. "Shall we move outside? It is a quiet night, and I think we can hear."

The camp was asleep when they went out. There were no lights in the other buildings. Stillness hung heavily over the wilderness. Stars gleamed dimly in the skies and under these stars the steady murmur of the river and the whispering of the forest was a soft melody of restfulness and peace. Denis wet his forefinger and held it above his head. The gently stirring wind was in the right direction to bring sound from the north.

206

The three girls stood in a little group. They seemed scarcely to move or breathe as the minutes passed. Their eyes glowed and their faces were tense and pale in the starlight as they waited. Denis struck a match and lighted a cigaret. The tiny flare illuminated the set lines in his face. He looked at his watch before the flame went out.

"Twenty-seven minutes past twelve," he said softly.

Antoinette stood with Angelique's warm fingers clasped in her hand. Catherine was a step aside, her golden head high, listening, her eyes shining, an infinite pride and faith in her attitude.

"Oh, Vincent!" she whispered. "Do it! *Do it!*"

Denis could hear the swift ticking of his watch.

"Listen hard," he said. "It is time!"

Every sound seemed to grow in volume then, the murmur of the river, the whisperings in the forest, the beating of their hearts—and through it all at last came a sound that was like a smothered moan that disturbed the length and breadth of the night, a sound that rose through a second or two until the earth and the air seemed to tremble with it, faint, illusive, gone—a ghost of a sound that came and passed and left the stillness of the night heavier than before.

"Done!" cried Colonel Denis.

A sobbing cry of triumph came from Catherine. "I knew he'd do it! Oh, I knew he'd do it!"

They went back into the lighted cabin. Denis, even in his triumph, was amazed at Antoinette St. Ives. He had never seen the look that was in her eyes. Her cheeks were no longer pale but were flooded with a wild color and wet with tears. She made no effort to hide them or wipe them away. A strange pride and glory were in her face as well as in Catherine Clamart's. Angelique saw it, and wanted to cry out in her joy—cry out so that Clifton might hear, miles and miles up the river.

Denis looked at his watch again.

"You'd better return to your beds, young ladies," he advised paternally. "The dam is out, but it will take hours for the water to get down to us. You would be sleeping now if it were not for the promise I gave you, and so I must insist that you resume your broken rest. I am going to set you an example immediately."

Half an hour later his light was out, but looking from the darkened window of their own cabin Antoinette knew that he was not asleep, but wide awake, and that he was waiting for any word that might come over the telephone, and for the arrival of dawn.

"It is impossible to sleep," said Catherine. "I am going to finish doing up my hair." They could hear her brushing it in the darkness. "If I could talk with Vincent over the telephone I would give—almost anything!"

207

"And if I could be with Gaspard, helping him shove logs into the river, I'd give more than that!" whispered Angelique, as the flip, flip, flip of her boot-laces told them that she was further preparing herself for action instead of undressing for bed. "Ugh!" she shivered. "Can't you see them?— three hundred men working like demons all through this darkness, three hundred men straining and fighting almost for their lives, three hundred of them—while every cabin in the woods is lighted, and women and children are awake, listening, waiting—a lot of them praying! Dear Mother, it's almost like *war*!"

A quick breath came from Antoinette at the window.

"I was thinking of that," she said, and in her voice, low and soft though it was, came clearly a note that made Angelique pause in the lacing of her boots. "As we were riding in an automobile from Brantford one day Colonel Denis told me of another night like this, years ago, when the work of Captain Brant and three hundred men turned the tide of the next day's battle. He said they accomplished what it would have seemed impossible for a thousand men to do, and because they were three hundred then, as tonight, and were working against such odds—just as they are doing now —I, was thinking, too, Angelique!"

There was a moment of silence in the room, broken only by the flip of Angelique's laces and the silken swish of Catherine's hair.

"That was in the winter of nineteen-fifteen, near St. Eloi," continued Antoinette softly. "It was terrible—in the trenches. And ahead of those trenches Captain Brant and his three hundred heroes were digging through ice and snow—almost with their naked hands, with the German guns tearing at them through darkness that was like black pitch, Colonel Denis says. Thinking of that—makes me want to go out—and fight with them tonight!"

"With him, you mean," said Angelique, but the words were whispered only to herself.

And Catherine said, resting her brush for an instant, "Vincent has told me that everything depends on this night!"

"Yes, everything," said Antoinette. "And yet—"

"What?"

"Nothing. I was only thinking again."

"And so was I," said Angelique. "I was thinking. What if this night does end in failure, God granting that it gives back to us these men of ours! *Ours*, I said, Antoinette! Did you hear me?"

She heard very faintly the answer from the window. "Yes, I heard you."

In the darkness Angelique's face was afire with triumph and joy. But her lips were silent. She went to the window and took Antoinette's head in her arms, and kissed her. From one or the other of them Catherine heard a little sob.

Through the night they kept their vigil, whispering of a hundred happenings of the winter, and at times if Denis had stood outside he would have listened to soft laughter breaking the tension of the hours.

In the deeper blackness of approaching dawn there came suddenly the swift clatter of hoofs out of the forest trail. The girls hurried to the window and could faintly see the shadow of a horseman passing. The hoof-beats stopped at the depot office. They heard a beating at the door. In another half-minute a light was burning in Denis's room.

"Something—has happened!" gasped Catherine, fear choking her voice. "He was galloping—in the dark!"

It was Antoinette who groped her way first toward the door. Out in the night Angelique found her hand and it was cold as ice.

"I think—if anything had happened—the word would come by telephone—"

But they were dead white when they entered the office where Denis had made up Bolduc's cot near the telephone.

Denis was already at the telephone, his back toward them.

He was at Cambrai and Sanctuary Wood again! His voice rang out with military sharpness, sending a thrilling command to the watchers who had leaped to their telephones along the line at the first signal of the bell.

"This is Colonel Denis at Depot Number Two Wherever Captain Brant is, get him immediately! Tell him it is a matter of life and death and that I must talk with him at the earliest possible moment! Send every available man after him—*and hurry!*"

Scarcely were the words out of his mouth when a dull tremor ran through the earth. The tremor was followed by a second and a third; the log walls shivered; a roar swept out of the night—a roar that seemed to fill the whole world, tearing at the sky, upheaving the wilderness, shaking the earth, and sweeping off into distance like the crashing thunder of a thousand mighty cart-wheels rolling on pavements above the clouds.

A sharp cry came with the explosion—and that cry was in the cabin. It came from a figure standing in half gloom, a figure with a white and staring face and cavernous eyes whose sunken flame devoured Antoinette St. Ives as she stood in the yellow glow of the lamp.

It was Alphonse the monk.

And before shock could give way to a word of greeting, before she could find strength to move or reach out her hands, Alphonse darted with the swiftness of an animal to the door and disappeared into the night. In an instant she followed and called his name. The abandoned horse whinnied. The last whisperings of the convulsion that had shaken the universe were dying away. A moment she listened—holding her breath—and then turned to confront the ironically smiling, deathlike face of John Denis.

CHAPTER XXV

"What is it?" she demanded. "Alphonse riding in like that—the explosion—"

"It is Ivan Hurd playing his last card," said Denis, the smile remaining on his white lips. "He has blown the top of Sandstone Mountain into the Mistassini down there a mile or so, where the river is shallow and scarcely two hundred feet wide. Alphonse only learned tonight that the mines have been laid for three weeks past. They were to have been fired when high water came and our logs were in the river, but in some way Hurd discovered the meaning of our activities and has sent an avalanche into the Mistassini at a peculiarly embarrassing moment for us. If his plans work out there will be the biggest and most impossible log jam in the river's history at that particular point. And the logs will be our logs, forming a monster dam which will hold back the water of our lake reservoir long enough to allow Hurd to get a great quantity of his own timber into the river. Pretty, isn't it?"

Catherine drew in a gasping breath.

"You mean—he is going to steal the water from Vincent's dam?"

"That's it, partly. And while he is doing that, if his dynamite has been successful, our logs will be tying themselves into knots which will be enormously difficult to untangle, even when the spring floods come. Father Alphonse will return with definite information regarding the success of Hurd's exploded mines within an hour or two. Meanwhile—"

The jangling of the telephone bell interrupted him. He took down the receiver and in answer to his hello the girls could hear an indistinct voice at the other end. Then it grew silent, and in the pause Denis said:

"Thank God, Captain Brant has just come into Depot Number Four! They'll have him on the line—" He turned suddenly to the telephone. "What? Yes, this is Denis—Colonel Denis—at Number Two! Is that you, Clifton? Can you hear me clearly—"

Scarcely breathing, the girls listened as Denis briefly and without apparent excitement or waste of words described the new and sinister situation that had developed a mile and a half inside the Hurd-Foy limits. When he had finished they could hear Clifton's voice snapping with almost electrical sharpness over the line. They caught the words dynamite—high water—logs passing down—twenty-four miles—three or four hours—and then it ended. Denis hung up the receiver.

"What did he say?" demanded Antoinette.

Denis was a little nervous.

"He said the reservoir water was at its peak at Depot Number Four and that logs had been rushing toward us for an hour! He said there was only one way for him to get down to us within three or four hours and that was by taking a chance on the high water in a canoe! If he can escape the logs —"

"And you stood there and made no objection to that?" cried Antoinette, springing toward him. "My God, it is death! I know—because I saw it happen a long time ago—and the men I looked at were crushed to pieces like bits of paper! It can't happen again! It shall not! I won't let Gaspard come down among the logs—and—*I won't let Captain Brant do it*."

She was at the telephone before she had finished speaking and was ringing desperately. The voice answered again. Was Captain Brant there? Was it too late to get him? They must try!

An interval followed—minute after minute, each almost without end; and then the voice returned. Antoinette St. Ives listened to it for a moment. She made no answer. Slowly she faced Colonel Denis.

"It is too late! He is risking his life to come down and do what you are not man enough to do!"

She seemed not to see Angelique or Catherine as she left the office, white to the lips. In a moment or two they followed her. Colonel Denis stood alone, like one stricken. Then a shadow of a smile twitched at the corners of his mouth.

"Lucky Clifton! If you could only know you are coming—to *that*!" he breathed softly, and went to the door to find that dawn was breaking.

In the gray of that dawn Clifton was shooting down the river with Delphis Bolduc in the stern of his canoe. Half a dozen times they seemed to be facing death, but each time crept out. Twice the logs almost carried them over rock-ramparted falls where their bodies would have been beaten to pulp. The tremendous strain they were under Clifton could see in Bolduc's face. He had never seen Delphis so white and gaunt. He seemed to have lost flesh.

When at last the prow of their canoe shoved in on the sand-bar at Depot Number Three he wondered if he looked as badly as Delphis. He tried to laugh, and Delphis tried to laugh, but their voices were strained and unreal. Probably no one would ever quite guess the hell they had gone through, with a million logs tearing ahead of them and behind them and racing shoulder to shoulder with the canoe.

It annoyed him that a tremble should be in his voice—something which he could not control. He did not feel nervous or afraid. At least he assured himself this was so.

They swallowed hot coffee and food hurriedly while the clerk got Denis on the telephone. Clifton talked with him. The logs had not yet begun to arrive at Depot Number Two. But Hurd's mountain-slide was a diabolical success. The logs would jam. A huge mass of stone had settled in the middle of that narrow part of the stream, and between that mass and both shores great boulders had flung themselves like monster dragon teeth, waiting for the timber. Clifton's last instruction was for Denis to get dynamite and all available men at the scene of the anticipated jam. He and Delphis would be with them in an hour and a half—if nothing happened.

Two hours later they passed the deserted lower depot and came to a group of people waiting on a projecting bar just above Sandstone Mountain. Their canoe was ragged and leaking water. Their faces were whiter, thinner, more terrible looking. They were like two men who had come out of something ghastly and indescribable. Those ashore were tense and dumb with a kind of hopelessness that had settled on them like a shock, but the ghostly terribleness of the two men who got stiffly out of the canoe relieved them of their own emotions for a few moments.

Clifton looked them over at a glance, and a grunt told him that Delphis had done the same. There were thirty or forty, some of them women and children. Every available river-man had been enlisted in the work upstream, and here were only the roustabouts of the camp, half a dozen teamsters, the cook's outfit and a few others.

Clifton saw none of Hurd's people. But he did see Antoinette St. Ives, Angelique Fanchon and Catherine Clamart only a few steps away from him, white-faced and staring as Denis met him and Bolduc. Denis gripped their hands. But he did not speak. There was little need of that. Clifton and Delphis could see for themselves.

They turned their backs to the little crowd, and for the first time in hours a smile broke Clifton's lips as he saw in a more leisurely manner what Ivan Hurd had done. It was a good job. He looked up at the top of Sandstone Mountain, and then back again. In war Hurd's mind would have been an asset to the Huns. It was trickery, well done, absolutely effective, and somehow his mind flashed back to those days of Langemarck, in this very month of April in 1915, when the Huns first used poison gas. He could see again the French colonial Turcos and African Zouaves as they stampeded, fainting and choking and dying in the mysterious scourge as they ran—and then the Canadians filling that horrible gap that opened up the roads to Ypres, Calais and the English Channel—and holding the Germans back. Ivan Hurds were behind that gas-death. And here was an Ivan Hurd again, doing the last thing in the world that a white man would have expected him to do!

He forgot the little crowd of breathless, waiting men and women behind them as he surveyed Hurd's work. But he did not forget Antoinette St. Ives! She was there, watching him—and what an infinite contempt must fill her soul now as she saw him utterly beaten, the Laurentian Company beaten, herself beaten—because he had not possessed sufficient foresight to watch the top of Sandstone Mountain!

For beaten they were, as surely as the sun was shining upon them from out of the east! He heard Bolduc groan the words under his breath. And he could see.

A moaning roar and turmoil of water filled the air, and where the channel had been there was no longer a channel but a piled-up chaos of logs. Over this mass and about it the flood from the upper lake, filled with its volleys of timber, was crashing and beating with increasing violence, and as the two surveyed the pile there came suddenly a great upheaval in the center of it which lifted the growing mountain of logs half a dozen feet in less than thirty seconds.

Bolduc gave a sharp exclamation as his hand gripped Clifton's arm. That upheaval had revealed to them where the keystone to the great jam lay. The thought was in Clifton's eyes as he looked at Delphis. They walked on, alone, until they were half a hundred paces away from the little crowd of spectators—for in this crisis Clifton regarded them as no more than that.

Again their eyes met.

"Yes, it's the mass of stone in the center," said Bolduc, as if Clifton had spoken the thought in his mind. "A charge of dynamite in the right place—"

He paused, waiting for Clifton to give expression in words to what he saw. Clifton's lips were set hard. He was not afraid. But he was white. And Bolduc's face was like flesh that had hardened into wood, with its myriad little lines accentuated and its eyes looking out of half closed slits.

"There's a million horse-power of water crowding behind it," answered Clifton. "A charge of dynamite would loosen that central pile, and once loosened, even a little, the mass of rock would be leveled and scattered by the sheer force of the water and timber shoving from behind—"

"Yes, *but*!" challenged Delphis.

"A man would not come out alive."

"Possibly. But the timber would go down."

"Yes, it would go down."

They stood shoulder to shoulder. Bolduc laughed, but his laugh was not as hard as it had been at another time that day.

213

"I wouldn't do it for Denis," he said. "I wouldn't do it for any man or company on earth. But—I hate to have Hurd beat us like this!"

Clifton spoke as quietly. "If you will get the dynamite, Delphis, and tell Denis to keep himself and the people back—especially the people—"

No one saw the close, sudden grip of their hands in front of them.

Bolduc was gone no more than a minute or two and until he returned Clifton did not take his eyes from the jam.

"I told them we were going to try a little experiment along the edge, and warned them to get back," said Denis. "The charges are ready, with two-minute fuses. One each is enough."

They faced the boiling caldron of logs between them and the piled-up mass in the middle of the stream. This was the death-trap. They could cross it with caution and luck; but to get back again, and within those precious two minutes after the fuse was lighted—

"The instant the charge goes off the mass will begin to move," Delphis was saying, "and that will give more freedom between us and the main pile. It is clear, Monsieur, that when we have placed the charges *we must hurry*!"

For a moment some force drew Clifton about so that he was seeking Antoinette St. Ives. She was standing with Colonel Denis a little in advance of the others, looking at him. He turned to Bolduc again.

"Shall we go?"

"Yes—straight across for that spout of white froth. Don't wait or watch for me. Get to the pile first. If either of us slips—the other must go on *alone*."

A cry so shrill that it was almost a scream came from behind them as they leaped out into the twisting maelstrom of timber. Clifton heard the cry and it was like a knife running through him, and with it he heard his name, and then all sound was drowned in the grind and roar of rushing water and of logs in moaning turmoil. He did not see Bolduc. He did not raise his eyes as he made the death-race for the firmer footing ahead. Twice they opened and let him down to his knees. Once he slipped almost to his waist but got out with lightning quickness before the timber trap closed again to grip and crush him. It was all over in three-quarters of a minute. He reached the solid jam. And Bolduc came staggering up, white as ash, a limp in his last steps, and dripping water.

In another half-minute they had found a hollow in the heart of the jam almost directly back of the obstructing mass of rock and gravel. Here they could hear more clearly the tearing force of the water on both sides of them. They had guessed correctly. If they could free this central leverage a ten-thousand-ton battering-ram of timber behind would scatter Hurd's avalanche as if it were made of paper!

214

Delphis had taken his waterproof match-box from his pocket. Clifton held the dynamite, with the ends of the two fuses close together. The instant they were lighted he would drop them in a deep crevice that ran down at the back of the rock.

Until the match was sputtering between Bolduc's thumb and forefinger he had not noticed that the other's hand was shaking. He looked up. Bolduc's face was twisted with pain.

A sputter—a sudden snake-like hiss—

"Drop it!"

The dynamite fell from Clifton's hands, dropping dully into the depths of the timber. A pungent film of smoke rose out of the crevice.

In half a second Clifton was away from it and climbing with the swiftness of a cat out of the hollow. He came over the crest and saw the crowd on shore. It had come closer to the river. He could see Denis. And then Antoinette. She stood with her booted feet in the shore wash of foam and water sent up by the flood. It struck him then that everyone was behind her—even Denis; that she was alone, poised almost as if on the point of coming out to meet him, and that even Catherine and Angelique did not come to her side, but left for her alone that one position on a projecting shelf of rock that was nearest him. She had reached her arms out as he appeared, and he could see that she was calling to him, or to someone behind him, though he could not hear her voice.

He turned as he came to the edge of the solid jam and looked for Bolduc.

Delphis had been slow—terribly slow. His head and shoulders were just appearing out of the hollow. And then, as he came out, horror and shock swept over Clifton, when he saw that Delphis was dragging himself on his hands and knees!

He ran back, and as he ran he could hear now the cry that came from the people on shore. Delphis fell almost to his face, and then pulled himself up with an effort, like a drunken man. He was crumpling back again when Clifton reached him and flung an arm about him. Delphis's white lips spoke.

"My leg. I can't use it. Smashed—I think—"

He swayed almost a dead weight for a few precious seconds, and then Clifton got in front of him, with his back doubled over. Like a bag of wheat he pulled Delphis on his shoulders. His eyes were on a level with the shore as he staggered over the uneven, swaying mass of pulpwood, and he saw the change that was keeping help back from the other side of the channel. For a few moments the channel had opened between the rocks, and logs in a crashing bombardment were smashing their way through it. They

215

jammed again even as he looked. But no living thing could get across that space now.

Bolduc almost forced himself from his shoulder.

"Go on—alone!" he demanded. "You can't make it—with me—"

Clifton dug his fingers more tightly into his arms. Then he slipped, and they fell. In that moment he saw the white-faced crowd, and Antoinette standing at the end of the slim finger of rock. He looked at her, and smiled. She must have seen it, for her hands suddenly covered her face, and while he was still looking—and straining to get up with Bolduc on his shoulders —the explosion came, one, and then another, so close together that there was scarcely an interval between them. There was a lurch in the great mass, a roar that seemed to work deep down into the bowels of the river, upheavals, and a cataclysmic eruption at the center of the pile which set the earth and the mountains atremble with its force.

And then a mighty arm seemed to reach out and possess itself of Clifton. It jerked him away from Bolduc. It flung him back, tossed him up with a sudden spurt of timber, and when he recovered from the shock the place where he had been standing was gone, Delphis was gone, and all about him the freed masses were breaking up—and from the shore came such a cry as he had never heard in all his life!

It was a crowd cry, a shriek of women, a moaning protest of men, a cry of amazement and of horror and of shock.

And a still more terrible cry came from Clifton.

It was not because he was facing certain death, and was about to die as Delphis had died under the eyes of the people ashore. That was terrible enough. But this that was happening was more than the mere spectacle of death—men's death.

Antoinette St. Ives had leaped straight out from the tip of the rock into the milling swirl of logs between him and the shore!

"I am coming!" he heard her cry. "*I am coming!*"

A figure ran and leaped close behind her. It was Alphonse. He missed, a log struck him ashore, hands seized him—and held him.

But no hand could reach Antoinette. It was a miracle, a divine intuition that carried her feet over the maelstrom of flood and twisting, foam-hidden logs. A slip, a misstep, and death lay ready to engulf and crush the life from her. And she seemed to be looking at nothing—caring for nothing—but Clifton.

The cry that was in his soul died there as he sprang toward her, no longer caring what might happen to himself if he could reach her before the fatal moment came. There was no hope for either of them now. He could see that, and those ashore could see it. The whole jam was giving way. The

216

wall of water was moaning and roaring behind. Half a minute more—twenty seconds—maybe less—

They met on a footing of timber half as big as the floor of a small room, and as Antoinette came to him out of mist and spray that was golden with the morning sun the glory in her face and eyes was that of one who had come to a great triumph, and in that triumph had forgotten the thing called death.

There were a few moments left to them. He caught her as her slim body came within his reach. Her hands went swiftly to his face and then around his neck. It was she who spoke in his hour of horror and despair when God had taken the power of speech from his tongue.

"*I love you,*" she was saying. "*I love you—I love you.*"

Her lips were against his, not cold with the chill of fear and death, but warm—warmer than on that night of the great storm!

"*I love you—*"

Death was about them—upon them. It rolled and shuddered under them. Clifton crushed her in his arms, and his eyes sought the hopeless shore. Yet he leaped toward it as the floor of timber melted away from under their feet.

And then the boiling floods reached up. Light and the world disappeared as the chaos engulfed them. But he had her in his arms as they went —so close that death would never be able to separate them. That was his thought. *Death would not separate them.*

CHAPTER XXVI

In the rumble and roar that filled his ears he was conscious of but one necessity—to keep his arms about the one who had given herself to him in the moment when he was about to die.

They were under water and he could hear the moaning and sweep and drumming of it in his ears, and above all that the steady thunder of timber above them, and a still more terrible sound where in places the crowded logs were reaching down and tearing at the river-bed itself. Caught in this drag they would be torn and shredded into pieces like cloth, and so his first struggle was upward—up to a more merciful death of clean drowning or to be beaten lifeless but not so terribly obliterated by the upper logs.

He was amazed at the swiftness with which the water was carrying them and its freedom from obstruction. A thrill leaped suddenly into his brain and sped to the nerves and sinews of his body. His left arm was about Antoinette, holding her head close to him. He freed his right. With that and his legs he struggled upward. The current caught and twisted him, and suddenly he felt himself in a powerful undertow that swirled him about like a chip and then sent him to the surface in the boiling heart of it.

Fresh air struck his face and filled his nostrils and his lungs, and in that same instant he felt the undertow dragging him back again. He flung out his free arm and something sped under it. It was a spruce log, barkless, not over six inches in diameter and four feet long—a mere pencil in the flood, but enough. He could bring his face out of the water, and Antoinette's. She was gasping and choking for air. But she was unhurt. Her eyes were open *and looking at him*. He thanked God, and for the first time was inspired by the thought that they were going to live.

And in this same moment there began to possess him the almost unbelievable force of the thing that had sent Antoinette to him. It battled against the roaring in his head. It cleared his vision, swept doubt from his mind, and in the twistings of the flood with its hundred chances of death his heart and soul leaped to the glorious thrill of it. All life was reaching ahead of him again—life filled with Antoinette! She loved him and had come to him in an hour of hopelessness that they might go down and out together!

And now he knew they would live! The logs would not crush them, the floods could not drown them! For an instant so swift in passing that it seemed a dream he saw Antoinette's eyes looking up at him from a white face framed in a swirl of water. And he saw in them what her lips had spoken!

As he raised himself an inch or two higher he saw how closely death had missed them. The spout of the undertow had forced them up through an embrasure in the mass of grinding timber—into a pool, a *soupirail*, a tiny lakelet of clear water about which the logs had crowded and tangled themselves. It was not more than twenty feet across, and now he saw that the small spruce log had been part of a boom and that a chain fastened somewhere ahead was dragging it.

His mind gathered itself swiftly. Such an opening in the mass of timber could last only for a few minutes. A few key timbers were holding it temporarily. A change in the current, a shallower part of the stream, an up-jutting rock—any one of a dozen things and the key timbers would be disturbed and the mass would crowd in and crush them.

He began to work along the log and then along the chain, keeping it under the pit of his arm. He fought with all his strength, working against the backlash of the water, and Antoinette's free hand gripped the chain and helped him. It took him no more than two or three minutes to reach the edge of the mass and pull himself up. There he sank down, exhausted, his wind gone, but with Antoinette held so closely in his arms that her head could not move from its place on his breast.

For a little while they did not move or speak but lay in a crumpled, sodden heap with their hearts pounding against each other. Then the white face on Clifton's breast raised itself to him. Two dripping arms crept up around his neck. A pair of lips sought his and kissed him. And the soft mouth did not draw away but pressed sweetly to his own when Clifton kissed it again as he had done on the night of the storm.

Then Clifton stood up and drew Antoinette with him, his arms still closely about her.

Sandstone Mountain with its ragged perpendicular walls had slipped behind them. They could see the rapids through which they had come, its boiling water filled with logs that leaped and plunged like playing porpoises. On either side of them was dense forest. The water was quieter but the swift and sullen way in which the broken drifts of timber were speeding downstream told Clifton they were on the crest of the flood and that the mighty force which was propelling them would rend itself in still greater fury at the next fall and rapids. At the rate they were drifting they would reach this new danger in less than a dozen minutes.

Shoreward lay their hope.

Antoinette looked again at Clifton. And now, with her eyes clear of water and mist she saw that he was not the man who had swayed out of the canoe with Delphis Bolduc. The hard lines were gone from his face. Age had died out of his eyes, and it came to her that he was all at once the old Clifton Brant of the highways again, the Clifton Brant whose smiling eyes and debonair wave of hand she had first seen on the road from Brantford Town, the man who had made chums of Joe and Bim and who from the very beginning of things had laughed in the face of the world and had made light of everything that was black and grim. For he was smiling, and about him there was no sign of uncertainty or fear but only that monumental confidence which at first had disheveled her pride but which now made her want to get down on her knees and thank God for being good and gracious enough to give it to him.

There was gladness in her low cry as she put her hands to his face.

"Oh, I've loved you from the beginning—from that very first hour in Hurd's room! And if it happens that you despise me for what I have said and done to you I shall want to die here, just so that you are kind enough to hold your arms about me while we are going. I am not afraid!"

In sheer madness of joy he laughed as he kissed her upturned lips and eyes and the wet hair that framed her face.

"We're going ashore!" he cried. "Come, *cara sposa*—" And his joy rose above the moaning tumult of the water and logs. "It's going to be easy now."

Yet he knew he was lying to himself, and to her. And Antoinette St. Ives knew the same thing as hand in hand they faced the hazard with happiness swelling in their hearts.

He was measuring his time, even with that lightsomeness in his voice and the joy in his heart, and he knew there was not a second or a half-second to lose. They hurried to the edge of the floating timbers and Antoinette did not hesitate or question him when the logs thinned out and no longer made a floor for them. The pressure of his hand and the light in his face were all the surety she needed, and when he dared turn his eyes swiftly to look at her for an instant her lips flashed him a smile and her eyes were dark and glowing with the splendor of her love and faith and fearlessness.

"We'll go as far as we can," he told her cheerfully, as the log footing began to sway and sink under them at each step. "Then we'll jump in, and get ashore."

She wondered for a moment if there really was great danger—if Clifton could talk like that, with a half-smile on his lips and a struggle for their lives ahead of them! She looked a last time at the distance between them and the shore. It was not great, not more than thirty or forty yards. But it seemed to her like a mill-race through which individual logs were rushing with terrific speed and the force of battering-rams. Was it possible Clifton saw no great difficulty in passing through *that*?

Very gently the river seemed to reach up and seize her, and at first she went into it to her knees and then to her waist and her shoulders—and at that level the logs seemed flashing past her and beside her at still greater speed. And that half-smile was on Clifton's lips even then as he held her again with his left arm and began to fight the crowding logs with his right.

Ten minutes—possibly no more than seven or eight were left to them now! His only chance was to pull himself through the logs as they sped down-stream, make them crowd and batter him shoreward, fight his way inch by inch and foot by foot—and every instant keep his own body between Antoinette and their blows.

And he did that thing. Wrenched and torn he was thrown at last into the top of a fallen birch. He dragged himself ashore and pulled himself up to safety with Antoinette in his arms. The smile was gone. A twist of agony had settled in his face. Maybe his ribs were gone or his back caved in. It felt like that, he thought. He tried to force back his cheer as he sank to the ground.

"Beastly—wind—gone," he gasped. "A close rub, little girl—"

There was no use smiling now. White horror was in Antoinette's face as she caught his sinking head in her arms. A red discoloring of blood began to stain her torn and sodden dress. She cried out to him passionately, and he tried to answer as he felt himself going back more heavily into her arms. And then he could hear her sobbing voice dying away. It was his eyes he was conscious of last—the warmth of her lips against them.

Then came darkness.

The darkness lasted for only a little while, he thought, and as it began to break away he was conscious of voices, far away at first and then quite near him. With light and sound came swiftly an adjustment of his thinking faculties. It had been a close shave! That was his first mental sensation—and the logs must have pummeled him unmercifully to lay him out like this at the last moment, when he should be comforting Antoinette in place of frightening her to death with his stupid helplessness.

This thought made him try to get up, even before the darkness was gone or sound came clearly, and as he made the effort he called to Antoinette. Something held him back. Then she answered him. Her voice was very close. He felt her arms about his head. And it was all so comforting and the thought of her safety was so immeasurably satisfying that he sighed deeply and made no effort to raise himself just then.

Lights and shadows came and went for a time. He could feel a hand stroking through his hair and caressing his face. But for the life of him he could not speak or open his eyes—could not call Antoinette's name again, and he wanted to do that more than anything else. The effort seemed to bring darkness about him once more and when he came out of that darkness a second time his eyes opened with the returning light and he found himself staring up to find a log ceiling where there should have been tree tops and log walls where there should have been the open wilderness with the moaning tumult of rushing water whispering through it.

Then it came on him suddenly that he was in the girls' cabin at Camp Number Two.

This was amazing and in the shock and unexpectedness of his discovery he did not so much as move a finger.

There came a movement from the other side of the room, a sudden quick breath close to him and Antoinette was on her knees at his bedside. Seeing his eyes wide open and looking at her she gave a little cry, and another came quickly across the room and stood over him. This last was a little thin man with a shaven head and a face that radiated immeasurable cheer. A puzzled look came into Clifton's eyes as he recognized him. Why had Father Joseph come up to Depot Number Two from the monastery at Mistassini? A bit of illuminating truth began suddenly to possess him. Father Joseph was a graduate of a surgical college. It meant—

Antoinette saw him struggling to understand, and then with Father Joseph smiling on them she pressed her face down so closely that for a few moments Clifton could feel only the sweet smother of her hair and the warm thrill of her lips and cheek. When she raised her head her face was radiant in its happiness and as infinitely tender as an angel's.

"The logs hurt you," she said, "and we telephoned to the monastery for Father Joseph, and he came quickly. And now you are well again, Clifton, and mine—*all mine*. And, oh, I do thank our dear Mother in Heaven and will never forget to thank Her every day of my life so long as I live!"

Her shining eyes were filling with tears, and slowly she drew away from him and Father Joseph took her place at his side. The door from the room was behind him and he could hear Antoinette when she went out and closed it softly.

Father Joseph was counting his pulse, and then ran a hand over his right side, where he was beginning to feel a dull pain.

And then the tongue which had lain helpless in Clifton's mouth came to life.

"What time is it, Father?"

"About four o'clock in the afternoon, my son."

"And the jam went out this morning?"

"Yes, this morning."

"And it was—a success?"

222

A humorous twinkle filled the monk's eyes. "Very successful, my son, if I can believe the remarkable story which your wife has told me."

"*My wife?*"

"Yes, the beautiful young woman who left your side just now, and who —until my arrival at eleven o'clock this morning—was Mademoiselle St. Ives. Did you not hear her when she said '*You are mine—all mine*'?"

Clifton lay as if stunned by a blow, staring at the priest. And Father Joseph had straightened himself and was rubbing his hands and smiling.

"It was perhaps an unforgivable thing for me to do," he explained, with an almost joyous exultation in his voice, "for at no time have you really been in danger. The logs pounded you and you lost consciousness at the last, but since then your condition has been due almost entirely to extreme exhaustion and not to injury, though I think you have a fractured rib or two that it will take a little time to mend.

"But I could not make Mademoiselle Antoinette believe that. She thought you might die, and when we two were alone in this room she told me the story I have referred to, and said that never again would she believe in God or the Church or Heaven unless I made you man and wife, even though you could not lift a finger in protest; and when I told her of the impossibility of it she called in two other amazing creatures of similar beauty and insistence, and the three of them compelled me almost by force to do a thing which, I must confess, holds a most holy sentimental value but which cannot bind you legally if you care to object—though I know that Mademoiselle Antoinette would have lived to the letter and the spirit of that act through all the years of her life had you died.

"That was her fear—that you might die before she could call herself your wife." Suddenly the humor and light went out of the priest's eyes and face and left a softer radiance in their place. "I have known Antoinette St. Ives for many years, my son," he added. "Our Mother in Heaven loves her, else I would not have done this thing—and I pray that God's blessing will come here and eternally to you both," and for the space of a moment or two he bowed his head in prayer.

Clifton raised himself, speechless, and the priest laid a hand gently on his head. They could hear footsteps and low voices outside the cabin door.

"Only we five know of it," he confided softly, "and if you are displeased at what has happened—"

"You are—telling me the truth?" gasped Clifton. "It isn't—something monstrous—a joke—a *lie*—"

"Would I destroy myself, my son?"

"And she is—*my wife?*"

"Yes, if it is so you desire our act to be taken."

223

"Then God has been good to me," breathed Clifton, sinking back. "I thank you, Father. And if you will let her come to me now—*my wife*—" His voice was trembling like a boy's.

"I think—probably—she is outside the door."

The monk moved away, but before he went he took his cowl and robe from a chair near the bedside. The door opened and closed. And a few moments later it opened again, so very softly that Clifton scarce could hear it, and it closed even more softly, and there came the thrilling click of a lock and footsteps that were like a fairy's.

And then Antoinette stood in the light of the sun that came through the western window, only a step away from him, but hesitating for a moment as they looked into each other's eyes—and Clifton reached out his arms, powerless to utter the two precious words which he had meant to come first from his lips, and Antoinette came into his arms, and put her head on his breast and cried there in her happiness—yet in that happiness, it seemed to Clifton, was something of grief far back.

He learned what it was in the early dusk of evening. Antoinette was gone. John Denis had taken her place.

"Father Joseph says you will be up and moving about on your feet tomorrow, Clifton. If anything had happened to you, old man—to you or Antoinette—only God knows what I would have done! Even as it is we have paid too great a price."

"You mean—Bolduc—died."

"Yes. The timber went down. We have beaten the Hurd-Foy crowd. But Delphis went with it."

For a little space they were silent. It seemed to Clifton that Denis had not spoken all that was in his mind.

"I liked Delphis," said Clifton then. "I liked him more than most men. And it seems—to me—that Hurd is going to have another debt to pay."

"He has paid," said John Denis quietly.

Their eyes met in a level gaze.

"You mean—"

"When you and Antoinette went under with the logs Alphonse the monk was like a maniac, and ran laughing and screaming into the forest. He returned to Ivan Hurd. Later I was called to witness what had happened. It was in Hurd's room, and must have been terrible. Alphonse had a knife and Hurd, his naked hands and whatever else he could get hold of. He was literally slashed to pieces and the other beaten to pieces. Both were dead. But Alphonse must have died last for I found gripped tightly in his hand something which could not possibly have been there during the struggle. A curl of brown hair—very much like—Antoinette's. I closed his hand more tightly about it, Clifton. It will go with him into his grave."

224

Clifton had placed a hand over his eyes.

"I shall tell Antoinette—some day," he said. "I want her to know. She has learned about the monk's death, and Hurd's?"

"Yes. The tragedy is common news in both camps. We are taking Alphonse back to Depot Number One and will bury him in the edge of the forest near the monastery. Antoinette and Gaspard have selected the place, where years ago Alphonse saved Antoinette from death in the river. They will accompany the body in the morning."

"And I shall go, too," said Clifton. "I can ride if I cannot walk, John."

It was in the deeper dusk of evening that Clifton sat alone, bolstered high up in his bed. And it was in this dusk that Antoinette came to him again, and sat beside him, and placed her head so that he could press his lips in her hair and kiss her when she raised her face a little. And in this dusk sorrow and happiness became one between them, and precious secrets crept out of their hearts, and hope and glory and God grew about them as the stars came out in the sky and the benediction of night closed about the little cabin in the wilderness.